INTO THE BLACK

WITHDRAWN

Printed in the United States of America.

Published by 47North
P.O. Box 400818
Las Vegas, NV 89140

ISBN-13: 9781612182346
ISBN-10: 1612182348

INTO THE BLACK

odyssey one

EVAN CURRIE

47NORTH

▼

CHAPTER 1

▲

▶AS HIS FIGHTER broke clear of the atmosphere, Eric Weston reached forward and flipped a series of switches to disengage the Scramjet intake and engage the pressurized oxygen flow to the twin engines. The rush of air across the fuselage had long since faded, thinning to nothing as he angled the nose down and aimed for geosync orbit. Beyond the cockpit glass, the curve of Earth was clearly visible as he casually flipped the plane over and took a moment to admire the view so far below.

Things look so much nicer from up here. So serene compared to what I've seen. Japan, California, Hong Kong…None of them look like the battlefields I've fought over, Eric Weston thought soberly as he flashed back to his first engagements during World War III. When the war broke out, his company was one of the first strike targets for the Block forces. In the few minutes' warning the coastal defenses bought them, Weston had organized the other test pilots and got the prototypes off the ground to save them from the bombers.

Unarmed, they couldn't do anything but watch as the enemies' heavy weapons annihilated the facility and killed nearly everyone he considered a colleague and friend. After that, staying out of the fight wasn't really an option for Weston.

He flipped his plane back around so he could take a long look at his destination instead of wallowing in his origins.

Hanging in the Lagrange Four point like some serene floating sentinel, his new command, the North American Confederation Ship *Odyssey*, stood waiting to receive him. The ship floated in front of him, placidly awaiting her captain as he sailed toward her on a fast intercept vector.

Huh, I suppose it does look like an old sailing ship. Though, as he forced himself to admit a few moments later, he probably wouldn't have seen it if the designers hadn't kept pointing it out.

The *Odyssey*'s cylindrical habitats could only be seen as the hull of a sailing vessel if one had the most liberal of imaginations. The rest, though, was easier to understand. A long keel that appeared to mark the vessel's "bottom" was actually an enclosed flight deck, built to house shuttles and fighters. Similarly, mast-like sensor spires dotted her "top." The rear engine compartment looked like the stern of an old frigate, and her bow was marked by long antennae that reached dozens of meters out from the ship.

"Odyssey Control to Archangel Zero One, please change your approach vector to oh-two-four-mark-three. You have been cleared for standard approach on deck two," the voice relayed over his headset induction receiver, sounding clearer than if the person had been in the cockpit with him.

Weston acknowledged the signal and slid his fighter along the new approach path.

It didn't take long for the cat officer to come over his radio, taking over from the Bridge Control Team.

"Archangel Zero One, I have you on approach," the voice crackled over the radio as the signal began to suffer from the mutual interference of the counter-mass (CM) fields that surrounded both his fighter and the NACS *Odyssey*. "Call the ball, Captain."

"Roger, Cat. I have the ball."

"Confirmed. Glide path is clear. The deck is green. Come on in, the air is fine."

Weston guided the sleek Archangel Zero One toward the *Odyssey*, vectoring toward her bow and aligning toward the enclosed carrier deck in the ship's massive keel. The forward section of the deck was open to space, offering entry to the ship for fighters and shuttles at speed, while heavy side locks permitted more controlled docking. As the starry depths of space were eclipsed by the cavernous interior of the carrier deck, Weston felt the hairs on his arms and neck stand at attention. He recognized the sensation and knew that the ship's flight crew had caught him with "the trap," a powerful counter-gravity field that slowed the fighter down drastically without putting him through the effects of deceleration.

Minutes later, his fighter came to a stop and he regained control as he carefully steered it to one of the deck's lifts. Once he was in one of the eight hangars built into the *Odyssey*'s keel, Weston powered down and checked the external atmosphere on reflex. He carefully equalized the pressure in the fighter to that of the hangar and popped the canopy, waiting as it slid back. He pulled himself clear and, with a slight tug, floated free of the cockpit.

As he drifted toward the hangar's ceiling, Weston heard the reverberating clang of magnetic boots and looked up—or rather, down—toward the floor.

"Howdy there, Commande…whoops, I mean Captain!" the cheerful voice echoed through the hangar as its originator jumped up, did a neat little flip, and floated up to where Weston was just planting his own pair of Magboots on the metal deck plating.

Stephen "Stephanos" Michaels was Weston's wingman in the Archangel Flight Group, or had been until Weston officially accepted command of the *Odyssey*. During the war, Weston, Stephanos, and a small handful of others were among the only people qualified on the specialized Archangel fighters, among the only air superiority fighters that could stand up to the new Block frontline fighter aircraft. After three years of leading the Archangels, and the end of the war, Weston had accepted the promotion with the hopes of a place to start over, somewhere that wasn't filled with memories. At that point, Stephanos was Weston's choice to succeed him, taking his place as the flight leader of the Archangels.

Stephanos had not changed much since their younger days. Just over six feet, with a decidedly nonregulation haircut, he had an affable quality that hung off him like a comfortable set of clothes, something that served him well in the after-hours clubs he was known to frequent. Weston knew that he had been waiting for years to take over the Angels, and Stephanos seemed pretty happy about it today.

"Hey, Steph." Weston popped his helmet as he greeted his friend. "How are you and the others fitting in?"

Stephanos managed a humble sort of shrug that would have looked ridiculous on most anyone else, but just seemed to make him look like some good ol' boy straight off the farm. "Nothing to complain about."

Weston laughed. "Right. What that means is you've got complaints, but no one gives a damn."

Stephanos chuckled in turn as the two old friends walked side by side to the far end of the hangar, chatting about the ship and the mission, and finally entered one of the small doors that led them to the ship's internal lift. Inside the capsule-like pod that served to ferry the *Odyssey*'s crew, Weston signaled the lift to head for the ship's command center in the forward habitat cylinder.

Weston waited, glancing at his young friend, noting his occasional nervous fidgeting. He figured that his wingman had earned the right to be nervous by now, though. They had flown alongside each other since the inception of the Archangels, eight years previously, and through some of the most vicious air battles in the history of humankind.

All that set aside, Weston could hardly fault the man when he himself was on the verge of shaking. The *Odyssey* was the first ship constructed that made use of the new transition drive system that was supposed to allow faster-than-light travel, and his rather public position as the flight leader of the Archangels had put him on the short list to captain her.

The pod glided to a stop in the center of the forward habitation cylinder, and Weston felt gravity return as the pod slowly matched the cylinder's rotation before the hatch whirred open and allowed them to leave.

"Urk." Weston staggered as he stepped off, a wave a nausea sweeping over him as his body adjusted to the cylinder's rotation.

"It'll pass. First time you're on one of these things it takes your inner ear a while to adjust to the motion," Stephanos commented as his arm snaked out to steady Weston.

"I know." Weston straightened himself, fighting off another wave of sickness, and started down the hallway. "Not my first time on the ship, Steph. Was up here maybe a dozen times during the pre-commissioning—damn thing hit me every time."

The pair made their way through the halls toward the *Odyssey*'s command center, a large room with curving floors and ceilings. It was already bustling with activity as two full-maintenance details crowded the room, checking the circuitry for the nth time as they analyzed every system on the ship prior to her maiden voyage. A tall black man wearing a commander's uniform approached them on the bridge. Wide across the shoulders and taller than Steph by at least four inches, the commander caused the metal plates of the deck to reverberate under his feet, leaving Weston to think of an oncoming giant and wonder for a brief moment if he'd packed his sling.

"Commander Michaels." He bowed his head politely toward Stephanos before turning his attention to Weston. "Welcome aboard the *Odyssey*, Captain. I'm Commander Jason Roberts, your first officer."

"Commander." Weston returned the gesture while glancing around the room.

"Excuse me, Captain? I don't mean to question you, but would you prefer to change now?"

Weston startled, looked down at his well-worn flight suit and the helmet cradled under one arm, and grinned. "Don't much look like the captain of the fleet's pride and joy, now, do I? Well, let's transfer the command codes now; I'll come back in full dress whites for the camera ops in an hour."

"Yes, sir."

Roberts moved over to the captain's command seat and thumbed a print scanner, motioning Weston to do the same. After Weston's thumb had been scanned, twin lights lit up and the computer voice broke in.

"Command transfer initiated. Please confirm identities and desire to initiate transfer protocol."

"Identify Commander Roberts, Jason, NACS *Odyssey*. Transfer all command access rights to Captain Eric Weston."

"Confirmed. Captain Weston, please identify and confirm."

"Identify Captain Weston, Eric, NACS *Odyssey*. Confirm access transfer."

"All command access rights have been transferred. Welcome aboard, Captain."

Weston removed his thumb from the scanner and glanced over at Stephanos, who by now looked like he was about to float away—rotational gravity be damned.

"Well, Commander, the Angels are yours." Weston waited for a moment, permitting Stephanos his time in the sun, then continued. "I'll be expecting a full report on the squadron—weapons, flight status, and roster—by tomorrow."

Steph's smile dropped several degrees, probably at the thought of the paperwork he had just inherited. Weston started to smirk in response, until he, too, remembered the increased paperwork awaiting his attention.

Recovering, Steph saluted with a smile and, turning on his heel, strode off to his new duties.

"I'll be in my quarters preparing for the ceremony, Commander," Weston said, before he, too, turned to leave.

He headed down two decks to the officers' quarters, finally finding his room after a couple wrong turns. He stripped out of his flight suit, peeling the liner off his skin, and tossed it into a hamper built into the wall. A few minutes later, he was in the shower, washing the last remnants of his fighter suit off his body and hair.

After an all-too-short shower, Weston dried off and checked his closet. He found that all his things had preceded him to the ship and were all perfectly laid out.

I guess there are some perks to command, after all.

He pulled his dress whites out and laid them on his bed. Forty-five minutes after he had entered his quarters, an entirely new man emerged and headed back to Odyssey Command.

▶▶▶

The shuttle rolled to a stop and shuddered as the huge pylons stabilized the delta-shaped craft in the zero-g of the hangar deck. A few minutes passed as the craft was secured. The lift readied as her passengers floated over to it, dropped onto the steel plate, and activated their Magboots. Loud reverberations echoed through the air as they all locked into place on the lift, waiting for it to drop.

Machinery hummed and the lift dropped down until it came into contact with the flight deck of the big mother ship, and the passengers found themselves staring at a pair of armed sentries. Lt. Sean Bermont, former member of the Canadian Joint Task Force 2, was the first to step forward, handing his identification to the Marine sentry.

"Lieutenant Bermont, to join ship's company," he said, passing the sheet with his orders to the Marine.

The sentry glanced down at it, but his eyes weren't looking at the formal orders and ID; instead, they moved farther down to the lieutenant's dog tags.

The information came up, along with a countersigned security voucher from the ship's computer, and the Marine signed off on the arrival. "Very good, sir. Lift to the habitation decks is twenty meters behind you, and you should check in with the XO as soon as you settle in."

Bermont nodded and turned on his heel—as well as he could in zero-g—and moved toward the lift.

Behind him, he could hear the next man handing over his ID to the Marine.

▶▶▶

Weston left his quarters, dreading the press conference. When Commander Roberts met him at the entry to Command, Weston acknowledged him and everyone around the bridge before addressing his new XO.

"Commander, I think we should finish up the publicity ceremonies as quickly as possible. We do have a mission to begin," Weston said, wanting to get his new command underway. Although he had to play to the press, he didn't have to like it.

"Yes, sir. I'll contact the admiral, and we'll set up the public transfer."

Weston walked around the command chair, lowering himself slowly into it.

Huh, it is more comfortable than my fighter. Still...It just feels off, somehow. He fidgeted a bit in the large chair, familiarizing himself with the displays available at his fingertips, checking and rechecking the emergency restraints. Finally, he gave up the attempt to force a level of comfort that he didn't yet feel and turned his attention to work.

Weston glanced through the massive amount of reports from the ship's stations, noticing that there were remarkably few from the tactical stations concerning the ship's defensive systems. All the internal diagnostics were available, but there were no practical numbers; it was all theoretical. Weston was still examining the defensive systems when Roberts returned.

"Captain, the admiral is waiting in the conference room for the transfer of title."

"Good," Weston agreed, "let's get this over with."

Roberts and Weston left the bridge, riding an internal lift down to one of the outer decks, and entered the conference room. Admiral Gracen was surrounded by aides and several members of national and international presses, all with their whirring cameras focused on Weston's entrance.

She was a striking woman, one who knew how to manipulate a group with her tall, aristocratic bearing, as she proved while carefully guiding the press in the direction of the captain. "Ah, Captain Weston. Come in, come in," she said. "I'm certain that you're anxious to begin your new command."

"Yes, ma'am." Weston engaged his best professional face, smiling blandly as he stood ramrod straight for the cameras. "I'm eager to put the new systems to the test."

"Good. Good. Well, let's get this done. Is everybody ready?"

After all had voiced their readiness, the admiral pressed a control and the lights dimmed. Weston knew that the ship's recorders had just activated to document the transfer for the military archives.

The admiral leaned down and withdrew a small gold patch from a box by her seat.

"Eric Weston, former commander of the Archangel Flight Group, you have been promoted to the level of captain of the NACS *Odyssey*, with all the responsibilities and privileges therein."

The cameras whirred, focusing on the admiral's hand as she placed the gold patch on his left shoulder and stepped back. She extended her hand to Weston and shook his firmly.

"Congratulations, Captain."

"Thank you, Admiral. Now, if I may be excused, I'll—"

"It's not that easy, Captain. You *are* the guest of honor here, and there is protocol to be observed."

Weston sighed as he realized that he wouldn't be escaping after all. Still, the rest of the evening flew by as he was introduced to various dignitaries and members of the press. The press conference went by in a blur; about half the questions put to him received a standard "no comment," in slightly more flowery language, leading him to the after-party with a sensation in his gut remarkably similar to how he felt after flying triple back-to-back missions during the war.

He did his best not to look too eager to be gone as he picked at the buffet and said all the expected things in passing. The food was good, even if the conversation was lacking, but he did have trouble evading one particular reporter.

"Captain Weston! Excuse me, Captain."

Weston turned, already knowing whom the voice belonged to, but still startled when she appeared only inches away.

"Miss Lynn, nice to see you again."

A smirk crossed her face. "I'm sure, Captain. I still have a couple questions to ask you."

"Please, Miss Lynn, I've already answered your questions to the best of my ability. Much of the *Odyssey*'s mission and crew remains classified, as I'm sure you understand."

The woman gave Weston a knowing look, her expression making her confidence, or lack thereof, in Weston's answers quite clear. The young reporter was a representative of the Eastern Block, including China, parts of the old Soviet Union, Korea, India, and many other countries, which had been enough of a force that the United States formed a new defense treaty with Canada and Mexico. Although both sides had avoided using nuclear weapons, the massive damage to all the nations' infrastructures had been one of the deciding factors in the inception of the Confederation. Weston had previously met her when he had been forced to scrounge through Beijing in search of materials to repair his downed fighter. She'd nearly gotten him killed, and he had the distinct impression that she was now out to finish the job.

"Captain, what are your thoughts on a military presence being the first thing we, as human beings, send to the stars?" she probed. "Should we really be carrying our problems with us when we break free of the solar system?"

Weston sighed. "Miss Lynn, I can't comment on matters of philosophy. I'm sorry." He couldn't see it, but he knew that her microphone and camera were focused on him, and he had to select each word carefully.

"But, Captain, what about—"

Commander Roberts slid between Miss Lynn and Weston.

"Captain, your presence is required by the admiral."

Weston bowed out gratefully. "If you'll excuse me, Miss Lynn." As they left, he whispered aside to Roberts, "Thanks for getting me out of that."

"Don't thank me, sir. The admiral noticed Miss Lynn circling and thought you might need backup."

Admiral Gracen always did know how to smell trouble.

"Admiral, I understand I owe you my thanks." Weston slipped alongside the stern-looking admiral as she took a sip of her champagne.

Gracen looked him over seriously for a moment, her dark eyes piercing him through and through before she deigned to crook her lips and speak. "Nonsense, Captain, just doing my duty. The last thing the NAC needs is an Eastern Block 'exclusive' slicing our highest-profile captain to shreds."

"They have become better at manipulating public opinion lately, haven't they?" Weston grimaced.

"Yes, well…They tried by force of arms and very nearly succeeded," she said. "I suppose it was natural that they would begin applying alternative pressure."

"Yeah, and Lynn is far too good at her job."

"She ought to be." Gracen let a small smile grace her stern face. "We trained her, after all."

"Why is it that the best terrorists, the worst enemies, and the most dangerous people in the world always seem to be schooled in the North American Confederation?" Weston asked. "Just once can't they have graduated from some obscure school in Africa or something?"

Gracen shrugged. "Know thine enemy, I suppose. Where better for them to learn to stick it to us?"

"Do we honestly have to keep training the people doing the sticking?"

"Ah, but if someone else did it, we wouldn't have such *detailed* files on them," Gracen said.

Weston chuckled as he conceded the point. "Touché, I suppose, Admiral. Still, in any case, I think I'll remove myself from the chopping block and retire for the evening. I have a big day tomorrow."

Weston excused himself from the party, navigating the long corridors to his quarters. Although he knew that this first mission was just a shakedown cruise, he was glad to get away from the postwar politics. Even though there was still a space race of sorts, the Eastern Block was nowhere near the development of transition technology. The *Odyssey* was built primarily as a test bed for a host of new technologies and to defend the outer system facilities against potential Block attacks. With the addition of the transition drive, the mission became much more, however. Weston didn't hope to find anything specific, but the scheduled experiments would cover everything from long-term physical effects of space travel to looking for life in various star systems.

He entered his quarters and collapsed on the bed. Diplomacy. Up until now it hadn't been that much of a factor in his career; leading the Archangels had been mostly a matter of flying and firing, the same as when he was a Marine aviator for the United States.

Luckily, diplomacy would be over once he was out of communication with Earth, and that wouldn't be much longer, now. A few moments later, the events of the day exacted their toll and Weston fell fast asleep.

CHAPTER 2

▶ "COMMANDER ROBERTS, HAS the ship been cleared for departure?" Captain Weston asked.

"Yes, sir, Station Liberty cleared us several minutes ago," the imposing commander said, his voice carrying nonetheless. "We received final clearance from the tower during the night, and Commander Harris wishes you luck."

Weston was satisfied; tower clearance had been the final, official word they needed to begin. "Send him my thanks, Commander. Are we a go for thruster release?"

Roberts tapped out a command on his tablet PDA. "Aye, sir."

"All right, then. Helm, clear the moorings and take us out. Dead slow."

"Dead slow. Aye, sir."

The *Odyssey* shared space with many of the government construction projects of the North American Confederacy, including the space station that had eventually been built to replace the ISS after the aging construct was finally decommissioned and left to burn up in the atmosphere as its orbit failed. The new Liberty Station was built to last a great deal longer than its predecessor, and as the *Odyssey* cleared the big station's shadow, Weston admired the silhouette of the station against the blue and white of Earth below.

The deck rumbled as the thrusters pushed the big ship out of orbit, bringing Weston's focus back to the task at hand. Lieutenant Daniels tapped away on the touch screen in front of him, making course corrections on the fly via the computer interface.

Weston shivered. Watching Daniels work, he really didn't trust the "fly-by-keyboard" systems much. He'd always preferred the stick and throttle in his hand, but the designers had made that type of flying a last resort for the *Odyssey*.

Daniels continued with his work and slid his hands along the solid composite surface in front of him. The sensors within the sealed interface detected his finger placement, and the integrated display lit up like the proverbial Christmas tree as Daniels brought the systems online and cleared the mooring.

The *Odyssey*, now free of the mooring cables, drifted clear under soft thruster guidance until Daniels opened up the ship's reactor and sent a low rumble through her. The ship accelerated away from the station and Earth's orbit, leaving behind the cluttered section of space that had given birth to her.

"Helm, as soon as we're clear of Earth space, power up the navigation beams and accelerate to one-third of light," Weston commanded.

"Yes, sir."

As the *Odyssey* cleared the section of space claimed by Earth, the forward field generators powered up and began sweeping the ship's path of debris. Then the *Odyssey*'s massive engines came into play and the big ship began to steam up the huge gravity well generated by Sol.

"Approaching point-oh-five light-speed, Captain," Daniels said. "Request clearance for CM release."

"Granted," Weston replied.

The counter-mass system was the heart of the *Odyssey's* sub-light propulsion systems, a series of generators along the keel of the massive ship that threw up an energy field around the entire vessel. The math involved gave Weston a headache, though he understood it enough to comprehend what was happening as the fields began to charge.

Around the *Odyssey*, a bubble began to form as one generator reinforced the next, establishing an oval pocket that began to segregate the ship and its occupants from the "real" universe. Within the bubble, the effective mass of the ship began to drop, at least so far as the rest of the universe was concerned, rendering the massive ship uniquely less massive.

It wasn't *quite* cheating Einstein, Weston knew, but it was a way to bend the rules, just a little bit. The big drive reactors that powered the *Odyssey* stuck out just to the edge of the field, and when the system was in full operation, they threw out plasma at near light-speed—plasma that massed exactly what it was supposed to as it broke the edge of the field, pushing against the ship whose total mass was fooling the laws of physics into thinking it was 10 percent of what it was.

Without the field, the *Odyssey* could throw down a sprint mode that made a turtle look like a Formula One racer, and its top end clocked in just under a tenth the speed of light, or 0.1c. With the field active, there wasn't a thing built by man that could hope to catch her.

"Navigation." Weston paused and then chastised himself mentally: *Use their names, Eric.* "Lieutenant Daniels, plot a course to bring us on a close flyby of the Demos station and the Jovian research platforms. I want to say hello to an old friend."

Weston heard the young lieutenant at navigation acknowledge the order and, a few moments later, felt the shudder run through the ship as it realigned along its new course. The *Odyssey* was now reaching a quarter the speed of light and still accelerating as it roared along toward the ship repair facility in the Mars orbit.

As the ship approached the "Red Planet," an officer behind Weston called out, "Incoming call, sir. It's from Commodore Wolfe at Demos base."

"How close are we now?" Weston asked.

"About two light-minutes, sir."

"Acknowledge audio only. Inform them of our ETA and tell the commodore that we'll have visual in seven minutes."

"Yes, sir."

▶▶▶

"Excuse me, Chief..." Lieutenant Bermont said as he stepped up close to a squat and solidly built woman wearing the uniform of a chief petty officer.

She glanced up from where she had popped open a conduit panel and was checking diagnostics, her eyes falling to the bars on his uniform.

"Corrin, sir," she saluted.

Bermont returned the salute. "I'm looking for the rec deck, Chief Corrin. 'Fraid I got turned around." He had always felt more at home in the field than in this synthetic environment. Once he got out of the city, he never looked back, finding that he loved the rawness of nature more than anything. Pavement and concrete stopped being his home when he first

discovered jungles and swamps, so Sean became sniper certified with the Canadian Joint Task Force 2 (JTF2) and spent as
much of his time away from cities as he could.

She gave him a sour look and jerked her head over her
shoulder. "Down the hall you'll find a tube. Take it back to
Hab Two, lower decks."

"Thanks, Chief." Bermont nodded and started off. From
behind, he heard a muffled "groundhog" coming from Corrin.

▶▶▶

The seven minutes flew by as Weston carefully watched the
officers under his command, keeping track of their reactions
to the multitude of minor crises that were part of the type of
shakedown mission they were on.

"Captain, Commodore Wolfe for you on visual."

Weston looked up from the terminal he was working on
at the gruff face looking back at him from the screen. "Hello,
Jeff, good to see you again."

"You're telling me! This is about the last place I expected
you to turn up. I should've known that it would take something like that heap to pull you away from the Angels." The
commodore's gruff words were belied by the grin on his face.

"Who said I left the Angels? Got 'em stored tight and
secure on our flight deck."

The commodore laughed. "Now, how on earth did you
manage that?"

"It wasn't that hard," Weston said. "It made for pretty
good PR, and it's good training for the younger members
of the group. Besides, since the war ended, the Angels have
started to be a pain in the collective ass of the Public Relations
Department. They aren't exactly peacekeepers, you know."

"Well, that's a hard point to deny. Not that I regret it one little bit, Eric. Warriors are never appreciated in peacetime, except by those they saved during the war. Looks like we've both come a long way from Japan, my friend." The commodore's smile faded for an instant at the intrusion of old memories.

"We have at that, Jeff, and I can't say that I'm sorry," Weston responded. His eyes clouded as he thought back to the carnage over Japan when he'd first met Wolfe.

The commodore, then Captain Wolfe of the US Marine Corps, had been a flight leader in the Battle of Japan. The Chinese Advanced Mantis Fighters had poured over the beleaguered island state like locusts, faster and more lethal than the aging corps-issued joint strike fighter, short takeoff vertical landing (STVL) models that Wolfe had flown, taking the defense forces by surprise.

The first shots of World War III had been fired less than three miles from where the final moments of World War II had ended for the Pacific Theater.

The commodore grimaced for a moment. "I never had a chance to thank you for that, Eric. If you and the Archangels hadn't shown up…"

Weston waved him off. "It's history, Commodore. Japan was a whole different world and a completely different time. No need for thanks."

The somber moment lasted only a few seconds. "Well, I'll surely be expecting your thanks when you bring that shiny new toy of yours to my station for repairs."

The quiet mood broken, Weston laughed out loud and concluded the conversation as the *Odyssey* began arcing away from the Mars orbit. "Looks like we're starting to pull away from you, Commodore. Is that tanker waiting on us?"

"She's all yours. Been on high-velocity orbit of Saturn for the past several hours. I would imagine her crew is getting impatient."

"I won't keep them waiting too much longer, Commodore. *Odyssey* out." The commodore threw Weston a two-fingered salute before the screen flickered back to a forward view.

Weston looked back over his displays, watching the numbers flash by as the ship arced away from the Mars orbit and hit one-third light-speed, roughly half her maximum cruise speed. The big reactors grew quiet as the crew watched the Red Planet dwindle rapidly in the void. Weston glanced away from the screen, his attention turning toward his own terminal.

"Helm, what's our fuel status?" Weston asked some time later.

"More than sufficient until we refuel, sir," Daniels responded.

"That's not what I asked, Lieutenant." Weston's voice grew sharper, his eyes boring into the back of the young man's head.

"Sorry, sir." Daniels took a few seconds. "We're at about ten percent, sir. We burned about a third of that so far. Mostly during the initial burn at port speed."

"Thank you, Daniels. Begin plotting a retro-burn and take us into the Trojan Belt."

Silence answered him and Weston knew that several eyes had swiveled to watch him as Commander Roberts stepped over.

"Uh, sir, we have a rendezvous to make; you heard the commodore," Commander Roberts reminded him under his breath.

"Yes, I did, but it's going to have to wait," Weston said, gazing at him evenly.

"Yes, sir."

Roberts retreated and Weston felt the shudder run through the deck plates as the *Odyssey*'s course altered and her retrofiring sequence was initiated. Ahead of them loomed the huge face of Jupiter, marked as it had been for centuries by the violent storm in its southern hemisphere. The *Odyssey* arced off to one side, heading for one of the Trojan asteroid belts that hung ominously on either side of the huge planet.

▶ ▶ ▶

Bermont sighed as he settled back into the relatively comfortable couch that lined one entire wall of the crew lounge.

There was a screen embedded in the upper wall across from him that showed the rather impressive image of Jupiter from a link to the exterior cameras. It was nice, he supposed, but definitely not his thing.

He glanced around the room and noticed that a few groups had formed in their off-duty hours, including a couple of tables that seemed reserved for the glory boys of the Archangel Fighter Wing. He shrugged and dropped into an empty seat at a table populated by men in similar uniforms to his own.

Behind him, Bermont listened to the flyboys laughing over something he hadn't heard.

"The main difference between a fighter pilot and God is that God doesn't think he was a fighter pilot," said a man leaning over in his direction, grinning.

Before Bermont could say anything else, someone else cut in. "Yeah, but Archangels are slightly more humble than most fighter pilots."

Most of the men around the table seemed to think that was quite funny.

The Archangels were willing to settle for being God's right hand rather than the Big Guy himself.

Bermont chuckled with the rest and introduced himself. "Bermont."

"Savoy" was the return response, the two shaking hands. "Tech geek."

Bermont noted the ranger tab on the man's shoulder, along with several rockers and a bud on his chest, and didn't even consider making any of the normally requisite geek jokes. Maybe he would later, when he knew the man, but he tried not to make a habit of annoying anyone who could both survive SEAL training and program a video recorder. They tended to be creative when it came to getting even.

He noted Savoy's eyes skimming over his own uniform and couldn't quite stop from smiling when the man looked confused at the total lack of insignia. Unlike the American elite units, JTF2 didn't much go in for things like identification. Until they'd been swept up into the North American Confederation Armed Forces (NACAF), Bermont's normal uniform was a black SAS sweater, BDU pants, and boots. No rank, no insignia, no medals.

"Canadian," Bermont said.

Savoy's eyes widened in recognition. "Ah. Good to have you on board."

"Good to be here."

The pilots behind them roared again, laughing at something, and broke up the conversation. Bermont shifted his attention to check them out. The Archangels were infamous, possibly the most well-known faces in the Confed. The government had used them as poster boys, recruiting tools, and general all-around hero types in order to keep morale up during the war. A lot of troops Bermont knew didn't really like them much, figuring they were all show and no go. Their list of battle honors pretty much put paid to that idea, however.

Bermont didn't have the pedigree to match up with them, but he didn't want reporters shoving cameras up his ass while he took a dump, either. He'd served with the Canadian Joint Task Force 2 before the War Act instituted the Confederation between the United States, Canada, and Mexico. After the Confederation, JTF2 remained viable for a few years, while the armed forces spent more time fighting than worrying about who went where and in what.

Later, when all the old spec ops units got re-prioritized after the war, he'd been offered a slot on the *Odyssey*. He'd been leery of the offer at first, until he was briefed on the types they were calling up for the "security" complement of the starship.

Actual shipboard security was being managed by the marines, which was what he'd expected, of course, but the majority of the ground-based military presence on the ship was actually drawn from all the old "snake-eater" groups. He'd recognized a lot of the names on that list and had signed up without another thought.

His superior, Col. Jackson Neill, had told him that someone had decided it'd be a bright idea if the military people on the ship were already trained in hostile environments and survival techniques beyond the norm.

Bermont figured it was a load of crap himself. After all, even if they did find themselves in an alien world where they could breathe, what were the odds that the snakes there would be edible?

But what was a special operations trooper to do in a postwar world? Apparently, the Powers That Be thought there might be some use for a few of them, eating *alien* snakes, if that's what it took.

Bermont shrugged and leaned back, smiling to himself.

▶▶▶

Weston watched the screens carefully as the crew guided the *Odyssey* into the L4 Trojan point, its powerful navigation beams shouldering aside the larger nickel-iron rocks and sending shudders through the ship as it slowed. He checked off a point in his journal and noted the success of the beams under full-load stress.

"All right, Waters..."

"Sir," Waters said, turning to the captain.

"Power up the primary weapons array."

"Sir?"

"You heard me."

"Aye, sir."

Weston understood the man's hesitation; ironclad treaties existed concerning the firing of weapons anywhere, even close to Earth space. Those treaties didn't extend past the orbit of Mars, however, so Weston fully intended to see how well the systems were integrated into the *Odyssey*'s infrastructure.

"Pick a rock, Ensign," he said, "and then erase it from my universe."

"Aye, aye, Captain." Waters leaned forward, his voice eager.

▶▶▶

It only took a few minutes for the sounds of the shipboard weapons fire to die down, and throughout the ship, those without immediate access to the telemetry plots waited with half-held breaths for the results of the impromptu tests.

"Captain to all hands," Weston's voice sounded over the speakers in the Damage Control Command Center, as it did around the rest of the ship. "Congratulations on a textbook weapons test. Outstanding."

"If you slackers don't get off your flat butts double-time… I'm going to start knocking heads!" Chief Rachel Corrin said as she stalked through the DCCC.

The crew members scrambled to their feet as the harsh voice of the chief growled out at them. They snapped to as she marched down the length of the curved room and glared at them.

"Damage control drills—now!" she hissed, her tone brooking no argument as the crew snapped into action, grabbing their gear and rushing out the door.

Corrin sighed as she watched them go, letting her mask drop for a second once she was alone.

She shook her head, moving along behind the retreating figures. *This crew needs more than drills, in the worst way.*

Whoever had been behind the formation of the *Odyssey's* crew had either been complete imbeciles or hidden geniuses.

Corrin wasn't sure which, though she had money on the former.

The individual crew members had been drawn from some of the best pools of military talent available, and in the postwar economy of the North American Confederacy she served, that meant they had some damned fine people on board.

The problem was so very few of them had ever served with any of their shipmates before.

And that was a recipe for disaster if Chief Petty Officer Corrin ever saw one.

▶▶▶

The *Odyssey*, now back en route to the Saturn refueling rendezvous, accelerated back to its "in-system" cruise speed of 0.3 light-speed. Ahead of the massive ship, its navigation beams blasted aside any debris unlucky enough to be caught in its path, causing the occasional shudder to run through the ship.

Shortly thereafter, the rings of Saturn became visible as the vessel roared toward the orbit of the sixth planet. Out of the rings, a black shape became visible, its trajectory altering almost as soon as it was spotted. It rocketed free of the big planet's gravity well and slid into a parallel course with the *Odyssey*.

"Odyssey Command, this is the *Indigo*. Welcome to Saturn."

"*Indigo*, this is the *Odyssey*. Thanks for the welcome, but I don't think we'll have time to sightsee."

"Pity, we've taken in the sights for the past day while waiting for you. Least you could do is hang around and keep us company for a while."

"'Fraid not, *Indigo*. We have a mission to start, and I understand you have something to help us along?"

"Roger that, *Odyssey*. Lines are coming across now."

Snaking out from the *Indigo*, thick hoses glided across the space between the two ships, reducing their distance to a few hundred feet before the tanker altered its course and paralleled the *Odyssey*. Small pods were in place on the ends of the hoses, each containing a two-man crew that guided the hoses into place. The five hoses were soon locked into the *Odyssey*'s rear compartment, and the tanker began emptying its cargo.

By tanking up at speed in the outer system, the *Odyssey* would be able to keep from wasting a large percentage of its fuel during the initial boost phase of the trip. The pull of the sun's gravity was less here, and they already had built momentum while the ship was still significantly lighter due to its largely empty tanks.

Because of those same empty tanks, however, the fueling would take the better part of what remained of the night. Weston retired shortly after the process had begun, leaving third watch to look after the ship while they were being resupplied. When he woke, the low hum he felt through the deck assured him that the ship was again under full thrust and moving toward the edge of the Sol System.

On the bridge everything was running smoothly. They had just crossed the orbit of Pluto, and although the planet itself was nowhere in sight, it was a cheerful milestone in itself since they were the first humans to reach that far. Roberts had relieved the night watch a couple hours earlier and was sifting through crew assignments when the captain stepped onto the bridge.

"Captain on the bridge!"

"Status," Weston ordered as he stepped over to the command chair.

"We just crossed the orbit of Pluto thirty minutes ago, sir. Technically, we can engage the drive when ready, sir," Roberts replied crisply. "Though, the official heliopause is still a few minutes away."

"Good. Helm, calculate the trajectory—and be precise."

Lieutenant Daniels bent over his console and began the calculations. "Yes, sir."

"Mr. Roberts, contact the transition team. Tell them to charge the system."

Roberts turned to a console on his left, tapping a series of commands. "Transition team reports ready, sir. We can engage the drive at any time," he said into a recessed microphone.

"Good." Weston flipped a switch on his console and activated the ship-wide intercom. "Attention, this is Captain Weston speaking. We are preparing to engage the ship's transition drive system. We have all been briefed on what to expect and the psychological impact of what we are about to experience. Please brace yourselves and report any problems to the medical labs. That is all."

"Helm, do you have that trajectory for me?" he asked.

"Yes, sir, I just fed it into the system. We're ready on this end."

"All right. I want a go, no-go check from all stations."

"Helm…go."

"Transition Control…go." The speakers didn't convey any uncertainty, and Weston wished that he shared the sentiment.

"Reactor Control…go."

The list ran through all of the ship's stations, each confirming in turn that their section had prepared for the effects of the jump until Roberts spoke the final phrase.

"Odyssey Command…go."

"All systems, we are a go for transition in T-minus…" Weston glanced down and punched a series of commands. "Two minutes."

CHAPTER 3

▶ THE TENSION ON the bridge continued to build as the count ticked down, the numbers dropping rapidly until the crew was confronted with the final ten seconds.

Weston shifted nervously in his seat as the number ten went by. The transition effects had been kept highly classified for a reason. He knew what to expect, as did the entire crew, but in this case, that was worse than ignorance.

Next to him, Weston noted Commander Roberts forcing his hands to unclench; small bloodred marks were left to decorate his palms.

Weston viewed people all through the ship holding tightly to things, as if preparing for massive acceleration despite what they had been trained to expect. In one room, a nervous crewman had accidently knocked himself out while trying to strap himself to a chair; in retrospect, he was considered lucky.

A high-pitched whine began to reverberate through the ship. Usually felt long before heard, the sound continued to rise.

On the bridge, Captain Weston watched the small red light flicker on as the count went past five seconds and noted a slight relaxation that swept through him when it did. They were now past the point of no return. The *Odyssey* and her crew were about to make history.

The whine had reached painful levels in some areas of the ship, causing people to cover their ears and close their eyes in the vain attempt to shut out the sound. Outside the ship, a strange disturbance was affecting the ship's forward sensor spires, causing the *Odyssey* computers to begin insisting that the spires were no longer present.

The disturbance had begun making its way toward the aft of the ship. One by one, key systems appeared to go offline, each system insisting that it simply wasn't there.

The count hit zero. Weston's eyes widened as the disturbance intersected the bridge, and the entire forward section, including the view screen, disintegrated into uncountable particles that were swept away into the void of space. Weston found himself sitting on the edge of the void, grasping his chair for protection, as the effect encompassed his crew, one by one. When the maelstrom engulfed him and the universe went black, Weston's last conscious thought echoed through what was left of his universe.

If we survive this, I'm going to have a very serious talk with the techs back home about what constitutes "need to know."

▶▶▶

Four and a half light-years from where the *Odyssey* vanished, in the Alpha Centauri star system, a cloud of particles decelerated, apparently from nowhere, and rapidly reformed themselves. First, the long forward spires of the *Odyssey*'s primary communications array, and soon the rest of the vessel, were reconstituted as the tachyon disruption faded and left the massive ship hurtling sunward into the system's primary.

Odyssey Command recovered before the rest of the ship, the transition shock rippling through them even as they turned their attention back to the status reports that began filtering in. Weston had almost slipped from the command chair after they reentered dimensional space and was quick to correct his posture. A moment later, his head stopped screaming long enough for him to begin reacting.

"Report! All stations," he snapped, hoping his voice was steadier than his vision.

"Ship is undamaged, sir. Minor wear evident on the tachyon reactors. The tachyon-based sensors are out of alignment, however. Two hours to repair." The technician behind him sounded bad. Weston rose to look at him closer.

"Ensign Waters, you are relieved. Go to the med-lab and get yourself checked out."

As Waters headed for the back of the room, Weston glanced around the room again, searching harder for any evidence of trouble. The rest seemed all right, but he would have to keep a closer eye on them until they had a chance for some rest. He returned to his seat and thumbed an intercom switch after tapping in the channel number.

"Med-lab, how bad is it down there?"

Dr. Stevens's voice sounded shaky, even over the intercom. "Pretty bad, Captain. Over thirty crew members have reported in for various reasons…" The pause in the doctor's speech seemed ominous. "And we have at least one who we have to confine to the labs…Lieutenant Tearborn snapped, Captain. Security picked her up in Engineering. Apparently, she witnessed the reactor vaporize and she thought it was a breach."

Weston's words were uttered too quietly for anyone to hear him, but his body language transmitted the message to anyone on the bridge unfortunate enough to be watching. It had been hard enough watching the ship, apparently disintegrating into a vacuum, but to watch the reactor fall apart? Too many horror stories had been told about reactor breaches on board ships for that to be easily dismissed.

Weston let out a breath he hadn't known he was holding. "All right, Doctor. Do what you can. Oh, by the way, I just sent Ensign Waters down to you. He should be arriving soon."

"Yes, sir, we'll clear some space. Med-lab out."

Weston thumbed the switch back and sank into his seat. Tearborn was a good engineer, not someone he would expect to snap. *When I get home, I think I'll recommend sedatives for nonessential crew members prior to entering transitional space.* He thumbed open a notepad on his console and tapped one-handed, his eyes flickering between the log and the rest of the bridge.

He compartmentalized his thoughts and emotions, then straightened and locked an iron grip on his command persona. "Helm, plot us a nice long hyperbolic course. Commander Roberts, tell the labs to make good use of the time, because we'll transition out when we clear the gravity well."

"Aye, sir," both Daniels and Roberts chorused as they turned to their tasks.

The *Odyssey* sailed into the system, sails almost literally unfurling as the ship's massive retractable sensor arrays rose and locked into position, strengthening the impression of an ancient sailing ship.

Weston watched on his monitors as researchers rushed from lab to lab and console to console as they struggled to shake off the transitional effects and complete their work in the shortest time possible. The rear module entered a state of barely controlled chaos as the military crew stepped back and watched the civilian scientists, half in awe and half in disgust.

Weston oversaw the initial setup of schedules and sensor times, but as he had worked way past his shift without rest, he decided to leave it to his officers and allowed himself to retire and recover from the shock he had not allowed his system to work out. In his quarters, Weston felt his control slip away, and his hands shook as he collapsed on the bed, finally permitting himself to simply let go. Sleep didn't come easily, but it came.

▶▶▶

Chief Corrin growled as she yanked a crewman up by the scruff of his neck, twisting him away from her so he didn't puke on her polished boots.

"Get to the med-lab!" she growled, shoving him along in front of her. She stayed with him just long enough to flag down another crewman who looked to be in moderately better shape. "Med-lab?"

He nodded.

"Here." She shoved the still-retching crewman into his arms. "Take him."

"Yes, ma'am."

Corrin watched them stumble down the hall and steeled her stomach once again, heading into Marine Country to see what kind of mess the groundhogs had done to her bulkheads.

The sound of yelling up ahead caused her to quicken her pace, but the tone made her stop before she came into sight. She curiously glanced around the corner into one of the soldier's lounges, and her eyes widened at what she saw.

"OH YEAH!" The lieutenant who had asked her for directions earlier was boosting his hands in the air and yelling at the top of his lungs. "I want to go again!"

He grinned as half the men around him laughed openly and the other half glared at him with sickly green faces.

Corrin shook her head and backed out.

They couldn't give us marines...Noooo...They had to recruit a bunch of Rambo wannabes. Marines are bad enough, but at least I KNOW marines.

▶▶▶

"Captain to the bridge! Captain to the bridge!"

Weston was clear of his bed and halfway to the door before his senses focused enough to realize that running around the ship in his underwear probably wouldn't do much for morale. Well, his morale, anyway. In less than two minutes, he hurried onto the bridge, fastening the last couple buttons on his collar and looking around for the emergency.

"Captain, over here." Commander Roberts was looking at a display on one of the terminals linked to the research labs below.

"Roberts, I hardly think that a research breakthrough necessitated getting me out of bed. It could have waited until morning."

"No, sir—at least not according to the techs in the tachyon lab."

Weston's eyes narrowed. "Is it trouble with the reactors?"

Trouble with the tachyon reactors would be bad news; the transition drive was all that kept them from having to limp home at slightly under two-thirds light-speed.

"No, sir. Our tachyon-based sensing arrays started picking up a tachyon signal about an hour ago, sir. It took us this long to figure out even part of it."

"Figure out? We pick up stray signals all the time; tachyons are generated by at least a dozen special events." Weston wasn't sure, but he felt like his mind hadn't fully woken up.

"This isn't a stray, Captain. It's modulated."

Weston was silent for a moment. Modulated tachyon signals were considered impossible back home. It was a classic chicken-and-egg scenario. You couldn't modulate a superlight signal without a superlight computer, but of course, without modulated superlight signals, no one could build a computer that fast. The best anyone had really come up with was a complicated form of Morse code that sufficed for most in-system communications but required massive directional transmitters.

Transmitters that, unfortunately, didn't fit on the *Odyssey*. The best a ship her size could manage was an infinitesimal "ping" that allowed her to perform short- and long-range scans but didn't allow for any form of communication unless she managed to perfectly hit the intended receiver with the minute burst.

From within a star system, that was just barely possible.

At anything greater, they had a better chance of sailing off the edge of the universe.

More's the pity. "How the hell did we just happen to walk into this?" Weston frowned at the readout.

Roberts swallowed. "It appears to be omnidirectional, sir."

"What?"

Roberts just shrugged.

Weston blinked in shock. "My God."

That was unbelievable. An omnidirectional signal from a tachyon source would require immense power reserves, entire levels of magnitude above and beyond what the *Odyssey* could possibly *hope* to pump out. And the *Odyssey* had one of the most advanced reactors in existence.

"Yes, sir."

Weston tried to shake off the awe. "I guess science scores another foul ball; someone must have done the impossible again. Where's it from? Mars? Earth? One of the outposts?"

"No, sir. It's from a white giant about twenty-eight light-years from here."

For the third time in as many minutes, Weston was floored. "I don't suppose anybody we know is out there?"

Roberts just shook his head as Weston tried to wrap his mind around the situation. "No, sir. This is as close to absolute proof as you get. It's definitely not from Earth, sir."

Weston quickly recovered from the surprise. "Okay, it's alien. Any idea what it says?"

"Not exactly, sir. But Decryption thinks it's an SOS. They seem fairly confident."

"Yeah, I remember how confident they were thirteen years ago when they swore that the Block was calling for a retreat. I lost twelve planes before we managed to get our ass out of the middle of the Block's reinforcements," Weston muttered.

Still, his dry reply was belied by the look of interest that flared across his face. History was afoot here, and it seemed that the *Odyssey* was about to plunge right through the center of it. He paused for a moment, his eyes staring at the screens without seeing them, considering his options. The sheer odds of running into something like this were incalculable, though he'd actually seen similar things in his life. Hell, much of Earth's history rested on pivot points of sheer coincidence.

If someone out here was popping off omnidirectional tachyon bursts, why the hell hadn't they been detected before this?

Weston supposed that part of it was that human detection systems were both incredibly new (less than a decade old) and, frankly, not particularly good. He knew that the detection threshold for the *Odyssey*'s arrays were quite high; the power needed to blip her systems with an omnidirectional signal was staggering.

Oh, who was he kidding? He was out here now, and there was no way in hell he wasn't going to check it out. It struck him then that he was probably the first ship's captain in a couple centuries at best who didn't have the option of calling for orders when presented with something new. He'd known it before he took the assignment, of course, but there was something visceral about having that feeling forced on him like this.

"How long until we're clear of Alpha Centauri?" Weston asked.

"We've had to correct to avoid passing though the gravity tides of Beta Centauri, but still, we'll be clear in about an hour."

"Good. I'm going back to talk with some of the lab techs. Especially those Decryption boys…" Weston scoffed. "We'll see how certain they really are. Inform me when we're cleared for transition. In the meantime, have a course plotted to intercept the signal's source."

"Yes, sir."

▶ ▶ ▶

Weston took the first-available tube back to the rear habitat, following the smoothly arcing corridors until they led him to the com-lab. When the doors cycled open, noise assualted Weston from at least half a dozen stations as they analyzed the signal. The combined blaring was almost deafening.

"Is that really necessary?" Weston raised his voice as high as he could, trying to communicate past the ambient sounds to a man in a white lab coat.

The man glanced up at him, almost ignoring him until a glimmer of recognition flickered across his face, and his hand reached out and slapped a bank of switches, mercifully silencing the room. Weston glanced around and realized that only the tech he had talked to was actually listening to the sounds; the rest were wincing beneath heavy ear guards.

Wish I'd known to bring a pair...My ears are going to ring for hours. Weston winced and rubbed the sides of his head.

"I'm terribly sorry, Captain. I was just seeing if I could decipher the meaning," the man said apologetically. Almost immediately, the man seemed to forget he was there.

"Ahem," Weston cleared his throat, startling the man, as he shook his head in an attempt to clear the ringing. "How on earth could you possibly decipher anything from that mess?"

"Mess? Hardly. So far I've been able to tell at least three words apart, although I can only be sure of one—'escouros.' It seems to mean 'help' or perhaps 'rescue.'"

Weston did a double take and stared at the tech. "I don't take well to jokes at times like this Mr...."

The man looked startled for a moment, then grabbed Weston's hand and shook it energetically. "I'm so sorry, Captain! I'm Dr. Palin. I see you haven't had a chance to read my file yet, so I'll apologize for my apparent levity. I'm the *Odyssey*'s token linguist." The man grinned wryly at the word *token.* "My previous supervisor recommended me for the position, probably to get rid of me, I suppose, but I really am the best at what I do, Captain."

Weston was taken aback by the man's quick change of tack, his hand limply following Palin's. "Uh, all right. So you're the one who thinks it's a distress call?"

"No. I *know* it's a distress call. Unfortunately, I can't seem to find any specifics in the signal." Palin frowned.

Weston spent the next few minutes talking with Dr. Palin, occasionally interrupted by the lab technicians as they attempted to disassociate themselves from Palin, who was clearly considered a heretic.

Weston ignored them, as they didn't have any thoughts of their own to add to the discussion. He didn't have much patience for people who were only willing to toe the company line. While they were responsible for what they *knew*, he wanted to hear what people *thought* as well. Whether he was right or not, Palin was at least willing to step up to the plate, as it were.

"I'm going to take the *Odyssey* to investigate. If you're right, it's our duty to respond." Weston paused a moment. "And besides, even if you're wrong, it's something we really *have* to see for ourselves. Oh, and Doc? I think it would be best if you used the headphones for a while, give the others a break."

"Very well, Captain. I suppose I could restrict myself." Palin's voice sounded disappointed. "For a little while, at least."

Weston retreated from the lab, tapping the signal key to activate the induction microphone on his jaw. "Commander Roberts."

Roberts responded, "Yes, sir?"

"I'm heading to my office for a while. Contact me when we clear the gravity well."

"Yes, sir."

▶▶▶

Weston took the tube back to the forward habitat and navigated through the rolling corridors to his office. Once inside, he called up Dr. Palin's file on his local terminal, determined to find out what kind of man he was going to trust his ship's future to.

This is strange. To say that Palin's file was nondescript was an understatement. There were no particularly impressive achievements, nor were there any notes of discipline problems, something which drew his attention rather quickly after his first meeting with the man. *This can't be his record. A clerical error?* Weston began sweeping through dossiers that were stored in the computer's fractal core, sifting through terabytes of information as he had the computer cross-reference the good doctor's past.

Bingo. The computer flashed a "restricted information" block as he tried to call up one of the buried files that the computer had matched with Palin. A few moments later, his override code gave him access to the file he wanted.

He leaned back and skimmed through the file, skipping the basic biographical information to get to the meat of the situation.

Jesus Christ, what on earth is this? Weston scanned through the document, comparing the embedded picture quickly against his memory. *Yes, this is Palin—a lot younger, maybe, but definitely him.* The old CIA document described Dr. Edward Palin's contribution to their Black Ops projects in the early years after the turn of the millennium. Hundreds of experiments and documented evidence revolving around Palin's reported abilities.

Dr. Palin was classified as a linguistic telepath. *Whatever the hell that is.* Weston's mood had grown darker. *And you'd think that whoever assigned him would have thought to inform me about his alleged abilities.* Still, Weston had to admit that the file was impressive; it documented cases of Palin cracking encrypted algorithms faster than an array of networked supercomputers, as well as his uncanny ability to learn spoken languages literally overnight. Weston was still delving into Palin's rather extensive record when Roberts's voice came over the ship's intercom.

"Captain, we're about to clear the tidal range."

"On my way, Commander. Notify the ship to be ready for another hop through transitional space."

"Yes, sir." Weston could hear the distaste in the commander's voice.

Once more into the abyss. Weston smiled to himself, shoving aside his misgivings and personal dislike of the transition drive. He couldn't afford to show the crew that their captain didn't trust the very thing they were depending on.

▶▶▶

"All right!" the former Marine Force Recon sergeant said. "I've got thirty bucks that says I can make the all-time standing long-jump record, here and now, and *not* toss my cookies when I land!"

"You're on!" Bermont grinned, slapping a pair of bills down on the table. "I saw your face after the last one, Rogers, and you just ate, so I *know* you're gonna spatter the deck."

Loud cries echoed around the room as others got in on the wager, some betting with the marine, some with the JTF2 lieutenant. Chief Corrin shook her head and tried to pretend that the rank and file weren't betting on who was going to vomit all over her decks.

▶▶▶

Back on the ship's command deck, Weston appraised each officer in an attempt to determine their stress levels. He was satisfied that his command staff was up to the task. And even Waters seemed well recovered from his earlier state.

"We are a go in three minutes." The navigation officer didn't glance up from his instruments as he configured the course corrections.

"Engage transition drive when ready."

"Aye, sir."

Seconds ticked down as the *Odyssey* pulled itself clear of the star's gravity well, reaching for deep space as its massive reactors charged the tachyon transition system. Captain Weston involuntarily gripped the arms of his chair as the countdown started at one minute; he imagined that the rest of the crew felt the same. Transitional space was hardly a vacation.

"Engaging transition now," Lieutenant Daniels said, sounding fearful.

Outside, the nightmare replayed across the ship as the great vessel transitioned out of dimensional space and was flung across time and space by the ship's powerful engines. Weston's thoughts echoed infinitely through his awareness, locked in time and mind by the ship's passage through the universe: *I sure hope this gets easier with practice.*

CHAPTER 4

▶APPARENTLY, IT JUST wasn't going to get any easier. The *Odyssey* reentered dimensional space with emergency alarms blaring. The sound penetrated aching skulls and got even the sickest of the crew moving, as much in the hopes of shutting the things off as anything else.

"Sensors! What's going on?" Weston barely finished his sentence when the vessel rocked violently, forcing him to clutch the command chair.

"Debris field, sir! Shouldn't be here, though!" Waters's replacement, Ensign Bremen, muttered fearfully.

Apparently, the sensors aren't going to be much help, either.

"We came in well clear of system Trojans, sir."

"He's right, Captain," Daniels said. "I specifically set our course to keep us safely away from any Lagrange points. Whatever this is, it hasn't been here very long!"

"Hold on, data coming in," Bremen spoke up before falling silent with a shocked look on his face.

Weston prodded the young man. "Ensign? What is it?"

"It's…It's wreckage, sir. Sweet Jesus! It looks like an entire fleet died out here," Bremen said, his voice struck with a kind of awe and horror all at once. "Still reading heat dissipating from some of the wrecks, sir. They've only been here days at most, if they use the same materials we do."

Silence reined on the bridge for a long moment. Weston could see on their faces the question that was on the mind of every person on the bridge: *What have we gotten ourselves into?*

Weston was the first to break the silence, checking a monitor beside his chair. "Breman, I want a complete scan of the system. If whatever did this is still here, I want to know it. Daniels, triangulate and plot a course for the tachyon source."

"Lost the signal, sir," Lieutenant Daniels said, face downcast. "Best I can do is a general area—about two-and-a-half-thousand-kilometer diameter."

Weston grimaced. He should have known it wouldn't be that easy. "All right, take us to the area and initiate a search grid."

Weston slumped back into the chair, acknowledging multiple reports from the various stations regarding negative contacts in each sector. Reports were still coming in from the labs concerning the tachyon signal and its peculiar modulation. Palin still swore it was an SOS, and judging from the debris they had just seen, that conclusion didn't take a rocket scientist, as the old expression went.

"Captain! We just picked up something along the search pattern. Looks like a ship."

"Let me see it."

The massive screen focused on a floating hulk—no running lights, no apparent drive activity, no life support. The ship was so dead that the *Odyssey*'s computers had to enhance the image from the ship's lidar- and radar-based sensors to allow it to be seen against the black backdrop of space. The screen automatically cut back on magnification as the *Odyssey* approached the derelict craft. The ship was covered with carbon scoring from dozens of weapon strikes. Little of the original exterior appeared intact, although penetrating sensors detected that the interior atmosphere was possibly intact.

"Fascinating," Weston said. "Commander Roberts, have the landing shuttle prepped and take a team over there. Full environmental protocol. You'd better assume that it's a class-six environment."

"Yes, sir." Roberts sent a signal to the shuttle bay and exited the bridge.

▶▶▶

"Pay up!" Bermont grinned as Sergeant Rogers curled on the ground after his more-than-ten-light-year standing long jump, emptying his stomach across the deck.

Rogers groaned but shoveled a ten and twenty into Lieutenant Bermont's hand just as the alert station's call rang through the deck.

The laughing, joking, retching, and cursing ended abruptly as every man shoved his bitching stomach back down his throat and stumbled for the door.

▶▶▶

It didn't take long for Commander Roberts to reach the flight deck, and the crews were already prepping the Prometheus Class shuttle when he stepped onto the deck, boots echoing against the metal floor.

From another lift he saw a group of soldiers double-time their way across the zero-g deck, heading toward the shuttle that was prepping, and noted with concern the sickly color of a few of their faces.

One of them, a sergeant from the marines—Rogers, he recalled—was currently the palest black man that Commander Roberts had ever seen in his life. He shook his head in sympathy. Anyone that sick didn't want to move, let alone strap into a shuttle, but he didn't comment as the soldier began fitting himself into armor and grabbing a rifle from the rack. Instead, he suited himself up in likewise fashion, grabbed a sidearm and rifle, and followed the men onto the shuttle.

Roberts strapped himself into a troop seat on board one of the *Odyssey's* recon shuttles, pulling the harness tightly down across his shoulders. Around him, a small team of Special Forces troops followed suit, some of them strapping weapons above their seats and others breaking their arms down in preparation for the mission.

"All right, Jenny, take us out," Roberts addressed the diminutive woman, Lt. Jenny Samuels, in the pilot's chair and thought he detected an evil grin playing across her face. "And none of that hotdogging, either. The Archangels already know you're a good pilot!"

A low chuckle rippled around the flight seat as the shuttle was jarred by the thrusters kicking in. Two of the older soldiers groaned, making Roberts wonder what they knew that he didn't. He found out a few moments later as the shuttle's retro-thrusters fired and he was pressed hard up into the biting straps that held him to his seat. Outside, the shuttle flew clear of the *Odyssey's* flight deck.

"Roger, Odyssey Control, Archangel Two and Three have taken up escort positions. We're burning to intercept vector now." Another jolt slammed him into the waiting embrace of the straps as he listened to the shuttle's radio chatter over the induction transceiver secured to his jaw.

"Confirmed, Shuttle One. We don't read any viable airlocks on board, so you'll have to burn through."

"Affirmative, Odyssey Control, the portable lock is being prepped now. We'll be ready."

The chatter died down as the shuttle approached the derelict craft, its huge spotlights playing across the carbon-scored exterior as the mission specialist, Lieutenant Matheson, searched for a solid section to attach to. The alien ship seemed remarkably intact, considering the appearance of its exterior hull, and the lieutenant had little trouble selecting a spot. One last jolt pushed Roberts deep into his seat as the shuttle's magnetic grapplers locked on and secured them to the ship. From below them they heard the portable airlock latch onto the ship, and then a hatch in the floor spiraled open.

"Everybody, lock up. Full environmental protection. McRaedy, get in there and cut through."

A hissing sound echoed through the shuttle's interior as the soldiers and pilots locked up their environmental suits and moved into position. Two soldiers covered McRaedy with their rifles as he began cutting through the metal hull of the derelict vessel, sending showers of sparks flying back into the shuttle.

"Damn tough material, sir!" McRaedy yelled back as he kept working.

"Can you do it, Soldier?" Roberts asked over the noise.

"Kin-a, sir," the man yelled back. "Just watch me go."

"Go, Soldier, go." Roberts permitted himself a smirk under the cover of his helmet.

Despite the slow nature of the work, McRaedy managed to cut through after a little less than an hour had passed, moving back as the circular piece of metal fell away and clanged inside the derelict.

Roberts looked at one of the soldiers speculatively. "Artificial gravity? Curiouser and curiouser."

Roberts dropped through the hole, followed instantly by two others who swung their rifles as they covered the length of the corridor. A third soldier dropped in between them, sweeping a hand-held sensor up and down the hall, tracing hidden circuits and power relays through the ship's deck, finally settling on a direction and heading toward the ship's apparent bow. The rest of the team took up positions around Roberts and the sensor tech, covering point and guarding the rear.

"This way." The tech analyzed the power relays and their nodes of intersection. "If we had designed this ship, the bridge would be forward another ten meters or so and up two decks."

Roberts waved the teams forward to an access passage that angled upward. They moved along slowly, the marines' rifles leading the way as the group inched along.

"What's this dirt on the deck?" Roberts growled. His eyes narrowed as he nudged a pile of crumbled material with his boot.

"Unknown. I've got a sample," the tech replied. "Complex compounds, a lot of organics. I'll have to run it through the spectrometer and other gear on the *Odyssey* to break it down for you."

"Right." Roberts scuffed his boot clean on the wall as he stepped over the mess and followed the marines up the access route.

Clearing the empty decks step by step was unnerving for men used to ships that thrummed with life and power; the lack of either in these corridors left them looking constantly over their shoulders for whatever it was that they'd missed in the first pass.

The bridge was up three decks and back twenty meters, but they found it quickly all the same. The access doors were sealed tight, forcing them to use cutters with mixed results. Certainly, they were able to burn through the door, but it was harder than Roberts would have expected, given the thickness of the armor. While the hallways were empty and deserted, the bridge was not. Bodies of the crew were slumped over their consoles—barely recognizable as such, but definitely the crew. They were mummy-like husks, all in the same utilitarian gold uniform.

"My God," one of the soldiers said, obviously gagging in his suit.

"Help him," Roberts directed another to help the soldier back to the shuttle. "What in the hell happened to them?"

"I don't know." The tech's voice relayed a grimness that matched the sight before them.

The bodies were completely desiccated, their skin reduced to leather on their bones, their hair waving about in the slightest breeze. Their eyes—or where their eyes should have been—were black sunken pits.

"No water or other liquids are present...But it's more than that. Their cell structure seems to have been ruptured. I'd say the loss of bodily fluids was a side effect, sir," the technician said.

"Go on," Roberts said.

"If it weren't for the state of the wreckage, I'd say that they've been here a long time. Internal heat, air, and other traces say otherwise, though."

"They look human," Roberts said, stepping around the bodies.

"Don't read too much into that, sir," the technician said. "We tend to see humans in everything. It's a known evolutionary trait that helps children recognize their parents instinctively. It's the same trait that causes people to see faces in things like burnt toast or think that baby anythings are cute. As messed up as these bodies are, it's hard to say what they looked like when they were alive."

Roberts just shook his head and stepped up beside the second tech, who was trying to interface with the ship's computer. "Any luck, Macklin?"

The tech shook his head. "No, sir. The computer's either beyond the tools I'm using or it's completely scrambled. Given the state of things around here, I wouldn't take any bets on which one it is."

Roberts was looking over the central seat, apparently the captain's position. He marveled at the similarities to the *Odyssey* in its layout and dimensions. Whoever these people were, they certainly seemed to be as close to human as you got.

"Commander Roberts."

His back inadvertently snapped straighter as he heard the captain's voice over the induction set on his jaw.

"Recall your team. We spotted the source of the transmission, and we don't want to risk leaving you there while we go investigate."

"Yes, sir." Roberts thumbed the induction set to wideband broadcast and relayed the captain's orders. "Okay, everybody. Pack it up. We've got an SOS to answer and the captain doesn't want to be late."

The team made it back to the lock in record time, climbing out of the derelict vessel and into the shuttle. A signal from the pilot closed the floor hatch, and the small ship lifted off, leaving the portable airlock behind, still sealed tight.

"Roger, Odyssey Control, Shuttle One is clear of the alien craft and coming home. Archangels One and Two providing escort."

The *Odyssey* was already accelerating away from the derelict vessel as Shuttle One and its escort glided in on a docking vector. Looking over the pilot's shoulder, Roberts could see the distant glow of four of the Archangels as they accelerated on maximum burn toward the signal source, mock contrails forming behind them as the superheated plasma from their twin reactors swirled a few moments before vanishing into the void.

"The captain's broken the Angels out." Jenny pointed out the multiple points of light flitting around the ship.

Roberts glanced at the pilot. "His prerogative, I suppose. Besides, he knows better than anyone what they're capable of."

"You got a point there, sir. Better strap in now, this one's gonna be bumpy," Lieutenant Samuels said.

Roberts hurriedly locked himself back into his seat. When Lieutenant Samuels said that a flight would be bumpy, even the fighter jocks asked for a transfer. The shuttle closed in on the *Odyssey*'s stern, slipping in under the massive engines and aligning carefully along the lower deck of the *Odyssey*'s carrier section. Samuels fired the thrusters, and the shuttle drifted along the enclosed deck, its speed arrested, as the big ship's fighter trap hooked the shuttle. Two loud clangs sounded as the magnetic grappler connected and hauled the shuttle down to the bay floor.

Wincing, Roberts unstrapped himself and rubbed his sore shoulders. "Last time I checked, it was a court-martial offense to assault a superior officer, Samuels. I don't care if you do use the shuttle as a weapon."

Several soldiers in similar condition laughed ruefully as they disembarked the shuttle. "You'd never get it through the courts, sir. Too many of the brass have identical bruises, and they feel that if they had to go through it, so does everybody else."

Laughter rang in their ears as the team headed for the shuttle pod along the central pylon. Before they got halfway there, Captain Weston stepped out and started toward them.

"Sir!" The team saluted as one, coming to rigorous attention.

"As you were," Weston told them after snapping a return salute. He turned to the pilot. "Samuels, I need you to take the shuttle out again. We've found what looks to be a life pod. She's dead in the water and is going to need some help coming in from the cold."

Jennifer walked alongside the captain as he headed toward the shuttle. "How big is it, sir?"

"About eight meters in diameter. Less than that in length. We'll have to use the Can-Arms to bring it in, though. The whole thing is paramagnetic; standard grapplers won't lock on."

Roberts had caught up to them. "Uh, sir? What do you mean by 'we'? You're needed on the bridge."

Weston waved him off. "Not this time, Commander. I'm qualified to run the Can-Arms and you aren't. Hell, since the magnetic grapplers came into use, we only have a handful of people checked out on those things, and they are all busy right now. I'm not."

Roberts moved to argue, then stopped, finally moving back toward the waiting shuttle. Samuels, her copilot, and Captain Weston loaded into the shuttle craft and started the preflight. The craft hummed as the twin power plants came online and the magnetic gear deactivated and retracted into the craft. A light burn from the lateral thrusters sent the bird gliding out of the bay before the main power plants engaged, sending the SAR team en route.

Once outside again, Samuels pivoted the shuttle and aimed the craft toward the bright glow of the Archangels' power plants circling an invisible point in space. The arbitrary point in space gradually coalesced into a faint outline against the star field, the drifting escape pod coming into view. Samuels aligned the shuttle with the drifting pod, deftly matching its angle and drift with small puffs from the shuttle's thrusters.

"I guess I'm up." Weston headed aft as the copilot booted up the shuttle's life-detection software (LDS) and began running the sensor data through the program.

"Whoa! Sir, it looks like we've got a live one here. There's a heat source in there..." Samuels announced.

Ensign Ryan stopped dead. "Uh, Captain, I'm not sure I believe this myself, but the sensors read the pod as having one human occupant. They read the match as having a ninety-seven percent certainty rating."

Weston stopped for a moment, staring incredulously. "Ninety-seven? We only get a ninety-three percent reading from our own ships."

"I know that, sir." The man shrugged helplessly. "I don't know how to explain it...The only thing I can think of is that, if it is a human in there, the pod is paramagnetic for some reason. The material seems to be designed for easy sensor penetration."

After a moment's silence, the ensign spoke up again, his tone facetious. "Of course, it could be an alien boogey man who's spoofing our sensors."

"I'll turn that idea over to the guys in the science division when we get back." Weston grinned wryly as he extended the Can-Arms toward the drifting pod. "In the meantime, let's prepare for a guest."

"Yes, sir," the copilot replied as Weston manipulated the controls.

The long robotic arms extended from the bottom of the shuttle, and long pincers on the arms closed over two obtrusions on the pod. As the clamps tightened, the pod slipped through their mechanical grip as he moved to compensate. As he tried to grab it again, the left arm overcompensated and struck the pod lightly, putting it into a tumble.

"Dammit," Weston cursed under his breath as the pincers slipped free and the pod began drifting away. "Samuels, adjust your vertical vector by point-three-two. The pod's trying to slip away."

"Yes, sir." The lieutenant deftly adjusted the shuttle's course, following the escaping pod.

"Thanks. Trying again." Weston's face beaded with sweat as he extended the arms again and closed the pincers over the obtrusions, this time tightly. "All right, got him hooked. Time to reel him in."

The two Can-Arms retracted, pulling the shuttle to the pod and locking them together. Once the arms were locked in place, Lieutenant Samuels fired the thrusters and started the shuttle on a return vector to the *Odyssey*.

"Sir, the contents of the pod read as oxygen-nitrogen—breathable but high on the carbon dioxide levels. Looks like it's a purification system on its last legs." The copilot shrugged. "Assuming he breathes air and my instruments aren't all screwed up."

"Damn. Okay, suit up, both of you. I'm going to open up the Spam can and see what we've won," Weston ordered as he grabbed for his own pressure helmet.

After they had sealed their environmental suits, Weston opened the pressure hatch in the floor, accessing the portable airlock.

"Ryan, get over here and pass me the laser cutter."

"Yes, sir." The copilot slid from his seat and grabbed the cutter from a locker amidships.

Weston primed the cutter and focused it on the pod's hull, slicing through the material like a knife through butter. "Hey, Ryan, I think I will send a sample of this to the research labs. The material is vaporizing rather than melting; we're not going to have to worry about slag floating around."

It took a few minutes before Weston completed a decent-sized circle and kicked the floating obstruction into the pod. Retrieving a lamp from Ensign Ryan, he peered into the pod to look for the survivor. Strapped into a harness along the curved side of the cylinder was the source of the life readings: a slumped form, wearing a gold coverall, limbs drifting in the null gravity of the pod, her delicate face obscured by flowing strands of shoulder-length, raven-black hair.

Weston slipped himself through the hole feet first and alit on the floor of the pod. Unstrapping the survivor took less than a minute. He passed the unfortunate woman back through the hole to Ensign Ryan. After a brief glance around, Weston followed suit, leaving the dark interior of the escape pod behind.

"Take us back to the *Odyssey*, Samuels. We'll disengage the pod near the port bay and let the tug push it in."

"Yes, sir. Strap yourselves in and make sure our passenger is comfortable. We're going home."

CHAPTER 5

▶ BACK ON THE *Odyssey*, the shuttle was met by an E-med team in full biohazard gear who hustled the unconscious survivor from the flight deck. Stephanos met Weston as he stepped down the shuttle gangplank.

"You just can't help yourself, can you?" Stephanos slipped into step with Weston as he headed for the ship's lift.

"What are you talking about, Steph?" Weston asked, knowing damn well what the younger man was complaining about.

"Christ on a crutch, Cap. Do you realize that half the Angels out there went weapons hot when they heard you were taking a shuttle out yourself? I had to hold them back from cleansing the entire sector! Though, frankly, I almost gave the okay."

Weston glanced over at his ex-wingman. "I appreciate the sentiment, but I was hardly defenseless. The Angels were on station, and the area was pacified."

Stephanos snorted as they stepped into the lift. "Pacified? Hell, we just arrived on the scene. We had no way of knowing what types of ordnances were still floating around out there. You know how many people we lost in the Bering, after the battle was over? Remember Clarke? He made it all the way back to base only to have an unexploded shell take him out on landing approach!"

Weston looked over at his friend, a wry grin playing across his mouth. "I was expecting Roberts to bring this up, not you, Steph. It was a calculated risk. Besides, the Angels and the *Odyssey* were in the area to cover me."

Stephanos just muttered something under his breath, the words lost as the lift's doors separated and they stepped out into the forward habitat section. Weston split away from Stephanos, heading straight for the bridge.

"You watch yourself, Cap!" the younger pilot said as a parting shot. "This isn't the Angels, and you aren't flying solo anymore."

Weston sighed as he watched him turn a corner and vanish from sight. He shook his head and continued to the bridge. He knew Steph was right. Things had changed from the early days of the war. When the Angels were first fielded, they barely had enough warm bodies to put a dozen planes in the air, let alone three times that required in tasking on an average day. Old habits and bad ones—they both died hard and, as often as not, killed you if you couldn't put them away. He was the captain of the NACS *Odyssey* now, and there was more to it than just flying like a bat out of hell without a thought to the future.

Command sucks.

▶▶▶

Commander Roberts was examining accumulated data on the debris field when Captain Weston stepped onto the bridge. Weston walked over and glanced at the data over the commander's shoulder for a brief second before speaking.

"How much is there?" Weston asked. Even before he had gone outside, Samuels had been forced to alter course no less than five times on the short trip; he knew the debris field was extraordinarily dense.

Roberts twisted in the chair to look up at Weston. "A lot, Captain; between ten and fifteen ships at the very least. The scary part is that they all appear to have been of the same origins, design, materials, and markings. Looks like some type of internal conflict, maybe a civil war, or they tangled with one nasty group of Tangos."

Weston picked up a PDA and searched through the highlights resulting from the *Odyssey*'s scanning. "Send out shuttles and retrieval probes to get samples of everything of interest, and tell all the labs to be ready to analyze what they bring back. I'm going down to the med-lab to check on the status of our guest. Contact Dr. Palin and ask him to meet me there."

"Yes, sir," Roberts said, tapping out a command on his console.

"And have the sensor techs see if they can't backtrack the trajectories," Weston said over his shoulder as he walked out. "I'd like to know where they came from."

"Aye, sir."

▶▶▶

He grabbed the nearest lift, heading straight for the med-lab. If the preliminary scans they had done with the shuttle's emergency gear were accurate, the woman they had picked up from the pod would likely be waking up soon. She'd been suffering from dehydration and lack of oxygen but was otherwise fit.

Weston was willing to bet that this was going to be one hell of a story, one worth more than a few rounds at a bar of her choice, if her society was anything like Earth. *Token linguist. Let's hope he's half as good as that file implied.*

Because, God help them all, it seemed that an awful lot was currently resting in the somewhat eccentric, if not downright mad, hands of Dr. Edward Palin. Weston was understandably perturbed when he stepped off the pod and nearly ran over the subject of his thoughts, who was kneeling on the floor in front of the lift door.

"Doctor! What are you doing down there?" Weston blinked as he caught himself against the wall, staring down at the not-quite-prostrate man.

"Oh, hello, Captain. I was waiting for you, of course," the doctor replied, standing up and brushing himself off as casually as if he'd just gotten up from a mess table.

Weston stopped for a moment, his mouth working as he tried to find words to convey the thoughts he wasn't certain he was having. "Okay...I can accept that. What you're doing on the floor in front of the lift, however, is still a mystery."

Palin paused for a moment, looking confused "The floor? Oh, the floor. Ah, yes...the floor..."

Weston waited, expecting Palin to continue, but the doctor just walked toward the med-lab, pausing only to look back at Weston for a few brief moments before shrugging his shoulders and continuing. With a disgusted shake of his head, Weston followed in the doctor's footsteps.

▶▶▶

Scientists swarmed the med-lab once word of the survivor had slipped out to the other science departments. Weston waded through the assembled lab coats, drawing their attention away from the beleaguered doctor standing between them and the object of their fascination.

"Everyone has two minutes to get out. If anybody but Dr. Rame, myself, and Dr. Palin is still in this area, I'll have them hauled off to the brig."

The room cleared out in less than a minute, despite the grumbles of the retreating white coats. Dr. Rame looked at Weston in gratitude. Normally, he was in full command of his medical facility. To lose control to a mob had obviously flustered him severely.

"Thank you, Captain. I assume you're here to check up on our guest?" The doctor wrapped his tongue deliberately around the word *guest,* as if trying it on for size, then shook his head, as if the word didn't quite fit.

"Yes, Doctor. How is she?"

"Human," Rame snorted, the word slipping out before he could stop it. "I mean, she's fine, Captain. Slight case of dehydration and some unusual cellular damage, but that seems to be healing quickly. Other than that, she's in great shape."

"When will she wake up?" Dr. Palin asked.

"I don't know for sure; probably within a few hours. She's also shown some signs of extreme fatigue, so it's best to let her rest at this point. We have an IV drip administering fluids, so she can sleep as long as necessary." The doctor picked up a tablet computer and jotted a note down with a stylus.

Odd habit, Weston thought and then just shrugged it off. Some people didn't like dictating to computers. Stephanos was one of them, though Weston knew that his former wingman had always used a standard keyboard rather than a stylus, claiming that he felt like a complete idiot talking to a computer as if he expected some intelligent response.

He, himself, was a technophile and didn't have that particular problem, let alone understand those who did. So he just shrugged it off and turned his attention back to the situation at hand.

As he considered the doctor's report, Weston glanced between Rame and the motionless figure lying in the isolation chamber. "All right, Doctor, but I want to be informed as soon as she wakes up, and you'd better inform Dr. Palin here as well. He'll be in charge of all communication attempts with her."

The chief medical officer (CMO) looked over at the quiet man in the corner, noting his vacant expression with some puzzlement, but nodded his assent. "Yes, sir. I'll be sure to call you both."

Weston left, hooking a right out the door and heading for his cabin. Dr. Palin followed his lead.

▶▶▶

Dr. Rame watched them leave, slowly shaking his head. *At least he didn't try to have her interrogated immediately...or give her to those ghouls down in the bio-lab.*

He shuddered. As a medical doctor, he didn't want to think what it would do to his career if he'd had to lock the ship's captain out of the med-lab.

Even so, Rame couldn't decide whether he trusted that odd little doctor. And so, still shaking his head, he turned back to his terminal and began to correlate the data he had gathered while treating his impromptu patient's injuries.

▶▶▶

"Well, well, what have we here?" The softly spoken words barely traveled to the commander's own ears and were totally lost in the ruckus that had overtaken the adjacent bridge and data management itself.

The slim blonde called up three different views of the same scan, grabbed two of the floating displays, and slid them together, superimposing them over the third. Her smile widened as the blue, green, and red lines joined to form a single white one.

"I'd say that's a match," she said to herself, enjoying the sensation of having puzzled out a particularly aggravating riddle.

"Have something, Winger?" Commander Roberts said.

Lt. Michelle Winger jumped. She hadn't heard him come up behind her. "Sir...I..."

"Relax, Lieutenant," Roberts said in a tone that made it an order as much as a suggestion.

Michelle swallowed. "Yes, sir."

"Did you find something?"

She nodded, pointing to the floating holographic display in front of her. "I think that's a wake, sir."

"A wake?" Roberts eyed the fluorescing colors superimposed over an image of interstellar space.

"Yes, sir." Michelle turned away from him, her fingers reaching up to punch the air as she keyed in a series of commands via the floating interface. "These are particles of ionized gas—plasma, sir. Solar winds have disrupted them heavily in-system, but I've had three of our long-range scanners probing outside the heliopause for the last couple hours and—"

"Whoa! A couple hours? The captain only issued the orders twenty minutes ago," Roberts objected. "Winger, those scanners were needed to keep an eye on the local area! We could have potential hostile ships in the area."

The lieutenant blurted, "I realize that, sir, but we can cover a full global scan with two primary scanners and the secondary. I was worried that something might be coming in… or going out, sir."

Roberts frowned. "All right. We'll let it go, for the moment. But I'll have a few words with the captain about this, Lieutenant."

She nodded, hiding a grimace. "Yes, sir."

"Tell me about this wake of yours," Roberts said, leaning against the desk that Winger rarely used and gazing at her.

▶▶▶

Weston was sitting at his desk, filing paperwork in triplicate on the search and rescue. It wasn't as bad as it used to be, he supposed, since a signature was digitally transferred to every document with his thumbprint, but it was still paperwork.

So even though he'd only just sat down at the job and was nowhere near being done, the call over the ship's intercom was something to be thankful for.

"Weston here," he said, leaning back.

"Sir, Commander Roberts."

"Commander…What's up?" Weston asked as he tapped a command in the air.

He loved the holographic systems since they let him keep a clean desk. That was something he'd never been able to do when he had his keyboard, mouse, monitor, and other requisite office materials.

Now all it took to clean up was a wave of his hand, shutting down the desktop office suite and activating the catering service. In the time it took Roberts to start with his report, Weston was already reaching for a hot cup of coffee.

"Lieutenant Winger thinks she may have found the entry path of the fleet," Roberts reported over the intercom.

Weston frowned, turning back to his desk. Another sweep of his hand and a poke in the appropriate place activated the floating screen again and he found himself looking at Roberts. "Oh? How certain?"

The imposing man shrugged. "As certain as anything gets right now, I suppose. It's not human technology, and it's sure as hell not one of our wakes, but it looks like someone dumped a lot of energy along a tight trajectory out there."

"Have you extrapolated a point of origin?"

"I'm afraid not, sir. Nothing along that path for a thousand light-years."

"Hell." Weston frowned, more than a little disappointed. It would have been nice to see an inhabited alien planet, even if they had to sneak a peek from way out past the system heliopause.

"Winger has an idea on that, sir..." Roberts said, with a twist of his lip.

"Oh? Do tell."

"There's one star system—it's within ten light-years of the path and only twenty light-years from here," Roberts said, tilting his head, his expression one of skepticism. "It's the closest system along the path."

Weston considered the information. It could be a longshot, but it was still worth it. "All right. When the shuttles are finished gathering samples, bring them back into the pen. In the meantime, have Waters plot us an escape trajectory that'll coincide with this wake. We'll do some tight scans and then transition out to the lieutenant's planet."

"Yes, sir," Roberts said, managing to sound elated and disappointed at the same time.

The display went blank, revealing the synthetic cherry wood grain of his desk. Weston could understand the commander's thoughts on the subject. This was turning into a very interesting maiden voyage. So interesting, in fact, that there seemed to be a strong case for going home right now and reporting it.

Although, Weston *would* order a tight transmission beam to be sent—it would take several years to get home, but if anything happened to the *Odyssey*, that was the best they'd have. He wasn't ready to cash in the mission just yet. He wanted to see what else was out here—and more importantly, who else.

▶▶▶

Dr. Rame was tired. He had been working for several hours straight, his mind refusing to let him take a break from the fascinating case study in front of him: a human who not only wasn't born on Earth but had never been in the Sol System at all. Her body registered as human on every scan the doctor could imagine; even the brain waves appeared completely normal. Since she'd come on board, hundreds of theories had evolved in Rame's mind, only to be discarded.

Perfectly parallel evolution was ridiculous, of course. At least by any modern theory of evolution he'd ever read. Evolution wasn't a blueprint; it was a series of mistakes that occasionally turned out to be beneficial. And the doctor knew those were few and far between. Evolutionary mutations were far more likely to result in the death of a species's offshoot than anything that might benefit them in the long term, or even short term.

That left the insane—at least in Rame's opinion. *Captured humans actually seem the most likely,* he thought as he waited for a test to run. The conspiracy theories surrounding the last century or two had continued to grow as humans reached into the stars, and even he, the scholar he considered himself to be, wasn't immune to their attraction.

Of course, there was always the off chance that humanity was actually an offshoot of their culture, in some way. It was a longshot, in Rame's opinion, but possible. No one had ever found the so-called missing link, and far too many of the discoveries that supported it had been proven to be hoaxes.

He was still compiling the data on his new patient when the computer sounded an insistent beeping, notifying him of his patient's movement. Straightening from his task, Dr. Rame turned to the one-way transparency that separated him and the ship's guest. She was moving around the room, pacing with increasing speed and intensity, pausing only to examine the door and mirrored glass, the few features in the otherwise drab medical isolation room.

He toggled the intercom switch on the wall. "Rame calling Captain Weston." He knew that he should wear one of the induction units that the Command staff used, but he despised the feedback they sent through his jaw.

"This is Commander Roberts, Doctor. The captain has left the bridge for a moment. Can I help you?"

"Contact the captain and inform him that my patient has woken up."

"Understood, Doctor."

Dr. Rame hesitated a moment before reaching out and toggling the switch again. "Dr. Palin, this is Dr. Rame. She just woke up."

"Gotcha, I'm heading down now."

Gotcha? Rame shook his head as he flipped the intercom off.

▶▶▶

Weston got the call from Roberts while in the gym, his daily workout time interrupted again by ship's business. He changed back into his uniform and headed for the med-lab. By the time he arrived, a heated discussion had erupted between Rame and Palin.

"I don't care what your qualifications are! She was just pulled out of a life pod that was floating in the middle of nowhere. I'm not going to let you break out the thumbscrews until I am certain she'll recover!"

Weston never heard Palin's retort since both of them fell silent when they noticed his entrance. "Hello again, doctors. I assume that we have a slight difference of opinion?"

Rame turned to Weston, infuriated. "This so-called doctor wants to interrogate my patient, and I simply will not allow him to drive her into a relapse."

"I'm hardly planning on breaking out the thumbscrews, Doctor," Palin countered. "And it's highly relevant and even vital that we get what information we can out of her as soon as possible. Isn't that correct, Captain?"

Before Weston could reply, Rame cut him off.

"You'll get nothing out of her if you shock her into a relapse! This patient requires delicate handling."

Weston listened to the two doctors bicker as he looked in on the very active patient who Dr. Rame was vehemently protecting. She moved purposely from place to place, examining every detail, her dark-brown eyes scanning every object in the room. Her eyes flickered in his direction, either examining her reflection or, more likely, looking for any hint of the faces she must suspect were behind the mirror. He didn't know how to feel about this, the sheer impossibility of it numbing him to the extraordinary implications of the very existence of the ship's newest guest.

He turned back to the dispute that was threatening to flare through the med-lab. "Dr. Rame, how is her recovery coming along?"

Rame turned to Weston. "Her recovery is remarkable, but that worries me as much as anything since I can't figure out why. Anything unpredictable at this point is dangerous."

"In other words, she's fine as far as you can tell, right, Doc?"

Rame stammered over his words. "Well, yes, but that's the point, Captain! I can't be sure about my readings. We *did* just pick her up over forty-five light-years from Earth, sir."

Weston looked at the doctor for a long moment. "All right, Doctor, point taken. What if you joined Dr. Palin while he addresses her in the room? You have full authority to pull the plug at any time you feel her health is threatened."

Palin's face darkened. He opened his mouth to object but shut it after a glance from Weston. Rame, on the other hand, appeared mollified.

"All right," Palin said. "But I'll hold you to that, Captain."

"Good. Both of you get into class-five environmental suits and pay our guest a visit," Weston ordered.

"Class five?" both of them objected.

"Captain, this type of situation only calls for a class-two suit." Rame looked between the isolation chamber and Captain Weston in confusion.

"I realize that, Doctor, but class-five units incorporate mirrored visors and full-body coverage. And I don't think I want our guest seeing us just yet."

"Captain! I object to putting that type of stress onto this woman so soon. It's despicable. There's no reason to terrify the young lady that way." Rame looked at the captain in indignation.

"I'm sorry, Doctor. But the fact that we found a human being floating in a life pod forty-eight light-years from home has been preying on my mind, and I refuse to give up too much information too soon."

And so, in spite of his objections, the doctor slowly began to fit himself into the one-piece garment. He sealed its seams until he looked like he was wearing a lightweight spacesuit with a colossal helmet. As Dr. Palin mimicked his actions, Rame's bulbous mass turned to take in the mirror image that had engulfed Dr. Palin. A muffled voice sounded from the suit.

"All right, Captain, we're both prepped. Will you be observing, or should we call you when we're done?"

"I'll watch for a while," the captain said as he waved them on.

Weston imagined for a moment that he saw the suits shrug before they turned away from him and entered the small airlock that separated the main med-lab from the isolation chamber. He sidestepped to position himself squarely in the center of the transparency and looked in at their visitor.

She swung her whole body around as the airlock's status lights changed and the slight difference in pressure caused a low hiss to sound throughout the room. He saw her eyes open wide when the two ominous figures shuffled into the room, advancing on her with their hands visible.

▼

CHAPTER 6

▲

▶ DR. PALIN SPOKE first, his voice clear and undistorted from the confines of his hazard suit.

"Hello, my dear. We are here to speak with you for a short while," he said easily in English, not worrying about comprehension just yet.

Weston marveled at the change in Palin's voice. His condescending tone was no longer present, and his words rang with confidence and compassion as he addressed the frightened young woman before him.

"My name is Edward." Palin pointed to himself, repeating both his words and actions several times. He was sweating in the biohazard suit and kicked himself for not adding the optional thermostat package when he had selected the garment.

Over the induction set attached to his jaw, Palin heard the captain's voice: "Doctor, please remember to activate the computer's translation algorithms so we can all benefit from this."

Palin acknowledged and tapped a quick command into the PDA strapped to his wrist.

"Computer translation systems are now activated. Please identify subject."

"Computer, apply translation algorithms to the patient now occupying the medical isolation chamber."

"Confirmed. Translation systems online. Begin when ready."

Palin looked back at the young woman, her eyes now roaming the room looking for the source of the computer's voice.

"It's all right, my dear, please remain calm." Palin almost laughed, telling her to remain calm when he was practically shaking.

He repeated his previous actions, pointing to himself and speaking his name, Edward Palin, with no results. Finally, he pointed to the other doctor, thumping him once on the chest, then pausing in confusion. "Say, what's your first name, anyway?"

Rame scowled at the little man. "My name is Simon, if you must—"

"Simon Rame," Palin cut him off, thumping him hard on the chest once more.

"Hey!" Dr. Rame tried to object, but Palin was already repeating the entire procedure, pointing first to himself and then again thumping Rame in the chest, stating their names in turn.

The woman stepped closer to Palin, tentatively reaching out her own arm and brushing his chest. "Edward?"

Her face was uncertain, but she smiled tentatively when the silver blob bobbed up and down. She then reached out and thumped Dr. Rame on the chest and repeated his name.

"Hey! Why do I always get thumped?"

Both Dr. Palin and the young woman ignored the doctor's plaintive outburst as she began to chatter unintelligibly to Dr. Palin's ominous form.

From the outside looking in, Weston had to suppress the occasional chuckle as he watched Dr. Rame become invisible to the other two in the room. Even through the suits, Weston could see the exasperation evident in Rame's stance and the rapt attention that flowed from Dr. Palin.

For several minutes, Palin just sat there listening to her speak, allowing the words to wash against him as his mind began processing the information and looking for correlations to the languages he knew. After about twenty minutes of listening, he spoke.

"Jan mest Dukto Edward Palin."

The young lady stopped speaking and stared in astonishment at the silver mask covering Palin's face. "Jan mest Ithan Milla Chans."

Palin leaned back in his chair and an audible sigh was heard. "Lovely to meet you, Milla."

"Captain, our lovely guest here is Milla Chans. She also has some title, but I am not certain what it means yet. It's actually quite fascinating; her language seems to be evolved from the same core that makes up the Romance languages on Earth: French, Italian, and Spanish. Although, it does appear to be more complex."

"How long do you think until we can communicate with her?"

Palin paused a moment. "Between my skills and the ship's computer, I think a few days and we'll be conversing quite well—that is, as long as you don't intend to start interrogating her about technical matters."

"For now, I just want to hear her story." Weston paused a moment. "And find out where she's from, so we can bring her home."

"Not long, then, Captain, not long at all."

Weston acknowledged the report and turned away from the scene in the isolation chamber, his head spinning from what he had just observed. Palin had decoded the first levels of a new language in minutes and planned to be finished within a few days. His file hadn't been exaggerating his skills in the slightest.

Good. The sooner this is concluded, the sooner we can find out what happened and whether or not it may be a threat to us. Weston strode from the med-lab and headed back to his bridge.

▶▶▶

Dr. Rame had backed off when it became apparent his patient wasn't going to enter a blind panic, and he'd decided his presence wasn't needed. As the airlock cycled around him, he reflected on what he had just seen. Dr. Palin wasn't the oaf he had taken him for. He treated the young woman with compassion and had relaxed her enough to begin working with her to translate her language. Palin's phenomenal linguistic skills bothered him because Palin was never mentioned as being impressive in any way. In his lab, Rame slipped behind his desk and activated his terminal, calling up the personnel files.

Back inside the isolation chamber, Dr. Palin immersed himself in the language problem, absorbing the words, phrases, and inflections that Milla uttered. The language seemed more elegant with every word he deciphered, but he knew he was missing a critical piece of information. There was something about the decidedly one-sided conversation that was troubling him. The words came quickly, but try as he might, the meanings slipped past him. Even so, the discourse slowly became a two-sided exchange as Palin's instinctive comprehension of the alien language was complemented by the computer's growing data file.

"Docteur Palin, what is this…shippe?" Milla's accent certainly bore out his earlier comparison of her language to the Terran Romance equivalents.

"This is the NACS *Odyssey*, a long-range exploration vessel." Palin wished the captain had told him how much he could reveal to their guest.

"Odisee? I do not understand that word."

"The word *odyssey* means 'voyage of destiny,' or something similar. It seemed to fit the purpose of this ship."

Milla's laugh rang through the room. "It was certainly a voyage of destiny, from my perspectif."

His mind ran through what she had just said and how she said it. *It's the inflections!* He surged up from the table and rushed to the terminal built into the wall.

"Computer, adjust translation matrix to include Asian inflection coding as well as the European Romance languages." Palin's fingers leapt across the small keypad as he modified minute details of the translation program.

"Confirmed. Translation algorithms have been adjusted. Estimated time to adapt current data to new codes—five minutes, twenty-seven seconds."

Palin turned back to Milla, somewhat surprised to find her almost cowering back from his sudden moves.

"It's all right, my dear, just stay calm." His calm voice floated out of the suit, soothing Milla's fear and bringing her back to the discussion.

Dr. Palin spent the next five minutes calming Milla down, getting her back into the same frame of mind she had before his outburst. When the computer chirped the completion of its task, Palin keyed it into the induction set.

"Do you understand me properly now?"

Milla's face lit up with recognition, which was quickly followed by extreme puzzlement. "Yes! I do...but...how?"

"It was quite simple, my dear. Your language uses changes in the timber of the voice to distinguish different meanings in the same basic word. Once I told the computer to add that to its decoding process, it simply went back through everything we had said in the past several hours and recompiled its program."

Milla smiled at the pride she heard echo through his voice; this man was not one to be humble about his accomplishments. Still, she supposed he had a right; translating a new language in just under eight hours was a remarkable accomplishment—even with computer assistance. Although she was still worried about these people, she wasn't as frightened as she had been. They weren't the Drasin—that had been obvious the moment Palin and Rame entered the room. Despite their concealed bodies, she could tell they were as human as she was. For a brief moment, she wondered what colony they were from, but she put it out of her mind since no one in the colonies would feel the need to conceal themselves from her.

One of the Others. That thought pleased and frightened her. If it were one of the Others, her people would have help at last. *But which? None are reported within a century of having dimensional technology, and they could not have gotten this far out without it.*

"My dear? Are you all right?" The visage of Dr. Palin's suit looming over her shook Milla from her thoughts.

"I'm fine, Docteur, just considering my...situation."

"Ahh, well that's understandable, my dear. I have a report to make to the captain. I'll return as soon as I can. In the meantime, do try and get some rest."

Milla watched the doctor as he stepped into the bulky airlock. "I'll do that, Docteur Palin."

An airlock…incredible. I must be in a medical facility, but why an airlock, of all things? Energy fields have replaced airlocks for centuries on all the colonies. Milla stood up and examined the room again, paying close attention to the terminal that Palin had uncovered when he altered his language program. *An ancient airlock, but computer systems far and above anything I've ever seen. How do they manage a voice interface?*

"Computer, where am I?"

"You are in the medical isolation chamber of the NAC Starship *Odyssey*."

Well, at least it responds to me as well. Milla cleared her throat. "What is the system of origin for this ship?"

"You have not been cleared for navigational data."

"Where was the *Odyssey* built?"

"You have not been cleared for historical data."

"What information have I been cleared for?"

"You have been cleared for limited access to the onboard com-channels, limited access to the onboard catering system, and limited access to the ship's entertainment library."

"Computer, may I please have a glass of water?"

"One moment."

She waited a short while, uncertain what to expect, when a recessed slot opened up in the wall underneath the huge mirror and a tall glass of water was nestled inside. *Well, that settles any doubt I may have had about the true nature of that mirror.*

"Computer, what is available to me in the entertainment section?"

"You have been cleared to access the following music selections."

Milla watched the titles flicker past on the small screen, wishing she could read the language they were written in. Unfortunately, the translation program only seemed to operate on a vocal level. Selecting one at random, she walked back over to the room's bed and lay down while the music washed over her.

▶▶▶

Captain Weston was examining the data they had gathered on the remnants of the shattered fleet when Dr. Palin strode onto the bridge.

Weston lifted a hand to him, causing the doctor to frown and back off as he watched the captain sign off on a report and turn to Commander Roberts. "How long to the heliopause?"

"Thirteen minutes," Roberts replied. "We're already picking up several times the data density on the wake scans, and Winger thinks that she's right about that planetary system she recommended. Of course, she thought that before we got the extra data."

"Of course she did. All right, we'll transition as soon as she's done with her scans. Have the helm calculate our exit from transitional space carefully; I don't want to arrive too closely in-system. At least three hours out, all right?"

"Aye, Captain. Three hours minimum," Roberts nodded, moving on.

"All right, Doctor." Weston turned back to Palin. "What is it?"

The academic grinned at the captain, his expression not quite insubordinate as he responded. "I'm pleased to say I've deciphered enough of their language for the computer to translate any conversation you might wish to have—that is, assuming you don't want to ask her about technical details."

Weston's eyes widened. "You said it would take you several days."

"On the contrary, I said it *might* take me a few days. I was wrong."

"All right. I'll want you present when I speak with her."

"Of course. I'll be waiting for the call."

"Good. Thank you for the report," Weston said, looking back down to the PDA. He had picked up four more forms to work on while he was talking to the commander and the doctor.

"Yes, sir," Palin replied after a long silence and, finally getting the clue, turned and left the bridge.

As the academic vanished from sight, Weston set down his PDA and turned to his first officer. "His records don't do him justice, you know."

"Perhaps, sir, but his attitude needs a lot of work." Roberts watched the retreating doctor with an odd expression on his face. "He's broken at least two assistants in the com-lab. They've been begging for transfers since Alpha Centauri."

"You're kidding," Weston blurted, his eyes widening.

"I'm afraid not, sir." Roberts shrugged. "I changed them to another shift in the same lab. That's holding them for now, but Palin has a habit of working odd hours, so I don't know how long it'll last. Everyone who knows him says he's insane."

"True, but genius has a way of tempering people." Weston shrugged. "If nothing else, it helps excuse eccentric behavior."

"I suppose, sir," Roberts said. As far as he was concerned, if the person wasn't capable of operating within proper military structure, he didn't have time for them. Genius or not.

Roberts turned away, returning to the sensor reports that were still flooding in. Weston toggled another switch on his armrest. "Dr. Rame, are you available?"

The call came back a moment later. "Yes, Captain. Anything I can do?"

"How's the patient, Doctor?"

"Fine, sir. She just requested a glass of water and accessed the entertainment library."

Weston's eyebrow rose. "Palin did a great job. What's she listening to?"

"Oddly enough, 'Brahms's Lullaby.' It seems to be doing her some good; she's resting comfortably."

"Good. I'll want to speak with her soon. Please see to it that she gets whatever she needs."

"Of course, sir." The doctor's tone indicated that he considered the order almost insulting.

"And, Doctor…" Weston hesitated.

"Yes, Captain?"

"We're going to transition to another system soon," Weston said with a degree of hesitance.

There was a long pause from the other end of the conversation, until finally the doctor sighed. "I can't say that I'm overjoyed to hear that, but thank you for the warning. I'll have my staff standing by with relaxants."

"Thank you, Doctor," Weston nodded. "And make sure you have someone in Engineering, will you?"

"Certainly. I'm just thankful my newest patient is asleep. She doesn't need any more stress."

"The thought had crossed my mind, Doctor. In fact, if you think it's wise, I'll support adding a sedative to her air mix. To be frank, I'm hardly happy with how trained personnel react to transition. I wouldn't want to deal with any untrained reactions, not if we can avoid it."

"Agreed," the doctor said after a moment. "I'll check her vitals and consider adding something to slip her a little deeper."

"Excellent, keep me apprized. Captain out."

▶▶▶

"Crossing the heliopause, sir."

Weston nodded, taking his command chair. "Thank you, Daniels. Commander?"

"Yes, Captain?"

"Advise Winger that she'd better wrap up her scans. Then signal a transition alert."

"Aye, Captain," Roberts said, his voice thick with distaste.

Capt. Eric Weston did what he'd always done before a dangerous mission: he masked anything resembling nerves with a cool facade and hoped to God that no one saw through it. There was no sense in giving anyone else the silly idea that the captain didn't trust the transition drive any more than they did.

Especially if the captain really *didn't* trust it.

So far, he'd been lucky. His crew was too busy building their own facades to notice his.

So he smiled, looking relaxed, and the bridge crew around him relaxed themselves, even as the blue lights that marked a transition alert began to flash.

Ah, the glory of command.

The alert lasted for twenty minutes, until all sections had checked in as being ready, and then Weston gave the reluctant order.

"Activate transition drive."

Everyone on the bridge winced as Lieutenant Daniels pressed the final command and slammed his eyes shut. Most everyone on the bridge did the same, except for Captain Weston and Commander Roberts.

Both men had time to note this fact and promise themselves they'd speak with the bridge crew about the dangers of entering a potentially hostile area with their eyes closed.

The swirling maelstrom of tachyon particles ripped them apart as the *Odyssey* transitioned out of the white giant system.

CHAPTER 7

▶ TWENTY LIGHT-YEARS FROM where it began, the NACS *Odyssey* reintegrated into normal space with no external sign that anything unfavorable had occurred.

Internally, however, was a different story.

"Commander! All posts, report!" Weston ordered, diplomatically ignoring the retching sound coming from the lieutenant's side.

Roberts waved a hand to an ensign, who took the hint and rushed to assist the unfortunate Lieutenant Daniels, who was losing his spaghetti dinner under the fire control station. As he was helped away, a young woman slid discreetly into his place, maneuvering her feet to avoid the mess on the floor.

"Passive sensors are picking up a disturbance on the fourth planet," Roberts said.

Weston could understand that; passive sensors were just picking up data from no less than twelve hours earlier. They'd have to wait for the tachyon generators to regain a charge before they'd get anything current. Even so, information from twelve hours ago might explain some piece of the puzzle they were unraveling. "Correlate and send it to my station, Commander."

"Aye, Captain." Roberts flipped over a manual control panel and typed in a quick command, supplementing the vocal orders that he snapped over his induction microphone.

Weston flipped open his own display screen and wished, not for the first time, that the holographic displays had been cleared for bridge use. Unfortunately, the displays were deemed potentially unstable and were not approved for use in critical systems. It was a decision that Weston approved, but he still felt a pang of loss as he stared at the fourteen-inch screen and missed the room-sized equivalent that his simple desk system provided.

▶▶▶

Lt. Michelle Winger was the *Odyssey*'s go-to girl when it came to the array of long-range sensors that studded nearly every exterior surface of the big ship, but just now, she scowled as she scanned the data stream and wished that she'd been able to hijack the same three arrays she had used earlier. The information pouring in from her long-range array was interesting, but correlating data across multiple frequencies was her forte.

Whoa. Her eyes narrowed as she spotted something. *What the hell is this?*

Her fingers flew over the keyboard as she cursed the power drain that transition caused. As the data began to coalesce into something resembling a picture, she shot a glance to one side to check the power display.

Bridge systems had full priority, with weapons and navigation following right behind. But her systems were on the list, too, and the reactors were providing enough power that she would be fully online in a couple minutes, at most. In the meantime, all her scanners were already up and functioning perfectly, so she would have to make do with the basic interface for another hundred seconds or so.

"Commander!" she spoke up, a little louder than she'd intended. "I'm sending over my initial findings to you!"

A rap of her fingers across the board sent the data packet flashing across the fiber to Commander Roberts's station. Only after it was gone did she let out a breath she'd barely been aware of holding, her eyes floating back across her screen to where the data was still highlighted.

A moment later, the rest of her interface touchpads lit up as power was fully restored, snapping Winger out of her daze as she returned to work in full form.

▶▶▶

"High-energy discharges?" Weston questioned as he looked at the data Roberts had redirected to his attention. He noticed something familiar in the information and looked up with a cocked eyebrow. "Weapons?"

"It seems likely," Roberts said. "Though we could be looking at a storm front on the planet."

"That powerful? Weston shook his head skeptically. "No… It'd have to be the size of Jupiter to flash that high."

"Probably, sir," Roberts agreed.

"All right. Helm, take us in slowly," Weston said, even as his heart raced. "Commander Roberts, anything on the passive tactical scan?"

"Negative. Just some background hiss from the star."

Weston nodded, his eyes rising to look at the yellow star that was the system primary. There was always some background hiss from anything the size of a star; the massive gravity made certain of that. "Helm, you are not to cross the heliopause until we have our tachyon generators recharged. I want a system-wide ping before we even think of becoming trapped in that gravity well."

"Aye, sir. A full system ping," Roberts said. "Wilco."

▶▶▶

"How's the patient, Doctor?" Weston asked as he stepped over the knee-knocker that separated the med-lab from the hallway. With hours to go before he could make any useful decisions on the bridge, he had decided to check in and see how things were running through the ship—and in particular, the woman resting in Rame's isolation ward.

"She's sleeping," Rame replied, not looking up from his current patient, who had displayed odd symptoms from the transition. "Something much of the crew would love to do. The transition effects are growing worse, sir."

"How bad?"

"Nothing quite as serious as Lieutenant Tearborn, thankfully." Rame straightened from his unconscious patient and wiped his brow. "But unless I'm completely off base, I believe that part of the crew is allergic to the process."

Weston snorted. "Doctor, trust me, all the crew is allergic to it."

"I didn't mean psychologically," Rame snapped, both frustrated and irritated. "I mean physical allergies. There has been a series of consistent symptoms in approximately twelve percent of the crew."

Twelve percent? Weston blinked. "That's almost forty people!"

"Really? I hadn't counted," Rame said sarcastically as he passed his hands under a dissolvent spray to remove the sterile coating he'd applied.

Weston let the sarcasm slide, knowing that the man was tired and stressed. "How serious is it?"

"Nothing permanent or debilitating—not yet, at any rate," Rame said. "But it has affected the eyesight of twenty-three crew members. Again, not permanent. But disturbing, just the same. Thirty crew members have developed a disturbing cellular degradation of the soft tissue of their noses, mouths, and throats. I'm not certain about the internal effects of these yet. I've scheduled a series of tests."

Rame slid the patient under a large panel and opened the crew member's hospital gown. He punched a command on his PDA and turned away as the panel began emitting a series of regular popping sounds.

"Infrared treatments seem to work against the degradation," Rame said. "In the long term, however, I just don't know."

"All right. Keep me posted and inform me when our guest wakes up."

"Of course, Captain."

▶▶▶

"Prepare to initiate tachyon pulse."

"All systems go, no go," Commander Roberts replied, following the book.

"Tachyon generators…go."

"Receptor array…go."

"Forward shielding…go."

Roberts nodded. "Drive system?"

Daniels turned and smiled. "We see anything spooky, we're ready to bolt, sir."

"We don't bolt, Ensign." Roberts smiled, but without amusement. "We advance cautiously to the front and quickly to the rear."

"Aye, sir."

"Initiate sensor ping."

Like submarines using sonar in the previous century, the *Odyssey*'s tachyon array was a powerful detection device, but it had many of its own drawbacks. Unlike infrared, radar, and other telemetry systems, the tachyon generators could produce real-time imaging data from a distance measured in light-years or more. However, tachyons were not cheap to generate and didn't last long once they had been generated.

Neither Roberts nor Weston were familiar with the mathematics of the subject, though both were aware that, on paper, tachyons didn't even exist. It was one of those amusing mathematical proofs that seemed to be at odds with the real universe. On paper, a tachyon didn't exist because its half-life was too short to be measured. However, in that period of nothingness where the particles existed, they could travel across the rim of the galaxy and back.

So when the tachyon generator on the *Odyssey* pulsed, a shotgun-like spread of those impossible little particles leapt out through the fabric of space and spread out from the ship, creating interference in the local area of space as they passed. When they hit something—anything from a single atom to the local star itself—they created a ripple effect that rebounded out from the object and traveled back to the waiting receiver on the *Odyssey*.

▶ ▶ ▶

"Report."

"Nothing out there, sir," Winger replied as Commander Roberts appeared behind her. She'd barely jumped this time and felt proud of herself.

"Nothing?"

"Nothing like a ship, sir. I've compared everything we got to the readings from yesterday." She shrugged. "We've got a debris field around the fourth planet that looks artificial. Alloys, atomic decay, and some configurations match, but they're dead as doornails, sir."

"I'll inform the captain that we have nothing to fear from the doornails," Roberts replied, with a twinge of sarcasm. "Stay with the facts."

"Uh…yes, sir," Winger said, her face flushing. "Sorry, sir."

"Don't apologize. Just don't do it again."

"Yes, sir."

Roberts left Winger's station and headed back to the captain. "It looks clear, sir. There is some debris in the system that matches the debris we found at the battle scene, however."

"Nothing active?" Weston looked up.

"Nothing that we can see."

The captain spoke up for the benefit of the bridge crew. "Ensign Waters. Take us into the orbit of the fourth planet."

"Orbit. Aye, sir."

The big ship shook as its massive drives rumbled into action, vibrations reverberating through the entire vessel as it began to move through the depths of interstellar space and cross the invisible line that separated it from the star system. As the ship crossed the heliopause, the yellow star began to act on it, pulling it deeper into the system with the inexorable grip of its gravity.

The speed built slowly at first as the *Odyssey*'s huge engines and integral CM fields worked in conjunction to chip away at the inertia of the ship, increasing quickly as the grip of the star's gravity joined in. Soon the ship was speeding down the well fast enough that Lieutenant Daniels powered down both the thrusters and the CM fields until the *Odyssey* was free-falling toward the star.

Watching his trajectories, Lieutenant Daniels was less worried about the path of the *Odyssey* as he was about the path of anything the *Odyssey* might run into. Even with the powerful navigation fields shouldering aside anything in their path, he still kept an obsessive eye on the screens. Attention to detail was the bread and butter of his job, especially since certain electrical- and magnetic-neutral composites could penetrate the navigation fields with ease.

Such things didn't exist often in nature. However, as the debris ring around the fourth planet would testify, this system wasn't as pure as the driven snow.

▶▶▶

An hour into the drop, Weston excused himself from the bridge and headed to the mess deck for something to eat. The course Daniels had plotted to the fourth planet would take them about twenty-four hours, including acceleration and deceleration.

The mess was as busy as he'd expected. A large portion of the crew had taken advantage of the projected course to refuel.

Weston smiled as he spotted a group talking at a table in the corner. *Some of them are just here because they have nothing better to do.*

He walked over, wiping the smile from his face. "So, I see we've got a bunch of laze-abouts, huh?"

Everyone at the table jumped, save one.

"Gee, Cap," Stephanos said, grinning at him from where he was seated in the corner, "why don't you tell us how you really feel?"

Weston resisted the urge to laugh or roll his eyes since both reactions would have been too much, and besides, he knew that the Archangels would be able to read him without anything that overt. Instead, he just sat down. "So, how do you all enjoy being passengers on this cruise?"

The fighter jocks laughed, relaxing as they recognized their old flight leader in the captain, and they began to joke back with him.

"Just fine, Raz." A big beefy man who went by the call sign "Brute" smirked. "But when are you going to find us some real work to do?"

Weston shrugged. "Looks like we may have something coming down the pipe for you. Be patient."

Blaze, one of the first women in the unit, snorted softly. "Do as you say, not as you do, huh, Raz?"

"Precisely."

Weston reclined back in his seat, ordered some food, and let himself remember the glory days.

▶ ▶ ▶

The waking world came back slowly to Milla. Her mind lost in sleep for a few moments, she forgot where she was or what had transpired.

The transition from that moment of blissful ignorance to the painful reality of her situation was like a physical blow to her chest. The petite woman curled up on the stiff hospital bed and didn't move. As much as she wanted to lie there and die, she knew she couldn't. She couldn't make any sense of her emotions, how she felt. It seemed to change without warning and without any real idea of what was coming next. That, more than anything, drove her mad inside.

Out there, beyond the walls of this unknown vessel, lay the Drasin, and they were killing her people. She couldn't die when she knew that her people desperately needed her.

So she moved, sliding off the firm bed and onto the cold floor. She danced around for a moment, until her feet adjusted to the floor's temperature, and frowned at the offending material.

Milla knelt down and ran her fingers along the cool surface, feeling it suck the heat from her flesh.

Metal floors. No one builds a starship with metal...It's just not done! She sighed to herself and looked around, refusing to think of how much insulation the walls must have to make up for the intolerable properties of construction.

It wasn't just the metal, though. The entire place was completely off. The lighting was too bright, the spectrum shift was harsh, and now that she thought about it, she felt heavier than normal. It was like a bad copy of a starship, instead of the real thing.

And what is that sensation of constant falling, anyway? She shook her head, giving up that thought for a second before her mind stubbornly grabbed at it again. She knew that the ship had to have certain technologies.

Dimensional shifting was a given, she figured. Otherwise, where had they come from to pick her up? However, what she couldn't understand was how in the oath they had managed that and still used metal to construct the ship in the first place. The entire situation was like an impossible conundrum to her.

She gave in to the pit in her stomach and called up the computer terminal. It took a long time to load, for some reason, but finally, she was into the catering services.

After staring at the incomprehensible script for some time, Milla sighed and punched in a few items at random.

▶▶▶

The call came just as Weston was taking the first sip from the steaming cup of tea at the table in the mess.

"A captain's job…" He shrugged, reaching for his induction set.

Steph snorted. "They're probably calling to make sure you haven't drowned in your sink. Everyone knows that captains have to be watched *all* the time."

Another round of chuckles sounded among the pilots, though the comment had garnered a shocked look from the yeoman who had dropped off the tea. Weston ignored both as he affixed the induction set to his jaw and waited for the squirming sensation to fade as the unit molded itself to him.

"Weston here."

"Captain," Dr. Rame said over the unit, "you wished to be informed when our patient awoke?"

"Yes, Doctor, is she well?"

"She's well enough to request food," Rame replied, "though I don't believe that she *quite* understands the menu."

Weston frowned, drawing curious looks from the fighter jocks. "Why's that?"

"Because, frankly, I don't believe that any sentient being would ever order ice cream with oil-packed tuna on purpose." Rame shuddered.

Weston started chuckling, low at first, but rising until he was genuinely laughing at the comment. Around the table, everyone looked at him with puzzlement, but he didn't bother to enlighten them. Stephanos in particular looked like he was just itching to ask what was so funny.

Tough. Weston got up to leave. "I'm afraid I have to go. I'll see you all later."

To a man, their faces dropped as they realized that their former CAG had zero intention of sharing, and Weston took exquisite pleasure in the look of disappointment on Stephanos's face.

"Doctor, contact Palin and have him meet me in the med-lab," Weston ordered over the induction unit, smirking as he again glanced at his old squad and their disappointed expressions.

Some days it was good to be the captain.

▶▶▶

Weston walked into the med-lab as Rame and Palin were snapping at each other, trying to decide which protocols they would follow while talking with the survivor.

"Dr. Rame," Weston interrupted, silencing the doctors, "in your opinion, what was her reaction to the hazard suits?" *It's amazing how two well-educated and grown men are capable of this sort of childishness.*

"It was strange. At first, she was tense, but after she got a good look at us, she relaxed and remained remarkably calm, considering the situation she's found herself in."

Weston snorted with no small amount of satisfaction. "Good, I think we can dispense with the suits, then, assuming she isn't a medical danger."

Dr. Rame looked at him strangely. "Well, she has a whole cornucopia of new antibodies, but with the blood samples I've taken, we can develop cures and vaccines for anything she might pass on. What made you change your mind about the hazard suits?"

"I wanted to see her reaction. If her attackers had been human, or even humanoid, she would have been a lot more concerned about the suits. I'd say we're looking at an even more interesting story than we thought."

Dr. Rame looked thoughtful for a moment, considering that.

"You realize, Captain, that isn't the only possible interpretation of her reactions," Palin stated flatly.

"Of course I do, Doctor, but it's the best I have to go on right now."

Weston broke from the discussion and walked over to the transparency. "All right, Dr. Palin, let's go in."

▶▶▶

Milla was lying back listening to a musical composition the computer had told her was called "Ride of the Valkyries." Despite the strict limits the computer had placed on her entertainment selections, she had managed to find several pieces that she enjoyed.

"Milla?"

Milla jumped up, her eyes widening when she saw two men step into the room without their rather bulky suits. *Are these the same two men?*

"I suppose I should reintroduce myself. I'm Dr. Palin. This is the captain of the *Odyssey*, Eric Weston."

The captain... This will be a more serious session than the previous one. Hopefully we can settle the captain's concerns so I can get back to my duty, she thought as she looked to the captain, appraising him.

He was tall, taller than most people she knew, though not quite the tallest man she'd ever seen. She'd met the commandant of the Colonial Ground Forces once, and he would actually tower over this Captain Weston. Milla put that aside after a moment and turned her focus on the captain again, taking in his appearance. His close-trimmed black hair hugged his head, his face was stern, and she realized that he was, in turn, appraising her. The thought discomforted her for a moment, but she quickly regained her poise.

"Captaine Weston." Her head nodded respectfully in greeting.

"Ithan Chans." Weston imitated her slight nod and returned the greeting.

"I'm honored by your use of my title, Captaine. Dr. Palin never seems to refer to me in any way except as 'dear.' Which the computer informs me is a quadruped of some type." Milla smiled with a confused air about her.

Palin stammered a moment, trying to explain himself before Weston stepped in. "Actually, the word has several different meanings, which are differentiated by spelling. In this case, it is a term of affection older people use in reference to those younger than themselves."

"I see." Milla threw a look at Palin, enjoying the red tinge his face had assumed.

"Milla, could you please tell us what happened to the ship you were traveling on?" Weston asked.

She looked at the captain, trying to gauge him, but found herself unable to pierce his outward demeanor. She decided to go with the simple truth.

"I wasn't traveling. I was serving aboard the space vessel *Carlache* and we were attacked."

"We had gathered that much. Would you be so kind as to tell us by whom and why they decided to reduce a fleet of your vessels to scrap?"

Milla winced at that. She had known that it was unlikely any had survived the massacre, but it pained her to think of her comrades floating dead in the inhospitable depths of this radiation-seared system.

"They are called Drasin, and they attack us because it is their way. They are born to kill, they were created to kill, and they do it very well."

Dr. Palin glanced over at the hard shell that had formed across the captain's face. He knew that Weston was contemplating the implications of Milla's story, if it were true. Palin himself shuddered at the thought of a race of born killers stalking the galaxy, the nightmare of a thousand horror stories since the birth of science fiction. The idea that it may be true would cause havoc at home.

"Created? By whom?" Weston asked after a moment, taking a seat as he gazed at the young woman.

As he watched her consider her response, Weston took the opportunity to evaluate her. Milla Chans was pretty, he decided after a long moment, with an exotic air to her eyes that added interest to her face. She was petite and probably didn't weigh more than 110 pounds. But she was obviously strong, or she would still be under Rame's expert care, so Weston was willing to give her the benefit of the doubt on that matter. He was still examining her when Milla started to respond.

"I do not think you are ready for that yet. If you were, you wouldn't need to ask such a question, Captain. May I ask a question of you now?"

Weston hesitated a moment, frowning at the evasion. In the end, he decided that it wouldn't lose him anything to play along for a moment. "Yes, if you like. However, like you, I do not promise to answer."

Ithan Chans looked at him appraisingly; she had expected no less. "Of course, but I must ask this anyway. Where are you from? I know it is not one of the colonies because your ship's technology is completely wrong."

"I can't answer that, other than that we are a long-range exploration vessel. As for our technology, what do you mean 'wrong'?" Weston asked, raising an eyebrow.

Milla's arms swept around the room. "I mean *wrong*. You use archaic airlocks, metal to construct your vessel, or at least the floors and walls here, and yet you have dimensional access, and your computer...talks."

She blinked, shaking her head over that last comment before speaking again. "It is painfully obvious, even from what little I've seen, that you must be one of the Others."

Weston's eyes narrowed at the way she pronounced the word *Others*, like it was almost a curse. "Who are the Others, Ithan?"

Milla's lips curled. "The Others are those who broke their oath."

By this point, Weston was completely confused. "Oath?"

She looked up into his eyes, realizing that he didn't know what she meant. "There is a history to the universe of which you are completely unaware, one which I am ill-equipped to relate."

"Oh?" Dr. Palin leaned forward, rapt with attention. "Could you tell me more?"

Milla hesitated, shaking her head. "I don't believe that I should. There are some things in this universe that are better left unknown. Some knowledge changes you...That knowledge exacts a terrible toll."

Well, isn't that melodramatic? Weston thought, noting with amusement that Palin was utterly fascinated. Weston was about to ask something further when a message chirped through his induction unit.

"Weston here."

"Captain, we're approaching the fourth planet," Roberts's voice reverberated through his jaw and into his ear. "I thought you might like to be up here for this."

Weston nodded, standing up. "I'll be right up."

He looked over to Milla. "I have to go. Feel free to ask if you need anything, and I believe that we can get someone in here to translate the menu for you."

Milla looked puzzled as Weston smiled, but he didn't comment further. Instead, he turned to Dr. Palin. "Doctor, you're with me. I want you on the bridge for this."

"Huh?" Palin looked up in surprise. "Oh, yes. Of course, Captain."

Weston nodded to Milla and led Palin out through the isolation ward airlock.

▶▶▶

The planet hung in space, glittering in the reflected and refracted light of its primary like a jewel in black satin. The shattered fragments that passed over the sea-green orb marred the beauty of the scene, a testament to the fact that the world's defenders had not gone easily.

The low rumble of the *Odyssey*'s reactors sounded ominous to the crew as they watched the planet approach. There was something about the world on the viewer that felt wrong.

"Launch orbital drones," Weston ordered as the *Odyssey* slid to a stop, relative to the planet, already punching up a link to the main sensor array.

"Drones launching," Roberts replied, the report punctuated by the brief shudders that they felt through the deck. "Moving to take up orbital positions."

Weston nodded, distracted as he examined the information on the screen. The numbers didn't look right, but he couldn't tell what was off. After a moment, he looked up. "Analysis!"

"Sir..." a voice from behind him spoke up.

Weston turned toward the young female ensign. He had to think hard, but he placed her name quickly. "Yes, Ensign Rodriguez?"

"The numbers are all wrong, sir," Emma Rodriguez replied, frowning. "We're getting a serious shift in the oxygen content of the atmosphere. That's why the continents are red-shifted."

"Tell me why that's wrong, Ensign."

"Because we're getting indications of the same plant life we'd see on Earth. In fact, this world is extremely rich in photosensitive plankton," she replied, shaking her head. "No, Captain. There is something wrong here."

Weston turned back to his own display. That pretty much jived with what he felt in his gut but added a substance to his misgivings. "All right. Show me what the drones are seeing."

▶▶▶

Carnivore combat drones were catapult-launched, unmanned, reconnaissance vehicles designed as stealthy platforms to conduct surveillance over combat zones that had been previously cleared of more conventional platforms, like, for example, satellites.

Equipped with the same CM generators that permitted the *Odyssey* to approach two-thirds light-speed without a prohibitive fuel cost, the carnivores could accelerate to a tenth of light-speed in under eight seconds and crash to a halt in just under ten.

And that was in an atmosphere.

In orbital space the drones literally ricocheted around, altering courses on a dime, until they reached their preprogrammed orbital trajectories and slowed to a ballistic course that gave each of the five drones a stable orbit.

Then the heavily shielded bottoms of the drones slid open, revealing sophisticated optics and intercept sensors, and they got down to the nuts and bolts of their job.

▶▶▶

"Well, it looks…normal," Lieutenant Daniels said.

His comment was accompanied by a quiet murmur of agreement from the rest of the bridge crew, though neither Weston nor Roberts commented.

"Wait…" Roberts frowned. "Pan back on Drone Three. Was that a city?"

The screen changed as an operator followed the order, panning the image back and tilting to the optics of Drone Three so they could zoom in on the site of interest.

"Certainly looks like one," Weston said after a moment. "Bring the drone back around. Put it in a stationary orbit over the city."

"Aye, Captain."

The drone swung around, the stabilized optics staying focused on their target as it came back and slowed to a stop over the city.

"Zoom in," Weston whispered, watching as the city doubled in size several times. After a moment, they were looking at an area that the computer listed as about the size of eight city blocks, but Weston only counted three massive buildings within that area.

Someone whistled, but nobody else paid attention.

"Well, something's alive down there," Roberts replied, noting the movement of traffic on the streets.

Weston nodded. "Yeah. Anything on radio?"

"Negative," Ensign Waters replied. "Nothing from the tachyon lab, either."

"Zoom in again. Let's get a picture of these people," Weston ordered, leaning forward as he looked at the image.

An actual alien world. An actual alien city. It was utterly incredible and awe-inspiring.

And nightmarish.

The scene flickered again, zooming in close enough to read a paper over someone's shoulder, and the crew of the *Odyssey* got their first look at the inhabitants of the city below.

"Sweet mother of God. What the hell are those things?" Roberts asked in utter shock as he stared at the viewer.

Weston shook his head. "I don't have the slightest clue. But maybe our guest could enlighten us. Commander, I'll be in the med-lab. Have the drones finish mapping the surface, and continue to investigate."

"Aye, Captain."

▶ ▶ ▶

Milla Chans blanched white with shock and fear as she watched the screen. Weston, Palin, and Rame, who was worried about a possible relapse in her shocked state, took note of her reactions as they entered the isolation room.

On the screen, there was a swarm. No other word could quite describe it, and even that seemed to fall short.

The creatures were black with mottled brown and red across their carapaces. They moved through the remains of the once proud city, slowly dismantling the buildings piece by piece. They looked like arachnids in some ways, like other Terran insects in others, except that they were much larger.

In fact, they were hundreds of times larger than insects. The carnivore drone's scale meter on the head's-up display (HUD) indicated that the creatures averaged five feet in height, their long spindly legs extending beyond that.

They roamed through the city's streets like ants, carrying the dismantled building materials down into tunnels below. There was no sign of anything living, other than the arachnid creatures, and no sign that anything had been living there, other than the city itself.

"They are…Drasin," Milla said softly, pronouncing the word *Drah-sin*. "I…I had no idea that they would become so numerous…so fast."

"What are they, Ithan?" Weston whispered. "It's obvious they didn't build that city. So what are they…and who built the city?"

"My people did," Milla said, sounding almost helpless. "This was one of our…colonies…for…foodstuffs."

"Agricultural," Palin supplied.

"Quah," Milla replied, nodding, though the word had not been caught by the translator.

"She means yes," Palin said, keying the word in. "It's slang…like *yeah* or *yep*."

"I understand, Doctor," Weston said. "Miss Chans… Milla…What happened here?"

Milla took a shallow, ragged breath, staring at the screen as her eyes filled with tears. She closed them so as to shut out the horrible scene.

"Very well, Captain, I shall relate my story to you…to the best of my ability," she said, her voice quivering.

"Thank you, Miss Chans," Weston said softly.

She took a deep breath and began to speak.

CHAPTER 8

Weeks earlier, aboard the stellar cruiser *Carlache*

▶ "LIEUTENANT CHANS!"

The deck of the *Carlache* hummed under her as Milla Chans spun on her heel and found herself staring at her new commanding officer. "Yes, Commander Rath?"

"Lieutenant, I need you to work with Stavrim and Mailyn for the next several days. They need your expertise with the new weapons systems we've installed." The commander scowled at the word *weapons,* as if it tasted bitter to him.

"I'll contact them right away, Commander." Milla understood his distaste, even if she didn't share it.

Why do all commanding officers act insulted when they're forced to equip their ships with weapon systems? Well, all except the captain, and even he doesn't like them. Milla strode off, heading for the new control room to find crewmen Stavrim and Mailyn. Preparations had been progressing well over the past few months, since the tachyon burst from the frontier had changed her culture forever.

It still felt like a dream to her. The transmission hadn't contained any information. Not even the most basic of modulation. It had been nothing more than a trip wire of sorts. A warning, or alarm, given by a system so ancient that no one had known it was there until the Central World-Mind began giving the strangest orders.

No one questioned the orders at first, though they had been out of character for the World-Mind. Production on transports had slowed as new plans were spit out of the ancient database. Plans that no ship had included in centuries.

Weapons.

Milla shook her head, clearing it as she stepped into the control room and looked around.

"Ah, Lieutenant. We are having some difficulties adjusting the target-acquisition system that was recently installed."

Milla frowned, shaking her head. "Have you tried reintegrating the software? All those circuits should have been triple-checked before installation."

Stavrim had the good grace to look chastised. "No, we didn't. No one here is checked out on the software."

Of course not. Milla sighed, dropping into a crouch by the open panel. She looked over the systems but didn't see anything damaged. That was a good thing. The shipyards were all occupied with new constructions or conversions, like the *Carlache*, which made replacement components pricy.

"All right, make sure you haven't damaged the crystals, and close up that panel. I'll check the software," Milla said as she began the task, her fingers flying over the panel.

It took only minutes to find the problem: a minor software conflict had shunted the targeting sensors off alignment by two degrees. A small error, perhaps, but at any realistic combat range, it would result in missing the target by thousands of meters. Not something she could allow to slip by so easily.

Even though they hadn't known what to do about it, she was glad that the two had managed to spot the error.

The feat was made even more impressive by the fact that both of the technicians were mining engineers whose work didn't rely on split-second arming and aiming. Milla dismissed them, sending them off to other work, and walked over to the wall.

"Chans to Captain Tal." Milla palmed the intercom's switch with a graceful sweep of her hand.

"Tal here. Go ahead, Lieutenant."

"The problem has been resolved. All systems have been cleared for service."

"Good, we'll be breaking orbit shortly. Two outer colonies have reported unknown ships approaching their outer perimeters." The captain's voice sounded grim. "Configurations appear to match the historical records."

Milla signed off and sank back into the programmer's chair. The Drasin had been little more than folklore to her and her people until now. Scary stories that were bandied about on dark nights. They weren't supposed to be real. They certainly weren't supposed to be approaching the outer worlds.

Milla forced herself to relax. *Real or imagined, they won't be allowed to harm anyone. Our new systems are the best that can be made. We'll meet these Drasin, and if they are hostile, we'll deal with them on their own terms.*

She had returned to her quarters when she felt the shudder run through the deck plates as the ship's engines powered up. She instinctively reached out and grabbed the nearest wall as the ship accelerated out of orbit. A second later, the ship's artificial gravity field compensated, and the feeling passed. She knew they were now powering away from Ranqil, her home world, and were underway to the outer colonies.

I never really believed that upholding the oath would fall to me and my generation. Like the Drasin, it was just a story, Milla thought as she stripped down, pulling the silicon-covered garments away from her body and grimacing as the gel and powder clung to her skin and hair.

Being an engineer aboard any ship, let alone a hastily refitted *war*ship, was dirty business. On a ship like the *Carlache*, it was doubly so. The carbon crystals used to align the new weapons systems had a tendency to overheat, so each one had to be smeared with a messy silicone gel that contained suspended heat-dispersion capsules.

As she activated the shower, letting the recycled water cascade over her, she wondered about the new ships with the integrated diamond crystals and heat-dispersion systems. The ones with the triple redundancy built in, armored bulkheads, and energy shields that were supposed to be ten times as dense as the ones the *Carlache* produced.

Those would be interesting to see in action. And even more interesting to work on.

Milla hoped she could see one before it was broken up for scrap.

They weren't likely to actually *need* such things, and warships were illegal in peacetime.

Milla shucked her clothing, taking advantage of the downtime to use a cleanser. As she was finishing up, the lurch of the ship let her know that the *Carlache* had made the jump to dimensional space.

They were underway.

The thrum of the ship's engines echoed in her ears as she got dressed. *We should be about three days out from the nearest outer colonies. I think I'll recommend to the captain that we test the systems before entering a possible danger zone.*

▶▶▶

The next two days, Milla tested and retested the prototype systems they had just installed on the cruiser until she and the captain were satisfied that the weapons would perform as intended. Commander Rath tended to avoid the subject as much as possible. Rath had been the first officer of an exploration ship, and while a few offensive devices were always present, actual weaponry was quite foreign to the ship. Most of the equipment that could be used to defend his ship had multiple purposes. The laser drills, explosive charges, and even the hand weapons were primarily used as tools rather than defensive items. The new systems were another matter entirely, and no one pretended they had an alternate use. His vessel had become a warship almost overnight, and while the explorer within him resisted the changes, his warrior side had adapted too quickly for comfort.

The *Carlache* decelerated into the colony three days after they had left Ranqil. After their arrival, the captain called Milla to the bridge.

"Lieutenant Chans, I want you to examine the data we are gathering on what's left of the colony." The captain's voice twitched, and she thought he was going to break down and weep. A moment later she saw why.

The sensors were reporting back the state of the planet, and for a moment, she hadn't seen what the captain had. When she did, she paled until her ivory skin turned a ghastly white.

The planet was there and the sensors even registered life that seemed almost normal.

But the entire upper register of the life-detection gradient, the part that indicated human life, was dead.

There wasn't a single human alive in the entire system. Or if there was, something was eclipsing their readings.

But Milla knew that nothing could fool the sensors like that. Not while leaving a clean slate in the upper register.

She reached out and braced herself against the console, keeping herself from pitching forward. *Great Creator! There were…over twenty million people here just…just a day ago.*

"Take us in," Tal ordered, his voice steady now. "I want to see it with my own eyes."

"Aye, sir."

The *Carlache* flew into the system, sliding to a halt in the high orbital range of the sea-green planet.

"Optics," Tal called, "show me the capital."

The system capital was the only city worthy of the name on the entire planet, housing 90 percent of the planet's population while managing the processing, administration, transport, and various other nongrowing aspects of the world economy.

When it appeared on the screen, it looked like a ghost town.

The streets were empty, miles of ancient stonework broken up by massive buildings that towered over the terrain. It was heartrending.

"Hey…Something moved!" someone shouted. Milla didn't know who. She was too busy looking for the motions.

Something *had* moved. Something that was staying very close to the shadows.

"Grid three-twelve," Tal snapped. "Enlarge and enhance."

The computer responded and the bridge was silent as they stared at the face of nightmares.

The seconds stretched into minutes, until the captain managed to speak without a strangled voice, an accomplishment that Milla admired. "Database, search. Classify life-form."

When there was no response, Tal turned in his seat. "Now!"

The crewwoman at the terminal shook herself and quickly entered the request into the computer. It took only a few seconds before the computer spit back the answer that everyone already knew was coming.

"I...It fits the parameters of a Drasin soldier, Captain."

Tal nodded, accepting the confirmation. He already knew it was the Drasin and had only asked so that it would be entered on the permanent log. "All right. We need to—"

He was cut off when Milla's station chirped a warning as it completed a complex algorithm.

Milla heard a sob from one of the rear stations but forced herself to focus on the information pouring in. "Captain, the energy-decay readings indicate that this was just done a few hours ago. They could still be here."

"Full alert. All personnel to"—she heard the brief pause and the bitter sound in his voice—"battle stations."

The bridge erupted into fervor as the ship's recorders were examining every square meter of the surrounding system. It wasn't long before they found what they were looking for.

"Captain, there is a fading energy trail leading out of the system. Looks like it's on course for the Deserada System, sir."

"Lay in a pursuit course! Communications, start calling in all available cruisers. We need to stop them before they strike again."

A chorus of "yes, sir" echoed across the bridge as the ship accelerated into trans-luminary speeds in pursuit.

▶▶▶

For two days, the *Carlache* pursued the decaying trail, gathering ships from surrounding sectors and drilling their crews in the unfamiliar techniques of battle. On the third day, the *Carlache* found what they had been searching for and dreading.

"Captain, there is a ship on the extreme long-range scanners. It matches the historical configuration for a Drasin vessel."

"Full alert! Tell all ships target has been spotted. Adjust course by"—Tal glanced down at his displays—"point-two-three-by-eight degrees."

"All ships confirm. We are moving in an interception vector."

For the next three hours, the tension on the bridge built to the point where Milla entertained the notion that the friction from it would make walking across the bridge feel like moving through water. Then it was cut. They had caught up to the Drasin vessel. It was a mottled brown-and-black mass that resembled a seedpod more than anything else. Ugly bulges along its hull spoke of weapons ports or something worse. The alien vessel filled their screens as they approached, no longer in any hurry to escape.

It was turning as they approached, their energy fields blazing at maximum intensity.

"Hail them."

Milla turned to look at the captain in shock. These creatures had just wiped out an entire colony system, and he was going to talk? Stunned, she sat there listening to the conversation going on behind her.

"No answer, Captain."

Of course they're not. They're butchers, Milla thought in derision. She wouldn't let it reach her voice, but she couldn't help feeling something she'd never felt before.

Hate.

"Tell the other vessels to spread out."

"Yes, sir."

The Drasin vessel floated serenely in space—or as serenely as anything that ugly could be—before firing an energy bolt that rocked the *Carlache*.

The bridge was a furor of activity—at least half of it unnecessary. People yelled, people prayed, and some just stared with open-mouthed wonder.

"They're firing at us!"

No kidding. Milla's fingers played across her panel, her sarcastic thoughts echoing in the back of her mind. "Weapons are primed, Captain."

The captain's hesitation was palpable, and the ship rocked under a new assault. "Fire. All ships, open fire."

Outside, the area glittered with the fire exchanges; every ship in the impromptu fleet joined the *Carlache* in focusing on the unmoving Drasin vessel. For a brief moment, the vessel was clouded in the deadly hail, then the debris cleared and the Drasin vessel turned on the *Carlache* and fired again as it passed. The *Carlache* rocked under the barrage, but defenses held as the Drasin's weapons raked along the other ships in the fleet.

"No damage, Captain!" someone yelled.

The captain turned on Milla's position. "What's wrong?"

Milla shook her head, her hair cascading around her face. The frustration was evident on her face as she glared at the console and tried to wring some sense out of it. "I don't know, Captain. The systems are working fine. They should have had *some* effect."

"Well, they don't, Lieutenant! Find out why!" Tal snapped, his voice brittle with tension.

"Yes, sir." Milla was in a state of near panic as she frantically examined the logged readings taken during the assault.

She removed several safety systems, throwing more power through them than the official capacity was registered at. It was the only thing she could think of at the moment, and she prayed that it was enough.

"I've uploaded the changes to the fleet, Captain!" Milla cried out as she finished.

"Fire!" Tal ordered, turning back to glare at the screen, as if his anger could damage the ship outside.

The fleet fired on the lone Drasin ship again, the lethal halo of energy enveloping the alien ship for a brief moment in time before lashing back with another barrage.

"Captain, we hurt 'em this time. Not much, but we did hurt 'em!"

Tal leaned forward. "How are our shields?"

"Not good—down by seven-eighths, sir. The *Ronako* is reporting a complete shield failure and…" The young man faltered as he read something new on his console. "Captain! The *Ronako* is gone, sir. They just burned up."

A brief silence permeated the bridge, terminated by the violent shaking of the ship as they took another hit from the Drasin vessel. The *Carlache* rocked with every focused blast.

"All ships, this is Captain Tal. Pour it on! Every eighth of energy you have. Put it all into the new systems and keep firing!" Tal ordered over the fleet communicator, clutching his armrest as the ship seemed to shake itself apart around them.

Outside, the gathered vessels obeyed and the battlefield flashed with the massive discharge of all their combined weaponry. Gradually, they saw results. The Drasin vessel fired less often and with less force. Many of the Drasin's weapons protrusions melted off, leaving entire arcs of the ship's hull open to attack. The massive circular area began to buckle and rupture under the constant attack.

Tal leaned forward, showing a humorless smile. "We are doing it! Keep firing!"

"Captain, we're reading something strange from the *Ronako*!"

"The *Ronako* is lost! Keep firing!" Tal snapped, not even wanting to think about all the dead comrades on that fallen ship.

On the view screen, however, it became evident that the *Ronako* had once again become a factor in the battle. An energy distortion surrounded the vessel in a pale-blue light, growing in intensity as a thin funnel appeared in the swirling mass and spired across empty space to the dying Drasin vessel. Moments later, both vessels were covered in the same blue light as something was transferred from the drifting hulk of the *Ronako* to the Drasin ship.

A scant few instants later, the Drasin emerged from its glowing cocoon of energy and left the entire bridge looking in dismay at a fully repaired Drasin destroyer. Tal gaped for a moment, not believing what his own eyes and the ship's sensors were telling him. He shook himself out of it.

"All ships, evasive maneuvers and keep firing. Keep your shields up. They'd have done that to us by now if they could get through the shield systems!"

The fleet vessels spun on their flaring drives, firing wildly at the repaired destroyer and dancing away from the Drasin's lethal beams. When the fleet had evaded pursuit and recharged slightly, they ducked back in to repeat the maneuver. It was slow and brutal, but the tactic was working for them as the Drasin fire slackened.

"Captain, the incoming vessel is on an interception course!"

"Ours?" Tal gripped his command chair, looking over to the operations console.

"No, sir! Definitely Drasin configurations, sir." The young crewman looked sick.

"How many?"

The young man gulped as he looked up from his boards in terror. "Twenty-three, sir."

This time Captain Tal didn't hesitate, not for an instant. He hit the fleet communicator and yelled in no uncertain terms, "This is Captain Tal! All ships break and run! Vector zero-two-zero-mark-three! I repeat, all ships retreat!"

The fleet vessels turned and ran sprinting for the only opening they had left: a white giant system a few light-minutes away.

They needed to buy enough time to escape into dimensional drive, something they couldn't do with the drain the weapons placed on their systems. Most species had a choice when they were in a situation like this—fight or flight—and in this case, they could only choose one.

Tal was pale and haggard as he realized that he had chosen the wrong one.

They couldn't outrun the Drasin in deep space—that was obvious even from the short battle. They could only hope to trap them within a gravity well. Then if things went right, they could escape the well and enter dimensional drive while the Drasin were recovering.

If things went well.

Milla heard the captain order the ships to deploy their mines, which shocked her since those nuclear devices were a last resort. The small fighter craft they had worked on for months, refitting from passenger shuttles and small freighters, were launched into the maelstrom. Their pilots could hope only to buy a few more minutes for the retreating fleet. Even that wasn't enough, and the Drasin were soon upon them.

As if through a dream, she heard Tal give the order to abandon ship, but when she moved to object, his stare silenced her words and she left the battle-scarred bridge. Her last sight of Tal was his proud posture sitting in his command chair, staring at the damaged viewer.

At the pod, Milla looked wildly about. It was the last one, and she didn't want to leave anyone behind, but no one else came. Stumbling inside the small craft, she thumped the controls, sealing the pod off and firing the ejection thrusters. The *Carlache* spun wildly, framed in the small window of the pod, taking massive hits from the Drasin ships. Its weapons systems fired one last time as they returned fire with as much fury as futility. The last thing Milla saw was a fatally wounded Drasin fighter spinning in her direction; then the pod spun violently and the universe went dark.

A long time passed without her knowing it. Time that saw the rest of her fleet destroyed. Time that saw the Drasin hunt down life pods just like hers as her shipmates began to broadcast their plaintive cry for help.

Through all of that time, Milla floated in the microgravity of the pod, held in place only by her restraint system as she tumbled over and over in space.

After a long time, the Drasin left, apparently satisfied that they had finished their task. Satisfied that there was nothing left alive in the white giant system. And after they were gone, the circuits of Milla's life pod waited patiently for a command.

The computer decided something was wrong. It had been launched, and yet neither the automatic nor the manual triggers had been flipped. That was not correct. So it attempted to contact its ship, in case it had been ejected by accident.

No response.

The computer paused for an infinitesimal moment, accessed its internal scanners, and analyzed the air. When it detected the increase in carbon dioxide, the computer made a calculation and decided that perhaps it hadn't been an accident.

So, unbeknownst to the single occupant of the life pod, the onboard computer overrode its own programming and flipped a bank of virtual switches.

And above the unconscious woman's head, a small device began to beep.

CHAPTER 9

▶ MILA AND HER listeners sat in silence for a long moment after the story ended, each thinking about the loss from their own perspective, each affected to one degree or another.

"And, as far as I can make out, your people came soon after. I suppose I'm extremely lucky that your ship was en route to that system, but," Milla said before pausing and looking at Weston curiously, "why would you be going there? There is nothing useful in that system."

Dr. Palin spoke for the first time: "We were—"

"Doctor, not now," Weston said, shaking his head. He wasn't willing to share that they had a faster method of interstellar travel just yet.

Milla blinked as she looked to the screen. "Great Creator! How long have I been here? That's Duorchin. It's two weeks from where we were. I…" Her voice trailed off.

Weston and Palin watched the young woman hold back tears as the images of lost ships and comrades crossed her mind. After a moment, Weston shrugged and spoke.

"Apparently, you've been out for some time."

Milla looked at them, knowing that something was wrong in what she was hearing but not realizing what. After a long moment, she gave up and let out a shuddering sigh. "At any rate, I thank you for rescuing my pod."

"No need, Ithan Chans. Search and rescue operations are a part of our mandate," Weston replied, the response an ingrained reaction. You don't leave anyone lost at sea, on land, or in space. Period."

"Nonetheless, I am grateful." Milla's lips twisted. "In spite of the accommodations."

Palin chuckled. "I'm afraid that is also standard practice, my dear."

"You were an unknown. Our procedures require several days in isolation while medical tests are performed. I admit that the mirrored visors were my idea—and not from any book," Weston explained.

"They were most...disconcerting." Milla pursed her lips.

Weston smiled. "That was intentional."

Captain Weston walked over to the intercom and flipped a switch. "Dr. Rame, has Milla been cleared from isolation yet?"

"Yes, Captain," the doctor's voice floated back through the speaker.

"Good, we're coming out."

The three of them cycled through the airlock and stepped into the open med-lab. The on-duty personnel and their patients greeted Milla with stares. Her looks, normal as they were, only added to their curiosity. Weston led her through the lab and out into the corridors of the *Odyssey*.

"Doctor." Weston half turned to Palin.

"Yes, Captain?"

"Miss Chans needs living quarters and a change of clothes. See to it that the quartermaster assigns her something suitable."

"Uh…yes, sir." Palin blinked.

"All right." Weston smiled at Milla. "The doctor will get you set up. I have duties to attend to."

"Thank you, Captain. I appreciate your help."

"Not at all," he replied as he parted company. "Just doing my duty, ma'am."

As soon as Weston left the area, the doctor took charge. "Here we go," Palin said as the door opened. "Watch your step."

Milla nodded, stepping over the barrier that separated the small cabin from the hall.

"I've called the quartermaster, so we'll get you fitted for some different clothes," Palin said, a tad uneasily as he gestured to her thin hospital attire. "In the meantime, let me show you around."

▶▶▶

"Status reports," Weston demanded as he stepped onto the bridge, glancing around at the bustle of motion.

"Not much has changed, Captain," Roberts said, looking at the screens. "The carnivore drones have located another three…nests, but nothing near the size of the first one. Those things seem to be taking the planet apart piece by piece, sir."

"Explain."

Roberts turned around, placing a hand on the shoulder of a computer technician. "Bring up the pictures from the city again."

Weston watched as the screen's picture changed. "Is that the same area?"

"No, sir. This one is closer to the center of the population," Roberts replied. "Notice the state of the buildings."

They were demolished and the spiderlike things were dragging the building pieces underground.

"They look like bastardized spiders, Captain. But they act like ants," Roberts replied. "Watch this…"

Weston saw the screen shift focus on the army of creatures as they picked at a towering skyscraper. As the tower began to shudder and topple over, the creatures scrambled, but most couldn't move fast enough to avoid the colossal building's tumble.

For a brief moment there was no motion other than the rolling dust, and then some of the debris moved as some of the buried creatures dug themselves out. In minutes, the scene was back to normal as thousands of the creatures began picking the rubble apart and transporting it underground.

"Damn," Weston whispered. "What are they doing with all that stuff?"

"I don't know, sir," Roberts said uneasily. "They're grabbing everything—buildings, roads, trees, and animals when they catch them."

"And they drag it all underground?"

"Yes, sir."

Weston shook his head. "They must have miles of tunnels built, but it doesn't make sense."

"Sir?"

"According to Milla, this world was only invaded a short while ago," Weston explained. "Maybe less than a month, depending on how long she was floating out there before we picked her up."

"Damn," Roberts muttered, but with a hint of real emotion. "That's scary, sir. But they do have the numbers in place to—"

"That's just it, Commander," Weston interrupted him. "According to her, there were only a few of them in the city after the invasion. Maybe they were just underground by then, but if she's right…"

"Then these things take the expression 'go forth and multiply' to a whole new level." Roberts frowned, looking again at the screen.

"Right you are, Commander," Weston said. "Right you are."

▶▶▶

Milla Chans looked around her cabin, deep in thought. It was small but well appointed, she decided. Everything she needed was here, including access to food and water services, as well as a place to sleep and wash up. The colors were simple, even drab, she supposed, but the room had a feel of newness to it, like she was the first person to inhabit the space.

On one of her ships she'd have more room, but for the moment, this would suffice. At least it had shower facilities.

Palin had just left, along with the man he'd called a "quartermaster," but had promised to return with acceptable clothing. In the meantime, she'd been advised to clean up, and she intended to do just that.

There were backward parts of the colonies that still used running water, so she wasn't surprised when she saw the *Odyssey* did as well. She'd prefer a cleanser, but this would do in a pinch.

The soap, on the other hand, was a bit strange. She decided it would take some getting used to, but it smelled okay and the lather was interesting, if nothing else.

She shed the flimsy gown that had replaced her spacer gear, wondering what had happened to the gear. She stepped into the shower and punched in temperature settings. The water cascaded over her, causing her to flinch from the heat. But she eased back into it once her skin acclimated.

Cleansers feel better, she thought. *I hope they didn't destroy my spacer equipment. That takes weeks to form.*

She shook her head and grabbed the soap. It smelled different under the water, she thought, but it always paid to adjust to the local customs.

Especially when you've been rescued by them.

▶▶▶

"Is this information verified?" Weston looked up from the PDA he'd been scanning.

"No, sir. It's just an educated guess on the computer's part," Roberts said, shaking his head. "There's no way to be absolutely certain of the growth rate, but…"

"But?" Weston raised an eyebrow.

"But that's the low end, sir," the commander replied. "The high-end figures are a nightmare."

"I'll bet," Weston sighed, sitting back in his chair as he looked down at the numbers again.

Doubling their numbers every three days. Jesus.

The high-end number would *have* to be a nightmare. Whatever they were, they put rabbits to shame. His lips twisted at the thought.

"Commander, you have the bridge," he said, heading toward the exit. "I'm going to have another word with our guest."

"Aye, Captain." Roberts nodded. "Good luck, sir."

"Thank you, Commander," Weston said. "Let's hope I don't need it with a single young woman."

▶▶▶

Once the shower was complete, Milla stepped out hesitantly and wondered what she was supposed to use to get dry.

If I remember my cultures lessons, there should be something...Ah, here we are.

She located some dark-blue wads of cloth that seemed in the right place to do the job. If they weren't, she just hoped that she wasn't desecrating anything as she rubbed herself down. After all, one never knew with an alien culture. Even within the colonies, people could create the strangest icons.

There was a knock at the cabin door, so she stuck her head out of the washroom and yelled, "Come in!" before she ducked back in and closed the door with a thoughtful frown.

Now...Do they have a nudity taboo or not?

Milla sighed, rubbing her head. This just wasn't her specialty. She wasn't a social engineer; she blew things up. Granted, she usually blew up mine sites and other excavations, but the point was still valid. Her specialty wasn't exactly the most social of professions.

Outside, she could hear people talking and figured it was probably Dr. Palin back again.

"Excuse me, ma'am?" he said, after knocking on the washroom door.

The quartermaster. Milla recognized his voice. "Yes?"

"Clothes, ma'am," the voice said. "If you'll just open up a bit, I'll hand them in. I won't look. I swear, ma'am."

Hmmm...Does that mean they do have a nudity taboo or that they're worried that I do? Milla shrugged it off and opened the door a crack, accepting the dark-blue bundles that were handed in to her, and then slid the door shut again. "Thank you."

"No problem, ma'am," said the deferential voice. "Just doing my job."

She doubted that, but didn't press. No one with a title of "master" on a colonies ship would be required to stoop to personal deliveries. More than likely, he wanted to see the alien for himself. Not that she had a problem with that. She'd probably have done the same.

"Ithan?" another voice called after a moment.

Her eyes widened in surprise. "Captaine?"

"That's right, Ithan Chans," Weston's voice replied. "When you have a moment, I'd like to speak with you."

"Certainly, Captaine," she said, hurriedly slipping into the clothes provided.

The lower part of the clothing was easy to figure out, as was the top, but she puzzled over the two black tubes for a moment before deciding that they must be for her feet. They'd make for an insane hindrance on her hands. Once she had those on, along with the pants and shirt, she frowned at the two pieces left.

What in the world is this? She puzzled over them for a while, not able to place either the one with the two cups or the other slip of cloth with anything she'd seen anyone else wear. Finally, she just shrugged and tossed them aside. *If they're important, I'm sure someone will tell me.*

Weston smiled as Milla stepped out of her bathroom, wearing a basic crew member's uniform with no insignias. The *Odyssey*'s wardrobe supply was limited, but they had standard uniforms in pretty much any size.

"Ithan," he said as she pinched and pulled at the clothes.

Beside him, Dr. Palin, who had shown up a short while earlier, was silent.

"Captaine. Docteur." Milla nodded back. "My apologies for my...motions. I'm afraid that this clothing doesn't feel exactly right. It is stiff in...odd places."

Weston nodded, smiling. "It takes a while to wear them in so that they are just right for you. Don't worry about it too much."

"Very well," she said, not happy with it, but determined not to complain, either.

"I was wondering if I might interest you in a tour of the ship's facilities, Ithan," Weston offered. He'd been debating that since he'd talked to her, but it seemed like a harmless way to converse with her and see what her reactions would be. More importantly, it would let him try to get her measure, and that was something he found himself feeling in desperate need of.

Milla nodded. "I would be most fascinated, Capitaine."

"Good." Weston tapped the side of the induction mic on his jaw to connect with Commander Roberts. "Commander, I'm taking our guest on a short tour of the ship. Contact me if I'm needed."

"Yes, sir."

"This way, Milla." Weston gestured down the curving hallway, noting her unsure steps as she accustomed herself to the corridors. "We noted that your vessels have artificial gravity included in the design. Unfortunately, we don't have that ability yet. You're standing in a huge rotation drum, which serves as one of the two primary habitats on board the *Odyssey*."

Milla looked down the corridor and glanced back along the curve that she had just traversed. "I see, I don't think that my people have ever used such a technique. Our first ship designs were null-gravity freighters. The artificial-gravity technology came along quickly and was incorporated into our second-generation ships."

"Well, I suppose we weren't content to wait," Weston said. "We do have some ideas on creating an artificial-gravity field, but they are still in the design stage. The *Odyssey* was created after we discovered technology that allows us to travel faster than light."

Milla acknowledged his words, and all three continued on their walk through the habitat.

"This section contains laboratories and some living quarters. The forward module houses the command staff, bridge, the rest of the living quarters, and recreation facilities. Engineering is a null-gravity area and is off limits to most personnel," Weston said. "They don't even like me going in there."

"Engineers are engineers, Captaine. It may be your ship, but it's their engines."

Weston laughed. "True enough, Milla. True enough."

Their walk had brought them to one of the ship's lifts, and the trio stepped into the small capsule.

"Hangar bay."

The capsule whirred off while Milla looked around the small area.

"Here, put these on."

The captain's voice startled her for a moment before she took what he was offering her. "What are these?"

"Magnetic boots. The hangar bay is below decks, an area of the ship outside the rotating habitats."

"Oh."

Why is he showing me this? I'm not one of his people, Milla couldn't help but wonder as the gravity in the lift lightened until she could feel her hair floating up away from her skull.

The lift arrived at the hangar bay and the door hissed open, revealing the cavernous expanse of the ship's hangar. She felt almost lost as she looked up and around herself.

"Some of the shuttles are designed for trans-atmospheric flight and require more room for their controls," Weston explained, noting her slightly overawed expression. "That and the fact that they are used to transport large items to and from the ship."

The sharp clanking of their steps attracted the attention of several of the crew members in the hangar, but only one decided to approach them.

"Heya, Cap." Stephanos's cheerful face was sidetracked as he locked his attention onto Milla. "G'day there. Now, who's this?" Stephanos hadn't seen the pod's survivor when they had offloaded her from the SAR shuttle; he had been too busy locking his own plane down at the time. But others had noticed while the E-med team had been hauling her to the med-lab, and with all the rumors that had begun to flood the *Odyssey*, he realized that this wasn't a crew member.

"Is this the little lady we fished out of the drink a while back?" he asked, mostly just to hear himself talk.

Weston laughed again, leaving Milla wondering if the translation she received over her induction set was an error, since it sounded to her like this man was being rather flippant in front of the ship's captain.

"Yes, this is Ithan Milla Chans," Weston said, introducing the two. "And, Milla, this is Commander Stephen Michaels, but we call him Steph. Steph, Milla here was a duty officer assigned to one of the ships we found out there."

Milla winced as the translation came through. Her eyes then widened in surprise as she noticed that the young man standing in front of them winced, too.

"Sorry to hear that, ma'am." Stephanos's joking face had dropped into a serious expression. The loss of shipmates wasn't a joking matter to the young pilot, or to anyone who'd ever served.

Milla accepted his condolences without much reaction, concealing her feelings by looking around the massive chamber. A short distance away, she saw a shuttle that fit Captain Weston's description of what he called a "trans-atmospheric" vehicle. At the other end of the bay, however, several sleeker shuttles sat in tight formation, with people scurrying around them with some urgency.

"Captain Weston, what is the activity over near those shuttles?" she asked, her voice laden with curiosity.

Milla watched Weston and Stephanos scan the area, as if uncertain where she meant.

"What? Where?" Steph asked, confused.

"There," she said, pointing to the activity near the shuttles.

Dr. Palin followed her gaze, seemingly as confused as he was before, but the real reactions came from Weston and the man he had introduced as Stephanos.

He broke out laughing. "Missy, you call them shuttles?" A wry grin was growing across the pilot's face. From anyone else those would have been fighting words, but the confused look drifting across Milla's face had instantly quelled any indignation he felt. *Must be getting soft! I've decked 250-pound marines for less than that.*

Stephanos glanced from her to the captain, who was trying hard not to laugh again. "With your permission, Captain?"

Weston looked thoughtful for a moment before another chuckling fit overtook him. "All right, Steph, standard VIP tour. Nothing more. You know what I mean."

"Yes, sir, sure do." The cocky young pilot grinned, flipping a smart salute that somehow managed to look half-assed while still being within military protocols.

Weston shook his head as Stephanos turned away. *One of these days I'm going to have to figure out how he manages that.*

Stephanos guided Milla away from the captain and Dr. Palin and began walking the long stretch down to Milla's "shuttles," the ready wing of the Archangel group. As they approached the fighters in the ready flight position, several other pilots greeted Stephanos, many of whom had approached to appraise Milla, only to be sent back to their tasks with a word from the tall pilot.

"This is an Archangel fighter, Milla, and it's a far cry from any shuttle you're likely to see." Steph reached out to slide an appreciative hand along the smooth armor of the sleek craft.

"Fighter craft?" Milla spoke the words slowly, almost tasting them. This ship in front of her was the *Odyssey*'s counterpart to the small fighters her ship had launched in the final moments of their encounter with the Drasin.

He's right, though, she realized, examining the fighter. *I could have called our ships shuttles, because that's what they were. Not these. These ships are made for war—no wasted space like our refitted freighters.*

It was an eye-opener, forcing Milla to revise her thoughts on the controversy that had raged through her home world before she'd left. Many people, including herself at the time, felt the commissioning of dedicated warships were unnecessary, as refitted fleet craft had seemed to pack all the power needed.

Now she wasn't remotely as confident.

It was a good thing that she had never minded admitting a mistake. Well, not much, anyway.

Stephanos rattled on: "Trans-atmospheric superiority fighter. The original design is about twenty-eight years old, but most of the systems have been updated over the past quarter century. The space-maneuvering systems, for instance, were added to the design only two years ago. We never had much use for it, until the *Odyssey* hit the drawing boards, aside from one or two harebrained assault plans during the war."

Space maneuvering was pushing the envelope to the nth degree, and for a pilot like himself, it was the height of his craft.

"We even changed the airframes three times, so they just sort of look like the original Angels."

"Atmospheric fighters?" The phrase awakened a sense of horror in her. "You flew these against your own people?"

We've been taught that the Others often warred amongst themselves...but to see proof of it? Milla shuddered at the thought of this magnificent machine mowing down the very people who had built it. *People like this. We would probably have been better off if they had stayed on their own be-damned planet.*

Stephanos caught her reaction and the little shiver that ran through her body—a reaction that he was used to, in all too many ways. His face hardened, the way it always did when someone questioned the morality of his choice to serve in the military. "When we had to. These planes were built for one reason—defense. Millions would have died if these hadn't been built. Billions more would be under the oppression of a dictatorship. Don't get too caught up in moralizing before you learn the whole story, lady."

Milla swallowed her revulsion for the moment; it would do her no good here. "Tell me more, Stephan."

"That's 'Stephanos.' It's a call sign, not my name. Fighter jocks use call signs as a badge of pride in their abilities." Stephanos turned his attention back to the fighter in front of him. "The Archangel fighter is the fastest, most maneuverable plane we've ever devised. We normally measure aircraft speed by multiples of Mach, the speed of sound through our atmosphere, but the Archangel is a little different. The designers learned early on that the Archangel wasn't limited to the same factors that its predecessors were. A good pilot could bring an Archangel fighter to speeds measured in fractions of light-speed—even in Earth's atmosphere."

"Light-speed!" Milla was shocked. Fractions, or even near light-speed, inside an atmosphere were possible, but she'd never heard of a pilot who could keep control at those speeds. Perhaps in a very high atmosphere, but at lower altitudes the pilot's first mistake would be his last—and, most likely, take a considerable number of people with him when he hit the ground with the force of a nuclear detonation.

"Yeah, the CM field systems that give the ship its VTOL—that's vertical takeoff and landing capabilities—also allow the pilot to create a vacuum pocket around the fighter. Sort of a bubble that the air slides around so you don't get the friction that would normally destroy the plane," Steph said.

Like all pilots, Stephanos was required to know almost as much about his plane as the people who had built it. Knowing just which doodad had to be attached to which thingamajig had saved more than one pilot.

"The same thing also prevents any shock waves that might be caused by something flying at those speeds." Stephanos smirked. "In practice, though, we don't go much above Mach Ten…"

"I realize that. We developed a similar system to transport materials into orbit." Milla frowned, considering that. "What I do not understand is what type of system you use to allow control at those speeds."

Stephanos looked uncomfortable but shook it off and climbed up a ladder, dropping into the cockpit as he waved her up. "Well, come on up."

Milla climbed the small ladder so she could get a view of the cockpit. "Yes?"

"Well, the pilot controls the plane's movement with the foot pedals you see down there, as well as the throttle and the control stick on either side of the seat." Stephanos reached down and toyed with the control stick. "You can see that it allows for full movement over six different axes—or any combination of the six."

Milla just nodded her head and accepted the pilot's obvious omission without comment. She knew that the system was efficient, but it couldn't handle a plane at a tenth light-speed within a planetary atmosphere. Obviously, these people had their secrets, and it wasn't as if she were going to trust them with any of the defense secrets of her people.

The rest of the pilot's tour was interesting, but for her, the highlights had already been hit. She listened with mild interest as he described the fighter's engines and safety features, noted with mild amusement that he skimmed quickly over the weapons systems without really saying anything, and found herself instead studying the man rather than the machine. Stephanos was tall, over six feet, his hair a little rougher than most of the people milling around. She couldn't decide what color his hair was because in places it seemed dark brown and in others it was a reddish hue.

He seemed to have a permanent smile etched on his face, a jovial glint in his eyes that was echoed by the lines drawn in his flesh from years of laughter.

Milla tried to remind herself that this was a self-confessed killer, a man who hunted his own kind. It was hard to keep that in mind when confronted with the cheerful visage he presented.

He simply didn't fit her image of the bloodthirsty barbarians in the legends of the Others.

"Are you done yet, Steph?"

Milla blinked, startled by Weston's voice. *How did I miss the sound of his boots on the floor?*

"Huh? Oh, sure, Chief," he said, flipping another not-quite-sloppy salute at the captain. "Standard VIP stuff all done."

"Good. I think we'll head back to the bridge to see how the system survey is coming," Weston said.

"I'm going to go over some of the maintenance logs with Riley over there," Stephanos said. "I noticed some slack in the throttle when we were on the SAR." He turned and headed over to a small man holding an oversized PDA.

"'SAR,' Captaine?" Milla asked.

"Search and rescue operation," Weston replied offhandedly. "When we went out to pick you up."

"Oh."

"This way back to the lift, Milla," Weston gestured, leading them back to the ship's lift. Milla could see Dr. Palin standing nervously beside it. "What is wrong with the docteur?"

Weston looked at Palin for a moment. "He doesn't like the null gravity. He probably has a sensitive stomach."

Milla grinned. She had known his like in the fleet. Despite the artificial gravity on their ships, null gravity was a commonplace occurrence, and many fleet candidates found out the hard way that space service wasn't their optimal career choice.

A moment later they were on the lift, and Milla felt the rotational gravity return as the lift matched the speed of the *Odyssey*'s habitat module.

Captain Weston retrieved the Magboots from Milla and Palin, stowing them away in the lift's compartment. "Bridge."

CHAPTER 10

▶ DR. PALIN LEFT Weston and Milla in the lift when he exited to head for his lab and the data they had retrieved from the pod and derelict vessel.

"Bridge," Weston instructed the computer.

"Captain on deck!" The crewman's announcement brought the officers manning their stations to attention.

"As you were," Weston said. He didn't want his presence to disturb the work that had to be done. "Commander Roberts, what's our position?"

The commander looked at Milla, appraising her intently. After a moment, he shrugged and looked back to the captain. "Completing another orbit, sir. The carnivore drones have finished the planetary survey, unless you want something else?"

"No. Call them back," Weston said after a moment, looking at the screen, a frown forming on his face. "No signals from the surface?"

"No, sir."

Milla recognized the world that filled the large screen from the last time she'd been in this very position, though on a different vessel. She shivered, thinking about the pictures

Captain Weston had shown her, and felt the urge to be anywhere but here.

She felt a flush of guilt and steeled herself against it. She may not be able to do anything for the people who'd died there, but she would not disgrace herself or them by running from her own weakness. Not that she actually could run far.

Her reactions went unnoticed by the others as Weston continued speaking with his first officer.

"When the drones are back, we'll break orbit. How long until the transition threshold?"

"Fourteen hours, sir," Roberts replied without hesitation. It had been the first thing he'd checked before anything else, including the recon data from the carnivore drones.

"All right. Break orbit as soon as the flight deck reports the drone has been recovered," Weston ordered, more for the record than anything else. "Best speed out of the system."

Transition threshold? Milla looked from one officer to another, hoping for some clue to the meaning of the words. She searched each face, finding nothing more than a look of disgust, a wince of pain glimmering across one face, and the occasional look of controlled terror.

"What destination, sir?" Roberts asked.

Weston started to speak but stopped. Technically, he was only responsible for dropping Milla off at the next port of call—at least under the revised Maritime Act to which all space-going vessels adhered to in the Sol System. In practice, that meant returning the rescued to Earth, though they had dropped off some at the Mars base or the Jovian research platforms. This was a different situation. In the Sol System, the longest wait would have been a few weeks. A month or two at the outside. Taking Milla to Earth, however, could delay another authorized expedition for several years or longer.

Especially considering the carnivore data they'd just picked up.

He turned to Milla. "Ithan Chans, would you be so kind as to tell us where we should transport you?"

Milla looked at the captain for a moment. Where could she direct these people that would worry the council the least? Her home world was out of the question. It was one of the Five, the core worlds of the Priminae government, and was central to the defense of the colonies. Even though the people on this ship seemed to be potential allies, she couldn't lead them to one of the central systems. *Perhaps one of the agricultural colonies. One with a star dock.*

She considered her options, remembering what worlds were out here on the frontier.

Yes, Port Fuielles is near this area, only a few days' travel from here. That will do.

"Well, Ithan?" Weston prodded. "Unless you'd like to accompany us home after we've completed our shakedown tour."

Milla smiled. "No, Captaine, that won't be necessary. Please show me your charts of this area, and I will show you to Port Fuielles, a small outpost orbiting an agricultural world. It will do."

Weston led Milla to a navigation display showing the local star systems. She quickly located her system, a small yellow star about twenty light-years away, and pointed it out.

"Right here, if you don't mind."

Captain Weston nodded. "No problem, Ithan Chans. Commander, direct the coordinates to the helm."

"Aye, Captain."

Weston stepped over to Milla. "I would recommend you report to the med-lab. I'll clear a mild sedative with the doctor."

Milla looked at Weston in alarm. "Sedative? Why?" *These people mean to* drug *me!*

"It is only a recommendation. The transition drive can be"—Weston paused, looking for the right word; after a moment, he gave up and selected one that was inadequate for the task—"*trying* for someone who doesn't know what to expect. We know firsthand."

Milla looked at him speculatively. "You'll be receiving one of these *sedatives* as well?"

Weston listened with some amusement to the way she spat the word *sedatives.*

"No, I won't have that luxury."

"Then I, too, refuse the luxury."

"Very well, Milla, but I expect you will regret that decision once we enter transition." Weston shook his head. He couldn't blame her. He'd have done the same in her place. It was just funny how often being smart got you into trouble. *Ignorance is bliss,* he thought.

"Perhaps." Milla looked smug, having avoided the sinister trap.

Weston looked her over and smiled, knowing full well what she was thinking, and he knew that he couldn't convince her that she was wrong. *Oh well, her loss.* He shrugged, letting it go. It wasn't his problem anymore.

"Well then, we seem to have the better part of a day or so before we're clear for transition. Perhaps a visit to the recreation areas?"

Milla seemed to consider his offer and nodded. Weston guided her off the bridge and back to the ship's lift.

"Recreation decks," Weston said.

The efficient lift whirred away, dropping them to the outer levels of the forward habitat cylinder in mere seconds. The two of them stepped out into a cafeteria, with several exits leading to other parts of the recreation facilities.

"Are you hungry?" Weston asked, glancing sideways at her. Milla shook her head.

"I'm glad you don't want to eat before your first transition."

What is he talking about? Milla just shrugged her shoulders and looked around.

The ship's mess hall was crowded, as many of the ship's officers and researchers had decided to take the last hour in this system to refuel themselves before returning to their instruments and stations. Most of the crew had gathered in small groups and were engaged in some fervent conversation. Milla did notice a few who were sitting on their own, however. In one corner, Stephanos sat drinking something and staring at a large view screen.

"What is he doing over there?"

Weston followed her eyes to where the pilot sat. "Steph likes his moments of solitude. He's probably trying to watch the video."

"Oh." *Strange, I wouldn't have seen him as the sort to be a loner.*

Milla eyed the young pilot for a moment too long, but shook it off as Captain Weston led her into the rec hall.

Weston and Milla toured the room, drawing stares and hushed murmurs from the crew who recognized her. Milla's eyes roamed the area, taking in the facilities as well as the crew, stopping at the viewer she had noticed Stephanos watching. On the screen, a man was firing some type of weapon at several assailants, managing to hit his targets in spite of the most ludicrous distractions.

Weston followed his guest's eyes and barely suppressed a snort of disgust. "I wouldn't put much stock in that, if I were you. It's just entertainment. None of it's real."

"Entertainment?" Milla looked at the video again with new eyes. *Watching death is entertainment?*

"Just barely. This is strictly designed to hold the interest of the lowest common denominator of the population. Even people like you, who obviously dislike violence, have a hard time pulling their attention away."

She had to admit to herself that Weston had a point; it was difficult to turn away from the continual action on the screen. Looking around, she noticed no one was really watching except Stephanos, and something about his face belied his apparent interest in the entertainment.

"This must be a rather large vessel, Captain. Most ships I've seen don't provide as well for the after-duty time of their crews."

Weston's eyebrows arched. "This is only a small section of the *Odyssey*'s recreational facilities, Milla. About a third of this deck is dedicated to the recreation section. We have two full gyms, a small theater, half a dozen simulators, and a small library room."

Milla did a double take. "That much? This must be a huge vessel to warrant that level of luxury for the crew."

"That depends. We do build larger vessels, but they are primarily for cargo. The *Odyssey* is a carrier-class ship, designed with a large flight deck for the shuttles and the Archangels, as well as extensive research labs. Since we found it necessary to have a crew of about three hundred, we've included several amenities."

Three hundred? We run crews of twice that size with less than a quarter of the facilities this crew is afforded. Milla nodded distractedly. "Would you mind if we sat down while we talked?"

"Not at all." Weston slipped down into one of the seats across the table from Milla.

"Captaine, may I ask you a question?"

"Certainly."

"Why is it that you address me by my rank, where the others I have met seem to prefer my name?"

Weston looked at her. He hadn't actually noticed that and had to consider his answer for a moment. "The position of captain instills certain habits into a person. The only people on board who I refer to without using rank are Stephanos and the other Archangels, and I don't use their names, either. I use their call signs because I used to be their wing commander."

He flew one of those fighters? "You were a pilot, Captaine?"

"Yes, I flew with the Angels from the beginning. I met Stephanos when he was fifteen years old and only dreamed of flying a jet." Weston smiled at the memory. "At fifteen, he managed to break into the research facilities that designed the Archangel-class fighter over five times before we finally gave in and offered him a job there. Might have been more. He still won't tell me the real number." *Good thing we weren't working for the military back then*—Weston didn't add aloud, but smiled at the thought—*or he'd have probably spent the next fifty years buried in the deepest dungeon the MPs could find.*

Milla smiled. "I, too, have known people like that, and they have much to endear themselves, don't they?"

Weston chuckled. "Definitely."

Weston saw Milla's eyes focus behind him, her face reddening.

"He's standing behind me, isn't he?" Not waiting for her to respond, Weston turned and looked up at the glint in Stephanos's eyes.

"Telling stories about me already, Captain?"

"Sit down," Weston growled, a grin struggling beneath the air of command he had affected.

Stephanos grinned. "I do believe I will—at least to better defend my honor against the torrent of lies you're undoubtedly telling our dear guest here."

"Lies? You mean, like the time you convinced an entire bar full of drunks that I was covering their tabs for the night?" Weston asked.

Stephanos coughed awkwardly. "Well, it was like this…"

"Or maybe the time you had three different women drop in on Steffer, announcing that he was the father of their child…on his wedding night?"

"Hey! He had that coming," the pilot defended himself.

Weston looked back to Milla. "It took us two weeks to convince Steffer's wife not to have the marriage annulled."

Milla snickered, as much at Stephanos's feeble claims of innocence as the stories Weston was telling. The casual exchange between Weston and Stephanos was a relief from the stiff formality that she had observed on board any fleet vessel. This type of joking about was limited to the junior officers and crew members, and it was odd to watch two senior officers banter in public.

"It seems to me that you've pulled a few practical jokes yourself, Cap."

Weston could see Stephanos's eyes light up as he began to formulate his next sentence.

Weston stayed serene, then interrupted his friend. "Does the word *grounded* mean anything to you?"

Milla looked between them in confusion. *Grounded? What ground? We are on a space vessel.*

Stephanos looked at her with an expression of mock pain on his face. "The captain doesn't play by the rules. 'Grounded' is an expression that means 'removed from active flight duty.'"

Milla looked across at Weston, noting the laughter in his eyes. "One of the perks…of command?"

"Just so, Ithan. Just so."

The three of them broke out laughing, drawing stares from dozens of people who wondered what the captain and the space lady found so funny.

Weston was about to say something when a call from the bridge interrupted them. "Captain, we'll be breaking orbit shortly. The transition vectors have been calculated."

Weston tapped the switch on the side of the induction mic. "Good. I'll be up shortly."

He turned to Milla. "I'm afraid that I have duties to attend to, Ithan. If you'd like to stay here for a while, Stephanos can show you to your room when you wish. I'll send for you prior to transition, if you would like."

Milla looked across at Stephanos, who nodded. "All right, Captain. I'll stay out of your way until we…transition."

Weston smiled at her words; although, he did wonder about the way she seemed to almost taste the word *transition*. *She's in for a nasty shock if she's planning on a smooth ride.*

Weston strode out of the room, heading for the lift that would take him back to the bridge. Stephanos watched him leave before turning back to Milla.

"You interested in seeing some more of the sights?"

Milla looked around for a moment. "Certainly, Stephanos, I would be most delighted."

Stephanos stood and motioned her out of the room toward the closest lift. "We'll catch a lift running along the axis of the rotating habitats. There's something in the stern of the ship I think you'd like to see."

"Really? And what would that be?" Milla looked at Stephanos out of the corner of her eye, trying to guess his intentions.

Stephanos, apparently oblivious to her scrutiny, just stood there smiling. "It wouldn't be much of a surprise if I told you that, now, would it?"

▶▶▶

They boarded a lift that sped along the central axis, reducing its rotation until it stopped and they were floating free. Stephanos slipped a pair of Magboots across the lift to Milla, and they stepped out onto the *Odyssey*'s observation deck.

They approached the enormous transparent steel windows that looked over both rotation drums of the *Odyssey* as they spun counter to each other. There were long lines of cable tracing paths through the stars as they interconnected different portions of the ship, providing guidelines for the currently collapsed sensory arrays. And just off to one side, the blue-green world hung suspended amongst the stars.

Milla's breath caught at the panoramic view the windows provided. "It's beautiful," she said.

"Yeah. I like this place. Normally, you get quite a few people up here, but lately, we've been a tad busy."

Stephanos led her through the room, sidestepping tables that were bolted to the floor as they approached the glass. "The tables and chairs are remnants from the early design stage. There were plans to incorporate an artificial-gravity system into the *Odyssey*. They even built the main bridge about two decks up before they realized that the artificial-gravity systems drew more power than the all rest of the ship's systems combined."

Milla looked out at the starry expanse through the huge windows. "So you do have artificial-gravity technology."

"Well, no, not really." Steph frowned. "I don't get it all myself, but the technology they were going to use is based on the antigravity tech that we use in the Archangels. It's not true gravity, but a way to simulate it. The system was only activated during construction. From what I hear, the workers used this level as recreation area."

"I can easily understand why—it's a lovely place to be. But if the power drain was so bad, why was it used?"

Stephanos shrugged. "Probably because the reactor was online and none of the other systems, except limited life support, drew power. The *Odyssey*'s reactor outputs a constant amount of power, so if it isn't used, it's lost. The work crew wouldn't have had any trouble securing permission for the expenditure."

"I see. Lucky for them, I suppose," Milla said absently as she continued to take in the view.

"Definitely," Stephanos said. "This was the only orbital place they had, at the time, with a gravity field. The construction was based out of the old International Space Station at the same time as the new orbital platforms were being built."

Milla smiled. "That would provide the workers with a sense of home, I would imagine. It has been a long time since our ships were forced to travel without gravity. Even our small fighter craft have gravity fields."

"Really? I would think that gravity fields would hamper the response times in a fighter. We expand the field that provides us with antigravity to eliminate our own mass along with the fighters. No mass equals no inertia. Gravity is inconsequential once inertia is dealt with."

Milla shrugged. Ship design wasn't really her specialty.

Steph sensed that she didn't have anything more to say, so he just turned to look out over the rotating drums of the main habitats.

▶ ▶ ▶

Sometime later, the sudden blaring of the ship's PA system startled them.

"Ithan Chans, if you wish to be present on the bridge during the transition, you should make your way to the bridge now."

Stephanos looked up and replied, "All right, Commander Roberts, we'll be heading straight there."

"Very good, Lieutenant. The captain is waiting."

Stephanos closed the connection. "Translation: Get our backsides up there—now."

Milla followed behind him as the two of them headed back toward the lift, the clanking of their boots echoing through the room.

CHAPTER 11

▶MILLA AND STEPHANOS stepped onto the bridge while Weston was ordering for long-range scans of the target system.

"Tachyon scanners powered up, Captain. We should have preliminary telemetry in a few seconds," answered an ensign.

"Excellent. Send the data to helm as it comes in."

"Aye, sir."

Weston turned and looked back at the two recent arrivals on the bridge. "Ah, welcome back, Milla," he said, then turned to Stephanos. "We'll be transitioning out of this system in a few minutes and should have just enough time for you to get to the hangar bay. I've scrambled the rest of the Angels."

Stephanos stood to attention, acknowledged the captain, pivoted on his heel, and strode off the bridge.

Milla watched Stephanos leave and turned back to Weston. "You are preparing your fighters for launch? Why?"

"Ithan Chans, whatever hit your people out here was remarkably efficient. We still haven't determined why you survived or even what they did to the rest of your ships out there. I won't take unnecessary chances with my crew."

Milla nodded. She would be hard-pressed to find fault in his position, even if she had a say in the outcome.

Preparations on the bridge continued at a feverish pace as the tachyon telemetry came streaming back. Milla was shown to a seat that folded out of the rear wall and was strapped in tightly while the commotion on the bridge wound down. Finally, with all the preparations finished, the captain sat back and waited.

"Stephanos to the bridge," Weston called over the intercom. He leaned forward when his friend's voice came over. "Yes, Steph?"

"The Angels are ready to fly, Captain. Give the word and we'll burn out of here."

"Understood. Stand by, Archangels."

It was only at this moment that Milla realized what was bothering her. *They act as if we'll be in the Fuielles System within a few minutes. That system is days away; these people couldn't possibly have that kind of ability.*

She heard the captain give the order to engage, and she forced her mind back to the action on the bridge.

"Captain, forward spires have transitioned. The effect will overtake the bridge in thirty-two seconds."

Effect? What effect? Thirty seconds later she found out. Milla just stared in horror as the bridge view screen vaporized, the particles spinning away into the emptiness of space.

This is madness! It wasn't until the effect had overtaken the junior officers, spinning their atoms away into space, that Milla came unfrozen. Her hands clawed at the restraints that kept her pinned to the chair as she tried in vain to loosen them, her panic mounting with each passing instant. Then, almost the same second, she saw something that caused her to stop.

Capt. Eric Weston was sitting in his chair, simply staring at the approaching maelstrom, an expression of slight distaste decorating his features but nothing more. She looked at him and was instantly calmed by his relaxed form. She might not have been so calmed had she seen Weston's bone-white knuckles or the bloodred holes he was drilling into his palms with his clenched fists, but she wasn't supposed to see that and so she didn't.

Weston focused all his considerable willpower on projecting a commanding presence to everyone on the bridge, but the transition effect took its toll on him as well.

In a markedly different system over twenty light-years away, the unique signature of the *Odyssey* reentering dimensional space unfolded. Section by section and deck by deck, the giant ship stepped down from the tachyon stream and rebuilt itself particle by particle.

Throughout the ship, its crew began the arduous steps to ensure that the ship had reintegrated the entire myriad of its systems successfully. On the flight deck, Stephanos ordered the first of the Archangel fighters into position on the ship's catapults and had their backup take positions on the elevators that separated the vacuum of the flight deck from the hangar bay.

On the bridge, the scene was much the same as elsewhere, with the notable exception of a very pale and seemingly very cold young woman strapped into her seat.

"Get the sensors back online. I need a full scan of the system," Weston snapped as crisply as his nauseated stomach would allow.

"Aye, sir. Full scan in three minutes, sir."

Weston glanced back to Milla and motioned a young ensign over to check on her. As the young woman moved to respond to his order, Weston pulled another display forward and tapped in a command to echo the sensor displays.

Milla looked up, shivering, as a warming hand was laid on her shoulder.

The ensign looked at her with a gentle smile. "Are you okay, ma'am?"

Milla's eyes bored into the young woman. "That was among the most disturbing thing I've ever seen."

The ensign smiled sheepishly. "Yes, ma'am, the transition drive is hard to take. Here, let me help you." She unlocked the restraint straps that held Milla in place and slipped them back into their rollers.

Milla pitched forward, but the woman caught her easily. It took a few moments for the shivering and weakness to pass. Milla nodded slowly and then began to move of her own accord. She stood up and stretched. "Thank you…?"

"Ensign Lamont, ma'am. Susan Lamont."

"Thank you, Susan. I am Milla."

Ensign Lamont smiled. "I know. Most everybody on board knows your name by now, ma'am."

"I should have guessed that. A ship's gossip network is always the most efficient system on board, no?"

Susan shrugged. "Always has been as far as I know, ma'am."

Milla turned her attention back to the activities on the bridge; the captain's attention had been drawn to the incoming telemetry from the ship's radar and lidar sensors. Milla took a step closer to examine the diagram that appeared on the main screen.

She gasped, her mouth opening into a round "O" of shock, and stumbled forward, barely catching the back of the captain's command chair to steady herself. Behind her, she felt Ensign Lamont approach and loop an arm under hers to bolster her up, but she couldn't seem to martial the presence of mind to thank the woman or even throw her a grateful glance.

My God.

It was impossible, but it *was* the Fuielles System that floated on those screens, outlined with red and blue by the computer. The primary was a midsized yellow star with eleven planets circling it. Milla stared in shock, taking an involuntary step forward and clutching at the chair back as she tried to find her voice.

"How?" Milla's voice was soft, floating on breath only a few feet, but her hesitant question caught the attention of Captain Weston.

He half turned and smiled at her, or perhaps the ensign behind her, then gave Milla an apologetic look.

"I should have tried to explain it to you, but suffice to say, our method of travel is somewhat faster than what you described in your story. Less pleasant, I'll bet, though."

"Yes, you could say that," Milla said, her stomach still churning as the memories twisted at the back of her mind.

Weston nodded, seeing the emotion hidden in her eyes. The transition drive was one of, if not the most, disturbing things he'd ever endured. Certainly, it was *the* most disturbing thing outside of a battlefield. He took a breath as he glanced back around the bridge, then nodded and waved her closer.

Milla returned a few steps up to the chair that Weston had set up for her. The captain tapped a command into one of his smaller displays. A graphic appeared on it a second later, and Milla blinked as she recognized the general outline of the *Odyssey* from the many map plates posted about the ship.

"Our system charges every molecule in the ship with a tachyon surge," he told her as the graphic surged with color and the ship began to break apart. "Since tachyons aren't particularly fond of existing in this universe…"

The graphic vanished from the screen.

"What happens," he said, "is that we are actually broken down to sub-molecular components, which flash across the intervening space. When the tachyon surge runs out of power…"

The graphic on the screen reintegrated automatically.

"…so do we, and we come to a stop. Hopefully, right on target," he snickered, "if we've done our calculations right."

Milla nodded, not really understanding the details in the slightest but following the general principle easily enough.

"I'm told that the ship actually jumps instantaneously. The effect that we see is a result of a subjective time distortion." Weston paused a moment, then smiled. "Of course, that doesn't make it any easier to handle the effect."

"Fascinating," she said, and she *was* fascinated. Instantaneous travel between star systems was an incredible achievement.

Beyond that, even, it flew in the face of everything she had ever been taught. It was supposed to be impossible, utterly and completely.

"We think so," Weston said. "We actually have a few theories about traveling like you do…well, something close, anyway. The problem is that we can't navigate at superlight speeds. Our nav computers aren't fast enough."

Milla simply nodded. She understood the problem. Navigating at faster-than-light speeds required tachyon-based computing systems, something these people hadn't developed. Otherwise, you were forced to constantly stop and start as you checked your position and, perhaps, more importantly, the path you had chosen to ensure that it was clear of debris.

Remarkable, they couldn't do it the easy way, so they cut through the problem and made another option, Milla thought to herself, looking around the bridge of the starship just as something galvanized one of the men sitting ahead of her.

"Captain, readings are coming in from the long-range scanners."

"Report." Weston's attention snapped back to the task at hand.

Milla fell back a step, her eyes still intent on the actions of the people around her, until she felt a hand on her shoulder and turned to see Ensign Lamont standing behind her.

"This way, ma'am." The young ensign gestured her back to the chair. "You'll be better off here."

Milla allowed herself to be guided back as the people around her went to work.

▶▶▶

"Yellow star—similar to ours. Eleven planets." Ensign Waters paused as the data fed through his station. "No life signs anywhere."

Waters's quiet statement froze most of the bridge. Those without vital duties couldn't help but spare a glance to the young woman seated at the back of the room. Milla had gone white. She couldn't believe it. It wasn't possible. The Fuielles System should have millions of people and enough life-forms to have registered on even weak sensors from outside the system.

"You are mistaken." Her voice was firm.

Waters gulped and bent back to his station, rechecking the readings and directing the sensors more carefully at the system's planets.

"No, ma'am. There is a debris ring around the fourth planet that looks artificial, but no life signs. I...I'm sorry, ma'am," the young man said after a moment, his voice tense as his fingers automatically rechecked the numbers that the computers were sending him.

"Helm, plot a course to take us around the fourth planet. We'll do a qui—" Weston began to say.

He was cut off by an exclamation from Ensign Waters. "Captain! There's an object incoming on an interception course. Silhouette coming in now, sir."

"Put it up, Mr. Waters," Weston ordered, his voice quiet, yet firm.

Waters swallowed, tapping in the command. "Aye, sir."

A moment later, the dark silhouette of the approaching vessel was on the main screen. The ship read out as relatively small, only fifty meters or so, but it seemed to be fast.

"Trying to get a clearer shot, sir. The material seems to be absorbing the lidar and radar signals."

"Switch to the tachyon sensors," Weston ordered.

"Aye, sir, but at this range, they probably won't be much better."

Waters was proven wrong a moment later when the silhouette on the screen snapped into focus, showing the ship in more detail. Weston was studying the vessel thoughtfully when he heard a sharp intake of breath from behind him and turned to see Milla's face blanche.

As if I have to guess what that means. Out loud, Weston spoke calmly: "I take it you recognize the ship?"

Milla nodded dumbly. "It's a Drasin reconnaissance vessel. The same type as the one we encountered after..."

After another star system was sterilized...leaving only those things behind, Weston finished silently.

"Tactical analysis, Mr. Waters," Weston demanded tersely. "Can we run?"

Waters barely had to glance at the numbers. "Not a chance in hell, sir."

"Combat alert. All crew members to their duty stations."

The captain's voice rang out on all decks as the military crew of the exploration vessel snapped to their duties, going to full battle station alert in an instant. Commander Roberts slid into his station and began activating controls. Shudders ran though the *Odyssey* as armor plating slid aside from the weapons they protected and the ominous devices were freed from their captivity.

Weston nodded in satisfaction as he watched his people react smoothly to the situation, their training kicking in as they brought the ship from a 90 percent stand-down to full military power.

"Full power to the navigational deflectors. Waters, try to hail them. Commander, power up all weapons systems, and get a passive lock on that ship. Don't ping them yet."

"Aye, sir," they both chorused as they bent to their tasks.

"Captain, we have a passive lock, but it's only at eighty-three percent. The vessel isn't radiating any tachyons, so a real-time lock is impossible, unless we hit them with active tachyon sensors. The computer is doing course estimations," Commander Roberts reported a moment later, his voice showing exactly what he thought of the computer's estimates. The error margins alone were enough to disgust the man, particularly as he was about to bet his life and the lives of every crew member of the *Odyssey* on them.

"That'll have to do for now, Commander. Ensign Waters, is there any response?" Weston asked.

"Negative. No response to our hails. Initial sensor data is coming back, sir," the ensign said, sounding nervous as he leaned over his console.

"Send it to my station, Ensign."

Weston turned his attention to the data feeding into his terminal, looking for any information he could use to either prevent or win what looked to be an inevitable conflict. Frowning, he looked at the data closer before realizing what had struck him as odd.

"Ensign, did you run this through the fractal imaging program? All I'm getting here are echoes."

Waters stammered for a moment and reexamined the data himself. "What you have is correct, sir. I don't recognize the pattern. The material seems to be refracting the sensors. We can't get a good scan."

Weston cursed once under his breath. "That figures. Any response to the hails?"

"Still nothing, sir...Captain, they just increased their velocity, and the sensors are reading an energy buildup from the same locus as the alien ship!"

"Ping them," Weston's voice echoed coldly across the bridge.

"Aye, sir. Tachyon echo-location going active." A moment later, Waters's voice continued. "We've locked their position into the combat systems." Waters stiffened at his console, reading the numbers that flashed past his eyes instinctively. "Incoming!"

"Launch drones! Sideslip two hundred meters to starboard!" Weston called up Waters's intel. "Prepare to engage the enemy vessel. Give the Archangels the green light, and tell Commander Michaels godspeed."

"Aye, sir."

The *Odyssey*'s CM field pulsed once as the navigation computers briefly transferred a large chunk of power into the generators and fired up the maneuvering thrusters. The small but powerful thrusts pushed out from the port side, and the big ship groaned and shuddered as its remaining mass objected to the maneuver.

The objections were futile, though, as the ship slid away diagonally, even as the blast shields that protected the enclosed flight decks rumbled open against the silent backdrop of space.

The *Odyssey*'s flight deck buzzed as the Archangels screamed out into space, their twin reactors blazing as the nimble ships formed up and flew ahead of the *Odyssey*. The ship's thrusters burned hard, pushing the *Odyssey* to the side.

"We've slid by two hundred meters, sir, and the Angels report that they're forming up for a strafing run, on your command," Roberts said.

"Good. Have them—" Weston began.

"Captain! The drones are gone, sir! They just…vaporized," Waters muttered in shock. "I'm trying to compile the last few seconds of information that we got from them…It looks like they registered a very powerful energy signature intersecting our previous position."

"Analyze it, Waters. I want to know what it was," Weston told him and then turned back to Roberts. "Have the Angels fly point for us until further notice."

"Aye, Captain."

Weston watched as Ensign Waters passed the data to the labs for analysis and waited impatiently for the response. On the screen, the Archangels maintained their range from the *Odyssey*, and Weston knew the pilots were waiting for his order to engage the fighters' combat interface.

"Captain, the analysis is coming back. The energy signature is one of…" Waters hesitated. "A very powerful class-one laser."

"Class one? That's it?" Weston's expression was incredulous.

"Yes, s…sir," Waters stammered. "They're pumping more power through the beam than I would have thought possible, but it's still only a class one."

"Adjust the forward armor plates to compensate and increase to combat velocity." Weston touched a button with his thumb. "Weston to Stephanos."

"Aye, Captain?" the answer came back from the lead fighter.

"Ensign Waters is transmitting frequency data on the laser the bogey is using. Adjust your armor resonance and engage combat interface."

"Aye, Captain." Stephanos switched over to the squadron's frequency a moment later. "All right, boys and girls, we're clear for combat maneuvering. Engage the interface."

Good-natured groans sounded across the channel as a few of the pilots mock-objected to the order; Stephanos himself hated pressing that button, but it had to be done. Depressing a small covered button on the side of his seat, Stephanos hissed in pain as two thin molecular needles snicked out of his helmet and entered the back of his neck on either side of his spinal cord.

The so-called interface consisted of two very sensitive conductors that acted as neural sensors after they had penetrated either side of the spinal cord. The needles themselves were thin enough that, the specs claimed, an operator would barely be able to feel the entry—though most pilots swore differently—and were certified not to cause undue damage to the nervous system.

In return, they continually monitored the pilot's nerve endings and interpolated gross motor functions into a sophisticated program that allowed the Angels to very precisely adjust their maneuvers.

System initiation complete, Stephanos flexed his muscles carefully, trying not to think about the foreign objects in his neck, and turned back to the task at hand.

"Okay, team, readjust the cam-plates to the frequency they sent over, and give me a flying wedge in front of the *Odyssey*. Match her speed and bring all combat systems online." He switched back over to his direct channel to Captain Weston. "We're ready here, Cap. You sure they're only using class ones?"

Back on the *Odyssey*, Weston had been asking that question himself. "Looks like it, Steph. All the scans match."

Weston watched the tight formation of fighters on his screen shimmer as each of the sleek little craft altered its armor to reflect the laser frequency. Seconds later, the tightly formed squad had visibly shifted color to adapt to their enemy's lasers.

Weston listened to Stephanos's acknowledgment and then closed the channel. "Waters, what's the estimated time to intercept?"

"Eighteen minutes, sir. Until then, we can easily evade any shots they take," the ensign responded, his nerves having either faded or been placed somewhere else for the moment.

"All right, we wait," Weston said, trying to sound calm as he watched the countdown to contact.

The tension rose on the bridge as the clock ran down and the two ships closed the gap between them.

▶ ▶ ▶

Outside, the Archangel fighters maintained their formation as the rapidly approaching ship appeared on their less-powerful scanners.

Stephanos adjusted his scanners as more information about the target transmitted to his fighter's onboard systems. The enemy vessel had some way of scrambling most of the sensors they used on it, resulting in apparently random profiles and energy readings. His fighter's tachyon array was having the same issues as the larger one on the *Odyssey*. Neither system seemed capable of detecting the approaching vessel unless it varied from its course or powered its weapons.

The pilot frowned. Most materials had tachyon signatures that could be used to get some type of lock at almost any range. The incoming ship not only must have been constructed of a material that was transparent to tachyons, but its energy systems must have been incredibly well shielded as well since energy fields normally disrupted local tachyon fields.

Stephanos's fighter banked slightly as the *Odyssey* ordered a course change. The squadron all moved in unison as the ship altered course behind them. The enemy intercept was less than five minutes out when their scanners picked up the smaller groupings of signals that erupted from the enemy ship.

"Weston to Angel Lead, we believe the target vessel has just launched fighters. Be warned they have adjusted their course again to intercept and are still not answering our hails."

"Confirmed, *Odyssey*. Angel squadron has gone to combat maneuvering and is ready to provide cover." Stephanos couldn't help the large part of him that was eagerly waiting for this encounter. He already knew that the Archangels were best on Earth; now they were getting a chance to take on the local bully in a much bigger neighborhood.

"*Odyssey*, Angel Lead is requesting permission to break formation with Angels Two and Three to scout ahead."

"Denied. Angel Lead, we'll meet them together." Weston's tone was dry, but Commander Stephanos recognized the old "follow orders, you idiot" admonition hidden under the tone.

"Yes, sir," Stephanos sighed. It was worth a shot.

Three minutes to intercept.

▶▶▶

Behind them all, at the back of the bridge, Milla had gone pale as she watched the intertwining of graphics on the sanitized computer screens in front of her. To her mind—part of it, at least—they were already dead. The Drasin were faster than the fastest ship. *No, they aren't faster than this ship*, she had to remind herself. However, the captain didn't seem to have any intention of running.

It was insane. It was suicide. And yet, she couldn't manage to open her mouth to object to it. Part of her wanted to do nothing more than run and hide, lest the same thing happen to her and these people as had happened to her comrades before. Another part, however, wanted to do anything, even if it were futile, to kick the Drasin in the teeth.

She shivered, knowing, of course, that it wasn't her choice to make.

At T-minus sixty seconds, the *Odyssey*'s scanners began to go wild as they reported massive energy surges from the alien vessel's general location. Before the crew could respond, the power surge had already become evident.

The *Odyssey* shuddered and the bridge crew stiffened in their chairs.

"Captain, we just took several direct hits. Class-one lasers, all of them," Waters said tensely.

"Same frequency?"

"Aye, sir. Minor damage to forward armor. Estimates say the forward armor reflected over ninety-eight percent of the power away from the *Odyssey*." Waters frowned. "The two percent that was left was enough to ablate away several layers of armor."

"Fine." Weston hated to ask stupid questions, but he knew this one had to be asked. "Any chance those were com-lasers?"

"Negative, sir. Not unless they habitually use power levels consistent with a quantum thermal explosion for communicating with other species," Waters said, then immediately flushed as he realized that he had just joked with his captain.

Weston chuckled silently. "If they do, then it's probably safer to have them as enemies than allies."

A soft round of laughter circled the bridge, killing some of the tension as Weston nodded firmly and spoke aloud.

"All right, full power to the forward defense array. Inform me as soon as you have a clear lock on the target using standard sensors. And keep hailing them."

"Aye, Captain."

Thumbing a control on the panel of his armrest, Weston opened a channel to Stephanos. "Angel One, this is the *Odyssey*. You are clear to attack; keep your squad out of the fire zone between the *Odyssey* and the enemy capital vessel. Good luck, Steph."

▼

CHAPTER 12

▲

▶STEPHANOS FELT THE kick of the fighter's acceleration push him back into his seat before the CM stabilizer activated and the pressure equalized. He didn't have to check to know that the other fighters were still in perfect formation around him. They were all Archangels, and that was all he needed to know. He had led them against more than one enemy group; he knew his people and he trusted them.

As the sleek fighters rocketed toward their target, the alien battle group sent a squad to intercept the twelve incoming Archangels.

Stephanos blinked twice as he looked at his screens. "Four! They're sending four fighters to intercept us?"

Archangel Eight, a young man nicknamed "Brute," was quick to respond: "Yeah, don't seem hardly right. You'd think they would treat us with some respect—at least in our first encounter."

"Their loss, Brute. Let's frag 'em and leave the debris for someone else to worry about," said the fourth Archangel, a reckless woman who went by the aptly chosen call sign "Flare."

"Angels Three, Four, and Eight, you're with me. The rest of you stay on vector to intercept the aliens' primary fighter group." Stephanos banked hard, slipping out of the formation and accelerating toward the four hostiles coming after them.

The four fighters slipped into a tightly stacked diamond formation, the front and rear fighters offset vertically so they didn't block each other's shots. They approached the curiously shaped alien fighters, each pilot trying to ride the edge of tension and relaxation that created the optimum reaction time.

The alien fighters, for their part, remained solidly on an intercept course for the bulk of the Archangel squadron and ignored the four fighters burning on vector toward them.

"All right, I'm sending you your targets. Finish them fast and head back to the main group." Stephanos figured that either the aliens were seriously underestimating them or they had something else up their sleeves.

The other Archangels acknowledged the order and locked onto their assigned targets. On Stephanos's order, they broke their diamond formation and flew in toward their individual targets.

Brute broke onto the tactical network (tac-net) seconds later: "I think they just locked on. Computer can't confirm it, but my instruments just went nuts."

"Roger that, stay clear and be ready to go evasive."

Brute acknowledged quickly, but Stephanos could see his emotions echoed as clearly in his flying as if he had a sign pointed at him saying "nervous."

"Relax, Brute, you'll screw up your stabilizers flying like that," Stephanos commanded, noting the shaky flying with annoyance. Brute knew better than that.

Being nervous was fine. Flying nervous was not.

Brute's sheepish chuckle echoed in his flying as Archangel Eight smoothed out and resumed its original intercept course.

Steph smiled. "Better, Brute."

On their scanners, the Archangels watched as one of the alien vessels altered course toward them.

"You think he's going to swat us?" Brute said.

Even Stephanos snickered at the irreverent smirk he heard over the tac-net.

He was cut off abruptly when Brute let out a shocked yell and his fighter rocked violently in space. "I'm hit! The cam-plate mods were useless!"

Commander Stephanos cursed under his breath, linking his HUD into Brute's systems and checking the other plane's diagnostics. In a flash, he found the problem.

"Brute! Calm down, have your system analyze the frequency and readjust. The fighter isn't using the same frequency as the capital ship!" Stephanos watched the Archangel shudder in front of him, reading the fear and panic in the plane's demeanor, just as he would have read it in the pilot's face. The hit didn't look bad; luckily, Brute had managed to evade a continuous beam.

Stephanos tapped in a few commands, bringing his own cam-plate modifications up and then setting the computer to automatically control the system.

Originally adapted from active camouflage technology, the cam-plates used on both the Archangel fighters and the *Odyssey* itself really came into its own as a laser defense. By adjusting the absorption and reflection properties of the nanometer-sized particulates in the coating, the plates could alternately absorb or reflect energy on various bands with efficiencies exceeding 98 percent. With old-style single frequency lasers, as had seen heavy use at the beginning of the war, a prepared cam-plate defense rendered the area it was protecting effectively invulnerable. Of course, the power levels the *Odyssey* and the Angels were now encountering were so far beyond the upper limits of the plates' stress testing that it was really anyone's guess as to their effectiveness.

Too bad.

So Stephanos and the rest of the Archangels would have to entrust their lives, yet again, to the computer's adaptive capabilities.

Well, it's better than nothing, Stephanos thought as the program self-tested and flashed all green across the board. "All fighters, switch to auto-adapt combat programs."

"O...okay," Brute stammered a bit as his hands flew over the controls, almost of their own volition, reacting instinctively, activating the analysis programs and algorithms that connected them to the plane's armor plating.

Stephanos was relieved to see Brute's plane smooth out as the computer adjusted its cam-plates to reflect the incoming laser attack. He was considerably more relieved when Brute's wing stopped smoking as the automated repair system put out the small electrical fire and rerouted the area's circuitry.

"Angel Lead, missile away."

The rocket flared briefly under Stephanos's wing and flew away from the plane, accelerating toward the first of the enemy fighters. The alien ship had barely begun to react to the attack when the missile impacted and delivered its payload.

The oddly spherical explosion that was unique to zero gravity blinded both pilots and sensors for a moment before it cleared.

"Angel Three, confirm the kill," Steph ordered.

Archangel Three, Racer, paused briefly to double-check his sensors. "Confirmed. Nothing left but some dust."

The Archangels growled in satisfaction.

None of them would admit it, but for a second there, they'd actually been afraid that the aliens would prove to be juggernauts, somehow able to take everything they could throw at them and keep on coming.

Evidence that they weren't was the most welcome news the team had heard yet.

Stephanos grinned. "All right...Lock on and let fly. I'll cover you from here."

He listened briefly to the acknowledgments and watched the rapidly expanding contrails of the three fighters as they roared into the now one-sided battle. Five minutes later, the battle was over, and the four flyers rocketed back to rendez-vous with the main group.

Stephanos watched the small signals representing the combatants converge on his screen. He knew that the Angels could handle the alien fighters in one-on-one, but they were outnumbered by the swarm that preceded the alien capital ship.

▶▶▶

On the *Odyssey*'s bridge, Captain Weston watched the four lights blink off his tactical display with no small amount of satisfaction. *Good job, Steph.*

"Commander Roberts, signal the Archangels' main group and tell them to prepare for an artillery barrage. We'll thin out their opposition for them," he ordered, leaning forward and designating corridors along the path between the *Odyssey* and the alien ship.

"Yes, sir."

A moment later, the commander turned back from his station. "They report ready. Tactical is coordinating firing vectors with them now."

"Good, tell them to fire for maximum effect when ready," Weston said, sitting back in his chair as his stomach churned. He watched the tiny lights that showed the Archangels and wished that he were out there with them.

▶▶▶

Outside, the *Odyssey*'s primary laser array began to glow as the massive energy banks were charged in preparation for the battle ahead. Seconds later, the massive weapons opened fire, aiming straight into the ranks of the Archangels and, beyond them, the enemy fighter craft.

As the laser crossed the stellar void, the Archangel squadron split smoothly apart, allowing the powerful energy beam to slice through the space they had previously occupied. The enemy craft were not so fortunate.

A dozen of the small enemy fighters went up like matchbooks in a furnace as the *Odyssey*'s big guns cut a swathe through their ranks. Most of the rest were caught in the explosions of their comrades as the tight laser beam vaporized fighter after fighter with its lethal glare.

By the time Stephanos had rejoined his team, the *Odyssey*'s judicious use of its long-range cannons had evened out the odds in the coming battle considerably. With war whoops echoing across the tac-net, the Archangels plunged back into the fray, their weapons blazing as they engaged the enemy.

The silently screaming turbines of the Archangel squadron left rapidly, dispersing twin contrails of expanding plasma in the vacuum of space as they roared through the Drasin fighters, wreaking havoc through the aliens' formation as they worked to clear the path for the *Odyssey*.

One-on-one, the enemy fighters were no match for the Archangels, and within minutes, Stephanos and his squadron had decimated the first wave of Drasin fighter craft. However, it soon became obvious to even the most gung ho Archangel that the Drasin learned from their mistakes.

The second wave of fighter craft came at the Archangels in trios, each Archangel suddenly faced with three enemy fighters. Stephanos was the first to realize the enemy's primary reason for this method of assault—or at least, the primary result.

"Watch it, Angels! Each ship uses a different laser frequency, so don't count on the cam-plates to save you," he snapped as he flipped his fighter in a barrel roll that dropped him under the line of fire of an enemy fighter. Invisible laser light scored space where he had been, but Steph just haloed the Drasin and flipped his fighter end for end as he loosed a missile up the alien's plasma stream.

The explosion that followed tore the alien fighter to shreds, and Steph righted his plane as he glanced around. "Stay with your wingman! Don't let them catch you alone!"

The tac-net echoed with replies from his team as Stephanos jigged his fighter into a tight roll, leaving two enemy fighter craft well behind. That still left him with one following tight to his six. Twisting the flight stick violently, Stephanos spun his plane around in a rapid spin, allowing the fighter's inertia to continue pulling it along its previous course and swinging his guns onto the alien craft. Hunter became hunted in a handful of seconds before Stephanos squeezed tight on the firing stud, turning the enemy fighter into a cloud of expanding debris.

Many of the other Archangels weren't faring so well. Stephanos could see the drifting fuselage of three of his squad floating dead in space.

Thank God the cockpits were all ejected. He pushed thoughts of those drifting hulks from his mind as the two Drasin fighters he had lost earlier swooped back onto a pursuit course with him. He found himself hard-pressed to avoid the crisscrossing lasers that dogged his fighter through his desperate evasions.

Sweat beaded above his eye when the second Drasin vessel suddenly went up in a blaze of blue-white flames.

"Thought you might need a hand, Stephanos." He heard the grin in Flare's voice as Archangel Four slid alongside him for a moment before the remaining Drasin moved in for another pass.

"Break on three, Flare. He can't follow us both."

"Roger that, Stephanos."

The two sleek fighters paralleled each other for a moment longer before breaking hard away from each other and leaving the Drasin fighter to follow its original target—Stephanos.

"Anytime you're ready, Flare!" Archangel Lead rocked quickly back and forth as incoming fire from the Drasin ship swept along its wingtips.

"Just lining him up, boss man." Flare's fighter dropped into position behind the Drasin ship, her vertical thrusters flaring as she bellied in on its six, giving him mere seconds to register her presence before the four linked-laser cannons on her wings glowed. Seconds later, a charred and drifting fighter was left in the place of the bogey who had been hunting Stephanos.

Stephanos thanked his savior briefly before turning his attention back to the battlefield. The Archangels had acquitted themselves well in the battle, but the sheer force of numbers was beginning to wear them down. He knew that if something didn't happen soon, things would go from bad to disastrous.

He needn't have worried. Captain Weston had commanded the squad long enough to realize their limits.

A shadow passed over his cockpit as the bulk of the *Odyssey* slid into the dogfight, its short-range weapons blazing as they intercepted enemy missiles and fighters alike. Within moments, the battle had been turned to a rout as the enemy fighters peeled off and fled back to their carrier.

▶▶▶

"They're firing again. Minimal damage effect. The cam-plate modifications are holding."

Captain Weston nodded. He hadn't expected anything else. The capital ship's lasers were only class one, so they couldn't adjust the beam frequency without severe modifications; the fighters, however, worried Weston. "Have all local defense weapons continue to fire on the enemy fighters," he ordered. "Then lock onto the Drasin mother ship and prepare to fire."

"Aye, Captain," Waters replied. "I have telemetry coming back from our targeting laser systems now, sir."

"Good," Weston replied. "Send the numbers to the computer, and have it adjust the heterodyne frequencies of our main array to match the highest absorption level we can hit."

"Yes, sir," the young man said, sending the command and data into the computer with a flick of his wrist.

It only took the computer moments to analyze the return bounce off the laser they had painted on the enemy ship, carefully filing away various snippets of information about its molecular structure, heat expenditure, and perhaps, most importantly, frequency absorption rates.

The computer took that information, sent it to the main laser array, and adjusted the frequencies of the primary heterodyne coils to produce what should be an energy beam that would induce massive, critical failure in the chosen target.

However, in that short time, something outside had changed.

"Captain! We're reading—" Waters began to speak, jolting in his seat as his displays went haywire for a second, then totally dead.

Weston tried to say something, but his breath caught in his throat as he clutched at his chest in shock. A sweeping wave of dizziness dropped him to one knee. Around him, the same thing was happening to the others on the bridge, and through the ship, the scene was the same.

In the space of seconds, the NACS *Odyssey* was drifting, unguided in space, her crew dropping to the deck plates like proverbial flies.

▶ ▶ ▶

"Jesus H. Christ, Steph...What the hell is that?" Brute asked in shock as the Archangels broke wide, circling back around.

The battle with the fighters was all but won when the enemy cruiser entered into the picture. The enemy ship had closed with the *Odyssey* while the Archangels had turned and burned with their alien counterparts and, using that damned stealth signature of theirs, had managed to get closer than anyone in the flight group had realized.

As the Archangels swept back around, they could see a spectacular sight, something straight out of a sci-fi film.

A crackling beam of energy had joined the two massive ships, a scene that Milla would have recognized in an instant had she not been trapped in the embrace of the Drasin weapon. The same weapon had turned the tide of battle against her comrades during their first engagement with the Drasin, and now it wreaked its havoc on the *Odyssey*.

The Archangels soon found themselves under heavy attack again as their artillery support drifted uselessly past, the enemy fire tripling as they struggled to stay clear of the killing zones.

Commander Stephanos didn't see any other options, so he immediately kicked the fighter he had strapped to his back up a few more notches. "Archangels, form up on me!"

Around him, the rest of the flight team responded in kind, forming up smoothly behind him as they swept out and around, skirting the edge of the enemy range, just before turning back into the fires.

Stephanos's voice rang out over the tac-net. "Teams Two, Three, and Four, cover us from the fighters. Team One, you're with me. Time for a strafing run on the big boy."

Acknowledgments echoed across the net as the squad broke up into teams and whirled in at the enemy fighters, weapons blazing. Stephanos's team broke through the enemy formation and centered on the source of the energy beam that was assaulting the *Odyssey*.

"Team One, fire at will."

The enemy cruiser appeared larger and larger as they rocketed down toward its surface, pulling up at the last moment as their weapons blazed and skimmed along the armor plates. The three fighters' missiles, lasers, and cannon fire lit up the local vacuum with a blazing light. They ripped along the surface of the enemy ship, skimming the mottled black-and-violet hull. Semi-spherical explosions erupted in the wake of the four Archangels, shuddering through the big Drasin ship with destructive energy.

"No good! It's too big. We'll have to try hitting it en mass!" Stephanos yelled over the warning alarms that jangled in his cockpit.

The Archangels who had been covering Team One broke from the dogfight and accelerated suicidally fast toward the enemy capital ship. They knew that there was no point in holding back now.

Lose this fight and there was no going home.

"We're with you, Lead. Call the shot!"

The anticipation in Flare's voice brought a wide grin to Stephanos's face. Flare was always the first in and the last out. *Stupid girl.*

"Target the center of that energy disturbance, and give it everything you've got!" he snapped, flipping up all the remaining safeties from his firing studs.

No holds barred, the eight remaining Archangels swept in on the enemy energy weapon, all guns firing with desperate fervor. Behind them, the enemy fighters were in hot pursuit, trying to destroy the Angels before they could accomplish their task. As the Terran fighters swept away from the target, it became painfully obvious that they had failed.

Despite their best efforts, the energy maelstrom still connected the *Odyssey* with the Drasin mother ship.

The silence on the tac-net was broken a moment later.

"Cover me, boss man. I have an idea."

Stephanos snapped his head around in time to see Flare's fighter peel off from the rest, plunging back through the enemy fighters and toward the Drasin vessel.

"Flare! What are you doing?" Not receiving a reply, Stephanos cursed and reluctantly backed the brash woman's play. "All right, everyone, cover her!"

The remaining Archangels fell into a loose formation and plowed after the errant flyer, letting loose with their few remaining missiles to clear the small fighters from her path. The lone fighter was well ahead of them by the time Stephanos realized her intentions, and if it had been anyone else, he would have ordered him or her back again. He knew that any such order would go unheeded by the hotheaded young woman.

So, gritting his teeth at the sudden feeling of impotence, he watched his fellow Angel accelerate into the jaws of the lion and wished her luck as he followed his own instructions and started haloing enemy fighters and opening up with everything his fighter had.

The rogue fighter broke through the enemy's defenses, its cam-plates shimmering with iridescent ripples as the onboard computer tried valiantly to reflect the incoming fire. Stephanos didn't know what was keeping the armor active. He'd have expected it to be long overwhelmed by this point, but Flare seemed to have a higher power flying on her wing. Fighting the damaged thrusters on her plane, Flare kept the reeling aircraft on a direct course for the alien weapon emitter that was holding the *Odyssey* in its clutching grasp.

Samantha Marie Clarke, call sign "Flare," second-generation Archangel and general pain in her superior's posterior, overrode the safety systems and threw full power to the CM field, even as she slammed her throttle full up.

The fighter accelerated from just under 0.1c, relative velocity, to almost 0.85c in about a second and a half.

Flare died before the first quarter-second passed, even the CM field unable to keep her from being crushed by the sudden acceleration, but her fighter continued on, slamming into the enemy's capital vessel at relativistic speed.

The explosion that followed tore through the enemy ship, ripping its weapons mount from the hull in a single instant and terminating the attack on the *Odyssey.*

CHAPTER 13

▶ GROANS ECHOED ACROSS the bridge of the *Odyssey* and across the entire ship as the crew began to struggle up from their fallen positions and retook their stations.

"Put the alien vessel on screen." Weston was having trouble swallowing. His mouth felt like it had been packed with cotton.

"Aye, sir."

Weston heard the dry rasp from Lieutenant Daniels and assumed that his symptoms were far from unique. The screen flickered and showed the alien ship, a tall plume of flame marking a gaping wound in the ship's hull.

"Sir, we have a signal coming in from the Archangels!"

"Tell them to hold on that for a moment and clear away from the alien ship. Target that ship with all weapons. Fire at will."

The barrage of cover fire the Archangels had provided for Flare had deteriorated into a vengeful blaze that swept alien fighter craft from existence. A blaze that Stephanos found himself angrily reluctant to end, but as ordered, he signaled the others.

"All Archangels, break off. Full burn. We have to get clear so the *Odyssey* can use the pulse torpedoes." Stephanos was angry, but he was still a military man, and the best path to victory was following orders.

Not exacting revenge.

And the Archangels, in turn, were all soldiers.

They broke off.

Not happily, nor enthusiastically, but they broke off.

As the Archangels swept past the Drasin vessel, putting the enemy between them and the *Odyssey*, the guns of the Earth vessel opened up. Blindingly fast bursts of pure white light marked the passage of the *Odyssey*'s pulse torpedoes, almost impossible to follow with the human eye. Yet, even before those lethal pulses left their firing tubes, white-hot holes were already appearing in the alien hull as invisible radiation from the *Odyssey*'s primary laser array poured a hellish heat into the Drasin vessel.

Milla stared in shock at the screen as the Drasin ship was dismantled in a manner of seconds, its hull reduced to a handful of fused slices of unrecognizable material. The remaining fighters were mopped up by a combination of the Archangels' precision maneuvers and the judicious application of the *Odyssey*'s pinpoint defense systems.

In one furious moment, the *Odyssey* had managed what her own people had failed to do in hours of battle.

Ithan Milla Chans of the Colonial Navy felt a numb shock spread through her as she looked to the screens and slumped into her seat.

And then it was over.

Captain Weston thumbed a command when it became obvious that the battle had ended. "Shuttles Three and Four, prep for SAR and salvage operations. Shuttle One will prep for planetary SAR." Weston turned to look at his first officer. "Mr. Roberts, have Major Brinks prepare the planetary expedition. Inform him that I want him to take a full Special Forces contingent and whatever else he thinks he might need."

Commander Roberts snapped to attention. "Yes, sir." On his way out, he noticed Milla. "Sir, permission to bring our guest along? She could be helpful if they find any survivors."

Weston looked at Milla, judging the look on her face and the tense nod she sent in his direction. "Granted. Be careful."

"Yes, sir." Roberts motioned Milla off the bridge. "This way, miss."

"Commander," Weston said.

"Yes, sir?"

"Have two carnivore drones included in the shuttle payload," Weston ordered.

Roberts nodded. "Aye, sir."

Weston turned back to the staff. "Someone dig out those sensor records and get the labs to figure out what the *hell* we just got hit with!"

▶▶▶

Roberts followed Milla off the bridge and led her down the corridors to the lift, calling for the flight deck once they were standing in the small pod. Tapping his induction mic, Roberts gave orders as the lift sped to its destination.

"Major Brinks, gather your men and report to the flight deck for an SAR mission. Standard equipment, plus full environmental gear. Tell Lieutenant Savoy that his team has been activated and have them report to you."

Milla couldn't hear the confirmation that apparently satisfied the tall black man. Commander Roberts was an enigma to her. Her ship didn't have his equivalent. Oh, they certainly had a first officer on board—that was a given—but Roberts's entire manner was alien to her. She had never seen anyone quite as disciplined as this man. His entire manner spoke of control—control of himself, his environment, and everyone around him.

They remained silent as the lift arrived at its destination. Milla shifted uncomfortably under the commander's scrutiny. The lift doors opened to reveal the shuttle bay and the chaotic flurry of activity around the three large trans-atmospheric craft Milla had seen earlier. For a moment, she found herself looking around for the sleek craft that Stephanos had shown her before; then she realized that they had been outside fighting the Drasin.

The commander led her across the huge room, veering toward a shuttle that had attracted more than its fair share of the attention. Gathered around its base was a large group of men in addition to the technicians—men whose uniforms didn't match any that she had seen on board so far.

As they approached, one of the men broke from the group, marching out to meet them. "Commander." The man snapped a salute to Roberts. "My team is good to go. Lieutenant Savoy and his geek squad are packed up and already on board."

Roberts looked surprised. "That was fast, Major."

"Not really, sir. It was anticipation," Maj. Wilhelm Brinks, formerly of the US Air Force, said. "Rumors trickled down to us after we arrived in-system; we knew there was a good chance of another SAR. Savoy's equipment was already down here, so when you called for his team, we just packed their gear while Savoy assembled his squad."

Roberts nodded approvingly. "All right, inform your men that you've drawn ground duty. We don't have much data on the planet, so do a few orbits. We've been informed that it is supposed to have people living on it."

The three of them began to walk toward the shuttle.

"Supposed to have?"

Roberts's expression became grim. "Sensors didn't pick up anything except some residual energy readings that happen to match our playmates' weapons fire. We might get something when we get in close."

"Any chance of Tangos?" Brinks asked, his voice pitched low as he considered the situation.

"If it's like the last one." Roberts just shrugged.

Brinks nodded as the trio marched toward the shuttle and the waiting people. As they arrived, Milla saw the row of men with the odd uniforms snap into a rigid stance, their hands snapping up into a salute like Brinks had given to Roberts. A moment later, Roberts returned the salute, and they dropped their hands to their sides, standing at attention.

Commander Roberts looked over the rather motley crew. He was aware that each of them was handpicked, the best of the best of the various Special Forces groups that had cropped up by the start of the World War III—Army Rangers, Marine Force Recon, Navy SEALs, Joint Task Force 2, etc., etc.

Each man chosen for being the best his unit could field.

Only one problem, Roberts thought, with a carefully hidden frown. They weren't yet more than the sum of their parts. They weren't the well-oiled teams that each man had been plucked from, and it showed even in how they stood at attention.

He took a breath and stepped forward. "I'm certain that the major has informed you of the situation, so I'm not going to add anything that you don't already know. You're going to do a SAR recon of the planet. If you pick up any signs of survivors, you're going to do your best for them. If you kiss dirt, watch each other's backs, and you'll all come back alive. Hear me?"

There was an interspersed return from the soldiers that varied from a "We hear you, sir!" to a roughly uttered "Huah!"

Roberts was disappointed, not because of any lack of enthusiasm, nor because their replies were wrong, but simply because he would have preferred if they had all replied as one.

Milla and Brinks held back while Roberts spoke to the men, then stepped back and nodded to Brinks.

Brinks nodded back and turned to address his team. "You heard the man! Double-check that your gear is all accounted for, then strap in. We're going for a little ride." Brinks watched with satisfaction as his team broke up, heading to the equipment to make certain it was all intact. He turned to Milla and looked her up and down appraisingly. "It was hard to find a fit for you, and we don't carry a lot of this stuff in your size. If you'd follow me," he said politely, but firmly.

Milla followed the man to a locker on the far side of the bay where he pulled out an armored suit, similar to the one he wore.

She looked at it warily. "Do I have to wear this?"

Brinks smiled. "You'll be glad of it soon enough. It is standard issue for entering hazardous areas. It's what we call a 'firm suit,' completely sealed environmental gear that can withstand pressures from near vacuum to fifteen standard atmospheres without endangering the wearer. It also has a few other gadgets packed tightly into it that could save your life." Brinks looked her over for a second until she stared back. She was surprised to see the rather rugged-looking man flush and turn away. "One moment, miss...I'll have a female officer help you get suited up."

Milla watched in confusion as the major cleared the locker room and stepped out. She looked down at the armor in hand, puzzling over the hard material. Unless she was missing her guess, it was made of some sort of ceramic material, though she couldn't be certain.

"Ma'am?"

Milla looked up and saw a female dressed in the same hard armor looking at her from the door. "Yes?"

"I'm here to help you suit up."

"Oh," Milla nodded. "All right…"

The woman looked at her and she looked back. After a moment, she saw the armored woman roll her eyes and let out a soft chuff of amusement. "Oh for…Look, I'm Jaime…"

Milla looked down at her extended hand before she slowly took it. "Milla."

"All right, Milla…" The woman smiled, then waved her hand. "I'm afraid that you're going to have to lose the clothes."

"Pardon?"

"The clothes," Jaime repeated. "You can't wear those in a battle suit. It'll screw up the monitors and get real messy if we're stuck planet-side for too long."

Milla was about to repeat her last word, but realization clicked in.

Of course! She felt like slapping herself for a moment as she realized that the suits were much like her own spacer gear. You could be in it for hours, even days, depending on the situation, and wearing clothing would prevent certain key functions.

Or at least render them disgustingly messy.

Milla shuddered but quickly began to shuck her borrowed clothing, looking at the armor with a new eye.

▶▶▶

A short while later, Jaime led Milla out of the locker area and back into the hangar. Surprisingly, Milla found that, despite its armor-hard exterior, the suit was fairly comfortable to wear, and she didn't feel encumbered by the bulky clothing. Though, she grimaced, as the burning sensation left from connecting its various plumbing connections wasn't something to be enjoyed. Thankfully, that was going away quickly; otherwise, the armor would be hellish beyond belief.

"It's lighter than it looks," Brinks said, when he noticed her look of surprise. "Has to be. Otherwise, it'd be a hindrance."

Milla nodded. "It is…" She gingerly tried moving. "But it feels strange to move in."

Brinks nodded, a knowing expression on his face. "The legs and arms have a series of nano-fiber enhancements. They take some getting used to, but they'll add about five hundred kilos to your lift capacity and let you jump about forty feet vertically. Take care, though, your step will be a little energetic until you get used to them, so you'd best start now."

Milla bit her lip as she found out what Brinks meant. A simple step had catapulted her two feet off the deck and landed her face first into a bulkhead. Groaning from the floor, she bent her legs under her and tried to rise to her feet. Instead of slowly rising from the deck, she snapped straight up, stopping only after her feet were six inches off the floor. Landing roughly on the balls of her feet, she balanced herself precariously on her toes while her right arm flailed around, looking for something to steady herself with.

"Whoa! I said take it slow." Brinks reached out and grabbed her outstretched arm, steadying the young woman with a firm hand. "You practically have to relearn how to walk with these things. The fibers make for a fun step. Don't make any sudden movements."

Milla began to shuffle along as Brinks continued his explanation and impromptu tutorial.

"The suit is adaptive. It'll learn to anticipate how much strength you actually need, but until it maps your habits, you'd better just scuff your feet. Okay?"

"O…okay," she replied.

Slowly, Milla progressed from shuffling movements to actual steps. She knew that the suit would undoubtedly prove useful, but it would be difficult to master. Watching the similarly suited men over by the shuttle, she marveled at the apparent ease of their motions.

Roberts walked over from checking the shuttle. "How is she handling the suit, Major?"

"Better than I did when I first tried one." Brinks chuckled, patting Milla's armor on the shoulder. "When I first wore one, I decided to see how good the system actually worked. Put my head through a two-inch scaffold and woke up in a hospital room with a concussion and a Purple Heart."

Milla was confused how he had injured his heart—and why it would be purple—but she nodded and continued to walk painfully across the shuttle bay. The suit's nano-fibers, combined with the lack of gravity in the large room, forced Brinks to follow closely behind her and occasionally pull her back down so the magnetic clamps on her boots could reconnect to the floor.

"Let's get onto the shuttle. The rest of my team is packing the last of the gear now. Once that's done, we'll be heading out," Brinks said, trying to get his charge safely strapped in where a null-grav leap wouldn't wind up breaking her neck.

"Okay, I'll be glad to sit still for a while," Milla replied, relieved at the prospect of a chance to sit still and try to assimilate the new skills that she had to master.

▶▶▶

Strapped into a tight-fitting bolster seat, Milla looked around the shuttle at the other occupants. She studied the men as they strapped themselves down into their own bolsters, cinching the four-inch-wide straps so tightly that they couldn't move in any direction.

Their uniforms, she noted, varied slightly from the one that Brinks had given her. The main difference was a crumpled bundle of green cloth strapped to some of their shoulders, black cloth on others, and some with no cloth at all. Milla couldn't fathom what purpose the bundles might serve and was baffled why some of them didn't have any cloth at all, to say nothing of the color differences.

The first vibrations of the shuttle's movement shook her from her observations. For a moment, she didn't understand the casual demeanor of the flight crew. They weren't even looking at their controls. Then she realized that the shuttle was dropping out of the shuttle bay through some massive airlock. It wasn't until the big elevator shuddered to a halt that the flight crew turned their attention to the job at hand.

"Shuttle One to Odyssey Command, requesting clearance on deck two," the pilot, Milla assumed, said as she flipped a bank of switches over and illuminated the projected HUD display.

The woman sitting behind the shuttle's controls seemed a consummate professional, reading off the preflight checklists and requesting clearance for departure with efficient, clipped tones.

"Confirmed, Shuttle One. You are cleared for departure on deck two. Good hunting, Samuels."

The anonymous voice from the control was the signal the crew was waiting for, and a moment later, the shuttle thundered off the deck, slamming Milla sideways into her bolster seat. Seconds later, the nimble little craft roared free of the confines of the *Odyssey* flight deck and into space.

"Odyssey Command, this is Shuttle One en route to the fourth planet," Jennifer Samuels said with an easy drawl as she adjusted the course and trimmed down the thruster control.

The shuttle banked and shifted its course toward the planet, its four powerful engines blazing brightly as the little ship accelerated. Behind them, two more shuttles blasted clear of the *Odyssey*'s flight deck, banking in the opposite direction toward the drifting debris that had once been a Drasin capital ship and the flashing beacons of the fallen Archangels.

The fourth planet came rapidly into view, forcing the shuttle to decelerate and alter its course to orbit the barren world. Samuels brought the shuttle into a polar orbit, trying to evade the debris ring that made the equatorial orbit treacherous. Even so, light shudders swept through the craft as the deflectors shouldered bits of debris away from their path.

"Okay, I'm going to start a fast series of orbits to see if the scanners can pick anything up. Lieutenant Savoy, get that portable tachyon array aligned with the shuttle's sensor column so we can scan for modulated signals," Jennifer Samuels called over her shoulder as she maneuvered the shuttle into a fast orbit.

"Aye, aye, ma'am," the lieutenant said as he unsnapped his restraints and floated over to his gear.

It was on the ninth orbit that Savoy succeeded in isolating an encoded signal from the planet's surface. After a few minutes of puzzling over the code, he was startled by a voice from behind his ear. It was the first and only signal they'd received that looked like life, with the exception of a few of the insect-like things that seemed preoccupied with whatever it was that they did on a conquered planet.

"It is a distress signal. Their equipment must be badly damaged, though, because we should have picked it up before we left your ship." Milla was looking over his shoulder at the signal form on the sensor display.

"You're certain?" asked Major Brinks, who had noticed Milla's interest in the signal and listened for her judgment.

"Yes."

Brinks looked at her for a moment and nodded. "All right. Jennifer?" Brinks waited until Lieutenant Samuels cocked her head in acknowledgment, never taking her eyes off of her instruments. "Launch the carnivores. Then take us down to the source of this signal. We'll do a land search for survivors."

"Aye, sir."

CHAPTER 14

▶ THE DELTA-SHAPED SHUTTLE descended through the planetary atmosphere, cutting a blazing swathe through the sky as it homed in on the source of the distress signal they had detected from orbit.

Lt. Jennifer Samuels leveled it out over a desiccated forest. Shuttle One banked into a light turn and headed toward a squat structure, the source of the signal, which sat squarely in the middle of a clearing. Samuels brought the chunky craft into a hover over a section of the desiccated forest, a short distance from the clearing.

"Major, we're going to need a landing area cut out or else this is going to be a mighty short rescue."

"Master Sergeant!" Brinks said.

"Sir!" one of the smallest men on the shuttle snapped, half rising from his seat as his restraints popped free.

"Deploy four men with cutters. Have them clear a space one hundred meters in diameter for Shuttle One," Brinks told him as he slid behind a console and accessed the carnivore information stream.

"Yes, sir," the master sergeant snapped, spinning, his finger picking four men, seemingly at random. "You heard the major! Cutters out. We're kissing dirt, boys!"

The belly of the shuttle slid open, and four rappelling lines dropped down. They were followed quickly by four figures, tiny in relation to the delta-shaped mass above them, sliding down the fifty-foot drop into the dry timber beneath them.

"Okay, we're clear."

The figures looked up as an equipment crate descended toward them. Two of the figures guided the swinging crate to a steady landing, while the other two began a sweeping survey of the area, their weapons held at ready. Within minutes, the crate was opened and the contents were assembled into two laser cutters, just small enough to be wielded by hand.

"Shuttle One, the cutter team is beginning procedure."

Powerful lasers sliced through the dry timber of the dead wood, the invisible beams vaporizing the material so quickly that it wasn't given the chance to burn. Foot by foot, the timber was roughly sliced and left where it fell. In less than a half hour, a circular area over one hundred meters in diameter had been cleared of all obstructions.

Above them, two carnivore drones lazily orbited the area, extending the shuttle's sensors by over a thousand times as they kept careful watch on the new inhabitants of the planet.

Brinks watched the surveillance information come in as the shuttle hovered on its CM-assisted jets. The Drasin, as Milla insisted on calling them, appeared to be much like drones from an ant colony back on Earth. They appeared to be dismantling a population center, about 150 kilometers north of the shuttle's location, much the same way Milla reported they had in the previous system they had conquered, but with far fewer numbers.

Major Brinks had the drones make an estimate on the visible drones and shunted the information to the shuttle's computer for comparison to the previous data. It would probably be useful, he decided, to see how they worked from an earlier point.

He was slightly puzzled over the signals he received because they weren't registering as living beings, according to his software. This explained why they didn't show up on their long-range sensors, of course, but didn't help him much in trying to determine what they were.

Living beings had certain side effects on their environment that could be measured from a distance. It wasn't an exact science, unfortunately, but it was the best they could do. A laser, for example, could be reflected off the atmosphere and return a chemical analysis of the planet to the long-range sensors.

Certain concentrations were a good indication of life.

Carbon dioxide, for one, was a common by-product of living beings—at least from Earth's history. So one could look at the CO_2 levels in the atmosphere and use it to make a guess. Levels within certain parameters meant life signs, especially when corroborated with other sensor returns, like a certain oxygen content and even signs of certain pollutants. If the CO_2 range was ridiculously high or low, it was probably a sign that life wasn't present.

At least, that's how the *Odyssey*'s current life-science programs were developed.

Unfortunately, it was rapidly becoming obvious that they weren't quite up to the task of looking for nonhuman life.

This world, for example, was throwing almost all the readings off the scale. The CO_2 readings were on the low side, though, close enough to be within limits, especially if the world were a sparsely populated agrarian world, as Milla had suggested. However, the O_2 levels were rapidly dropping, and the resultant chemical shift in the atmosphere was red-shifting a lot of his readings.

These insect things, the Drasin, didn't even register until the carnivore drones got close enough to detect motion. This meant that they weren't built like humans at all.

Which, in turn, meant that the major was going to have to get on the bio-lab boys' butts to turn out a new program that *did* read the little insect buggers.

More work, he grumbled to himself as he watched the drones gather in all the data they could.

For the moment, though, all he cared about was that they were a long distance away.

The shuttle slowly lowered itself into the cleared area, its immense landing gear shattering the remains of the cleared forest as the full weight of the twenty-meter craft came down. As the heavy craft settled on its gear, a long gangplank lowered, allowing the soldiers inside to rapidly step down and assemble at the base of the shuttle.

"Sir, the signal source is three hundred meters that way," Master Sergeant Kail growled, pointing off to the west as he addressed the major.

"All right. Sergeant, detail two men to stay behind and guard the shuttle. The rest of us are moving out to check the source of the distress call," Brinks ordered, grabbing his pack and dropping its braces into the mounting points built into his suit.

Kail waved two of his men over to stand guard at the shuttle's lowered lift platform, then joined the major and the rest of his team as they left the shuttle and headed toward the clearing. Traveling through the remains of the forest wasn't difficult, in spite of the tightly woven embrace of the branches. A swipe of a machete—or more often, simply their hands— would snap the brittle wood into splinters and clear the path for the marching soldiers.

Milla struggled to keep up with the group but found that the peculiar qualities of the armor suit were considerably different when gravity was present. Practically every second step, she found herself stumbling over an upturned root or stepping into a shallow depression and nearly falling into the man ahead of her. Only the presence of Major Brinks and Corporal Curtis kept her on her feet and moving forward with any reasonable degree of progress. In between falls, she noticed, with a certain level of chagrin, that the others moved easily and fluidly in their suits, apparently using the properties to maintain a steady pace that quickly ate away at the distance between them and their destination. By the time they arrived in the small clearing, Milla was sweating heavily and exhausted from the pace, yet none of the others were breathing more than normal or had even broken a sweat.

Jaime leaned over her as she doubled up in the clearing, helping support her balance as Milla drew deep, ragged breaths. "The first march in these things is always tough. I've seen men used to eight-hour, quick-time marches get worn out in ten minutes of trying to walk in one of these."

Milla looked up at her in between breaths. "How long does it take to get used to this armor?"

Brinks grinned as he glanced at them over his shoulder. Milla couldn't see his smile, though, as it was hidden behind the shimmer of his armor's faceplate. His words, however, came through loud and clear. "Oh, usually a soldier figures it out after a three-day forced hike through rough terrain. I think we'll try to spare you that ordeal, though."

"Thank you," she muttered, along with a word that the translator software screwed up. "I do not believe I could take one day of this torture, let alone three."

Brinks shook his head, his knowing expression wasted on those who couldn't see it. "You'd figure it out. Once they get the hang of it, most soldiers can maintain a full run for about six hours without rest. The suit makes movement a lot easier, once you learn to stop fighting it."

Milla glared at him, her body language, even in the suit, so obvious that a lieutenant burst out laughing, while Brinks turned his attention to where Savoy and his men were examining the structure in the center of the clearing.

"I've never seen material like this before, Major," Savoy told him. "It seems to have many of the same properties as the escape pod we found, but it seems to be designed to block signals rather than to be sensor transparent. We can't read what's inside."

By this time, Milla had regained her breath enough to interject a comment. "It's a survival bunker. The basic design has been in our archives for centuries." She shook her head. "I did not realize that any were left...Then again," she considered after a moment, "when the Drasin threat was broadcast, someone on this planet may have copied the schematics out of the database and built this in a rush."

"So there may be people inside?" Major Brinks asked after she had finished.

"What else would there be?" she said.

Brinks shook his head. He couldn't decide if these people were hopelessly naive or if Milla was simply a consummate actress. Either way, he had little choice but to play out the hand. "Can you open it?"

Milla shook her head, grimacing. "No, they probably transmitted the frequency code to the other colonies, but without it, I can do nothing."

"Any way we can talk to the people in there?"

This time Milla paused for a moment before shaking her head grimly. "No, we saw that their communications system was damaged. The only system they have active right now is a secure radio transmitter—no reception capabilities. It is a last-resort device, built to gather energy from the decay of an energy element. If it is active, then they have lost all power, including, perhaps, life support."

Brinks digested the information and finally nodded to Savoy. "Open it up."

Savoy signaled to two of his men, who advanced with a larger version of the laser cutters cradled between them. Approaching the bunker, Savoy took a lightweight hammer and pick from his belt and rapped the hard material three times in succession, pausing a moment before repeating the process. When no response was heard after a full two minutes, he signaled the men behind him and stepped back.

The laser cutter took a few moments to charge the capacitors as the two men began the process of slicing through the bunker material. A few minutes later, it was apparent that blocking sensors weren't the only way this material differed from what Milla's escape pod had been built of.

Wiping sweat from his brow, one of the cutters, Sergeant Mehn, looked up at Savoy. "This is going to take a while, Major. The material is turning to slag and then running into the cut behind the laser and hardening again. The worst thing is that it seems to get harder to cut after each successive cooling."

"All right," Savoy said, "we'll work along and slip laser-and heat-resistant braces into the cut as we go. Should be easy enough to remove them afterward."

The work progressed slowly. As each section was sliced open, a third man would slap a brace into the opening to keep the melted material from filling the hole. Savoy's team traded off on jobs as they cut their way through the bunker, evening out the harsh work among the group. Hours later, the man-sized cut was finally completed, and Savoy called to one of his men.

"Burke, we're going to need a special job on this one. Think you can blow that section *out?*"

The short man stepped up and began examining the area. Finally, turning to Savoy and his upper suit bobbing, he signaled the affirmative. "Yes, sir. With the braces in place, I could blow it inside out, if you want."

Savoy motioned the man to go ahead. The rest of the group began evacuating the immediate area, cleaning out the equipment as they relocated to a safer ground. Milla watched the man called "Burke" carefully lay explosives, triple-checking and meticulously measuring each charge. A half hour later, he finished and headed over to the group, an innocuous device resting in the palm of his hand.

Burke nodded to the man, then called out to the rest of the men: "Fire in the hole!"

Milla looked around for a moment, wondering at the sudden movements as everyone ducked their heads. Corporal Curtis reached up and pulled her down as well.

"Believe me, miss, you want to be down here right now," she told Milla as she placed an arm over her helmet and physically held her down.

That statement was punctuated by a loud explosion from the bunker and the sudden showering of rock pelting down on them. Milla was thankful for the tough armored suit and helmet she wore.

The group gradually stood up and dusted their armor off, admiring Burke's work. The explosives had cut a clean hole in the bunker, blowing most of the debris out and away from anyone inside the squat structure.

The group approached the building cautiously, their weapons held ready. The point men stopped at the makeshift entrance, expertly scanning the interior before they stepped inside. Once inside, they found themselves in an empty room that took up the entire interior of the bunker.

Brinks looked around at the unimpressive room before turning to where Milla had just joined the group. "Well, where are they?"

Milla scanned the room carefully. "Under us. The bunker should extend downward one hundred meters. Give me a moment, and I should be able to find the control panel."

Roberts stepped back, allowing Milla to search the room. Finally, she smiled and walked over to a blank wall. "Here it is."

Everyone stared at her for a moment until she waved her hand a few inches from the wall, causing a shimmering display of light to appear. The light coalesced into a floating control panel that Milla manipulated by brushing her hands along its shimmering surface.

"Projected-particle interface," Milla explained as she entered instructions into the surface. "It's activated by a three-dimensional grid of motion sensors built into the wall."

The major just nodded, but Savoy stepped up behind her, fascinated by the system.

"Are you receiving *tactile* feedback?"

Milla nodded, tapping another button with an audible click. "Yes, the particle field allows the computer to exert pressure so that you know when you've activated a control."

"How does it manage that?" the major asked, a tone of wonder in his voice. "I don't see any projectors…"

"No, you wouldn't. The wall is the projector. The same devices that are reading my input also display the interface," she said.

"Really? But how do you—"

Savoy found himself cut off as Milla entered the last command and the floor began vibrating. In the center of the room, a circular seam appeared in the floor and the round section began rising. After it had risen a short distance, it stopped and then rolled to one side, revealing a deep pit beneath it.

"You have got to be kidding me." One of the soldiers stared down the hole, trying vainly to see the bottom. The best he could do was follow the rungs of a ladder down until even they disappeared from sight.

"Sorry," Milla said. "It's the best I can do. Without the power being active, I can't bring the lift up."

"It'll do, Milla. If we can get a power source down there, do you think you can recharge the system?" Savoy cut in.

She thought it over for a brief moment. "Probably. The system should be a standard reactor."

"Good. We'll have to lug the power packs down there, so let's get started," Savoy decided, eyeing the pit in front of him. His finger caressed the firing stud of his rifle, the blackness below impenetrable to even his suit lights and night-vision systems.

CHAPTER 15

▶ DRAGGING FIVE 100-POUND power packs down a vertical shaft that had apparently been built precisely to spec at one hundred meters depth wasn't the easiest job in the world, but after a few hours, Savoy and his tech team had managed it.

Four of them found themselves standing on the roof of a lift car, waiting as Milla found the access panel and opened a hatch in the lift, allowing them to drop through and hand the packs down one at a time.

Inside the small lift, Savoy looked around. "What's on the other side of the doors?"

"They open up directly into the shelter. I wouldn't recommend you ask Mr. Burke to open this door." Milla's voice was dry, but some sense of humor managed to make it through the translation algorithms.

"I doubt that will be necessary," Lieutenant Savoy told her, chuckling as he looked up at the hatch. "Jackie, would you hand me the pry bar from the tool pack?"

He took the tool as it was offered, then sized up the door for a moment before moving.

Taking the pry bar firmly in one hand, Savoy rapped out a pattern on the door, paused for a moment, and then rapped the pattern again. After repeating the pattern several times with no response, he jammed the pry bar into the crack between the doors. The two soldiers who had squeezed into the lift with them took up flanking positions on either side as Savoy put his weight into the bar and began to force the doors open.

Sweat beaded on his forehead from the strain of leaning into the bar by the time the door was a quarter of the way open. Sweat that turned cold when an unfamiliar, but unmistakable, barrel of a weapon was pushed up against his visor from the other side of the lift doors. The titanium-alloyed bar clanged to the ground as Savoy cautiously raised his hands ahead of him, palms out, in an attempt to placate whoever was on the other side of the doors.

Harsh words rang out, mostly indistinguishable by their translators except for the word *open*. Savoy had little time to reflect on the situation as the lift doors slid open, exposing him to another person wielding a rifle-type weapon.

"Guys? I got a problem here. Two armed individuals," Savoy subvocalized into the induction mic on his jaw.

"Can you recognize what type they are?"

Savoy responded, his jaw barely moving as he spoke with the short and guttural sounds of subvocal phrases: "For Chrissakes, Hilliard! They're alien manufactured. For all I know, they're pea shooters."

Hilliard's calm voice came back. "All right, do you see any others with weapons?"

Savoy's eyes flicked around the dark room beyond the lift. "Negative, but there are a lot of people in there."

There was a long pause. Savoy saw Milla try to move forward out of the corner of his eye and breathed a sigh of relief when the soldier at her side, Jaime, clamped a solid hand down on her shoulder and held her back. The two armed men weren't professional soldiers—he could see that in their faces. They were scared kids, and that made them a thousand times more dangerous in this situation.

"All right, Savoy, we'll use maneuver Trojan-Twelve. Jenkins, Mallard, don't shoot unless you have to. Move to disarm rather than incapacitate," Hilliard decided on the spot, shuffling around as he and the others slipped into place.

The acknowledgments echoed through the radio links. Savoy tensed up as he prepared to play his part in the maneuver.

"Uh…hi." Savoy winced at how foolish that sounded, but forged ahead. "We come in peace…"

A single glance at the look on the faces of the two men facing him was enough to tell him that the translator had failed. Savoy was debating whether to risk asking Milla to translate when the choice was taken from him.

One of the gunmen uttered something unintelligible and roughly grabbed his arm and pulled him out of the lift, forcing him to the floor. As soon as he was on the ground, Savoy put up a token resistance, drawing the attention of both gunmen as they roughly forced him down, their weight pinning him hard. Then, seconds after the initial struggle, the weight abruptly vanished.

▶▶▶

Milla watched as the two men manhandled Savoy to the ground, stunned by the sudden violence from a people she had thought she knew. A blur of motion made her blink as her attention was captured by the two soldiers—Jenkins and Mallard—as they leapt into the fray. Jenkins launched into the top gunman and carried them both over a dozen meters into the shelter. Mallard limited her leap to a shallow arc that caught the second gunman low and tumbled them both to the ground, just beyond where Savoy had landed.

Just as she was about to rush into the room herself, Milla was roughly shoved aside as Hilliard dropped into the lift, allowing the fall's kinetic energy to be absorbed into the suit. He then launched himself into a long arc that landed him fifteen meters into the shelter, his rifle swinging side to side as he searched for more hostiles.

"Clear!" Mallard said as she kneeled on her target, his rifle knocked well out of the man's reach.

"Clear!" Jenkins crouched low over his man, his own weapon digging into the man's neck, even as his right foot was planted solidly over the gunman's weapon.

"Clear!" Savoy had his handgun out and was helping Hilliard cover the occupants of the shelter.

Major Brinks's voice came over the radio, surprising Milla for a moment. "Confirmed. Milla, you're clear to enter."

Milla stepped into the room, looking nervously around. Gathering her nerve, she stepped more firmly into the shelter, looking around for someone who might be in charge. Everywhere she looked, she was met by fear as the people cowered away from her, leaving her confused by the reaction.

Suddenly, she remembered how alien her armor actually looked. "Oh! Mr. Savoy? How do I remove this helmet?"

Savoy stepped up behind her and pointed out the release catches that sealed the helmet to the suit. Twin hisses echoed through the room as the suit pressure was balanced, and Milla tugged the helmet off.

She looked around at the people, who were all watching her now, and held up her hands in a comforting manner. "We are friends. I'm from Ranqil. We just arrived in-system a few hours ago."

One of the huddled survivors stepped forward cautiously, her face a mask that hid all but a small portion of her emotions. "You are from Ranqil?" Her voice was suspicious as she looked Milla up and down and then examined Savoy and the others.

Milla shook her head firmly. "I am from Ranqil. These people are not. They are not from the colonies; they are of the Others."

Distaste ran across the woman's features as she looked over the soldiers in the room. "We do not want them here."

Milla looked over her shoulder to where the soldiers waited, their eyes scanning the crowd, even as their weapons didn't *quite* cover the crowd. She thought about her own reactions to her rescuers. "You may not want them, but you do need them. They rescued me when my ship was destroyed by the Drasin. Now they come to rescue you as well."

A shiver of fear passed through the huddled mass of people at the mention of the word *Drasin*.

Their spokesperson paused for a moment before speaking again. "So the rumors were true. Few believed them to be when we heard of the first Drasin attacks. It was a struggle to get permission to begin construction of this shelter. How many survived the attack?"

Milla swallowed before answering. "You are the only survivors that we've found. No life signs were detected, and there were no other signals from the planet."

The silence in the room was palpable as Milla's words sank into the collective consciousness of the group.

Savoy cleared his throat behind Milla to remind her that they had things to finish.

"We have to restore power to your reactor so that we can evacuate your people."

The woman looked disturbed. "Why should we evacuate? The Drasin are gone now. We can rebuild."

Savoy stepped in, his translator having stepped up its effectiveness after he'd had it recompile its program from the spoken words they'd been recording. The local dialect wasn't completely identical to that which Milla spoke, which wasn't confusing for human ears, apparently, but it had thrown the computer out of whack for a moment.

Even as he started to speak, he was already starting to work out new algorithms in his mind to enhance the translation. The system simply wasn't designed to handle minor changes in pronunciation on the fly like this. Still, he'd have to worry about it later. For now, he and his team had more pressing concerns.

"I'm afraid that's not true, ma'am," he told the woman, who appeared to be the leader of the ragged band. "They're still out there. We have to get you and your people out before any of those drones find their way here."

Savoy had expected more shock, but only an air of resignation followed his statement.

The crowd deflated a little, as if he'd taken away some fancy they had embraced, but the reality hadn't been so far from their minds, after all. The leader nodded after a moment, then sort of half bowed to him and nodded.

"Very well. The reactor is this way." The woman gestured to the far wall and a small door.

"Thank you, ma'am," said Savoy. "Mallard, Jenkins, let those two up and help me lug those power packs over there.

We should be able to jump-start the system, if what Milla said about the reactors is right."

"I will have our engineer explain any systems necessary to you." The woman was now exerting a command influence, confirming Savoy's belief that she was of some importance to these people.

"Thank you, ma'am," he responded, keeping his tone respectful as he nodded his head to her.

The three soldiers each hefted a power pack, shouldering them and walking toward the door at the far end. The local engineer stepped up to the fourth pack, gesturing helpfully as he kneeled down to carry it.

"No! Wait!" Hilliard strode toward the man as he tried to heft the power pack.

Consternation turned to a pained look as the man strained his muscles in a vain attempt to move the heavy pack. Hilliard laid a hand on the man's shoulder and shook his head with a slight smile.

"Here, I'll carry it." Hilliard kneeled down and grasped the pack's handles, hefting it with ease and flipping it casually over his shoulder. "It's the suits, sir. They have a series of strength enhancers. Lead the way and I'll bring up the rear."

The man nodded as emotions wafted across his face, ranging from an unbelieving stare to a fascinated gaze. Finally, the man turned and led Hilliard to the door, taking long looks over his shoulder at Hilliard and the pack he carried with such ease.

The woman turned to Milla when Hilliard was out of earshot. "Can they be trusted? The Others are oath breakers. You know that."

Milla took a deep breath before she continued. "I don't know, but we have little choice, I'm afraid. And the oath breaking was a long time ago."

"Oath breakers are oath breakers."

"Perhaps. But as I said, they rescued me, and now they are saving you and your people. That should earn them at least the benefit of the doubt from us." Milla's face was earnest.

The older woman sighed after a moment, relenting. "Perhaps you are right." She paused a moment. "What is your name? I am—or rather, was—Titualar Saraf. Now, I suppose, it's just plain Saraf."

Milla looked around her. "Not to these people. You are still the titualar of this system to them. I am Ithan Milla Chans of the Ranqil merchant fleet. I was on an interception mission when the task force I was assigned to was destroyed by a Drasin battle fleet."

"The Drasin are that powerful?"

Milla nodded grimly. "They are more powerful than that, I fear. They annihilated our force with ease; our vessels had no chance against them."

"Then we are lost. They will overrun our defenses, finally. Over eight millennia of peace and we end like this." Saraf looked resigned.

Milla shook her head violently, refusing to accept that death was inevitable. "It is not over yet. The Five have several fleets of next-generation starships nearing completion. They should put us at nearly an equal footing with what I have seen of the Drasin fleet. The era of peace has come to an end, but not our civilization."

"What of your friends? I wasn't aware that any of the Others had achieved dimensional travel?" Seraf nodded to the soldiers.

"They haven't. Their technology is a puzzle to me. In many ways, their equipment is vastly inferior to ours. They have no knowledge of field manipulation or dimensional access. Their computers are almost laughably slow, and their medical technology is archaic." Milla stopped for a moment, her voice drifting away as she thought about the wonders she had seen. "Yet, they translated our language in less than a day. They have software that is superior to any I have seen and have the capability to jump between the stars in an instant."

Saraf looked toward the door that hid Savoy and the others from her sight. "Instantaneous star travel? Impressive, I admit. But I doubt if they will be of much help now that the Drasin have come."

Milla laughed mirthlessly, her tone a bitter, yet somehow satisfied sort of sound that Saraf didn't recognize. "There was a Drasin vessel in your system when we arrived. A vessel of the same class that survived a full assault by six of our heaviest reconfigured combat vessels. Their one vessel, smaller than one of our trade ships, destroyed it in less than ten minutes of actual fighting. From a military standpoint, I don't think that the colonies have seen this much combat power, in one place, in the last twelve thousand years."

"They are soldiers, then?" Saraf's voice was flat.

"They are—at least many of them are. In many ways, much of their ship seems dedicated to exploration and science, yet they do seem to believe in being capable of their own defense," Milla replied with an odd smile.

The conversation between the two women was cut off when a loud hum came from the far wall and glaring emergency lights ignited around them. A moment later, the four *Odyssey* soldiers and the local engineer stepped out of the reactor room.

Lieutenant Savoy headed back toward Milla. "We have the reactor back online, Milla. Major Brinks is coming down in the lift now. We'll have to prepare this group for evacuation immediately."

Milla and Saraf nodded and turned to the rest of the survivors, calling out instructions as they walked through the group. By the time the lift had returned with Major Brinks, the survivors had already begun to organize their affairs, and a rough sort of order descended on the room.

Milla stepped forward to greet the major when he stepped off the lift. "Major, this is Saraf," she said, extending a hand toward the older woman. "She is the leader of these people."

"Ma'am." Brinks tipped his head toward the woman as he surveyed the area. "May I ask how many people we are looking at?"

"Certainly, Major. There are nearly five hundred survivors here."

Brinks swore at that, looking around as he started crunching numbers in his head. "One moment, please."

They nodded as he switched to another channel. "Samuels, relay a query to the *Odyssey*. Five hundred refugees found. Orders?"

After Jennifer Samuels confirmed the order, he settled back on his heels and began pondering the situation. The *Odyssey* was built to handle a lot more capacity than it was being used for now, but five hundred additional lungs would stress the support systems.

The time it took for the light-speed message to crawl out to the starship, and then for its return journey, seemed like eons as Brinks tried to figure out what they'd do if the *Odyssey* couldn't handle it.

"Stand by for message from the *Odyssey*," Samuels said a couple minutes later.

"Roger," Brinks told her, then watched as a video window appeared on the screen.

Captain Weston looked out the screen at him. "Message received and understood. Organize the evacuation. The *Odyssey* is dispatching remaining shuttles to help. Godspeed, Major."

Brinks wanted to wipe the beading sweat from his forehead but couldn't because of the helmet, so he turned to the two women and ignored the infernal itching. "We'll begin evacuating as soon as possible. The *Odyssey* is standing by to treat any injuries and to provide succor. It'll be cramped, though."

"They will endure," Milla said firmly, receiving affirmation from Saraf.

"We will, Major," Saraf said, for the first time nodding with genuine gratitude. "And on behalf of my people, I thank you for your aid."

"Not a problem, ma'am. Believe it or not, most of my people signed up in the hopes of assisting in a situation like this. We have a clearing cut about fifty meters from the bunker topside. We need to get everybody out there, in groups of fifty to seventy people at a time."

"I understand, Major. I will inform my people. Please inform us when it is time for the first group." Saraf turned to leave, but was interrupted by Brinks.

"The first group can leave immediately, ma'am. Shuttle One is prepared to transport survivors as soon as the first group is loaded."

"Very well, Major. I will inform my people immediately."

CHAPTER 16

▶ WITH REPORTS COMING in from the surface, the bridge, and in fact, the whole of the *Odyssey*, everything was in a state as close to chaos as Weston ever wanted to see. Men and women moved from station to station, some just crunching numbers on whether the *Odyssey* could handle all the people being brought up, others trying to find the gear required to make it happen.

"Captain Weston, sir?"

Weston turned away from the view screen for a moment and made eye contact with the young ensign. "Yes?"

Ens. Susan Lamont hesitated a little under his gaze but firmed up a moment later and went on with her report. "Engineering reports that they've brought the recycling systems up to max, but for five hundred more sets of lungs, they're going to have to unbox the backup units, too."

Weston grimaced. "Tell them to go ahead and log my authorization on the paperwork."

"Aye, Captain," she said, heading back to her station.

Capt. Eric Weston thumbed his way through the PDA that held the list of materials that were being shifted, un-carted, installed, or torn out in order to make room for the five hundred refugees. It was a long list.

"Captain?" Waters looked up from his station.

"Yes, Lieutenant?"

"Lieutenant Samuels just radioed in, sir. The first shuttle with evacuees will be arriving in less than fifteen minutes."

"Good. Thank you, Lieutenant Waters," Weston said before turning to his first officer. "Commander Roberts, you have the bridge."

"I have the bridge. Aye, sir."

Weston turned back to the view screen for a last long look at the floating, spinning carnage that lay just outside the *Odyssey's* bulkheads before spinning on his heels and heading off the bridge.

It took Weston less than three minutes to navigate his way through the ship corridors and find Dr. Palin. The eccentric linguist was poring over notes from his earlier talks with Milla Chans and was too absorbed to notice Weston come in.

Palin looked up, finally recognizing the presence of the captain.

"Doctor," Weston said, "the first load of survivors is due in soon. I'd like you to be on hand to meet them."

"Of course, Captain. I've been compiling the tapes of all our conversations with Miss Chans. There should be no communication problems."

"Excellent, Doctor. Let's head down to the shuttle bay now."

On the shuttle deck, Weston and Dr. Palin waited as the *Odyssey's* flight control officer reported the shuttle's approach and landing. A few moments later, the deep, grating vibrations in the deck plates announced the final cycle of the combination airlock/elevator that brought the shuttle up from the lower flight deck.

Palin's eyes grew wide as he saw the tail fin of the huge trans-atmospheric shuttle rise from below, the ship slowly revealed as it rose on the powerful elevator. "Oh my…It never seemed that big before."

Weston glanced over at the vessel. "That's because when you boarded the shuttle planet-side, it was docked in a control building being refitted and refueled. You never saw the whole thing at once."

Palin watched in fascination as a yellow behemoth trundled over to the shuttle, backing slowly into place until the nose of the ship had been secured to a stout pin in the machine's back. The yellow loader stomped off, dragging the shuttle along with it toward the docking pylons. Palin stared at the approaching duo in consternation, finally turning to Weston, a question forming on his lips.

Weston cut him off before he could start. "Null grav."

"Huh?" Palin was more confused now than before.

"We use the walking loader because this deck is zero-g. A wheeled vehicle couldn't get any traction, and cats require too much maintenance. The feet on the walker are magnetic, the same as the boots you're wearing," Weston explained. "The loader holds the shuttle down, as well as moves it around, until it's locked into place."

"Oh," Palin said, blinking as he processed information that he'd not really considered before.

"You wouldn't want to see what kind of damage a shuttle could cause if it started floating around down here," Weston added.

Palin just paled at the thought.

It wasn't quite as bad as the captain let the linguist think, of course. The shuttle had its own magnetic locks that could hold it quite firmly in place in an emergency, but the threat was credible. All fighters, shuttles, and in fact, all equipment had to be locked down solidly before the ship could engage in sharp maneuvers.

Only the CM fields made the null-grav flight deck a reasonable design feature—at least as it currently stood on the *Odyssey*.

The loader had finally done its job, locking the shuttle into the docking pylon next to where the captain and Dr. Palin were waiting. Four huge servo-powered arms whined into position, locking the shuttle down. The shuttle's loading ramp lowered, and two of the Special Forces team stepped down.

"Fifty survivors aboard, sir. The major and the rest of the team are organizing the others into groups of seventy-five for transport. This group needs immediate medical care."

Weston nodded, returning the soldier's salute before waving the E-med teams in from where they were waiting. "Good work, men. Report to the infirmary after decontam, then hit the showers. You're relieved until your CO is back aboard."

"Sir." Both soldiers snapped quick salutes and double-timed off the ramp and out of the shuttle bay.

Weston stepped to one side as people were carted off the shuttle, the E-med teams rushing them through decontamination and sending them to the med-lab. As the last of the E-med units left the shuttle, a lone woman walked down. There were no obvious injuries, but none of them looked healthy, either. Stress or environmental issues had weakened them, from what he could see. Some were clutching children as they were guided along, others carrying what little belongings they'd managed to save. He'd seen scenes like this before, but they always caused his guts to roil up and a sense of helplessness to ball up deep inside.

How many others died down there? Only one shelter survived... Weston grimaced. Actually, there was every likelihood of others, but without beacons to guide them, there wasn't a damned thing he or anyone could do.

Lieutenant Samuels stepped forward to introduce an older-looking woman with a severe expression. "Captain, this is Titualar Saraf. She is the leader of these people."

"Very good, Samuels. You'd better get the shuttle prepped for another run. We've directed all available shuttles to help with the evacuation, but you'll have to do at least one more run after you've refueled."

"Aye, sir."

As Lieutenant Samuels turned back to her cockpit, Weston extended a hand to the woman, anchoring her to the floor as she moved forward. "This way, ma'am. We'll catch a lift up to the habitat levels after decontamination."

The woman blinked, then said something in return that came through as a garbled mess through his induction earpiece. Weston frowned, glancing over at Dr. Palin.

"I don't know, Captain. One moment and I'll..." the suddenly nervous linguist muttered, tapping away on his PDA.

"Just a moment, Captain," Samuels said, snapping her helmet down. After a moment, she looked up. "I'm sending you the new program now."

A tone signaled the download and Weston checked his PDA. He activated the new program and looked at Saraf. "Can you understand me now, ma'am?"

"Yes, Capitain," she told him, smiling patiently, "I can."

"They speak a different dialect, sir," Samuels told him. "It's close, but the differences give the computer some problems."

"Fascinating," Palin said, already digging through the source code for the new modifications. "Oh, I say, who coded this? It's quite remarkable."

"Lieutenant Savoy, sir," Samuels said. "Captain, if you don't mind?"

Weston nodded. "Go do your preflight, Lieutenant."

"Sir." She saluted, turned, and vanished back inside.

Weston turned back to Saraf. "We have to go through decontamination. I'll escort you up to the infirmary, where you can look in on your people. Will that be acceptable?"

The woman nodded, following as Weston guided her toward the far wall of the shuttle bay. Her expression was distracted, her thoughts obviously barely focusing on the conversation as she looked over her people. "Thank you, Capitain."

Weston smiled at her as they reached the far wall. "No problem, ma'am. All part of the service."

▶▶▶

The twenty-minute decontamination procedures left the survivors tired, slumping them in the lift's seats as the capsule carried them to the *Odyssey*'s second habitation cylinder.

"I do wish to see my people," Saraf said, in the peculiar accent that sounded almost, but not quite, French to Weston.

Weston looked up. "Of course, ma'am. We'll visit the infirmary first. After that, we'll move over to the recreation decks to find a place for your people to stay. That's the only place where we have room and normal gravity."

"I'm sure it will be fine," Saraf brushed off Weston's concerns.

Moments later, the two of them strode into the med-lab, Weston guiding his charge over to where Dr. Rame was working.

"Doctor, how are your new patients?"

"Arrogant." Rame didn't look up from his terminal.

"Doctor!" Weston snapped, catching the doctor up sharply.

Glancing up, Rame took in the woman at Weston's side and the captain's dark glare, a deep-red flush crossing his face.

"Sorry, sir, ma'am," he said quickly, then nodded to them both. "They'll all live. Mostly dehydration and nutritional deficiencies. A couple appear to be suffering from early stages of oxygen deprivation as well, but that is being remedied naturally."

Saraf nodded, diplomatically ignoring the doctor's first comment. "The youngest?"

"Ah, yes, the infant. She's fine. In better shape than many of the older children and adults. With youth comes remark-able resilience." Rame beamed as he glanced over toward a makeshift incubator in the corner.

Saraf didn't respond for a moment. Finally, she nodded, letting out a long and deep breath. "Yes. May I see my people now?"

"Certainly. This way," Dr. Rame said. "We've had to impro-vise a lot of our facilities, I'm afraid. We simply weren't expect-ing five hundred patients to drop in on us, so it's a lot more hectic in here than normal."

Weston allowed himself to fall behind, watching Dr. Rame show Titualar Saraf through the infirmary. His eyes wandered the room, moving from face to face as he tried to take in the scene. At his best guess, none of the patients were more than twenty years old, most considerably less, and at the far side of the area, he noted the tiny baby in an enclosed environment with medical equipment closely monitoring the child's condition.

Weston tapped the induction mic on his jaw to open a channel. "Commander Roberts, could you please come down to the med-lab? I want to be on hand when Milla returns from the planet, and I need to you show Titualur Saraf around and arrange accommodations for our passengers."

"Yes, sir," Roberts's voice sounded in his ear.

▶▶▶

Ten minutes later, Weston was on his way down to the shuttle bay, checking the ETA on the next transport and the passenger list. The subsequent shuttle wasn't due for over an hour, leaving Weston with the time to do something he had felt the need to do for several days.

He made his way over to the Archangel One, his own fighter, and pulled open a maintenance flap so he could do the customary check.

The Angels had a full maintenance staff, of course, and his own fighter had been checked out long since, but Weston had never believed that was quite sufficient. He'd been a student before enlisting in the old American Marine Corps, specializing in philosophy, oddly enough. One of the lines from the old books he read always came back to haunt him when he flew the last of the old joint strike fighters.

It was a foolish warrior who entrusted his weapons to the care of any man, save himself.

It was impossible for him to handle all maintenance on his fighter, of course, but he could check to ensure that the work had been done and done properly. So, despite the fact that his fighter was no longer his weapon, Weston settled in with the computer interface and called up the maintenance log, carefully moving down the checklist.

All the while he tried to keep his mind off what was happening outside the armor-plated hull of the *Odyssey*. Trying not to think about things he couldn't change and things he couldn't help.

▶▶▶

It was nearly forty-five minutes later when Weston was disturbed by the reverberating clang of the flight deck's massive airlock closing. Glancing up from his position, he noted that it was one of the Archangels returned from patrol. He was about to turn his attention back to the shakedown of his fighter when he noted the markings on the returned fighter craft.

Extracting himself from his position, Weston pushed off of Archangel One and glided across the null-grav bay until he snagged the docking pylon that locked down over the newly returned fighter. As he got closer, he saw the pilot pull off his helmet, revealing a very tired and frustrated looking Stephen Michaels.

"Stephanos, you look like hell," he told the younger man flatly.

A wry grin twitched the corners of Stephanos's mouth, though no humor entered the young man's eyes. "Thanks, Captain. You always know what to say, don't you?"

"I've already arranged the memorial service for Flare. You have a few hours to shower and change. From the look of you, I suggest you get some rest, too," Weston said, patting his young friend on the back. "Don't worry, I'll make sure it's handled."

The loss of Flare weighed heavily on Stephanos, and he knew that Weston was right. He did look like hell, and he needed the time to prepare for the memorial service.

"All right, Captain. I'll see you later."

Weston watched as the young pilot dropped to the floor. His Magboots snapped down, and then he walked away. In Weston's experience, losing a pilot under your command was one of the most difficult things a wing leader could experience. The added feelings of responsibility tripled the crushing weight that fell on a man's shoulders when he witnessed the death of a friend and comrade.

It was, unfortunately, not something that anyone else could really help with. Stephanos was on his own—for the moment, at least. Until he burned the initial rage from his system, his young friend would listen to no one.

Not even him.

Shaking his head, Weston walked back to his fighter to continue his work.

He wasn't interrupted again until the airlock cycled the next shuttle craft through. At that point, he had completed his inspection of his fighter's systems. Hefting himself out of the cockpit and drifting to the floor of the shuttle bay, he watched as the shuttle was trundled into place by the lumbering loader.

After the shuttle was locked into place, Weston walked over to the lowering ramp to greet the occupants as they disembarked. Savoy and his tech team were the first ones off.

"Captain." Savoy and his men saluted.

"At ease. How many on this trip?"

"Seventy, sir. With the two heavy lifters and the three shuttles following us in, we managed to pack 'em all aboard. They'll be here in less than ten minutes," Lieutenant Savoy replied, dropping his salute as the captain dropped his. "Major Brinks is in the last one."

"Of course he is," Weston said. "I've read his reports, and I believe that Dr. Palin was quite impressed with your alterations to his translation algorithms."

Savoy shrugged, actually feeling his face redden under his helmet. "It wasn't that hard. He has set up a fine system, Captain."

"Very well," Weston nodded. "As you were."

Weston stood his ground as the men saluted again and moved off. He watched and greeted the survivors who stumbled off the shuttle, another group like the last—a mix of adults and children, few elderly and still fewer with injuries that might indicate contact with the enemy. Either they got away clean or they simply didn't get away, he supposed. It was a wonder that anything had survived the holocaust that had hit their world, Weston knew. The initial readings, both from the *Odyssey*'s main array and the atmospheric reports from the team and the carnivore drones, indicated an event of biblical proportions.

He didn't know how those monstrosities had managed the damage they had inflicted, but it was obscene.

Genocide on a scale that Weston could never imagine, even in his worst nightmares.

The captain had to shake himself free of the sinking sensation that followed those thoughts, forcing himself to continue greeting the survivors as they descended.

When they had all been guided off, Weston turned back to his fighter. He looked at the sleek craft and wondered if there was anything else he could do while he waited. Since early on in his career, he had learned to understand the systems he entrusted his life to, often working on his fighter when he felt the need to relax.

"Captain?"

Weston turned to see Commander Roberts standing a short distance away. "Commander, have you gotten everybody settled?"

"Yes, sir. I've assigned Lieutenant McRaedy to act as liaison officer."

"Good. Good. Do you have the latest ETA on the last shuttles?" Weston asked.

"They're already here, sir. Just clearing the quarantine fields, I should expect."

Weston smiled. "Good. Have the helm take us on one more orbital pass of this system. Make sure we intersect the battle coordinates on the way out."

"Yes, sir. Gave the order fifteen minutes ago."

Weston looked at him in surprise. "You've been researching the Archangels?"

"Yes, sir," Roberts replied evenly.

"Good." Weston paused a long moment, then nodded. "That's very good, Commander."

Roberts turned his head as a low rumble echoed through the bay. "That'll be the first shuttle through the lock now, sir."

"All right, Commander. Return to the bridge. I'll be along shortly."

"Yes, sir." Commander Roberts pivoted on his heel and walked toward the exit while Weston waited for the shuttle to dock.

Weston's body was present as the next shuttle docked, but his mind was now focused on the loss of a woman he knew well. A small unit by necessity, the Archangels had managed to maintain one of the lowest casualty rates in any serving unit of the last war, but when they lost someone, it hit damn hard.

As soon as everyone was back on board, he and Stephanos had something very important to do.

CHAPTER 17

▶ AFTER SHE HAD SEEN the survivors settled into their temporary quarters, Milla found herself wandering the corridors of the *Odyssey*. The captain had been very clear that the majority of the survivors were not to leave their designated areas, but she and Saraf had been given exemptions. Even so, Milla wasn't certain where she was going. She had simply felt the need for a walk. She stopped at one of the vessel's unobtrusive computer terminals and asked it a question.

"Computer, where may I find Commander Stephanos?"

"There is no Commander Stephanos listed in the ship's directory."

Milla stopped for a moment, remembering her earlier conversation. "Then please direct me to the location of Commander Stephen Michaels."

"Commander Michaels is currently on deck eight, second habitat. Training facility."

It took her thirty minutes of wandering, but Milla finally found her way to the location the computer had specified. Standing outside the doors of the training area, she pressed the buzzer on the wall.

"It's not sealed!" The voice was muffled but audible from the other side of the door.

Milla walked in tentatively, not certain what to expect. She half thought to see rows of workout equipment and other physical-training devices. Instead, she found a long, empty room that seemed to stretch an immense distance for a ship-board area. Stephanos was standing idle a few meters away, with a chunky black rifle cradled casually in his arms.

"I...I didn't realize you were..." Milla stammered. Handheld weaponry was quite foreign to her despite her experience with shipboard batteries. The concept seemed so much more personal—and final.

"No worries. Just working off some steam." Stephanos looked relaxed, a sheen of sweat on his brow, but the smile she had become accustomed to was no longer present.

"With a weapon?" Milla shivered.

She saw a slight expression cross his face—annoyance, perhaps, but maybe not.

"For some people, shooting is the ultimate form of therapy. A lot of aggressions can be worked off in a very short while. Stay if you wish. I'll be here for a while, yet."

Milla watched in fascination as Stephanos turned back to his "therapy."

Stephanos turned his attention back to the weapon in his hands. It was identical to the ones carried by the Special Forces troops when they were planet-side. Comparatively short for a rifle, the weapon was built with versatility in mind. He thumbed the clip ejection switch, and the hefty clip dropped to the deck with a solid clang. Moving over to a small work-bench, Stephanos slapped open the rifle's grips and exposed two long blue-green cylinders, which he also ejected from the weapon. After examining the cylinders carefully, he reinserted them into the rifle and closed the breech. Pulling a full clip from the bench, he slapped it into place and flipped off the safety.

Milla, watching his motions with ill-disguised horror, found her voice again. "You actually enjoy this?"

Stephanos turned sharply after hearing the note of censure in her voice. "Enjoy? I suppose. Firing a rifle requires focus. It's almost meditative in its own way."

"But...You like being a soldier?"

His eyes narrowed at her tone. "Yes, I suppose I do. I've accomplished a lot of good in my life. Saved a lot of lives."

Milla digested this for a moment before trying another tack. "I suppose you see yourself as a warrior for peace, then?"

Stephanos felt his face harden. As many times as he had heard that fallacy, he could never understand the people who uttered it. Taking a deep breath, he called to mind all the patience he could muster before replying, "No soldier worth the title would ever make that claim, Milla. Peace is the one thing we don't fight for."

A look of shock crossed her face. "Then why?"

"Freedom. That's the core of why we do what we do. Peace is a fallacy in itself. Personally, I only know of two forms of peace—peace in death and the peace of slavery." He snorted in amusement. "And I'm not certain about death.

Milla found herself staring at him blankly for a time as he spoke, uncertain whether she abhorred or understood what he was saying. Perhaps it was both. Since her encounter with the Drasin, she'd found that many of her old belief systems had been shattered, and she had no idea how to even begin picking up the pieces.

"Obviously, fighting for peace is stupid. That's why we don't do it," he continued flatly. "If you make peace your only goal, then you lose sight of reality. We fight to be free, we fight to defend ourselves and others, and we fight to win." Stephanos paused, letting his words sink in. "Let me ask you something, Milla. What do you believe is a soldier's primary function?"

Her answer was as fast and wrong as Stephanos expected. "To fight."

"Wrong." Steph shook his head, his face an iron mask.

Milla looked startled. *What else is a soldier for?*

He looked at her calmly, considering his answer for a moment, but only for a moment. It was something he had often thought about himself, wondering if killing was what he existed to do or if there was something more.

He had decided that it was something more. Those who flung this accusation at him were people who had never worn a uniform, never made the commitment that Steph had.

"A soldier's first duty, his reason for being, is not to fight. Fighting is the final recourse for any civilized people. His duty is not even to preserve the peace; that is a police officer's job," Comdr. Stephen Michaels of the NAC military said by rote, remembering the many long nights of arguments and discussions that had brought this to his mind. "A soldier's first duty is simply to stand between his nation and any who might wish it harm."

Milla blinked at the simplicity of the statement as Stephanos went on.

"To stand there, with crossed arms, and say to the universe, 'You are not getting past me,'" Stephanos said. He stopped for another brief moment before continuing in a subdued manner. "The fighting happens when the universe decides to test his resolve. A soldier doesn't seek conflict, Milla, even if he often seems to find it."

Stephanos couldn't tell if she had listened to him, or even heard him, but it didn't matter much, anyway. It was a lesson she and her people would have to learn, one way or another. After a moment's consideration, he made a decision. "Here, don't knock something that you don't understand."

With that, he turned his attention back to the rifle and the range, this time taking care to include Milla in the exercise by describing as best he could what was happening and why. He half turned back to her, extending a hand that she took after a moment's hesitation. He drew her closer, holding out the rifle as he explained its workings.

"This is an MX One-Twelve infantry support rifle. It has been standard issue for the NAC military and most of our allies for the past eight years. This one's an MK A-Seven model, so it's been refitted a few times since the original weapon was put into service," Stephanos said as he thumbed a control on a spindly pedestal.

The computer's voice startled Milla as the lights dimmed and something glowed at the far end of the room. "Active program will begin in thirty seconds."

Stephanos pulled the rifle up to his shoulder and gazed down the long length of the room, looking for a target. "This one has been configured to fire 'virtual ammo' to give a realistic training experience without blowing holes through the hull. It's what we call a hybrid model, designed to maximize both old and new technology into a single…"

The weapon roared, causing Milla to jump and swing her head away from Stephanos. For a moment, she saw nothing, and then an armored form materialized and swung a similar weapon in Stephanos's direction.

"…seamless…"

The gun barked a second time, the armored form vanishing into the ether from whence it came.

"...design."

This time, two soldiers appeared, their weapons already pointed at Stephanos. Milla heard a motion and watched Stephanos move, ducking under the enemies' fire and returning fire in kind, the black rifle stuttering out a loud, steady beat as shots left it with a flash of blue-white light. In short order, the two soldiers had vanished and Stephanos straightened from his crouched position.

"Pause."

"Simulation paused." The computer's drone was punctuated by the lights returning to their former level.

"It uses a hybrid chemical-electromagnetic propellant system. The result is a peculiar mix of technologies."

Stephanos turned to Milla, offering the weapon to her.

Taking it gingerly, Milla almost dropped it as Stephanos let its entire weight fall into her hands. "It's heavy."

"Yeah, the mags are a partially reconstructed uranium alloy. Nonradioactive, but still quite solid. It's built that way to isolate the power cells in each clip from the chemical propellants in the shells." Stephanos reached over Milla's hand and hit the ejection button, dropping the heavy clip into his other hand. "Here, see? The clip is separated into two compartments: the first one holds the physical shells and propellant, while this smaller section contains a power cell and enough hydrocarbons to power the electromagnetic accelerators for eighty shots. Since a clip only holds sixty, it gives the soldier a nice margin of error in the field."

Stephanos grinned. "And, off the record, it also gives us another source for energy if our equipment runs dry...And

I've heard more than a few stories about guys using them as field expedient demolition packs."

Milla tentatively twisted the stocky weapon around, examining it from different angles. "It is uncomfortable to hold. Our lasers are much smaller, easier to manipulate." *And they have other uses than slaughter,* Milla thought to herself as she hefted the weapon.

Stephanos shrugged. "It takes a bit of getting used to, that's all. It's very well balanced and exceptionally accurate. It feels a bit big because it's designed to be used by soldiers in light-power armor."

Milla nodded as Stephanos showed her the workings of the rifle, but her attention waned rapidly as she glanced at his face. The man's normally jovial visage was hard, chiseled, and very stern in spite of his lilting tone. Without forethought, Milla reached up a hand, almost touching his face, before Stephanos turned away. In the last glimpse she had of him, before his face moved away, Milla saw a sheen across his eyes.

"Steph?" Milla was confused for a moment; she was at a loss to understand the emotions she saw flit across his face. She took a halting step forward, her hand reaching for his shoulder.

He was looking away, and as she touched him, Stephen flinched. He finally turned back, his hand coming up to signal her to give him space for a moment. Steph took a breath before finally speaking.

"I'm all right."

Stephanos stepped away from her, up to the control pedestal where he thumbed the simulator off. Turning, he hurried past the confused Milla and left the room, slapping the rifle into a cradle set in the wall as he went past.

Milla stared after him. Confusion and hurt swept across her face until she followed in the pilot's footsteps and left the target range.

▶▶▶

Captain Weston was standing at his desk, the chair pushed well out of the way and the entire top showing a holographic depiction of thousands and thousands of stars. He'd been staring at those stars for so long now he imagined he could see them without the holograph.

Weston had never had any particular interest in either astronomy or space, and here he was now, bound to study both like a drowning man seeking air. He was still poring over the images when his door chimed.

"Come in," he said, loud enough for the computer to hear and key the door sequence.

Footsteps approached and stopped on the other side of the desk, so Weston looked up and nodded when he saw whom it was.

"At ease, Commander."

Commander Roberts settled back and eyed the holographic starscape with mild interest for a moment before speaking. "Sir, have you considered our next transition coordinates?"

Weston's lips twisted, but he'd been expecting that question. "May I presume that you have a suggestion, Commander?"

"I don't see how it's a choice, sir," Roberts said frankly. "Things have gone far enough...Captain, it's time to go home."

Weston sighed, then stepped back and waved a hand at the holograph. "Do you recognize this, Commander?"

"Sir?" Roberts looked confused for a moment. Then he shrugged. "It's a star map, I presume?"

"Yes. But more specifically, it's of a section of the galactic arm that Earth lies in," Weston told him, reaching into the holograph and triggering a preset program. "Right...here."

A star lit up, bright blue, out along the edge of the map closest to Roberts, and the commander glanced at it with slightly more interest.

"The attacks we've encountered occurred here, here, and here," Weston said, gesturing as the program lit up three more stars in fiery red.

One of them, Roberts noted, was quite close to the blue point.

"That's where we found Milla," Weston told him. "Forty-five light-years from the Sol System. This one...is fifty-eight light-years from home."

Roberts nodded as Weston pointed out the second light.

"This one," Weston nodded to the third, "is where we are now. Port Fey. Almost ninety light-years and the latest attack of which we're aware. Tell me, Commander, do you see what I see?"

Commander Roberts frowned, suddenly looking closer at the four stars that were highlighted. Finally, he shook his head and looked back up at the captain. "Sir?"

"Do you remember the brief that I had filed concerning Milla's story?" Weston asked.

"Of course."

"The Drasin haven't been seen for thousands of years, according to her. That implies a lot of space for a spacefaring civilization to move around in. So tell me, Commander"—Weston lit up a swath of light across the galaxy of stars with a gesture—"why is the front in their war on this side of Milla's people?"

Commander Roberts blinked and actually paled as he registered what the captain was saying. The attacks had moved inward *from* Earth's direction, moving more or less away from Earth and into the area of space controlled by the Colonials. Roberts let out a long breath. "So either they're conducting a massive preplanned attack from all sides or—"

"Or their home world lies somewhere much closer to Earth than I'd like," Weston finished for him.

"Sir, this is all the more reason to return home," Roberts stated. "We have to warn the Admiralty and get production started on more ships."

Weston shook his head. "I don't think so, Commander. Not quite yet."

"Sir." Roberts looked quite grim. "If I may ask?"

"You may...In fact, I'd be disappointed if you didn't," Weston said, his tone light.

"Then, pardon my language, but why the hell not?"

"Because it would be pointless, Commander," Weston told him. "Either we would arrive far, far too late, because Earth simply does not have the resources to defend itself now or at any point in the near future, or there is simply no rush."

Roberts stared at him for a moment, not quite believing what he'd heard.

"Have you had a chance to look at the power estimates we registered from the alien ship, Commander?" Weston asked.

"Not yet, sir. I was busy..."

Weston nodded. "I know. I'm not implying anything, Commander. Just wondering if you'd had time. You should look at them. They're...revelatory."

"Sir?"

"The first beam the ship fired"—Weston paused, until he saw Roberts nod—"exceeded the entire output of our reactor by over three times."

"What?" Roberts had known that it was powerful, but not by that much. "Sir, that's insane. You're talking about more power than—"

"Than our entire fleet is capable of putting out. And damned few of them are equipped with our armor," Weston said. "And besides that, if Milla was telling us the truth—and I have no reason to doubt her—then the Drasin have committed at least twenty identical ships to this war."

Roberts took a breath, nodding. He wasn't questioning the story of Miss Chans, either; too much of it had been proven true now.

"So, assuming a worst-case scenario, how many of those do you think we could intercept if they attacked Earth?"

Roberts took a deep breath, thinking hard. Finally, he sighed and looked up. "If we abandon Demos and the outlying bases, no more than two on our own. Assuming that they were intent on getting to the planet. The fleet might be able to take another two, maybe three."

Weston nodded. "I guessed slightly more, but I assumed that we could get the Block to point their guns somewhere other than at our heads."

Roberts winced. He'd forgotten to calculate for the Block's fleet, meager though it was. Even so, he decided, it wouldn't make much difference. Block ships didn't have the reactive armor and would go up like matchbooks under laser fire that powerful.

Still, he nodded, accepting the captain's correction.

"No, Commander. I think I may just have to plot another course," Weston said after a moment, then checked the time and corrected himself. "After we complete one last duty in this system. Come along, Commander, and I'll explain my intentions along the way."

▶▶▶

Milla was wandering through habitat two, head down, deep in thought, when she ran into a solid form and was sent sprawling to the floor.

"Oh, dear me...I am sorry."

The man she had run into looked up and his eyes widened in surprise. "Miss Chans, are you all right?"

Milla's second glance identified him as Dr. Palin. "Yes, Docteur, I am fine. I apologize; I was not looking where I was going."

"Not to worry, my dear..." At the word *dear*, Palin's face turned red. "Ah...I mean, Miss Chans. I'm quite all right." Palin paused for a moment then looked at her curiously. "What has you roaming the halls in such a distracted manner?"

"I just had a most disturbing conversation with Commander Michaels. He was showing me something, and then he was very distracted and distant. I'm afraid I don't understand," Milla told him, uncertain whether she had done something wrong.

Palin looked solemn. "You don't know? I thought you were on the bridge during the battle?"

"I was." Milla became more confused.

Palin looked almost embarrassed. "Commander Michaels lost one of his team. She flew her fighter into the enemy ship to save the *Odyssey*."

A look of shocked understanding crossed her face. Milla suddenly realized she should be feeling the same as Stephanos, or worse. After all, hadn't she just lost her ship, a fleet, and two colonies? For a long moment, she just stood there, wondering why she felt nothing. Why hadn't she felt anything in the entire time since she had been rescued?

How can that be? I've lost hundreds of thousands of my people, dozens of friends, my shipmates, my captain, yet I feel nothing? And this man, this self-proclaimed warrior, is so devastated by the loss of one comrade that he is forced to hide his tears? Milla's silence stretched. *What does this say about him? And, perhaps, more importantly, what does this say about me?*

Palin cleared his throat, uncertain of how to react to the sudden silence. "There is a memorial about to start for the lost pilot on the observation deck—if you would like to attend, that is."

Milla looked around, as if expecting the answer to her unasked question to appear on the deck plates. Finally, she looked at Dr. Palin. "Yes, I believe I would like to attend—if it would not be an intrusion."

"No, no, I shouldn't think so. Here, I'll escort you up."

Milla followed Dr. Palin through the halls of the *Odyssey*, finally reaching the central lift.

When they stepped out of the lift onto the observation deck, they saw people congregating silently around a long casket-shaped object. All eyes faced the center of the room.

Captain Weston and Commander Stephanos were standing stiffly with their backs to the open vista of space that lay beyond the observation deck's huge windows. As Milla moved closer to the group, she could hear Weston's softly spoken words describing the battle that had transpired earlier and the debt everyone on board owed the fallen pilot.

"Lieutenant Samantha 'Flare' Clarke gave her life in the defense of her comrades and, in doing so, saved her ship, her wingmates, and the remaining civilian population of this system. No greater gift can be offered, no greater honor achieved. While we commend her body to the stars, we keep her memory alive, in our hearts and in our minds."

Weston stopped, silence reigning in the room for a long moment before Stephanos stepped forward, his stance at attention. "Beacon away!"

A low shudder passed through the deck plates as a small beacon launched from the forward hull of the *Odyssey*. It arced away from the ship, circling the debris field that had formed in the wake of the battle. Locking into position, the beacon began to broadcast its message, a log of Flare's accomplishments, from her first solo flight in the Archangels to the final run that saved her ship from destruction. A small ion engine came online and locked the beacon into place. The debris may drift, but the beacon would ensure that anyone who cared to hear it would remember the sacrifice that marked that spot forever in the annals of the Archangels.

CHAPTER 18

▶ THERE WAS AN aura of palpable frustration between the people in the captain's office.

"We cannot tell you that, Capitain," Saraf said firmly, shaking her head. "I am sorry, but it is not done."

"Titualar…" Weston paused, wrapping his tongue around the unfamiliar word. "I don't believe that you understand the situation I'm in at the moment."

"No, Capitain. I most certainly do not, nor must I," the woman said, with a wave of her hand. "We cannot give you the coordinates to one of our central worlds. It is not possible."

Weston nodded. "Very well. Then I have no choice but to set a course for home. I'll make certain that your people are well received, and we'll try to arrange some kind of return to your worlds, but it will most likely be some time."

"What?" Both she and Milla paled.

"I simply can't justify spending any more time out here," Weston said, clasping his hands in front of him as he settled onto his desk. "Not with the situation escalating like this. We lost a pilot today and several multimillion-dollar fighters. More than that, we discovered alien life that tried to kill us."

He shook his head. "No, I'm afraid that I can't risk this ship or the people and information it carries without something to leverage against the risk."

"What leverage?" Milla asked softly. "What is it you hope to accomplish?"

Weston shifted his attention to her. "One of your central worlds, as you say, will have the authority to send a diplomat back with us. Someone who our government can talk with, someone who can perhaps make deals."

"Deals?" Milla blinked.

"He means negotiating for our technology," Saraf muttered.

Weston shrugged. "There is that. There is also the possibility of you receiving some of our technology. There is mutual defense. Though, to be honest, I wouldn't expect that for a while."

"Why not?" Saraf asked, with a wry twist to her mouth and tone.

"Because our military power at this time isn't prepared to project past our solar system," Weston answered her, despite Roberts stiffening behind him. "The point is, the only way we can remain out here any longer is to bring back someone who can speak with authority. And that means going to the source."

Milla fell silent for a moment, while Saraf just shook her head.

"This isn't done," the older woman said firmly. "It's not an—"

"I'll tell you," Milla spoke up.

"Ithan!"

"He is right," Milla sighed. "He has his own council to answer to; we cannot expect more than he has given us already. I will tell him how to find Ranquil."

Saraf's eyes widened. "You cannot."

"What does it matter now? The Drasin have penetrated our borders. What will these people do that they won't?" Milla snarled. "I am sorry, Titualar Saraf, but I am with the fleet, and you are not. I will give him the coordinates."

Weston let out a low sigh as he settled back in his seat, wondering if he'd done the right thing.

▶▶▶

Later, on the refugee decks, Milla found even more problems to consider as she tried to get the refugees to accept sedation prior to the ship's transition.

"Why would we want to sleep?"

Milla sighed. "The technology of this ship is undoubtedly effective, but it is not pleasant. What they call 'transition' is… difficult to describe. Please accept my word that you would prefer not to experience it."

While some of the people were inclined to accept Milla at her word, the majority voiced strong objections when Dr. Rame walked in with a contingent of medical personnel.

"I'm afraid the captain has ordered short-term sedation for all passengers."

Immediately, protests were heard through the room, causing Titualar Saraf to step forward.

"I object, Docteur. You cannot drug us like this."

Rame sighed. "We don't have a choice, ma'am. Right now, your people outnumber our crew. We have had to completely clear most of this habitat and a sizable portion of the other decks to house your people. We don't have sufficient security or medical personnel to deal with the effects of transition on your people."

"If it's that dangerous, Docteur, why do you use it?" she demanded.

"The transition drive is physically harmless. However, none of your people have been cleared psychologically, and you are unprepared for the effect it may have on your minds," Rame told her flatly, without rancor in his voice.

Saraf was about to argue further when Weston stepped through the door into the room.

"I'm sorry, Titualar, but this is necessary." Weston paused for a moment, considering. "I will permit you and Milla to join us on the bridge while we transition. But the rest of your people must sleep through it."

Faced with Weston's implacable position, Saraf and the others backed down, leaving Weston breathing much easier. An uprising among the refugees would have complicated matters incredibly. He quietly lead Milla and Saraf toward the ship's lift, the three of them stepping aside to make way for the medical personnel.

"Why are all these medics here?" Saraf watched the men and women passing with suspicion.

"When we pump the anesthetic into the air system, they have to watch for potential allergies and the like. We want your people to sleep through the transition, but we're not willing to risk their lives or health for it."

Saraf and Milla nodded, accepting the captain at his word, for the moment. The trio took the next-available lift directly to the bridge, stepping into the *Odyssey*'s command center less than thirty minutes from the system's gravity threshold.

▶▶▶

Two minutes after the *Odyssey* completed its transition, a now familiar state of controlled chaos ruled on the bridge. Weston examined sensor reports from all decks while Commander Roberts coordinated system-wide checks to ensure no damage had occurred and been missed. All of the bridge crew was frantically trying to catch up with the data pouring in from the sensors, and Milla was trying fervently to calm down Titualar Saraf, who had just experienced her first transition.

Weston, for the most part, ignored the conversation going on behind him. The words were flying back and forth a bit too fast for the translators to adequately keep up with the conversation. Short buzzwords and phrases echoed back to him, eliciting the occasional grin around the bridge—"appalling," "unnatural," and "insane" being the bridge crew's favorites.

After the brief downtime caused by the transition, the sensor resumed feeding real-time data to the bridge terminals, resulting in a rapid cooling of humors around the bridge.

"Sir, we're reading the residuals of a firefight from in-system." Commander Roberts was the first to speak.

"Signature?"

"Two. The first matches the Drasin vessel we encountered earlier. Number two falls within estimated parameters for the fleet we found destroyed."

Milla's attention swiveled to lock onto the conversation and reports echoing across the bridge.

"Get their locations and plot us a safe course to observe the battle."

"Aye, Captain."

Milla took a step forward, her face tight. "Observe?"

Half turning in his seat, Weston caught a glimpse of outrage on her face. "Yes, observe. This isn't our war, Ithan Chans. If we can avoid fighting it, we will."

Beside Milla, Titualar Saraf just stared at the screens, her color gone a pasty white. The Drasin in one of the core worlds was worse than a nightmare; it was Armageddon.

"There are men and women—humans—fighting and dying out there, Captain Weston!" Milla pressed.

"Your military?" Weston asked

"Of course."

"Then it's their job to fight and to die, if the need should arise. It's not our job," he replied evenly, gritting his teeth against the words. He didn't like that fact any more than Milla did, no matter what she may think, but there it was.

Milla was outraged, barely able to keep from shouting, "You fought the Drasin at Port Fuielles."

"We defended ourselves at Port Fuielles. They initiated combat, most likely believing that we were one of your ships. This is a different matter."

Milla was searching for something else to say when Commander Roberts called the captain's attention back to the battle.

▶▶▶

In what might charitably be called a "bunker" on the fourth planet of the system, a group of uniformed people watched with frozen hearts as the drama above them unfolded on the screen in front of them.

"Captain Duclos has engaged the Drasin, sir."

The man in charge, an oddly small gentleman in an impeccable gold uniform cut the same as those around him, grunted once to acknowledge the comment but didn't look away from the screen. He was Adm. Rael Tanner and he was *nominally* in charge of systems defense—what little of it there was.

"What about the third ship?" he asked, his eyes flicking away from the battle.

The technician frowned, shaking his head. "Still nothing on them, sir. They're circling well clear of the battle…"

"Probably a freighter," the admiral replied, his eyes still drawn to the new ship. "They should be running, if they know what's good for them."

"Uh…yes, sir," the technician replied. "But…Well, where did they come from?"

That was the question, Tanner supposed. The new ship had just appeared from nowhere, literally, amidst a tachyon surge that lit up every sensor in the entire system. Whoever, or whatever, they were, though, they were of no importance at this moment.

He had a friend out there giving his life just to buy a few minutes more.

▶▶▶

"It's over, sir. The Drasin vessel is moving on the planet."

Milla looked at the starry view screen in a horror that was echoed across the bridge.

"Planetary defenses?" Weston asked in clipped tones, his heart dropping as he realized the position he was being pushed into.

"Minimal orbital defenses detected. One small station and maybe a dozen defensive satellites—as near as the sensors can tell." Roberts stared intently at the information relayed to him from the sensors and the many technicians assigned to interpret them.

"Any readings on ground-based defenses?"

"No, sir. Nothing even remotely close to the power rating needed for effective ground-to-orbit defenses."

Weston slumped back into his seat; he could feel the chill that permeated the bridge. The situation was forcing him into a decision he dearly wished to avoid. With a deep sigh that echoed across the bridge, he sat up in the seat and slapped the switch that opened a direct line to the *Odyssey*'s flight deck.

"All Archangels, scramble! All pilots to their planes. All deck personnel to their stations. This is not a drill. I say again, this is not a drill. Search and rescue crews, stand by for immediate deployment," the captain's voice echoed through the ship, snapping everyone into action.

Milla turned from the screen, looking at the captain in confusion. "But...I thought..."

"We won't sit back and let them kill all life in an entire world," Weston said. "No matter the circumstance, no one has that right. I would interfere no matter who was on that planet and no matter who was in that ship." Weston turned back to the matter at hand. "Helm, plot an intercept course. All available thrust."

Lieutenant Daniels bent to his task, the chill that permeated the bridge lifting as the *Odyssey* shifted to battle stations. "Aye, sir. Plotted and engaged, sir."

"Good. Bring all weapons online and increase power to forward sensing systems. I want to know the instant they notice us."

The *Odyssey* arced a long parabola, turning sunward to intercept the looming figure that was entering the planet's orbit. The *Odyssey*'s engines fired to life as the ship accelerated deeper into the system's gravity well. The giant ship was four minutes out from its target when it became apparent that they had been spotted.

▶▶▶

"Sir! The unidentified ship!" The technician's horrified voice snapped Tanner around.

He turned to the screen again, having looked away after their last defending ship had died, and his eyes widened. "What in the oath do they think they're doing?"

The ship had arced in from its nice safe course and was now closing on an intercept course with the Drasin cruiser.

Whoever they are, they are no transport, Tanner thought, with a mixture of disbelief and shock.

No transport captain in the colonies would be this stupid, and the merchant fleet habitually screened their people for insanity. The admiral growled to himself as he turned to his people.

"Order them off! There's nothing they can…" Rael Tanner paused, grimacing as he considered something else. That ship was as good as dead. He knew that they couldn't fight the Drasin. But maybe, just maybe, they could delay them just a little longer. It might even—by some unimaginable miracle, he supposed—be enough. He gritted his teeth, hating himself with every fiber of his being for what he was about to do, but he had a world to consider. "Cancel that," he said as the technician started to access the com-channels.

"Sir?"

"You heard me."

"But, sir, they'll be—"

An icy pit lodged in his stomach, but the small man just nodded. "I'm aware of that."

There was a long silence.

"Yes, sir."

▶ ▶ ▶

"Sir! Enemy vessel turning to port. They're adjusting course to intercept us."

"Stand down from passive sensors," Weston said. "Get an active lock on the enemy ship."

"Active lock, aye, sir." There was a brief pause as the ship's tachyon-based sensors locked on the Drasin ship's position. "Captain! They've launched fighters."

Weston thumbed the intercom switch again, his voice booming over the rumble of activity on the *Odyssey*'s flight deck. "The enemy has launched fighter craft. All fighters prepare to launch."

"Passive sensors are reading an outgoing transmission from the Drasin ship's radio frequency." Roberts looked up from the tactical display he was monitoring. A sharp look of concern crossed his features. "Captain, they've received a response!"

Weston sprang alert, his eyes gleaming with a mixture of fear and a sudden adrenaline. If they had picked up a radio transmission this soon and replied to it… "Step up the scanning! I want to know who answered them."

A long, tense moment passed before the answer was found. "Got them! Captain, two more enemy ships and full fighter complements closing. One was hiding behind the gas giant's second moon. The other is moving in from two-point-zero-three AU away."

"Estimated time to intercept?"

"At present speeds, the first bandit group will intercept us in eight minutes. Two and a half minutes later, group two will join in the fray, and ten minutes after that, we'll have to deal with group three," Roberts presented in a matter-of-fact tone that belied the grim look on his face.

Weston's face twisted as he considered his options. In a one-on-one confrontation, he could afford to wait and let the enemy make the first move. It was foolish, but it allowed him and his people to do as they had to without worrying about whether or not it could have been avoided. For a long time, it had been a proud tradition of Weston and the Archangels that they had never started a fight, but once started, they always finished it.

Apparently, however, he wasn't going to have that luxury this time. A three-on-one battle against relatively unknown enemies was already too foolish a situation for him to compound with an equally foolish act of chivalry.

"All right, let's make this spectacular. Lock the forward pulse torpedo launchers onto the lead ship. Fire a full barrage, then let the Archangels out of the pen."

"Aye, sir," the response came back instantly, and everyone bent to their tasks.

It took only moments to make the calculations.

"Target locked, Captain."

"Fire."

▶ ▶ ▶

"By the oath," someone swore under his breath into the shocked silence of the room.

The small man couldn't blame him. There were three Drasin cruisers in the system now, and they'd completely missed the other two.

Well, at least that poor bastard out there did us one favor, Rael Tanner thought to himself as he whispered a brief prayer for those who were about to die.

"Send a coded tight beam to the Forge. Inform them of this revelation...Tell them..." Tanner paused, shaking his head. "Tell them that we haven't much time left."

"Yes, sir."

CHAPTER 19

▶ THE *ODYSSEY* SHUDDERED as the blazing-white charges were expelled into space, streaming ahead in an ever-widening cone. The instant the lethal charges were out of range, sleek Archangel fighters poured from the dual flight decks, weapons and pilots both primed and raring for action.

On board the lead Angel, Stephanos took a deep breath before opening the tac-net and addressing his pilots. "All right, boys and girls, our threat board is all lit up, and this time around we're going to be heavily outnumbered and outgunned."

"So what else is new?" Paladin's wry grin carried well over the radio frequency, eliciting a laugh from those of the squad who remembered skirmishing with the Block's air force in days past.

The Archangels had never relied on numbers to win a fight.

They spread themselves out, keeping pace with the *Odyssey* and providing a flying wedge between their mother ship and the enemy. The small sensor screens in front of each pilot echoed the current displays on the *Odyssey*'s bridge, a countdown to the impact of the pulse torpedo barrage. The tac-net was silent as they watched the diverging path of the torpedoes.

The silent displays showed the paths of the torpedoes widen farther as they approached their targets, the similar charges inherent in the weapons repelling them away from each other lazily until the enemy vessels entered into their sphere of influence.

In that indefinable moment, the displays changed dramatically as the arcing trails of the torpedoes twisted and turned into an untraceable corkscrew that colored the entire screen. Sixty-five light-seconds from the *Odyssey*, the Drasin vessels were treated to an awesome light show as a dozen brilliant globes descended upon them, literally from the heavens. For many of them, this light show was the last thing they ever marveled at.

The first torpedo struck a tightly packed formation of Drasin fighters, annihilating one in the first blast and destroying the rest with secondary explosions. The next eight torpedoes had much the same effect, wreaking havoc on the Drasin fighter wing. The last four, however, breached the fighters' barrier and struck heavily into the Drasin mother ship. Four blazing plumes of fire rose from the stricken vessel as the effects of the torpedoes vaporized its hull.

On the *Odyssey*'s bridge, they had to wait an additional sixty-two seconds for the results of their efforts, but it was well worth it.

Captain Weston took a deep breath, nodding to the tactical controls and the man who had handled them. "My compliments, Mr. Waters. Time to recharge?"

"Tubes are recharging now, Captain, but it's going to take a while. Firing a dozen of those things has drained the reserve capacitors. We'll need to recharge them from the reactor, and it will take hours at our current power demands."

Weston nodded slightly and turned to Roberts for a report. "Damage?"

"The first enemy ship is turning from its intercept course. They're limping off." Even through his rigid demeanor, Weston could hear the satisfaction in Roberts's voice.

Weston wasn't quite so satisfied, though. Four direct hits from pulse torpedoes shouldn't have left much alive to limp off.

Tough bastards, Weston thought but didn't let it color his voice as he addressed the commander. "Let them go. Continue tracking the other two."

"Aye, sir."

The *Odyssey*, with its flying wing of escorts, continued to roar toward the next intercept point. It wasn't until they passed the debris caused by their long-range fire that they realized the situation had again changed. The farthest Drasin vessel had turned back to the planet, the energy from its charging weapons lighting up their sensors like a beacon in the black.

▶▶▶

This time, in the control room for the systems defense forces, no one cursed.

The shock was complete in the large command room in Mons Systema, and it was possible to hear the proverbial pin strike the floor.

"Identify that ship!" Adm. Rael Tanner snapped, breaking the shocked silence and jerking everyone back to work.

"There's still no transponder ID!" someone yelled. "It's a Spirit, sir..."

Several people shivered involuntarily at that, though logically they knew it was foolishness. Spirits and Spirit ships were nothing but folklore, tales told at night to chill the blood and enflame the senses. The idea of it was ludicrous, but then, so was the idea of an unknown ship coming from the black to save them from the Drasin.

"I do not believe in Spirits!" Admiral Tanner growled back. "Especially not ones that can cripple a Drasin cruiser with one attack. Find me that ship's identification. I do not care if you have to go outside with a telescope and read the name off its hull!"

"Yes, sir."

"Sir…One of the Drasin is looping back! They're coming here!"

Silence descended as they watched the cruiser circle back around and make for the planet.

"Alert the orbital defenses. Prepare to engage landers," Tanner replied, half turning to see the action in another section of the bunker.

A huge hulk of a man just in sight nodded to him, and Tanner turned back, assured that his counterpart was already on the job.

For all the good it was going to do.

Tanner left that job and worry in the hands of the one most able to accomplish it. He turned his focus back to the mystery ship that had managed to cripple one of the "invincible" Drasin cruisers.

Who are you? he asked as he glared at the purple dot on his threat board.

▶▶▶

Weston watched the tactical display, the cool-blue and red dots dancing across the screen like the display of some warped video game. It would be more than an hour before the capacitors for the torpedo tubes could be recharged, and the laser array was nearly worthless at this range. Weston found himself debating two bad options, looking for the lesser evil. Intercepting the closer enemy vessel would be the safest route for the *Odyssey*. With the support of the Archangels and the formidable close-range firepower of the *Odyssey*, the single enemy vessel could be dispatched of relatively quickly. However, the second enemy vessel would have thirty, perhaps forty, minutes or longer in orbit of the planet, an eternity to those on the surface. Even so, Weston hesitated to attempt an intercept of the second ship. Moving thus would place the *Odyssey* in the cross fire of both enemy vessels.

With seconds ticking down to conflict with the nearer enemy vessel, Weston reached a hard decision. "Helm, replot our course. Put the *Odyssey* between the second vessel and the planet. All available thrust."

As the ship began to rumble off its flight path into a tighter trajectory, Weston linked into the Archangels' tac-net. "Stephanos, I'm ordering the *Odyssey* to intercept the second ship. We have to cut them off before they can begin planetary bombardment. We're going to need you and the Archangels to stay on course to harass and delay the first ship so we can get into planetary defense position."

Stephanos replied with a simple acknowledgment, belying the concern he felt. Their earlier encounter with the enemy had nearly turned disastrous and had only been successful after the combined strengths of both the *Odyssey* and the Archangel fleet were pitted against their adversary. In spite of this, he knew that Weston could no more allow the bombardment of a helpless planet than he could have allowed a civilian town to be bombed back during the war.

"All right, Angels, form up and kick in the burners. Time for a little hit-'n-run!"

Snorts and chuckles echoed over the tac-net as the Angels checked in and joined up with Stephanos on an intercept course with their target's fighter wing.

"Just like the old days, Steph!" Racer said with a grin.

Stephanos groaned. "Don't remind me, Racer. The *Yangtana* wasn't exactly a bright point in my career. And this monster packs a slightly bigger wallop."

Snorts, catcalls, and cries of "not likely" echoed through the net as Stephanos thought back to the last time they tried this maneuver. The *Yangtana* was the Eastern Block's penultimate warship, a combat carrier capable of laying waste to a thousand-square-kilometer area from up to five thousand kilometers away. The Archangels had volunteered to prevent the *Yangtana* from reaching its launch zone, a point over a thousand kilometers off the west coast of California from which it would launch a crippling attack on the New York and Delaware regions of the North American Confederacy.

The Angels had lived in their planes, literally, for three and a half weeks, all the while running harassing attacks on the *Yangtana* and its fighter cohort. The *Yangtana* was the prototype for its class, the latest in a long line of ships deemed unsinkable. Surprisingly enough, Stephanos mused, in the *Yangtana*'s case, that turned out to be a truth. A hundred and twenty kilometers from the launch point, the Archangels had reformed for one last attack, their numbers having been depleted by over 60 percent during the last three weeks.

The massive Chinese warship had taken everything they could throw at her and a good deal more from the surface ships that had joined the attack. In the end, the NAC forces had won the day, but the *Yangtana* herself survived the attack.

In fact, she was still sitting there, where the Angels' attack had driven her, beached on a shallow reef that had become her final resting place.

That last battle had weighed heavily on Stephanos for months afterward. Of fourteen planes that went in, only eight had come out. A rate of attrition that Stephanos hadn't believed possible a month earlier. That was the first time he had realized that the Archangels weren't, in fact, angels, but only human, after all.

Stephanos shook his head clear, noting that he was less than a minute away from intercept range. *And this monster does, indeed, pack a more lethal punch than even the* Yangtana's *big-gun batteries. Not to mention that this bugger isn't limited to one plane of motion.*

The tight formation of fighters blazed in on their alien counterparts, taking continuous fire from the moment they entered within range. Every cockpit filled with warning alarms as the onboard computers struggled to adapt the cam-plates to deflect the incoming laser fire. From the outside, the sleek fighters shimmered with iridescent colors as the modifications occasionally altered the visible color of the fighters' armor.

The Archangels ignored their alien counterparts, trusting their over-beleaguered combat computers to defend them from the other fighters' laser fire. Stephanos and his team instead focused their weapons on the Drasin carrier ship, directing Havoc missiles, eighty-millimeter cannon rounds, and thirty-gigawatt laser fire at the big ship as they skirted along the very edge of their firing range. Due to the speed they were traveling and the shallow angle of their attack, Stephanos and his team had only engaged the enemy carrier for a few seconds before they were peeling off from the battle group and soaring back into open space.

"Great fun!"

"Yeah, yeah, quiet down, Racer. All right, peel back and initiate Assault Plan Twelve. Racer, you and Reaper start waxing those fighters as we slip past. If they get smart, they'll start nailing us with coordinated strikes. And you know what happens then…"

Stephanos's warning was unnecessary since every pilot in the Angels knew the limits of their fighters' laser-dispersion technology. Coordinated bursts from multiple frequency lasers would overload the system and crash the onboard software that handled the cam-plate reflection modifications. The resulting twenty-second reboot time often translated into eternity. Literally.

The fighters wheeled back into line with the Drasin ship, Angels Five and Eight flanking their brethren as their computers focused on the approaching line of enemy fighter craft. They watched the line of enemy fighters form up into a wall of defense between them and the enemy capital ship.

"Looks like we have to handle the fighters first, Angels."

The Archangel group acknowledged Stephanos's message, understanding it to be an order as much as a comment. The fighters split up into a group of two-fighter teams and increased speed toward the waiting line of fire.

▶ ▶ ▶

In the Mons Systema command center, the huge threat board lit up from one side to the other. Furious battles raged all through their system now, it seemed, and the key players were still closing in on the planet.

The Drasin had the lead, but the unknown ship was closing fast on a course that would swing it around the planet and bring it in between the Drasin cruiser and its objective.

The computers were unable to predict exactly who would win the race; all they could say at this point was that it was going to be close.

Too close.

▶▶▶

The *Odyssey* accelerated into the orbital plane of the nearby planet, hooking her powerful gravity field and swooping around just as the Drasin ship reached orbit, immediately aligning to bring its forward guns to bear on the target. It became obvious to everyone on the bridge of the Terran ship that the enemy cruiser had taken early notice of their intentions.

"Sensors to full sweep!" Weston ordered as the Drasin vessel slowly brought its own forward weapons to bear on the Terran vessel.

"Aye, sir."

The *Odyssey*'s formidable forward sensor array went active, painting the Drasin ship with an inescapable web of electronic and tachyonic signals. The Drasin ship accelerated, vectoring to intercept the *Odyssey*'s position as it did.

"Ping them," Weston said, his voice cold.

The *Odyssey* released a single, focused burst of tachyons and captured the reflected signals the barest slice of an instant later, locking the Drasin's course changes into the targeting computer.

"They're closing, Captain," Roberts reported from examining the combat display. "No sign of a weapons lock or firing as of yet."

They want to play a game of chicken, Weston thought. "Report on the second ship and the status of the Archangel group."

Roberts looked down, flicking the display aside for a second. "The Drasin ship is moving to bypass the Archangels while its fighter support keeps the squadron busy, Captain. They'll be here shortly if they aren't stopped."

"Keep tabs on him."

"Aye, Captain."

▶▶▶

"Yang-boy is making a break for it, Steph!" Paladin called out over the tac-net.

Stephanos looked up from his HUD for a second, glancing over his shoulder through the canopy of his fighter to where a huge alien capital ship was pulling away. Stephanos cursed. "All right, Wings Five through Eight, break off and start harassing maneuvers. One through Four, provide cover!"

The squad split apart, the first team targeting the fighters as they swung in on another pass. The second team accelerated out of the dogfight and vectored toward the enemy capital ship.

Stephanos haloed another fighter in his HUD and loosed a Havoc missile, forgetting the target as soon as he did. That fighter was dead the second the missile dropped from its pylon, and Stephanos had more things to worry about than some soon-to-be flotsam.

▶▶▶

Roberts sneered as he watched the Archangels break up and move to harass the enemy vessel. "Captain, Commander Michaels has initiated harassing maneuvers against the Drasin ship."

Weston kept his attention focused on the cruiser he was going head-to-head with. *He's not going to make the same mistake as the others. He's going to keep this up close and personal where we can't duck his shots and adapt to his laser frequency.* Weston could respect an opponent that was able to adapt as quickly as this. Which wasn't, of course, the same as liking said enemy.

"Lock the forward laser array, and fire a medium beam," he said.

Like any warrior, Weston liked the easy targets. The ones he could respect he'd rather have on his side than against him.

▶▶▶

Admiral Tanner watched the board, wondering at the miracle that was being given to him.

The back and forth of weapons signatures echoed on the threat board, and the occupants of the room watched in rapt attention as the computer displayed the exchange of fire in clean, sanitized graphics for their consumption.

He and his people had been prepared to die for a few minutes' delay, but this unidentified ship was buying them more time than they'd dared dream of.

Now, if only it would be enough.

▶▶▶

Waters spun around. "Captain Weston! The ship just launched fighters and what looks like a planetary assault squadron."

Weston focused on the descending ships, calling up the minimal profiles the *Odyssey*'s active sensors had managed to gather before they hit the atmosphere. "Project their landing point, Commander."

"Aye, sir." Roberts called up a vector projection and had the computer estimate probable landing sites. "Captain, looks like a major settlement on a continent in the northern hemisphere."

Milla stepped forward and looked at the data over Roberts's shoulder. She gasped slightly as she recognized the city on the data display. "That is Mons Systema! It's the government capital of this system."

Weston nodded, accepting that information quietly. "Roberts, go down to the shuttle bay and have Savoy prepare his men for some ground pounding."

"Aye, Captain." Roberts's face looked troubled, but he got up to leave the bridge, tapping the induction set on his jaw as he did.

"And Roberts?" Weston said.

"Yes, sir?" The Commander paused, glancing back.

"Once they're away, take command of the auxiliary bridge. I'll have a command crew waiting for you."

"Aye, Captain," Roberts said, turning back toward the lift.

Weston turned back to the tactical repeater that showed the situation outside. He could hear Roberts giving orders as he waited for the lift.

"Lieutenant Savoy, we have a situation developing," Roberts said. "Prepare your men for a hot insertion; you'll have to do an OILO."

The doors hissed open and shut, and Roberts was gone. But he focused on the situation outside that had become paramount to his thinking. Behind him, he didn't notice his young guest, Milla, hit the call switch for the lift while everyone else was busy with other matters.

▶▶▶

Stephanos jinked to the left as a stray missile detonated just off his wingtip, rocking the plane with the concussion but thankfully missing any major shrapnel impacts. He flipped the plane end for end on his directional thrusters, killing his main engines as he did, and let the plane's momentum take it along its previous course as he haloed the fighter that tried to ice him.

"Adios, sucker."

Stephanos's eighty-millimeter cannon blazed, ripping the pursuing fighter to shreds in an instant. He watched the blaze of flame and shrapnel for a second before he kicked his main engines back into full power and killed his momentum, swiveling around and accelerating toward another target.

Around him, the Archangels were faring well against their alien counterparts, often taking the enemy fighters by sheer element of surprise. The enemy pilots were obviously not used to targets that shot back.

▶▶▶

Roberts burst into the hangar bay just ahead of the assault team, the clangs of the Magboots echoing off the walls and ceiling as they headed for the shuttle. A few moments later, the lift doors opened again and a lone figure stepped out.

"Miss Chans," Roberts said as he recognized her, "I don't think that your presence is needed this time."

Milla finished snapping the armor on as she walked into the room, the helmet crooked in the bend of her arm. "I think that you will need someone on the surface who knows the people, Commander. And I do not think that anyone else on board fits that description and knows how to operate your 'firm suits.'"

Roberts scowled but had to acknowledge the point. "I don't suppose you've had any weapons training?"

Milla's face darkened. "I have had some with our own lasers, and Commander Michaels showed me the basics of your own rifles."

Brinks and Savoy looked at each other, a concerned look passing between them. Neither liked the idea of having an armed civilian at their backs.

Roberts would have agreed with them had they said anything, but he also knew that Milla brought other things to the mission. He looked at her and spoke again. "And you're probably not OILO qualified, either."

Milla raised her eyebrows. "OILO?"

▶▶▶

"The shuttle has launched, Captain."

Weston nodded, otherwise ignoring the update, and snapped another order. "Direct a new barrage at the enemy capital ship. Bracket it while the shuttle makes its approach."

"Aye, sir."

The weaponry officer tapped the commands into the keypad, and the low whine of charging capacitors was heard as the laser array charged for the next volley.

A moment later, the laser array flared briefly with the incidental illumination of its pulsed energy release just as the *Odyssey* engaged the enemy ship and its fighter complement with its smaller cannons, rockets, and laser systems.

The Drasin vessel rocked under the multiple impacts, saving itself from serious damage by reversing engines and slipping back past the dispersion range of the *Odyssey*'s weapons. As it did so, Lieutenant Samuels slipped her shuttle through the opening the *Odyssey* had prepared for her and rocketed for the planet ahead.

"The shuttle has broken through, Captain."

Weston nodded. "ETA to pulse torpedo recharge?"

"Thirty-eight minutes, sir."

Weston growled low in his throat, causing several bridge officers to pale and studiously examine their stations.

▶▶▶

"Christ, Samuels!" Brinks yelled as his armored body was slammed into the restraints for the eighth time in as many seconds. "Cut me some slack back here! I'm not as fond of acceleration bruises as you pilots!"

Samuels just grinned, showing her teeth as she favored the big man with a glance over her shoulder. Several other soldiers groaned at the sight and muttered amongst themselves. Samuels had been something of a legend in their circles, a truly insane pilot who did anything to get her squad into and out of the worst-possible missions imaginable. The only thing worse than her smiling during a flight was when she showed her teeth.

Samuels turned back to the controls, her eye flickering wistfully toward the distant flashes that marked the area of space where she knew the Archangels were fighting for their lives. A moment later, she hardened her eyes and turned back to the assault team.

"We're picking up signs of fighting near the capital on the southern continent!" the young pilot yelled back to where the fighting teams were preparing their equipment. "I'm moving into a geo-sync. Red light is off. We're at yellow now!"

Milla watched as the military people continued their work with cool precision, not bothering to respond to the announcement. The young pilot didn't seem to expect any answer, either; she turned back to her piloting and focused her attention on the instrument displays in front of her.

"Geo-sync?" Milla asked when she managed to get Savoy's attention.

He responded over the radio link, still examining her equipment along with his own. "Geosynchronous orbit. She's getting us in position for insertion."

"Ah…" Milla responded, her tone making it quite clear that she had little idea of what he meant. Savoy didn't take the hint; he finished checking her suit and equipment and then bent to his own equipment with cool professionalism. Milla let it drop.

Lieutenant Savoy looked around at everyone, noting that some of the faces were still visible within their armored helmets. "Combat standards, people."

Milla blinked at the odd words, glancing up just in time to see the clear faceplates of the armor soldiers around her suddenly shift and blacken until she was looking at a rank of faceless men in alien armor.

"You too," Savoy said, turning to her.

"H…how?" Milla asked in confusion.

"It's not difficult," he told her, opening his tac-net HUD as he did.

Milla jumped as a bank of lights and diagrams lit up inside her helmet, following the sweep of her eyes.

"Calm down," Savoy instructed her. "Watch the center of the screen. You see the highlighted square? It's red."

"Y…yes, I see it."

"Eyeball the screen. Watch for movement."

Milla did as he told her and watched as the square turned blue and another beside it turned red.

"Third square over...the one with the picture of a shield."

"S...shield?"

Savoy sighed. "The blue thing with the white star. Highlight that square."

"Oh...okay," she said when she had done it.

"Say 'activate.'"

Milla spoke hesitantly. "Activate."

To her, nothing seemed to change, except that the pictures grew smaller and lined the bottom of her screen.

Similar to, though less sophisticated and versatile than, the cam-plate armor technology that protected the *Odyssey* and the Archangels, the personal armor used faceplates designed from a hardened transparent aluminum originally created for the windscreens of military Hummer assault vehicles.

Since then, the material had been improved several times with nanoscopic-level upgrades, allowing it to change its molecular structure between a default clear mode and a laser-resistant opaque mode that required a constant power feed to maintain.

The power trickle was minute, but its requirement kept soldiers from being totally blinded on the field if, for one reason or another, they found themselves without power.

"Green in sixty!" the pilot announced. "Lockdown in five! We've got enemy fighters inbound! Prepare for combat maneuvering!"

Five seconds later, the hatch between the command deck and the troop section slid shut, sealing tightly. Milla jumped at the loud, metallic clang that echoed even through her suit. Around her, the troops snapped to their feet, or as close to it as they could manage in zero-g.

"Snap in, boyos!" Savoy yelled over the common tac-frequency. "I'm blowing the hatch!"

A soldier beside her grabbed a safety line from her belt and clipped her onto an overhead railing before doing the same to himself. "Hold on," he said, not unkindly.

Milla nodded inside her suit, not realizing that even if the soldier had stopped to wait for confirmation, he wouldn't have been able to see her movement inside her helmet. She wrapped her hands tightly around a rail that ran along the wall. *Now what?* she wondered to herself as Savoy tapped a code into a panel.

Suddenly, the hatch blew, exposing the interior of the shuttle to the hard vacuum of space. Milla felt the tug of the explosive decompression trying to pull her armored form into the depths of space. She tightened her grip even more.

"Are you people mad?" she demanded, in shock.

A group of chuckles floated back across the tac-channels.

"Mad? Naw…just crazy."

"We're worse, lady; we're spec ops."

"Ya know, I've been wondering the same thing ever since I signed up—pretty smart chick to get us pegged so quick."

"Awright, cut that out!" Savoy ordered tersely. "Playtime is now *over!*"

Savoy looped himself back toward where Milla was holding onto the wall as if her life depended on it. "You can relax now. Decompression is over, and your suit's integrity is rated to several hours in hard vacuum."

Milla glared at him from behind her mirrored visor, not realizing that he couldn't see it.

Savoy chuckled, however; he had years of reading emotions through the way a soldier held herself in her suit. "If you're pissed now, you're gonna be ready to kill me when I tell ya what comes next."

▶ ▶ ▶

Stephanos wheeled his fighter around in a 180-degree spin without killing his forward momentum, loosed a missile and two bursts from his cannon, and spun back. Behind him, the pursuing Drasin fighter stumbled directly into the hell storm barrage thirty-three seconds later, erupting into a ball of flame and expanding debris.

"Yee-haw!" Brute yelled over the tac-net. "Lovely shooting, boss man!"

Stephanos suppressed a smile, instead snapping an order into his mic: "Can the chitchat, Brute. And watch your six!"

Brute laughed over the net as he flipped his fighter in a graceful pirouette, his cannon blazing as he did. "No problemo, boss man! These jokers react like computer drones!"

Stephanos had to admit that Brute had a point; the enemy fighters flew well, but predictably. *We do this and they do that.* They were either relying heavily on computer interfaces or discipline was extremely rigid among the enemy flyers. Either way, the Archangels had a marked advantage over their flying foes in this fight.

He set his features as he considered it. "All right, Angels. Here's what we're going to do…"

CHAPTER 20

▶ "NO!" MILLA DECLARED firmly. "I will *not*!"

Major Brinks exchanged a snide look with Lieutenant Savoy. "You're the one who wanted to come along planet-side. This is the only way that's going to happen."

"This is insane!" she tried reasoning with him, or so it seemed to her mind. Objectively, she sounded very much like she was panicking, but Savoy was polite enough not to say so.

Savoy shrugged. "Welcome to the military. You think any organization with a quarter ounce of sanity would use the motto 'It's not a job! It's an adventure!'?"

"But...but..." Milla stammered.

"Look," Brinks began as reassuringly as possible, "I'll be with you all the way down. You're going to be perfectly safe—at least until we hit dirt."

Milla's armored form shifted back from Savoy, and Brinks could read shock in her stance. "Until?"

He shrugged again, an awkward motion in armor. "War is a funny thing. It doesn't allow any guarantees."

Milla finally acquiesced. "Very well...What do I have to do?"

"Whatever you're going to do, you'd better do it quick!" Samuels snarled over the intercom. "We've got three more bogeys joining this here party, and they look mighty pissed!"

Savoy pulled Milla around, standing her in front of Brinks so he could clip her armor to the major's with the built-in security clips. Then he floated the two of them toward the back of the shuttle, actually bouncing off the wall as Jennifer Samuels slammed the stick hard to avoid a burst of fire.

"Green light!" Samuels shouted over the intercom. "We're lined up! You've got a thirty-second window! Go, go, go!"

"I am not ready!" Milla screamed as she was pushed toward the open airlock.

"Too late." Savoy grinned and threw them both out of the orbiting shuttle craft.

He watched for ten seconds as the boss and the space lady floated clear. How many troops could say that they had just tossed their commanding officer out of an airlock and expected to get away with it?

Some days, I love my job. Savoy grinned, checking the shuttle's approach velocity and the telltale green light. All the numbers checked and he had another five seconds on his window, so he grabbed the bulkhead and threw himself after his boss.

▶▶▶

Jumping from orbit bears few similarities to skydiving in the classic sense. The first few moments are more akin to swimming or the types of dreams where you try and try to move but can never seem to budge. After that, however, the sudden acceleration as your orbit decays is, without a doubt, frightening. Your stomach feels like it's being driven into your spine, and you pity the poor person who made the mistake of eating before his first jump.

Milla, fortunately, hadn't been hungry during the preparations for entry into the system and only had to worry about the spinning planet that loomed ever closer beneath her. Tossing her cookies into a sealed helmet was asking for trouble, particularly when the next time you'd be able to remove said helmet was sixty vertical miles straight down.

Brinks's tight grip kept her from struggling much as the planet's gravity pulled them down, but it left him little time to properly guide their descent.

"Miss Chans!" Major Brinks yelled over the tactical sub channel. "Please stop struggling! I have to give this my entire attention."

Her struggles instantly died down, the young woman going limp in her suit as the fear of what might happen overrode the fear of what *was* happening.

The major thanked whatever god watched over lunatics as he examined the HUD system overlaying his visor. He could see the landing zone (LZ) lit up in green with colored concentric circles surrounding it. Yellow for a close drop, orange for a long walk. Red indicated a distance that would prevent him from being a factor in the coming battle and was a position to be avoided since his team would be relying on every combat hand they could get. He was fairly confident that he could hit the inner green dot.

The gravity of the planet had quickly caught them in an irrevocable tug as Brinks adjusted his trajectory with slight puffs from the manned maneuvering unit, or MMU system, he had attached to his backpack.

▶▶▶

An observer on the planet's surface would have had a very interesting sight on that chilly predawn morning. Earlier, great glowing orbs had sliced through the cold atmosphere, heating up the earth where they passed close on their approach to the great city. An attentive observer would have been able to hear the explosions and screams that marked the passage of those first orbs of blazing light.

But now there were new players in the predawn sky. Twenty-one separate points of light appeared, moving against the dimming starscape, organized into seven groups of three. Lights that quickly brightened to a nova-like intensity as they plummeted to earth, friction and heat buildup bleeding off of them in a trail of flame that stretched to the heavens.

The ablative outer three layers of their armored suits bled off first, leaving fiery trails of light behind each of the soldiers as they drifted together.

When that was gone, the inner armor began to heat up and glow as the heat friction continued to build, but the material held and the heat merely fed the thermocouples that shunted the extra juice to the suit's capacitors.

As the old Earth saying, and new Earth motto, went…

"Waste not, want not."

▶▶▶

In the Mons Systema command and control center, the local activity had jumped up a hundredfold as men and women rushed around, tracking the incoming objects and trying to rally support to their landing zones.

"There's a Drasin lander coming in over the city center!"

"Satellite defenses ineffective!"

"Admiral! The unidentified ship has launched a shuttle."

Tanner spun in his chair, glaring at the last speaker. "Where?"

"Entering polar orbit now, sir," the bewildered tech said, looking up. "Four of the landers have been destroyed, along with their fighter complements."

"Congratulate the gunners…"

"It wasn't us," the tech said, shaking his head.

Tanner growled as he turned back to the threat board. *Who are these people?*

▶▶▶

At twenty thousand feet, Brinks's visor finally lightened as the unearthly glow of superheated metal and composite material faded to a tolerable dull orange. He could see the spinning horizon and began shifting his weight and Milla's to guide the airflow around them and shift their fall in the desired direction.

When he hit five thousand feet, he triggered his "chute."

The chute wasn't a haphazard masse of rope and silk, nor even a carefully designed airfoil. It was a small block of metal that drew on the suit's internal power and energized its core with the same anti-mass technology that gave the Archangel fighter craft their VTOL capabilities.

This small pack separated from the armored suit, connected by two superstrong wire cables, leaving Brinks and Milla dangling under the floating pack.

▶▶▶

The other soldiers were in an OILO (orbital insertion low opening) operational stance and waited until they slipped under five hundred feet to trigger their own chutes. In teams of three, their aborted falls became great sweeping glides that brought them in low over the population center and the alien orbital pods.

Someone whistled over the intercom as the city below became clear enough for them to get a sense of scale. The towers were huge, dwarfing the largest built on Earth by a significant margin, but it was the three pyramids around which the city was built that really shook them up.

Each was the size of a small city on its own, straddling a series of bays and rivers that intertwined the skyscrapers. As they swept in, the computers in their suits kept updating the size estimates, finally settling on numbers that put the pyramids alone over three kilometers across at the base with potentially millions of people living within.

Amazing as it was, however, the major knew that none of them had time to be gawkers.

"Teams, this is One. Call by the numbers," Brinks ordered as he observed from his altitude.

"One, Two. No contact."

"One, Three. No contact."

"One, Four. Have a visual. Sector G-Ten…firefight in a populated area. Civilians…hostiles…no local soldiers yet… look like a couple cops, though."

"Four, One," Brinks interrupted the soldiers. "Cops?"

"Affirm. Two uniforms—cops or local militia. Resistance ineffective."

"Four, One. Render assistance. Three, provide backup for Four."

"Affirm."

"Affirm."

"Five through Seven, continue reporting."

"One, Five. Minor contact. Looks like a pod had a rough landing. No motion."

"One, Six. No contact."

"One, Seven. Contact. Major battle at I-Nine and J-One. Require assistance."

"Teams Two and Six, render assistance to Seven. Five, approach with caution. Remain in contact."

An echoing of "affirm" came back over the net as the soldiers moved to their tasks.

▶▶▶

Stephanos cursed into his mouthpiece as he jinked his fighter hard about, barely avoiding some type of compressed energy burst fired from the Drasin fighter dogging him.

"This bastard is better than the rest! Brute, give me a hand over here!"

Brute's voice came back over the tac-net almost instantly. "Righty-oh, boss man. Inbound on your nine, high."

Stephanos looked sharply to his left and spotted the twin burn of Brute's fighter as it angled around toward him. "Roger, Brute. Rope-a-dope?"

"You got it, boss man," Brute's voice came back.

As the Drasin moved in for another burst at Stephanos, Brute blasted in from above with his guns blazing. The Drasin was fast and skipped to the left to avoid the shells. While his attention was diverted by Brute's attack, Stephanos flipped his plane around, killed his momentum with a long burn, and rocketed down the enemy fighter's throat.

The Drasin was taken by surprise, angled his own thrust, and skipped just above the barrage of rounds that Stephanos sent his way. A second later, he was rocketing off at an angle from the fight and circling for another move.

"Damn!" Stephanos cursed. "Is it just me or does anyone else notice something different about that bastard?"

"Other than the fact that he's a competent pilot?" Brute answered.

"Yeah. Other than that."

"Nope."

Stephanos shook his head. "Something about this one is familiar…"

"Worry about it later, boss man! He's coming around for another pass."

Stephanos checked, and sure enough, the fighter was coming in for another try. "Peel out, Brute. I'm gonna bird-dog him."

"Got it."

As Brute's fighter peeled out of the area on full burn, Stephanos checked his displays and found what he was looking for. The Drasin was coming in tight on his six as he let out the throttle and showed the enemy a taste of what an Archangel was really capable of.

▶ ▶ ▶

Surrounded by towering buildings on all sides, Con. Tsari Reme depleted her small laser's charge into the thing that had just finished murdering no less than three of the people in her community. It wasn't a big community, actually, just a close-knit subsection of the capital. She had grown up here. Constable Tsari knew everyone here by their first names, and they all knew her.

As the laser whined dry, she tried to swallow, but her mouth was too dry. Her throat worked continuously, without any real function, as the thing turned its gaze on her. Some movement to the creature's rear shook her attention and her heart dropped.

Oh God, she thought in shock, *there are more of them.*

Five more of them, to be precise. And they all turned on Tsari and her junior partner, a young man named Nethan.

"Do you have a charge?" she yelled.

He shook his head wordlessly, his worthless laser held limply in his hand.

She growled, though not really at him. It wasn't his fault; the local constabulary wasn't supposed to be faced with this sort of thing. Hell, most of the time, they gave directions to lost people from Central Systema and the rest was spent on domestic calls. A ship crashing into their little community and disgorging six lumbering beasts with a taste for carnage wasn't in the handbook.

The things were huge, almost four times her height at the shoulders, and they moved with a purpose. Their purpose was destruction, and they were good at it. Tsari winced as another storefront was trashed by a casual backhanded swing from an armored fist. She wasn't sure what to do. *But, by the Maker, this is my community, and I'm going to do something.*

Nethan stared, goggle-eyed, as his normally sane and well-adjusted superior strode out into the middle of the street and pointed her empty weapon at the creatures.

"I don't know who you are or what you are, but I want you out of my neighborhood!"

▶▶▶

Cpl. Sam Deacon shook his head as the computer relayed the translation to his ear: "Brave lady, that one. Stupid as all hell, but brave."

Beside him, his two squadmates nodded their heads. "You got that right, Sam."

They watched from their perch on a building they'd used as a landing pad while the creatures actually paused mid-destruction and stared at the constable with a degree of confusion that was actually laughable. Unfortunately, it didn't last long, and the team could see them aiming their weapons at the lady cop.

"Move!" Deacon ordered as he kicked off the building and launched himself into the fray.

Behind him, the two men didn't bother to reply. They just followed his example and jumped from their perch into the middle of the battle on the street below.

▶ ▶ ▶

Tsari entertained a brief fantasy that they were actually listening when the things looked at her, then each other. When they lifted their weapons toward her, she tried in vain to swallow and consigned her soul to the afterlife.

She certainly didn't expect what happened next.

A sudden impact, a few feet to her left, jerked her attention to the side, just in time to see a blur of motion rebound off the ground and fly into her. She cried out in shock and heard the aliens' weapons open fire at the same moment, charring the place she had been standing to a cinder. She hit the ground with a heavy weight pressing down on her.

"Stay here, lady," the weight ordered as it got off her, slinging an odd-looking rifle from its shoulder and aiming it back down the street.

"Who are you?" she asked. *Military... They must have arrived, finally.*

"No time." He triggered his weapon, causing her to flinch back in horror as it let out a whining roar and a flash of firelight.

What kind of weapon is that? She couldn't place it. Certainly, it wasn't on the police standard-issue books, or even any of the military books that she knew of. Tsari shook her head and tried to make sense of the strange figure in armor that was kneeling over her and firing an imposing weapon back at the things that had trashed her community.

That last thought was enough for her. If this guy was shooting at those things, he was a friend.

"Hey, you got a charge pack for a Milosan Laser?"

She saw the figure twist to look at her and swore it looked somehow confused.

"Sorry, lady, got nothing like that."

She let out a curse under her breath, an atrocious habit, but one she'd picked up a long time ago and had never been able to break. To her surprise, the armor turned around to look at her again, and when it spoke, the voice was laughing.

"Here." It handed her a small hand weapon that was over four times the weight of her laser. "There's no safety. Point and pull the small lever."

▶▶▶

Deacon grinned under his helmet. He'd been hanging around these people for days on the *Odyssey* and they never cursed. It irritated him to no end how reasonable they always seemed to be. Nobody was that calm. Nobody. So when the translator actually whispered a few choice invectives in his ear, he did something that he never thought he'd do: he handed her his sidearm.

Then he returned his full focus to the creatures. The Drasin ship had landed in what looked to be a peaceful suburb. They were ugly—that much was certain. Their armored forms were covered in something slick and slimy that gave the gigantic things a decidedly sinister air. They had a vaguely insectoid appearance, just like the long-range scans indicated, but he'd seen that before. Any exoskeletal armor tends to take on insect-like features when it's taken far enough. God simply got things right when he made those things.

Sam Deacon leveled the big rifle on the thing again and opened fire. Across the street, he could see and hear the rifles of his two comrades joining in.

▶▶▶

The Drasin soldier drones were enjoying this run as much as they enjoyed anything. This group hadn't had a lot of chances to see action so far in the war, and it was only in the fighting that they found meaning.

The six members of the clutch walked through the area like they owned it. Local police were unable to mount an effective defense, and if the military's ground troops were anything like their navy, it was going to a pretty easy job.

The leader stopped when he saw a lone female human march out and demand that he leave her community. Laughter bounced back and forth between his clutch until he finally got himself under control and lifted his weapon toward the brave fool.

As he was about to fire, a blurring motion swept her from his sights, faster than he was able to track effectively as he fired on reflex. The particle beam erupted from his forward mandible, ripping up the stonework street but utterly missing its target.

He quickly summoned two others. Taking chances wasn't part of his makeup, and the three of them approached the building that the motion had vanished behind. When they were within only a short distance, a mottled black-and-gray figure appeared from behind the building and hefted a weapon.

Expecting no problems, despite the previous miss, the soldier took his time aiming. To date, the ground weapons on this world were laughably ineffective.

The roar of sound and light staggered him, and he fell back in surprise and shock, a burning pain erupting through his body. As if from a distance, he could hear the others calling for him, but it was too dark to find them, and soon their voices were lost in the blackness as well.

▶▶▶

With the immense acceleration that an Archangel was capable of, it took Stephanos only moments to find what he was looking for and reach it. He was mildly surprised when he realized that the Drasin was still on his tail but berated himself for assuming that he'd lose it that easily. He'd have to do better now that he had located one of the Trojan points of the system, and he'd use the asteroids in the area to make certain of it.

It was difficult to remember that the technological edge he was used to having in previous conflicts wasn't certain out here. The fact that the technologies they had encountered were so wildly different than Earth's made it even harder to understand, or even make an accurate guess.

He jinked the fighter under a tumbling mountain, firing his retro-thrusters as he passed it, cutting forward motion to almost a standstill in an instant and climbing vertically in relation to his fighter to hide behind the asteroid.

The CM field that surrounded his fighter allowed for such insane maneuvers, and it was one advantage that he seemed to hold over the enemy pilot. The Drasin fighter ripped past, decelerating wildly as it spun around to aim at him, but Steph had precious seconds in which he could react first.

He loosed three rockets, haloing the target in his helmet HUD long enough for each of the "fire and forget" munitions to accelerate away from his plane. Then he keyed the vertical thrusters again and dropped under the mountain, rotating back the way he'd come, and fired his main reactors.

▶ ▶ ▶

Behind Stephanos's fighter, the alien craft shook under its own heavy power as it decelerated toward the retreating target. Its sensors reached out ahead and detected the munitions that were hurtling through space toward it, and it briefly contemplated its options.

After a split second, it locked the rockets up and opened fire.

The Archangel standard munitions were powered by the same technology as the fighters themselves and were, in many ways, even more effective since the mass involved was considerably less.

As the rocket left the CM field that surrounded the fighter, it lurched into what could be described as real space, its acceleration limited enormously by the laws of physics as they applied to normal dimensional space.

It took only tenths of a second for the rocket's own CM fields to power up, reducing the appreciable mass of the munitions to a number that infinitely approached zero. When that happened, it accelerated on its predetermined course like a laser beam.

In those tenths of a second, however, the alien fighter had already fired its lasers and destroyed the three weapons, leaving nothing but a cone of rapidly dispersing fragments in their place.

"Damn!" Stephanos swore as his munitions blinked off the HUD, well short of their target. "This guy is no joke."

He risked an instinctive glance over his shoulder, but there was nothing to see, of course. The black of space prevented him from seeing much of anything at any reasonable range, and the fighter he was tangling with wasn't at what he would call a reasonable range.

Turning his focus back to the HUD, Steph checked the range and noted that the Drasin was once more closing the gap and coming up on his six—hard. Steph snarled, hitting his retro-rockets and flipping the Archangel end for end.

Two missiles left, he thought, checking the munitions stores from the corner of his eye as he armed the remaining Havoc missiles and haloed the incoming fighter.

Whatever else this guy was, Stephanos had to grant him a certain grudging respect. The enemy flyer was a real pilot, unlike most of the drones they were dealing with.

Stephanos blinked, a thought coming up to him from the past.

It clicked in, and the light came on.

"Drones," he said suddenly into an open com-channel.

"Pardon me, boss?" Racer asked a moment later as the time lag kicked in.

"They're drones! Just freaking drones!" he snapped. "There's only *one* real pilot out here! He's directing the rest!"

Another pause as the time lag filtered through. Steph didn't wait; he armed his seeker countermeasures as the countdown clock ticked down on his meeting with the only Drasin flyer he'd yet seen that was worth his time as a pilot.

"Are you sure, boss man?" This time it was Brute, sounding genuinely disbelieving.

Steph didn't blame him.

No one, *no one*, used drones for combat duty.

It was stupid, it was wasteful, and it gave the enemy a decided advantage.

The US Air Force, back when it still existed as a discrete military organization, had a plan, once upon a time. They used some old airframes from the venerable F16 platform, rebuilt them with the latest in technology, gave them combat programs, and placed a wing of them under the command of a single pilot.

The result was a clusterfuck of near epic proportions.

While marginally successful in simulations, the real-world effect of the birds was decidedly poor. In spite of having higher acceleration rates and tighter maneuvering than any manned vehicle, the drone birds were consistently shot out of the sky by vastly inferior planes.

Simply put, they were predictable in a way that humans never were.

Just like the fighters Stephanos was looking at now—all except one of them, that is.

"Yeah," Steph said dryly as he keyed up all his counter-measures and programmed a macro with a few flicks of his eyelids and motions of his fingers. "I'm sure…"

"Angel Lead…" he almost whispered as the Drasin fighter closed to within extreme targeting range. "Fox two."

Stephanos's finger snapped the firing stud shut, and the recessed missile rack dropped its final two birds from the limited space within the Archangel fighter, and his last two Havoc missiles screamed silently away.

▶▶▶

On the ground, amidst the towering city around him, Deacon hissed in victory as the soldier drone went down, its leg shattered in a dozen places by the burst from the squad's MX-112 rifles. They didn't pause to evaluate it; Corporal Deacon merely took a step forward and put another burst into the drone center mass while the other two fired as they moved, targeting the other enemy units.

Deacon held the rifle high as he stepped in, eyeing the downed target briefly, then hit it again when it twitched.

"Stop moving and die, you dumb bastard," he muttered, glancing over for the others in his squad.

A short distance away, the two troopers who he had with him caught one of the other drones in a blistering cross fire, the MX-112 auto-rifles spitting fire as they dropped the drone hard.

At close range, the MX-112 rifle wasn't at its most effective, but he was glad to see that it was enough.

He froze when his armor's HUD threw up a warning light from his eight o'clock, and he instantly threw himself hard to his left as a sizzling stream of energy fried the rubble behind him to a crackling sludge.

Deacon hit the ground, rolling, noting somewhere in his peripheral mind that the local cop had thrown herself to one side as well and came up firing.

This time the target was about fifty meters away, just outside the point-blank range for the MX-112.

The magnetic accelerator spit out the first of a ten-round burst, its muzzle velocity over three thousand meters per second. The round cracked the sound barrier instantly, punctuating the whine of the rifle with the snap of a sonic boom, and crossed the fifty-meter gap on momentum alone.

Then, just before slamming into its target, the round ignited a second-stage booster and began to accelerate again.

The overall effect at fifty meters wasn't much more effective than a ballistic round, but the ignited mini-rocket slammed into the drone with enough force to shatter its armor and penetrate through to its interior before the onboard explosives detonated.

The remaining ten rounds struck less than a second later.

As the drone dropped, a hissing and smoking fluid pouring out of its cracked shell, Deacon straightened up, slowly turning, with his rifle ready, as he surveyed the immediate area.

"Area clear."

▶▶▶

"We lost track of the groups when they slipped into the city proper, sir."

In the darkened room of the command center, Admiral Tanner turned on his heel, his eyes glancing up to the threat board as he addressed the technician. "Trajectories?"

"Analyzed." The technician handed him a crystal data plaque.

The admiral glowered down at the information, noting that the landing locations for the Drasin matched up with the projected approach of the group that had fallen from the unidentified ship's shuttle.

"Fine. Get me an observer on the ground in each of the reported hotspots," Tanner growled, slapping the plaque back into the tech's chest. "I want a pair of eyes on the enemy and *five* pairs on the objects that dropped from the unidentified shuttle."

"Yes, sir."

▶▶▶

Teams Two, Six, and Seven stood perched on the top of one of the scrapers of the immense population center and looked down at the scene below them.

It was awesome, in a bizarre sort of way.

The Drasin drones had landed on the rooftops and found that they had more than enough space to set up operations where they were.

This made sense, given that each rooftop was larger than a football field.

So they'd actually appropriated three of the huge sprawling buildings, and much to the annoyance or downright fear of the local military, they'd apparently decided to get ready and work their way down through the buildings.

The resulting firefight sprawled across the three buildings and through the intervening spaces while what the Terran teams took to be military vehicles engaged the drones as they hopped from place to place with apparent impunity.

The flashes of laser light and the odd sizzling sound of the invaders' energy weapons were easily seen and heard by the nine members of the NACS *Odyssey*'s Special Operations teams.

Lt. Sean Bermont looked down at the scene from where he was kneeling by the edge of the rooftop. The combined computer network had tallied all the Tangos, and the numbers weren't looking good.

"I read at least fifty of them," Corporal Givens said from behind him.

Sean didn't bother to remind the corporal that they had a shared data network, and whatever the corporal saw was what they all saw. It wouldn't change the numbers, nor would it make the defenders' actions any more effective.

Whatever the drones were packing in the way of armor, it was clearly effective against laser weapons.

Sean looked away from the battle zone, looking around the garden of skyscrapers. Finally, he tagged three buildings with his HUD, knowing that the tags would be transferred to the others.

"Rogers, you and Givens take the building to our right. Establish a presence and prepare to snipe at the enemy. Adams, Benoit, the middle. Jenkins, Carter, take the left," Bermont said. "Samms and Curtis, you're with me."

A quick chorus of acknowledgment was heard, and Sean nodded once.

"Move out."

The six men he'd assigned to sniper duty nodded once, then turned and took a running leap from the building, their assisted muscles driving them straight up over forty meters and out into the dizzying heights with deceptive ease.

▶▶▶

Gunnery Sergeant Rogers and Corporal Givens landed easily on their assigned rooftop, legs flexing as the nano-fibers in their armor absorbed the impact of the three hundred–meter, pack-assisted jump, and hastily got to work.

Rogers was a Marine Force Recon sniper specialist from way back and had been a career soldier all his adult life.

He dropped to one knee as Givens lay out prone near the edge of the roof. His rifle was the long variant of the MX-112, given to all the branches of the NAC military and its allies, and he'd spent many long hours learning every nuance of his particular rifle.

He casually flipped down the bipod and then flipped up the two reticule lenses of the rifle's integrated long-range sight.

Only then did he lie out beside his spotter and turn his HUD over to accept the targeting information that Givens had been gathering while he prepared.

"What have we got?"

"Three Tangos pinning down survivors from a crash. Looks like some military, but they aren't doing all that well against the Tangos, Sarge." Givens said, lighting up the HUD icons.

Rogers grunted, noting the display and checking the scene.

"Looks like they got one," he said, noting a downed Tango.

"Sure did, Sarge…But I think they hit it when they crashed the…whatever the hell that thing is," Givens replied.

"Probably," Rogers grunted, lining up his first target.

The Tango he'd chosen was making a real ass of itself, chewing through the cover that the survivors had fled to. In short order, it would probably open up the path; then those people would die.

Maybe in your next life, asshole, Rogers thought to himself as the reticle in his sights flashed red and he squeezed the trigger with the same cool, calm deliberation as he used on the range.

The long rifle bucked once against his shoulder, and it spat its heavy round out with the combined whine of its electronics and crack of the sonic boom.

The round left the barrel at three thousand meters per second, tearing through the atmosphere like the proverbial bat out of hell. Fifty meters from the rifle, the onboard rocket booster kicked in, and it quickly accelerated on target as a set of fins snapped out, stabilizing the round in flight.

It roared into the Drasin drone at over twenty thousand meters per second and still accelerating, the kinetic impact holing the hard shell of the drone just before its payload went off.

The Drasin stopped mid-motion, staggered to one side, and collapsed.

But by then, Rogers had already picked his next target and fired.

▶▶▶

Sean Bermont glanced back at the two soldiers he'd selected for his team.

Russell Samms and Jaime Curtis were both drawn from the old US Army Rangers Corps, while Sean himself was a former member of Joint Task Force 2 from back before the Confederation.

"All right, we drew shit duty," Sean told the other two with a wry smile that they could hear, even if they couldn't see. "We're going to get in close while the other groups cover us and make contact with the locals."

"What for?" Jaime asked, sounding disgusted. "It doesn't look like they're doing much good for themselves…"

"That's what for," Sean snapped. "We're going to pull them out if we have to…Then we'll hit these bastards with thermobarics, if all else fails."

"On top of a skyscraper?" Russell objected. "No offense, Sean, but are you nuts?"

Jaime snickered, but Sean just rolled his eyes. "Have you checked this thing out?"

He tapped his armored boot on the rooftop.

"It's like obsidian or something…" Sean shook his head. "A thermobaric pressure wave won't do fuck to all this…But I'll bet it knocks those bastards off their feet."

"If it doesn't, I wanna go home," Russell whined. "All right, let's do this."

"Hang on a second!" Jaime muttered. "Are you sure? I don't want to start collapsing the entire city here."

"Trust me, Curtis," Sean said calmly. "Me and Savoy are already running the numbers, but it's looking like this city could take a multimegaton nuke and come out in decent shape."

The slim trooper shook her head. "It's the boss's call…"

"Yep, so don't worry about it," Bermont said, looking around. "All right, we've got to get moving. Ready?"

"Ready!"

"On the bounce," Sean grinned, using an old phrase long embraced by troopers in powered armor, though no one really seemed to remember why. A few people insisted it had to do with some old sci-fi novel. Sean doubted it, but he'd seen stupider reasons for traditions.

For whatever reason, it fitted the situation as the three soldiers judged their position and then leapt from the rooftop toward the carefully marked landing zones on their HUDs.

▼

CHAPTER 21

▲

▶ COMMANDER ROBERTS SWUNG himself over the threshold, in the null gravity of the auxiliary bridge, letting his momentum propel him.

Compared to the main bridge, this room was at least twice the size and just as well equipped, mostly because it was the primary control center of the *Odyssey* in the original plans. When the artificial-gravity generators fell by the wayside due to their enormous power requirements, the bridge moved to the second cylindrical habitat, and this room had been turned into its backup.

"Commander." A lieutenant didn't bother to come to attention or even salute as he approached, entirely for practical purposes since standing at attention in zero-g was about as effective as equipping firefighters with flamethrowers.

Instead, the young man reached up as Roberts sailed past and hooked his hand, swinging the commander down into the command chair.

"Much obliged, Lieutenant," Roberts said calmly as he looked around.

The bridge was built into the top of the *Odyssey*'s control tower, which was more egotism than anything else, but provided a magnificent view on three sides through the transparent armor around them.

However, in battle, having transparent sections in your wall was contraindicated—if you were in to making understatements.

"Take us to battle stations, Lieutenant," Roberts commanded. "And bring us completely online."

"Aye, sir," the lieutenant replied, tapping in a command code. "Sealing the bridge now."

The incredible view offered by the transparent battle steel vanished as the armor shifted to block all wavelengths.

"Activating screens."

Rolls of transparent plastic slid down from the recessed ports in the ceiling, the thin film covering the walls with a milky coating for a moment before they flickered, and the external view once again returned in an ultra-high-definition display filtered through the computers and overlain with an electronic HUD.

Roberts finished clipping in his restraints just as the ship rumbled, the screens lighting up with the red on red of a direct fire warning.

"Status!"

▶▶▶

The main bridge of the *Odyssey* shuddered and rolled as the crew gripped tightly to their seats and consoles.

"Damage reports coming in!" Ensign Lamont yelled over the screeching of tearing metal that could be heard right through to their teeth.

Weston grabbed for the console and slid it over as he punched up the damage control code, bringing the reports up on his own screens.

Not good. We're venting atmosphere from the forward weapons stations. He ground his teeth. "Get damage-control crews down there!"

"Aye, Captain!" Lamont said, her hands already keying into the emergency channel as she spoke quickly and calmly over the emergency frequencies.

"Incoming!" Waters yelled.

"Take us up! All power to vertical thrusters!" Weston ordered, leaning forward in the command chair. "Pitch us forward! Bring the primary array and the forward HVM banks to bear!"

"Aye, Captain!"

The NACS *Odyssey* clawed for vertical altitude relative to its opponent, climbing above the lethal beam that scorched vacuum just shy of their position. As they did so, Ensign Waters stood on the proverbial stick as he pitched the nose down while the ship climbed.

Slowly, the *Odyssey*'s forward laser array came back into targeting range of the enemy just as her forward hyper-velocity missile (HVM) banks slid open.

As it climbed and twisted in space, the cutting beam of the Drasin laser followed suit, tracking its wayward target through space.

The forward bow of the *Odyssey* erupted as its laser array flashed to life just as her HVM banks were flushed. The gleam of the charging banks cast an eerie glow on the plasma exhaust of the HVM launch as both weapons tore out of the *Odyssey* and sought out their target.

The Drasin laser scorched the lower keel of the *Odyssey*, vaporizing metal and venting atmosphere as it blew out her lower flight deck.

Inside the *Odyssey*, the deck rocked as a five-person team tried to make its way down the zero-g corridor in hard suits.

"Shit!"

"Belay that chatter!" Chief Petty Officer Corrin growled, her harsh voice echoing over the suit intercoms of each man. "Move it, you pansies!"

The team kept moving, occasionally bouncing off the walls as the ship rocked around them, but finally got to their positions.

"We're here, Chief," the lead man said, glancing back from the sealed door. "We've got hard vac on the other side."

"All right," Corrin muttered, slapping a sealing switch beside her and dropping the heavy lock door behind them. "Break the seal and let's get to work."

The man nodded, turning back to the door as the corridor pitched and rolled around him. "On it, Chief."

As the men moved quickly about their jobs, the information concerning the battle continued to feed from their suits and from computers all over the ship into the main bridge systems.

Once there, the entire networked computing grid of the NACS *Odyssey* was sliced into bite-sized pieces, prioritized according to importance through a specialized computer algorithm, and then fed straight to the screens of Ens. Susan Lamont.

"We're bleeding air from the flight deck!" Lamont snapped over her shoulder, her fingers already cutting off the deck from the rest of the ship as she called up a list of the personnel still on the lower decks.

"Send rescue teams!" Weston barked. "Daniels, did we hit anything?"

▶ ▶ ▶

The Drasin cruiser pitched upward as it tracked its quarry, trying to keep a solid beam on the human ship as the vessel performed the most...unexpected actions.

As it reconnected the beam to its target, the controller had a moment of satisfaction before warning alarms went off through all its systems.

That moment was its last.

▶ ▶ ▶

Hyper-velocity missiles could accelerate to nearly 0.8c in the few seconds they took to cross their normal effective range. The ones that launched from the *Odyssey* were targeted at an enemy ship within half that radius.

Even so, they managed to accelerate to 0.63c before impacting on the Drasin cruiser, delivering their kinetic payload on target less than four seconds after they had launched.

By that time, the ship was already bubbling under the hellish heat of the *Odyssey*'s primary laser array.

▶ ▶ ▶

"We got him!" Daniels yelled, throwing his arms up as the cruiser vanished from his screens.

The bridge erupted into cheers, but Captain Weston didn't join in.

"Lamont...damage control?"

Ensign Lamont swallowed and nodded, turning back to her station as the brief exultation passed, and she began to coordinate the crews moving through the bowels of the ship.

▶▶▶

"They did it, Admiral."

Admiral Tanner nodded dumbly as the central computer painted the death of the Drasin cruiser on the threat board in brilliant detail.

Whomever that ship belonged to, it was a formidable force in and of itself.

However, since it had entered orbit, they had tried contacting the crew on every frequency used by the colonies, to no avail. It either wasn't answering or it didn't hear them.

In either case, it wasn't exactly comforting.

Tanner had no quarrel with the captain of the vessel; certainly, he had nothing but respect for the man's abilities, as well as those of the people under his command.

However, neither did he have any liking for an unidentified ship holding high orbit over his world.

Especially not one that was capable of defeating a Drasin cruiser in a close-range exchange.

Unfortunately, he found himself in a situation where he had little control, and less choice, over such things.

For the moment.

Tanner looked at the threat board for a moment and ducked his head to look at a different display.

Soon.

Very soon.

▶▶▶

A body floated past the crewman as he pulled open the hatch to the forward laser-control room, limbs floating freely as the iced eyes stared sightlessly.

"Oh fuck!" The crewman fell back, gagging in his helmet as he tried to keep from vomiting, more from the shock than anything else.

This time Chief Petty Officer Corrin didn't say anything to reprimand him. She just moved forward and dragged the body out of the way.

"This is why pressure suits are required during alerts," she growled over the tac-net, turning the body over and shoving it unceremoniously into another room. "And they don't do you any fuckin' good if you don't seal the helmet. Now find that fuckin' breach."

The men nodded, swimming forward, eyeing the debris path.

Anything that hadn't been locked down had been torn up by the decompression, throwing papers and smaller items through the rushing air and right to the source of the breach.

Of course, as it turned out, it wouldn't have been all that hard to find, anyway.

Crewman Jacynck slid over to the four-foot hole burned through the hull, passing his safety line back to his closest companion, then slid out into the black. He looked up along the front of the heavily armored bow of the *Odyssey*, then twisted and looked back down.

"Well, Chief…" his voice came dryly back over the intercom, "I don't think that we're gonna be able to slap a quick patch on this and call it a day."

Corrin snorted and waved to the other two. "Bring up the torch and start patching that up temporarily…I'll tell DC the bad news."

▶▶▶

The Havoc missiles had just dropped from the internal pylons when Stephanos launched every countermeasure in his fighter's stock.

Flares, dazzlers, EM screamers, and old-fashioned chaff erupted out from the fighter as the two missiles were briefly vulnerable to interception. This confused the Drasin's sensors for a split second as the Havoc CM fields firmed up and their rocket motors kicked into full burn.

Both missiles slammed into the fighter two and a half seconds later, hitting like the hammer of God.

As the fighter vanished in a cloud of expanding debris, Stephanos pivoted his fighter in place and slammed the throttle forward as he sought out the next fur ball.

He was halfway there when his theory was proven beyond the shadow of a doubt.

Two previously competent, though predictable, pilots slammed into each other in the middle of a tight maneuver, their communication obviously cut by the loss of the flight leader. In a few moments, the remaining fighters were mopped up by the superior flying of the Archangels.

"Good call, boss man!" Brute called over the tac-net as Stephanos slid into position between him and Racer.

"Thanks, Brute," Steph said, checking his HUD. "Where's the big boy?"

Across the few meters that separated them, Stephanos could see Brute nod his head in the distance. "Looks like he wants to play with the Cap, boss man."

"Dammit!" Steph snarled. "Roll call!"

▶▶▶

"Archangel Squadron reports that the enemy cruiser has slipped past them, Captain," Waters said grimly. "Commander Michaels intends to intercept."

"Belay that," Weston told him, looking at the course projections. "Tell him to take a least-time return course. The Archangels can get here an hour ahead of them. We'll meet him together."

"Aye, sir," Waters replied, keying into the channel.

"Sir." Lamont turned. "We don't have the lower flight deck at the moment, sir. Rescue crews are still pulling survivors out of there, and there's an eighteen-meter slash right up the trap."

Weston grimaced. "The upper deck?"

"Clear, sir…but it's meant for the SAR shuttles and—"

"I know what it's meant for, Ensign," he barked, turning back to Waters. "Tell the Angels that they'll have to come in softly. We don't have any traps for them."

"Aye, Captain."

"And tell Samuels to get her ass out there to pick up any survivors of the engagement!" he said, pulling his console close again as he started tallying up what they'd lost against what the last ship in the system still had.

"Aye, Captain."

▶▶▶

Major Brinks and Ithan Chans touched down on the roof of the tallest skyscraper the major could find, and he immediately cut the lines and let his chute float up and away on its own.

His HUD and suit computer collated the feeds from all the free chutes, using them much like the carnivore drones to provide real-time intel from the local hot spots.

Unlike the carnivore drones, though, the chutes were neither particularly stealthy, nor were they nearly as good at gathering the intel as the drones.

But they were what he had, and he had a lot of them.

"If you can get a hold of anyone in charge," Brinks told Milla as he crouched by the lip of the roof and looked down over the battle scene about a kilometer away, "do it now."

With that, he turned his focus on the fight below.

▶▶▶

Lt. Sean Bermont and his team landed "on the bounce," right in the middle of a firefight between three humans and one of the drones.

The drone twitched in their direction, causing the three to scatter as its weapon drew a line of fire in the obsidian roof of the building, their own guns firing in return.

Bermont rolled under the cover that the locals were using and glanced in their direction as they stared back. For a people under attack, they weren't exactly as jumpy as he'd have expected.

Though, frankly, they reminded him more of civilians than the military that he'd assumed they were from their weapons and uniforms.

"Stay down," he ordered them, hoping that the translator wouldn't give him any problems. Then he popped up with the MX-112 leveled at the drone.

The Drasin drone was firing at Curtis as the former ranger dove across the roof, the beam scorching her side. She fell and rolled to a stop some distance away as Russell and Bermont both opened fire.

They moved forward, weapons blazing as they did, and walked the fire right into the single drone in their sights with short bursts that ripped its carapace apart.

As it tumbled, Bermont waved Russell to Curtis's side, then turned back to the locals.

Corporal Samms, formerly of the US Army Rangers, crossed the distance between himself and his wounded teammate in a fraction of a second, sliding along the smoothly fused surface of the rooftop as he dropped to his knees beside the tough lady who had taken enemy fire.

"Jaime!" he muttered. "Come on, girl. You okay?"

When there wasn't a response, he flicked his HUD over to the tactical menu and then called up her medical stats.

The alien weapon had done one hell of a job along her side, either melting or maybe vaporizing away a large chunk of her armor and ravaging the flesh underneath.

Russell had to rely on what her armor sensors were telling him, though, because the military armor had automatically sprayed hardening foam over the breach to plug the gap and apply a coagulant to the wound. Her heart was still beating, which was a relief, but she wasn't responding.

"Got a problem, L.T.," he muttered as he linked into her suit pharmacy. "Curtis is out like a light. Heartbeat is strong. You want me to wake her?"

Lieutenant Bermont frowned, glancing over his shoulder for a brief moment. "Negative. Leave her as is for now. Recon and secure the area. I want to talk to the locals first. Then we'll see what to do about Jaime."

"Whatever you say, L.T." Russell nodded, rising to his feet, more than a little relieved.

Her injury wasn't going to be pleasant, and waking her from it was going to hurt the tough lady—a lot. The suit wouldn't dispense painkillers or tranquilizers without either her or a corpsman's authorization, either, so she was going to be in a lot of pain until she woke up enough to order a couple aspirin.

He hefted his rifle and glanced around, deciding on a rectangular block that looked like it was probably an access door to the skyscraper. He easily hopped the thirty-meter distance, landing on the block, and dropped almost instantly to his knees as the suit's sensors reached out and began identifying everything in range.

Behind him, Bermont had turned back to the trio of local soldiers who had been pinned down by the drone.

"You guys understand me?" he asked, eyeing them carefully.

They should, from what he'd been told. The commander had told them all in the pre-mission brief that this was the space lady's home world, and her dialect should be the best handled of the translation programs they had so far, though his suit memory also held an extensive library from the refugees as well.

One of the locals, a woman with a statuesque build and very hard eyes, nodded, her weapon not *quite* aimed in his direction.

That was fair. After all, his rifle wasn't *quite* aimed at them.

"Who are you?" she asked him.

"Introductions will have to wait," Bermont told her flatly, his HUD already linked to the others in the *Odyssey*'s assault force. "We've got at least another twenty of those drones inbound on our position, and frankly, I don't think we've got enough firepower to hold them off."

She and her two male companions looked around in nervous fear, but Bermont just shrugged and held up a hand.

"They're not here yet..." he told her, knowing that the drones were currently distracted by sniper fire from all sides.

With luck, they might have time to check out the corpse of the one that he and Russell had taken down.

"What I need you to do is pack up your shit...umm...gear." He had to backpedal and correct himself when he could tell from the look on their faces that the translator obviously flubbed the word.

Cursing wasn't something computer programs were generally much good at translating, as a rule.

"'Cause when we move, we'll be moving fast."

The woman blinked, then shook her head. "We can't jump like you..."

Bermont grinned, though they couldn't see it. "Don't worry about that, lady. We've got it covered."

▶▶▶

Milla Chans tore open the roof access panel by accident, completely misjudging the strength granted her by the armor, and tossed the panel away while blushing under her mirrored visor. She shook it off while moving down into the building.

The suit she wore was well equipped for communications but had nothing in its vast repertoire of com-channels, transceivers, amplifiers, and beam coms that would be picked up by the local defense forces.

And those were precisely the people who she had to get in touch with, hopefully before some misunderstanding resulted in the local militias opening fire against the soldiers from the *Odyssey*.

CHAPTER 22

▶ A SIGNAL CAME IN over the command channel as Brinks examined the rooftop battle in his HUD.

"One, this is Five."

He pushed the schematic aside for a moment, and a floating image of Lieutenant Bermont appeared.

"Five, this is One," Major Brinks responded. "Go ahead."

"We've got three locals, plus one injured, for pickup. You have a couple packs to spare?"

"One moment," the major said, tapping into the chute control programs with a flick of his finger. "Have two inbound. ETA—forty-five seconds. I'm showing five drones approaching your immediate position. You'd better pull out."

"Will do," Bermont said. "I just have one thing to do first."

"Right," Brinks confirmed, trusting his man to know what he was doing. "Once you get those locals clear, I'm going to drop a TB on your location. So when I say bounce…"

"We hit the sky," Bermont replied.

Major Brinks frowned but didn't bother saying anything else. One of the problems that you encountered when dealing with Special Operations units—especially when what you had wasn't a spec ops team, but rather a select gathering of the best spec ops individuals—was the fact that they had a, perhaps justifiable, sense of superiority.

And, of course, they were all insane.

He himself excluded, of course.

▶▶▶

Lt. Erin Mackay listened to the radio chatter from the other teams, letting it run in the background as he and the two soldiers with him moved over to the fallen drones. The streets were empty, but his suit sensors could read the occasional motion source flicker by a window, the people inside looking out at the destruction that had rained down on their neighborhood. The area was obviously a suburb of the city, and the buildings here were only twenty or so stories high, not the monstrous buggers that rose against the sky to his back.

Corporal Deacon moved across the fire zone while Mackay covered him and kneeled by the drone they'd taken out.

"A...Are you sure you should be doing that?" the local cop, or whatever she was, asked nervously.

Corporal Deacon glanced back at the local policewoman, exchanged a glance with Mackay, then shrugged in this armor, one of the grossly exaggerated motions that armored troops got used to using. "Just having a look."

Beside him, Sergeant Steward knelt and reached down to run his finger through the creature's blood. He instantly yanked back with a curse and drove his hand into a pile of rubble to scrape the liquid off.

"Motherfucker!" the sergeant cursed.

"What is it, Sarge?" Deacon jerked around, his weapon coming up.

"Fucking shit started eating away at my suit!" Steward growled, checking his finger. "Fuck!"

Deacon's rifle dropped. "No shit?"

"No shit."

"Whoa..." the younger man said, his voice filled with a kind of awe. "These things actually got acid for blood? Cool."

"Shut up," Steward growled, using a tone that made Deacon take a step back.

"It's not acid," Erin muttered, checking the basic analysis his HUD provided. "It's some kind of superheated compound. It just ate off some of the ablative material that survived your jump, Sarge."

"Oh," Deacon sighed, sounding disappointed.

"Deacon, you need to get your candy-ass out of the TV room once in a while and quit watching that sci-fi shit," Steward told him in no uncertain terms. "That stuff will rot your brain—what's left of it."

Deacon didn't have an audible reply, so Mackay just rolled his eyes as he spoke up. "These things have molten rock or something for *blood*. Would you two mind saving the mutual bitch session for when we're back on the *Odyssey*?"

"Molten rock..." Deacon sounded interested again, and he dropped down, checking out the corpse of the drone, flicking slowly through a series of computer-enhanced images on his armor HUD. "No way..."

Steward and Mackay waited patiently for him to explain what the hell he was talking about, but all the soldier did was let out a long, low whistle and repeat himself.

"No fuckin' way..."

"Deac!" Steward finally snapped.

"Huh?" Deacon jerked around. "Yeah, Sarge?"

"What the fuck are you jabbering about?"

"Wha...Oh, sorry, Sarge." The soldier flicked his fingers a couple times and sent a download over to the others' suit HUDs. "I think they've got silicon-based chemistry...But whatever it is, it's got a real high tolerance to heat..."

He glanced back at the cooling body for a moment, then back at the other two. "Nasty little things, for sure, but it might be good news for us."

"How?" Steward asked in a clipped tone.

"Well, that thing there," he gestured to the dead drone, "has a current body temp that's over one-eighty...I'm guessing that the living ones are hotter..."

"So we can use the IR sensors in our suits to spot them easier...all right..." Steward nodded. "All right, now *that* is what I like to hear, kid."

"More than that," Mackay added, thinking furiously. "Our bullets can track heat. If these things are that much hotter than humans, we can activate the thermal guidance chips without worrying about hitting locals."

"Bingo, L.T." Deacon grinned under his darkened face shield.

▶▶▶

Standing on overwatch atop one of the tallest buildings, Brinks acknowledged the communication he'd just received. "I hear you," Major Brinks said as he mulled over the information. "Hold back on the IR until I get back to you."

"Confirmed," Mackay replied.

Brinks frowned as he pondered the thought while quickly browsing the suit network until he found the person he was looking for. "Lieutenant."

"Sir?" Savoy's response was instantaneous, the whining crack of gunfire in the background.

"Got a problem for you."

"That's what we tech geeks like to hear, Major," Savoy smirked. "What's up?"

"These things are running a body temp over one-eighty," Brinks started to explain. "The thought that Corporal Deacon had was—"

"Crank up the sensitivity in the rifles," Savoy interrupted, grimacing. "Shit."

"What?"

"Nothing, sir," Savoy shook his head, jostling the image. "I just should have thought of it first. Give me two minutes."

Brinks signed off, leaving Savoy on the other side to mutter a mild curse for having missed something so obvious. He frowned, locating the team with the closest Drasin drones.

"Bermont, I need you to do something for me before you move out," he said a moment later.

Sean Bermont paused in his handling of the chute, cocking his head as Savoy told him what he needed.

"Gotcha, Sav," he said after a moment, then switched his tactical frequency to the squad level. "Russell, we need an IR scan of one of those things while they're still kicking!"

A few meters away, Corporal Russell knelt on the roof of the apparent access building. "No problem. We've got three of the bastards jogging over here right now."

"Great," Bermont muttered, yanking one of the guy wires from the chute and pulling one of the locals to his feet. "This isn't going to tickle."

While the man looked at him oddly, Bermont looped the wire under his arms and around his torso. He clipped it to a loop built in for just that purpose. Bermont then grabbed the second man and repeated the process.

"Two to evac," he signaled, then turned to see the next chute swoop in.

The two men looked confused and scared out of their minds as the line was suddenly drawn taught and they were pulled off their feet while the wire loop bit into their chests and underarms. They yelped in pain, but the remote-controlled chute didn't really care one way or another. It hung low, then dropped over the edge of the skyscraper, using the immense building itself as cover as Savoy guided the two to safer ground.

"Wait here," Bermont told the third, the woman who had appeared to be in charge. "I'll be right back."

Then he reached up and grabbed a handgrip on the bottom of the chute and kicked off the ground, skimming the rooftop over to where Curtis was still unconscious.

"Beautiful," Savoy whispered as the suit's tactical network grabbed the information from over a kilometer away. He tossed the numbers over to a module he had developed for on-the-fly programming.

From there, it was just an electronic hop, skip, and jump to recoding the computer buried deep in the carbon-fiber chassis of his rifle.

The MX-112 assault weapons system was a throwback to an earlier time. In a lot of ways, it was a twentieth century rifle masquerading in twenty-second century clothes. When the rest of the militarized world was moving to lighter, higher-velocity rounds, the USMC adopted the exact opposite stance.

The MX-112 was big, nasty, and it put equally big and nasty holes into whatever it was fired at. It didn't jam. It fired underwater if someone was stupid enough to try it, and if the barrel was clogged with sand, the first bullet simply cleared it and greased the way for the rest.

Put simply, the marines of the day were in love, from grunts to officers and beyond.

Despite this, however, the design mostly languished in obscurity until the outbreak of the war, since SWAT and anti-terrorist units had no use for a weapon that was going to perforate the target and then go on to do the same to any five others hiding behind it. When the Chinese attacked Japan at the start of the Block War, however, the Block soldiers were understandably perturbed to find that their opponents on the beaches carried rifles that were able to perforate light- to medium-armored vehicles and still retain enough energy to kill the soldiers inside.

The fires of the war burned away a lot of lesser weapons, but the MX-112 emerged with a legendary reputation. A legend that had continued to grow over the decades as the rifle underwent revisions and evolutionary changes, until the latest product found its way into the hands of one Lieutenant Savoy, NACS *Odyssey*, on an alien world over a hundred light-years from where the rifle was born.

Savoy flipped open a programming window in his HUD, keeping one eye on his threat indicator while calling up the onboard computer built into the rifle. The electronics were entirely optional on the weapon, but when they were in use, they offered several degrees of sophistication over any mere conventional weapon.

One of those degrees was what concerned Savoy at this moment in time. He tapped into the software that controlled the rudimentary seeker systems on the heavy-caliber bullets and tapped a single digit into them.

In about thirty-three seconds of programming—most of that time used just to find the appropriate line of code in the first place—he had altered the thermo-sensor's sensitivity from 96 degrees Celsius to a toasty 196 degrees. Then he smiled and squirted the program change to every man in his unit.

"Savoy to all teams. Apply incoming program change, and switch weapons to thermal-guidance."

▶▶▶

Milla Chans, ithan of the Colonial Fleet, found she was forced to pry open the lift doors within the immense construction's transport tubes. The maglev tubes were necessary for the transport needs of the pyramid's inhabitants.

Milla knew from personal experience that a great many people within the immense habitats never left them, and never wanted to. Each one was a city in its own right, and they were merely grouped this close together because of convenience.

She made her way through the tube, still moving a little awkwardly in the armor, looking out for a debarkation point.

She knew that, at this level in the pyramid, the local population would be sparse in spite of the marginally less room available at the apex of the huge tubular design. Those who lived in the apex habitat that was suspended directly below the point of the pyramid would be among the most influential families, and thus were able to secure the entire habitat for themselves.

She wasn't looking forward to bursting in on them in the slightest.

The debarkation point was fairly easy to locate, and she found herself wishing she'd been carrying one of the standard-issue lasers she normally had. The weapon they had provided her, grudgingly though it may have been, was almost certainly not suited to opening doors.

Milla sighed and looked over the debarkation doors in annoyance.

Finally, she reached forward and began to go to work prying them apart.

▶▶▶

Lieutenant Mackay sent the coded pulse to his rifle computer, then flipped the weapon over to burst mode as he glanced around at his squadmates.

"Come on. We'd better move out." He glanced along the lengthy street that led toward the three towering pyramids, which appeared to float eerily over the placid waters, supported by massive struts sunk into the ground below.

"'Fraid that might not be a great idea, sir."

"What's up?" he asked, turning back.

"Roving recon shows another squad of those suckers coming this way, Lieutenant," Sergeant Steward told him, pointing off to one side. "Not sure what the hell is going on with them, but the chutes are having trouble locking them down…"

"Hey, no sweat." Deacon grinned under his helmet. "We took these bozos easy. We've got the guns, and we've got the mobility…"

A screeching, hissing sound jerked all their heads straight up, just in time to see three of the Drasin drones clear one of the smaller buildings with a bound and come crashing down to street level.

"You were saying, Corporal?" Sergeant Steward growled as the three of them scattered, grabbing the local cop as they ran just ahead of the sizzling blast from the enemy weapons.

▶▶▶

"Sorry 'bout this, Jaime," Bermont muttered as he hooked the wounded soldier's arm and unceremoniously flipped her over.

Normally, he'd be worried about aggravating her injuries, but in this case, two things kept that from being a primary concern. First was the fact that the suit automatically held her immobile while unconscious for just this reason. Second was the fact that he could hear the rapid crack of the scramjet rounds, fired from Russell's MX-112, as they went supersonic.

Which meant that they were about to have company!

He yanked the wire down from the chute and slapped the clip onto the metal eyebolt, which was located just between the shoulder blades of Curtis's suit, and tapped an order into the chute's program.

The CM-powered device lifted off the building, drawing him and Curtis up with it, then smoothly glided back to where the sole remaining local militia woman was still taking cover.

"All righty!" Bermont said to her. "It's your turn now."

"Who *are* you people?" she finally ventured, surprising Bermont.

"We're here to help," he told her. "Now come on… arms up…"

She obeyed, her right fist still locked tightly around the handle of her weapon. Bermont clipped the line, then paused and glanced at the rifle-style weapon. "Hey. What does that thing fire?"

"What?"

He tapped the weapon. "This. What does it shoot?"

She looked at it and shrugged. "It is a laser."

"Laser, huh?" He plucked it out of her hand, despite her attempt to hang onto it.

"Hey!"

"Relax, lady," he muttered, flipping the rifle over in his hands. "Let's see. Control panel...can't read that shit...red light. That probably means it's hot. Let me guess, this must be the—"

The weapon hummed in his hand and a sharp crack and sizzling sound made him jump. He dropped the weapon in surprise while looking over at the section of wall he'd just melted down.

"Whoa! Holy shit," he whispered. "That's impressive."

▶▶▶

People screamed as Milla stepped through the mangled doors she'd bent and ripped open like paper. She really couldn't blame them. She knew firsthand how frightening it was to see a faceless figure, especially one that had just mangled a pair of security doors with its bare hands.

Not that the doors were all that strong, she had to admit. Strong enough for civilian use, but certainly not constructed out of anything that resembled actual armor. And since they were inside, they weren't designed to withstand the elements, either.

Just ordinary, average people who weren't using strength-augmenting alien armor.

Ironically, they'd probably have been less afraid if she'd used a laser to cut her way in.

Milla Chans took a moment to examine the area and noted that there were several people with palm lasers pointing shakily at her. She slowly held up her hands and made it a point to not make any sudden motions.

"I am Ithan Chans," she told them. "Colonial Navy."

The palm lasers stayed pointed at her, but the shaking subsided a little, so she breathed easier. Palm lasers were intended more for survival than anything else. They started fires, heated rocks, cut things, those sorts of utilities. However, they were powerful enough to injure a person, even fatally in extreme cases, and she had no desire to put the alien armor to a serious test.

There was, of course, absolutely no reason for any of these people to actually own them, but Milla found that people in the cities tended to do strange things for no apparent reason. She doubted any of them had ever actually *used* the small devices; however, it didn't stop them from acquiring them.

She wouldn't mind, really, if they would acquire a training course at the same time. Unfortunately, most people who wished to own such things really had no idea what they would do with them should they actually acquire them.

The people calmed a bit more, and Milla reached back and pulled the tabs that broke her suit's seal. She pulled the faceless helmet off and looked around. "I require a communications terminal."

They stared at her for a long moment before one of them finally stepped forward. "M…My rooms are through here."

Milla nodded, not realizing that her minute gesture was lost in the suit, and walked in the direction he was pointing. She had to duck a little to get through the door but still managed to scrape the top of the helmet along the frame. The armor only gave her a small increase over her normal height, but it felt like she was towering over everything she encountered.

The terminal was in a table in the center of the room, and she winced at the thud her hand made when she reached out to turn the system on.

"Sorry," she told the man who had followed her into his rooms, trying to ignore the rather large crack that had appeared in the terminal. Luckily, it didn't seem to affect operation, so she keyed her code into the military channels with extremely delicate precision and soon found herself face-to-helm with a rather shocked-looking secretary.

"This is Ithan Milla Chans, Colonial Navy, identification code Senthe Auros Bonis Kirof Bonis Senthe," she rattled off calmly. "I need to speak with the commander in charge of systems defense as soon as possible. I have information concerning the unidentified ship in orbit and the soldiers on the ground."

▶▶▶

Fleet Admiral Tanner was still trying to scrounge up any available assets to step between the sole remaining Drasin cruiser and, if necessary, the alien ship that had taken to hunting the Drasin, for no discernible reasons.

He'd left the command of the ground units in the hands of Cmdt. Nero Jehan, his alternate in the Colonial Army, but judging from the constant flow of contraband language flowing from the adjacent communications pit, Commandant Jehan wasn't having much more luck than he was.

Tanner sighed, taking care to do so quietly, wiped his brow as he crossed the short distance to his peer, and laid a hand on the roughly built man's shoulder.

Jehan was from one of the outer colonies, one that had so far only been populated for a few centuries and had grown up in real wilderness, not in the carefully monitored and tamed preserves that still existed here on Ranquil. That was undoubtedly one of the reasons the man had chosen a military career in the first place and certainly led him to his vocation in the ground forces.

It also made him a little rougher than most people from the Five Colonies were willing to tolerate.

"Calmly, Nero," Tanner said as the mountain of a man half jumped and spun on him.

Tanner stood a full head and a half shorter than his army counterpart, but he didn't flinch as the big man turned, and it was the bigger man who backed down first.

"Apologies, Rael," Nero Jehan mumbled, shaking his head.

"No need," Tanner assured him. "However, do check your language; it makes my naval personnel nervous."

The ogre of a man smiled ruefully, rubbing the back of his head in slight chagrin. The ultracivilized culture that his diminutive friend came from was hard for him to work his way around easily, as he'd grown up in a community of less than one million people that had been spread over several hundred square kilometers of rugged forest and brushland.

Here on Ranquil, with over five billion people living within only a few square kilometers, he had found that there were few people, indeed, who wanted to be around him.

Rael Tanner had been one of those few.

"Apologies again," he said, glancing back over his shoulder.

"How's it going?" Tanner asked, nodding in the direction of Jehan's staff.

Jehan grunted a sound that communicated more annoyance and disgust than all the illegal curses Tanner had ever heard. "I've lost three brigades so far. Enemy losses are negligible."

Tanner frowned.

It didn't make *sense*, dammit!

The weapons they carried, the shipboard tools of destruction, were more powerful than some suns! One laser rifle could render a small mountain to molten slag in short order, its beam able to radiate focused energy that was on par with the surface of a small star. The shipboard weapons were even more powerful.

The Drasin shouldn't be able to stand up to that. No one should be.

"Have your people seen any of the objects that fell from that alien shuttle?" Tanner asked.

"Soldiers, not objects," Jehan corrected.

Tanner hadn't heard that. He looked up sharply. "Oh?"

"Heavy armor. Loud weapons," Jehan told him in that clipped way of his. "*Their* weapons kill Drasin."

Tanner blinked.

Well, at least something was killing Drasin.

All he had to do was figure out who, what, and of course, why. Then maybe he might be able to save his world.

Tanner was about to reply when one of his aides came running up.

"Admiral, sir…We have a call for you."

"I don't have time for—" Tanner started to say.

"It's from Ithan Chans…assigned to the *Carlache*."

Tanner froze.

He turned slowly, his eyes falling on the flushed aide. "That is not possible."

"Her identification has been verified, sir."

"Show me."

The aide nodded, passing him a remote terminal. Tanner flipped it over, looking at the picture on it. "That is not any ensign I've ever encountered."

His dry tone caused the aide to flush. "She claims to be wearing body armor, Admiral."

"Armor? May I see?" Jehan asked.

Tanner handed him the terminal without question.

"This is the armor those soldiers wear," the big man said after a moment's glance. "I've been receiving reports on it from all over the city."

Tanner considered that thoughtfully. "So, what is she saying?"

"That she has information on the unknown ship and soldiers, Admiral," his aide replied. "She wants to be brought in."

"Do so. Send a detail. Make certain that she is alone and unarmed, then put her on a secure terminal," Tanner said finally. "I want to talk to this Ithan Chans."

"Yes, Admiral."

▶▶▶

"Listen to me carefully, Lieutenant," Major Brinks growled. "I don't care if that laser can play the 'Star-Spangled Banner.' I read over thirty of the damned ET spider things coming your way now, and I want you and the rest of your team out of there—now."

Lieutenant Bermont didn't look happy over the order, but he acknowledged it.

"All right, I'm sending in two more chutes to pick you up," the major told him, waving off a reply. "I'd suggest you don't miss them."

"Yes, sir," Bermont said over the network. "Understood."

"You'd better," Brinks growled, wiping the channel clear with a finger flick and an eye blink.

He was watching two full-fledged firefights and one cautious approach while at the same time eavesdropping on Milla as she talked to her boss. Of the four, he was firmly convinced that it was the conversation that would prove to be the most important, but he had an artillery barrage to direct.

"Sniper teams, prepare to direct a mortar barrage to Lieutenant Bermont's position," he ordered. "Thermobaric munitions are cleared for use."

▶▶▶

"Russell!" Bermont yelled, though he didn't have to. "Pack your shit, boy! We are leaving!"

Corporal Russell glanced back, nodded once, and emptied the rest of his clip into the approaching wave that was clambering up the slick, smooth sides of the pyramidal structure's tube-like pylons.

There were more and more of them now, as if they were attracted to anything that could kill one of their numbers.

Bermont wasn't sure if they had a tactical network of their own and were deployed to cover the hottest spots or...something else, but the net effect was the same. The soldier drones were converging on his and Russell's location, and with each one either of them took down, several more appeared out of the woodwork.

So to speak, of course, seeing as how Bermont had yet to actually see any wood.

He emptied his own clip, the heavy scramjet rounds blasting from the muzzle of his rifle accelerated by the rail gun to lethal speeds even before the scramjet engines ignited. He felt a warble through his suit as the weapon went dry. Then a flicker of motion from above caught his attention.

He hit the clip ejector with a smooth motion, rising from his kneeling position as he saw Russell do the same. The fresh clip slapped into the rifle, even as he looked up to see the CM chute swoop down over his position.

In a practiced maneuver, Bermont grabbed the chute's handle in his left hand as it flew past, letting the familiar sensation of giddy weightlessness pass over him as it enveloped him in its field. Then the building under him dropped away as he was pulled into the air.

A few meters away, Russell was already airborne and whooping out some mad war cry as he sprayed fire back in the direction he had just come from.

Bermont watched as the creatures converged on the top of the pyramid-shaped city, milling around in apparent confusion, as their intended targets were no longer waiting there for them. There were some halfhearted attempts to find them, he noted, but they didn't seem to be looking *up*.

Bermont wondered how long that would last.

Long enough, he hoped.

▶▶▶

"Mortar unit...hold fire," Major Brinks ordered, watching the scene on the top of the immense pyramid over a kilometer away.

He could see the drone things still arriving, even as the ones already there milled around as if lost. It was better than he'd hoped, and the former marine major couldn't resist taking advantage of it.

He flashed back to the information they had on these things, thinking about what they had done to the first planet the *Odyssey* had seen them on. How they had begun taking it apart, piece by piece.

How they had apparently increased their population.

Doubling every three days.

He knew that they had to be destroyed, not merely defeated. That wasn't enough. Every single one of them that had landed on this world had to be wiped out in detail, without exception. He didn't know how they bred and thus couldn't take a chance that one of them might, just might, be able to replenish their numbers in only a few weeks.

So, finally, as the arrival of new drones began to peter out and he saw some of those already there start to look antsy about leaving, Major Brinks opened his mouth to give the order.

CHAPTER 23

▶ ARCHANGEL LEAD SLID to a controlled stop only a few meters from the rear bulkhead, its reverse jets flaring brightly as Stephanos stepped on them in order to kill his inertia. Without the dedicated fighter traps used on the lower deck, landing the Archangels on the *Odyssey* required a great deal more skill than normal.

Even so, he stopped with a comfortable, though narrow, window and leaned his helmeted head back against the seat as one of the trundling loaders made its way out to him.

The entire flight operations staff was scuttling over the deck in their hard suits, working feverishly through the vacuum of the flight deck, and he could see that the large equipment elevators were moving nonstop as they transported men and equipment to the lower deck.

The fighter rocked, drawing Steph's attention as the loader backed into the blunt nose of his fighter and locked into place. Then, with the steady gait of the indefatigable machine, the fighter and its pilot were turned around and guided straight to one of the immense airlocks that transported shuttles to the repair bays above them.

He had to wait for three other Archangels to make the run and watched as they were moved into place beside him. He was itching to be out of his cockpit now that he was back aboard the *Odyssey* but forced himself to wait until the four fighters were in place and the airlock lift rumbled steadily upward.

From that point, it was only minutes to when his fighter was locked down, his cockpit pressure equalized, and Stephanos popped the seal. He crawled out of the tightly fitted bolster seat and accepted a hand from one of the flight crew as they, in turn, crawled all over his plane with their tools and scanners.

"How'd you do, sir?" one of them asked as Steph's feet clanged to the bare deck, boots locking him in place.

"Chalk five more up, Ben," he said, half smiling at the man.

"Yes, sir." The tech saluted him.

Stephanos moved to the closest call terminal and keyed in a request to speak to the captain.

Weston must have been waiting for the call, because in a few seconds he was looking back through the terminal screen. "Good to have you back, Steph."

"Good to be aboard, Captain," Stephanos said tiredly. "How long have we got?"

"That's the good news," Weston told him. "The mother ship you took on has apparently decided that it doesn't want to tangle with the two of us just now. It's adjusted its orbit to scale outside ours, about two-point-three AU out...It's not going away, but it's not coming any closer."

Steph let out a long sigh. "Thank God, sir. My team needs as much time as we can get."

"See to them, and get some rest. We'll call you if we need you."

"Aye, Captain." The pilot saluted, albeit somewhat sloppily, and smiled wearily as the picture flickered out.

Stephanos half turned, noting the three other pilots standing some distance behind him.

"Grab a shower and hug your bunks," he ordered them. "We're standing down for now."

They didn't cheer, or even comment much, which was a testament to how tired they were now that the fight-or-flight adrenaline surge had started to leave them. Instead, the three pilots just trudged toward the lifts, and Stephanos turned back to the airlock as it started to rumble back down to the flight deck.

Weston stood up, releasing the restraints that kept him secured to the command chair in case of extreme maneuvers or combat damage and walked over to where Ens. Susan Lamont was talking steadily over her damage-control channels.

"How bad is it, Susan?" he asked, leaning over her shoulder and resting a hand on the console.

"Could be worse, sir," she said, tapping in a command. "CPO Corrin's got the patch underway in the forward weapons control rooms. Should be another hour or so, and we'll be ready to repressurize them."

"Armor?"

"Four more hours, sir." Lamont replied, glancing up. "We have a crew outside putting the slab into place, but we'll have to recall them if that ship heads back in."

Weston nodded soberly.

They certainly couldn't leave men out in the black; if it came down to combat maneuvers, it would be nothing short of a death sentence.

"The flight deck?"

"That's a bit trickier," Lamont told him, calling up a schematic.

The picture on the screen showed an immense gash, right up the center of the lower flight deck. The edges were melted down from the extreme heat they'd experienced, and the beam width was over four meters wide at its worst.

"We didn't lose much there since the deck is almost never under pressure, anyway," Lamont said calmly, "but the enemy beam sliced through the CM circuits that made up the fighter traps. They've got to be rewired before we repair the deck damage. It's going to be at least twenty hours, sir."

"Fine. Good work, Susan."

"Thank you, sir," she said, back straightening.

Weston moved across the bridge to the tactical console. "Waters."

"Sir?" the kid said, looking up.

"How'd they get through our armor?"

Waters shook his head. "I'm afraid they just overpowered it, sir. No tricks, nothing fancy, they just burned right through it."

Weston winced.

That was bad.

The cam-plate modifications were capable of reflecting away over 98 percent of the beam energy of any class-one laser. That meant that the beam power they were facing was such that less than 2 percent was enough to kill them.

Weston didn't want to think of what would happen if they had to face more than one enemy vessel at once, or if one enemy got a lucky shot through one of the multitude of chinks in their armor where the cam-plates didn't cover.

"All right!" was all he said out loud, though. "Analyze everything we've got on these things, and make sure that our labs are doing the same. And, Waters?"

"Yes, sir?"

"Tell the eggheads that they're on a deadline here," Weston said. "I don't want answers two years from now; I want them *now*."

"Aye, aye, Captain."

▶▶▶

"Fire Plan Romeo, Mark," Brinks said as he watched the overview of the fight through his suit's HUD.

"Romeo confirmed," the signal came back an instant later.

"Engage," Brinks responded, his eyes watching the crowd of drones that had gathered at the top of the tubular pyramid that Bermont and his team had just pulled out of.

"Engaging," the calm answer came back.

From his position, it was anticlimactic—at least at first. The single word was spoken in confirmation and a series of lights lit up as the sniper teams opened fire according to the Plan Romeo schedule.

Their computer network controlled the exact timing, of course, and the fighting was far enough away that the launches were less than nothing to Brinks, even with suit enhancement, had he been inclined to watch for them.

He hadn't been.

Brinks watched the target zone instead, knowing that when the thermobaric rounds detonated, it would be climactic enough.

▶▶▶

Thermobaric weapons, sometimes also known as fuel air explosives, were a known quantity in military technology for a long time before they entered into truly widespread service in the early twenty-first century, moving from weapons that had to be deployed by large aircraft to forty-millimeter grenade versions placed solidly in the hands of individual soldiers.

Five separate shells were fired at Brinks's command; fins and computer controls guided the little kamikazes along a carefully selected course. As they topped their arc and started to fall toward the Drasin drones, the shells spread out in a geometric pentagon that kept the enemy mass at its center.

When they reached within forty meters of the targets, the first-stage explosion detonated.

The shells ruptured, blowing out their payloads with a sudden massive force and sprayed aerosol chemicals over the entire region. As the area became laden with the harsh, poisonous chemicals, the second-stage ignition detonated.

The resulting rumble was like a clap of thunder directly overhead and shook the air for over a kilometer.

A firestorm raced through the air, jumping from molecule to molecule of the harsh chemicals, erupting in an orgy of destructive power that forced the air aside with effects best compared to a nuclear weapon.

The overpressure wave erupted on all sides, casting out farther and farther as the chemicals ignited, until it met the Drasin and, by extension, the overpressure waves erupting from each of the other shells.

▶▶▶

"Identify yourself," Rael Tanner growled at the screen, looking straight at a face he didn't recognize but which matched the computer files they had for one Ithan Milla Chans.

The figure, clad in alien body armor, stiffened and saluted. "Ithan Milla Chans, Admiral."

"Ithan Chans died when the *Carlache* went down with all hands," Tanner told her coldly. "I lost a good friend on that ship, and I'm not inclined to be flippant about his fate."

The woman looking at him paled, her eyes widening, and her jaw locked momentarily. After a second, she got herself back under control. "Admiral, I survived the loss of the *Carlache* and was rescued by the Starship *Odyssey*."

"The ship in orbit?" Tanner asked, not willing to give up the chance to identify the ship in question.

"Yes, Admiral," the supposed Ithan Chans replied.

"Why don't you tell me who they are?" Tanner said coldly. "Assuming that you are who you claim to be."

"They are…" Milla's face twisted. "I believe them to be of the Others, Admiral."

Tanner heard a hissed intake of air, but ignored it. "Ithan, I don't believe in myths."

Milla looked shocked but didn't cross him on the statement.

Tanner ignored her look. "So what I'll presume you mean is that although they are not a Colonial vessel, however, they *are* human."

"That…that's correct, Admiral."

"What frequencies do they use?" Tanner asked. "I wish to speak with their captain."

"They communicate on radio frequency, sir."

Tanner grimaced.

Radio.

That was irritating. He wasn't even sure that they had anything that would transmit on so low a band.

He glanced over his shoulder. "Find me a way to talk to these people."

"What? But we…" The technician paled suddenly under a withering look. "Uh…yes, Admiral."

Tanner turned back to Milla. "What else?"

"Admiral, they have soldiers on the ground here and—"

"Yes, I am aware of that," Rael told her. "They are engaging the Drasin at several key points and have been—" A sudden explosion of curses erupting from the army control pit startled him, and Tanner looked over. "What the hell is going on over there?"

His naval ratings looked at him in shock, but he ignored them.

"Admiral," one of the army ratings came running over, "there has been an explosion over the third habitat."

"Damage?"

"Minimal, sir, if any," the rating replied. "But it was…unexpected…and very, very large, sir."

Rael glanced back at Milla. "Your friends?"

"I don't know, sir," she replied, hefting something. "One moment, I'll check."

▶ ▶ ▶

The overlapping compression waves ripped through the Drasin drones like five separate hurricanes of power all tearing and rending in different directions. One drone would be lifted into the air by the front of one wave and then slammed into a dozen other drones and torn in another direction completely as it intersected the front of a second overpressure wave.

From the outside, the scene was hellish, the sort of thing one might expect from an action movie, flames and smoke obscuring the deadly consequences of the eruption of power.

Several of the drones were thrown clear off the peak of the pyramid, flying out into the air hundreds of feet above the ground until gravity took over and guided them down to, what Brinks hoped would be, extremely rough landings.

Just in case, he tagged each of them in turn and sent orders to his outlying units to check on them as soon as possible.

More often, it was parts of the Drasin that flew out of the miniature holocaust, legs here, bodies there, and so forth.

Brinks had those tagged as well, but on a lower priority.

The rumbling sound died out slowly, the crackling thunder softening as he looked over the scene at maximum magnification.

▶▶▶

"We counted thirty-eight drones there, sir."

Nero nodded, looking at the information. Whatever those other soldiers had done, it had ripped through the Drasin group like nothing he'd ever seen. Fiery explosions were actually rare in combat. They normally were rather subdued events with a lot of noise, assuming you weren't in space, but very little else, other than smoke or shrapnel.

This, though, was something else.

The computers had registered at least twelve confirmed kills in that instant conflagration, and the tally was going up as the smoke cleared.

Across in the other control pit, Rael Tanner looked at the faceless visage that had been Milla Chans and waited for information that only she could provide him.

After a long moment, the face nodded and the armored hands came up and pulled the helmet off again.

Milla Chans looked a little pale, which Tanner could understand well enough, but in control as she spoke. "It was them, Admiral. They managed to group many of the Drasin together in one place…Major Brinks assures me that they analyzed the building structure for any danger before he ordered the attack."

Tanner forced himself to nod as if it made much sense to him. "Ithan, what are their intentions?"

"Sir?"

"Why are they helping us?"

Milla looked confused for a moment. He thought he saw her shrug, but it was hard to tell through the armor she wore. "I don't know for certain, Admiral. All I know is that their captain told me that he wouldn't—couldn't—stand by and watch an entire planet die. He saw what happened at Port Fuielles, sir—and at Duorkin."

Tanner winced.

"Port Fuielles as well?" he asked painfully.

"Yes, sir," Milla said. "The *Odyssey* rescued five hundred survivors…But that was all."

Five hundred.

Tanner closed his eyes, whispering a few words for the loss of fifty million people.

He shook his head. "Ithan, I think you should come to the command center. We need to communicate with these people, and for the moment, you are our only method."

"Of course, sir." Milla bowed her head. "I will arrive as soon as possible."

"Good," he told her. "I will await you."

▶▶▶

Bermont hit the rooftop running, letting the chute soar up and away from him as he skidded to a crouch by the edge of the insanely tall skyscraper and looked over at the clearing smoke that obscured the place he had just left.

He whistled, the sound audible only to him, as his HUD enhanced and magnified the scene of destruction for him.

"Goddamn," he muttered, switching to a thermal overlay.

For a moment, his HUD just went white as the temperature overloaded its initial settings, but in a second, the computer adapted and altered the sensitivity of the sensors until it could differentiate through the rapidly dispersing heat of the explosion.

"Oh shit," he breathed a few moments later. "Oh shit."

There were still moving heat sources in there.

"Major," he accessed the command channel, "we've got a problem."

▶▶▶

Brinks cursed. "How many?"

"About seventy percent of them survived, sir."

"Jesus Christ," the major cursed. "What the hell are these things?"

The words went out over the command channel and to all the members of the impromptu war council.

Savoy answered, "They're obviously adapted to a different environment than this, sir. I'm guessing that the TBs just didn't have enough heat to cook 'em, and the chemicals apparently aren't harmful to them, either."

"But the concussion should have been enough to rip them apart, anyway!" Sergeant Rogers objected over the line. "Nothing gets up after a blast like that!"

"Underground, you might be right, Sarge," Savoy told him. "But out in the open, even with the tandem controlled blasts...Apparently, there's at least one thing that can get up."

"I'm with Sav," Bermont said after a moment, frowning over the HUD. "I saw what that laser rifle could do...If that can't cook these things, they're not going to be burned by a little explosion. We ripped a few of them up with the concussion, but the ones that survived that weren't affected by the other components of the TB."

Brinks growled. "All right. We still have to clear them out. Suggestions?"

"Major," Bermont said, "I think we're just gonna have to get down and dirty with these guys. I don't see any slick trick that'll take 'em out."

"He's right, Major," Sergeant Rogers replied.

Brinks nodded slowly, almost unwillingly, and though he wasn't opposed to the idea, he'd rather not risk his men that much. "All right...Go to it."

"Yes, sir," the chorus came back.

▶▶▶

"Report coming back from Major Brinks, sir," Waters said as Weston turned around.

"How are the teams doing?"

"Not badly, sir." Waters frowned. "Some injuries, only one that looks serious. The major is requesting that we deploy carnivores so he can re-task his chutes for squad deployment."

Weston nodded. "Do it."

Launching carnivores during the firefight wouldn't have been possible, given that the drones required either the *Odyssey* or a shuttle to control them, and all of the above had been quite busy at the time. Now it was feasible, so he'd give the major whatever he could.

"What's his progress?"

"Unknown at this time." Waters shook his head. "They've eliminated some of the ground troops the enemy vessel launched, but they aren't certain of total numbers."

"Give him his drones, Mr. Waters," Weston said. "Have Commander Roberts and the auxiliary bridge take up their controls for the moment."

"Yes, sir."

"After that, consider yourself relieved," Weston told him. "Get yourself something to eat and a cup of coffee."

"Aye, aye, Captain."

Weston turned away from the young man and looked back at the screens that depicted the outside orbit of the remaining Drasin ship as it circled far out beyond the planet's orbit, waiting.

Waiting for what was the question.

CHAPTER 24

▶ THE FIRST OF the three carnivore recon drones slid into position over the city while Major Brinks looked out over the incredibly complicated mesh of buildings and structures that made up the population center.

"Switching carnivores to active thermal scanning," Commander Roberts's voice came crisply over the network. "Drones Two and Three are descending to two hundred meters...Drone One is being tasked at eighteen thousand meters. Please set waypoints for deployment, Major."

"Thank you, Commander," Brinks said, tagging several key points for close overflies. "I'm dispatching troops to these points now."

"Confirmed. I'll have detailed recon data waiting for them," Roberts replied.

"Excellent," Brinks said, eyeing another section. "I've also dispatched Savoy's team to investigate an apparent wreck. It looks dead, but I'd appreciate it if you could drop Drone One to a tactical altitude."

"Roger," Roberts replied. "Primary carnivore descending to eighteen thousand meters. Could you relay a waypoint for this wreck?"

"One second, Commander," Brinks said, tagging the location, then attaching all the information they had already gathered to the waypoint before shooting it up to the *Odyssey*. "Done."

"Confirmed. Wait, One."

Brinks waited as patiently as he could, knowing that the computers and technicians on the *Odyssey* were already meshing the various scans from his chutes and suit sensors into one high-resolution scan.

"Confirmed. Drone One will remain at a maximum tactical altitude. Good luck, Major."

"Thanks, Commander," Brinks said.

▶▶▶

"Man, this shit sucks," Corporal Deacon griped as he and the other two members of his squad ducked under a fallen wall, the huge slab of whatever-it-was still intact after having been blasted clear off the building.

Sergeant Steward made a face behind the anonymous plate of his armored helm but didn't respond as he lay back against the solid material and slowly pushed his gun over the edge and twisted it around.

"Looks like...five of them," he said after a moment, pulling his rifle back. "Everyone have their weapons set to thermal guidance?"

"Do I look like an officer?" Deacon asked in amusement.

"No, and you never will, if I have anything to say about it," Lieutenant Mackay replied in like manner. "We're good to go, Sarge."

Steward nodded in the exaggerated motions necessary when wearing powered armor. "All right. Spread out a little, and remember, at this range, we'll only have a two-, maybe three-degree flight correction…So don't pretend you're in an action flick, all right, Deac?"

Corporal Deacon rolled his eyes but only nodded tersely in response as the three of them spread out.

"Wait! What are you doing?" someone called.

Deacon glanced back, looking at the local cop who'd been tagging along with them. "Relax, stay low."

Constable Tsari didn't have much to say in response to that, so she did as she was told and hugged closely to the wreckage as the three soldiers spread out.

There was no traditional three count; the three of them didn't need one in this case. Their linked systems shared a few million calculations, estimated the location of the enemy from indirect heat sources, and flashed a green light on their HUDs.

Together, they rose up, weapons leveling as they brought them snug to their shoulders and squeezed the triggers. The air was immediately filled with the whining of the capacitors discharging in rapid-fire sequence and the roar of their bullets going supersonic, letting a hundred of the lethal little killers fill the air.

The Drasin reacted almost as fast, two of them jumping for height, their tough outer carapaces somehow letting them dig their mandible-like claws into the obsidian-smooth material of the surrounding buildings as they moved to bring their weapons to bear.

The other three spun around, weapon mandibles coming up, only to be chewed to shreds as the heavy rounds struck home. Each of the three caught the bullets originally intended for five as the guidance systems in each round redirected them away from the two escapees.

Even as those three Drasin fell, the two that had escaped opened fire and the sizzling beams slammed into the fallen wall, one of them tracking fast enough to catch Lieutenant Mackay as he twisted aside.

Flames and nauseous gases erupted from the armor as he fell, the material being vaporized by the extreme heat and force of the blast.

As Mackay hit the ground, Steward and Deacon raised their rifles, threw themselves aside, rolled in the air, and fired.

The weapons made their unique whine-crack once more, sending dozens of hefty killers upward in the reflex shots as the two troopers hit the ground hard and slid to a stop.

Neither of them had aimed particularly well, but it didn't really matter, because as the bullets leapt forward, their eager little forward sensors detected the heat of the Drasin drones above them almost before they even left the barrels of their rifles. The hardwired nano-circuitry took a moment to glimpse at the few lines of onboard software, just to confirm the target parameters. They happily raced off in search of the warmth they were designed to seek.

Less than a tenth of a second after the weapons fired, the Drasin drones were torn apart and fell to the ground.

Sergeant Steward ended his slide with a reverse shoulder roll and came back up to his feet, his rifle seeking out any other targets around them as he shouted over the tac-net, "Deac! Check on him!"

"You got it, Sarge!" Deacon said, already on the move.

The corporal hit the ground, skidding on his armored knees, and came to a stop by the fallen lieutenant, then automatically called up the medical information from Mackay's suit.

"Telemetry from his vitals aren't looking good!" he shouted, the suit already initiating defib.

Mackay jerked once, his back arching off the ground as the suit shunted a jolt through his body. His face mask cleared as the armor automatically shifted to medical mode, letting Deacon see Mackay's eyes open wide from the shock, stare around unblinkingly, and settle back down.

"Still nothing!"

Deacon hit him again, jolting the soldier off the ground as his suit finished applying foam to the breach and the drab-green substance started to harden.

A series of beeps and symbols flashed across Deacon's HUD and he let out a breath. "Got him back, Sarge, but he's in a bad way!"

Steward didn't answer as he finished his circuit and let his rifle drop from his shoulder as he shifted to the command emergency channel.

"Major, we've got a man down. I say again, man down."

"Roger that," Brinks replied tersely. "Am redirecting a chute for pickup. Stand by."

Steward confirmed the transmission and signed off, leaving Brinks to do his job. He now had two seriously injured soldiers and no immediate evac point. He directed the chute to pick up Mackay after shifting his com-suite to locate Milla.

"Miss Chans," he said after a moment.

"Yes, Major?" Milla paused, head cocked as she listened. She stopped mid-motion, not paying attention to the men escorting her to the command and control center, much to their annoyance.

They froze behind her, though the man in front moved on for a few steps before realizing that no one was following. He turned. "Ithan? What are you doing?"

She held up a hand. "One moment. Yes, Major, there are extremely good medical facilities in the city. Yes, Major, I am on my way to speak with the admiral in charge of systems defense. I will arrange it."

"Arrange what?" the third man demanded.

"Medical treatment for injured soldiers," she told him calmly. "There are two seriously injured men in need of medical attention."

"Ithan, we have to get you to the admiral. You can deal with them once we arrive."

"No, I will deal with it while we travel. You have a com, of course?"

"Of course, but—"

"Then contact the admiral," she told him coolly, starting forward again as she motioned to him with one hand. "Now."

▶▶▶

Across the city, far from the heavier built-up sections where the majority of the fighting was currently contained, Lieutenant Savoy and his geek squad were moving toward a badly chewed-up piece of machinery that looked more like a fallen rock than the remnants of a lander craft.

"What kind of radiation are we getting off this, L.T.?" Burke asked, his weapon traversing the wreckage as they moved forward.

"It's hot, but not smoking," Savoy responded, eyeing the levels carefully.

They were peaking at lethal levels for unprotected humans but nothing that would seriously endanger armored soldiers. The odd thing was where the spikes were in the EM field. Most of them were very low in the spectrum for radiation rather than the higher-energy wavelengths.

Another odd thing was the mist that had formed around the wreckage, making the entire approach feel like something out of an old horror flick.

"Jesus," Mehn whispered, watching as the mist curled up around his legs, reaching higher as it poured out from the wreck. "Where the fuck is this coming from?"

"Looks like water mist..." Savoy replied. "Probably a coolant breach, or maybe their reactor is running hot. The heat might pull water vapor out of the atmosphere."

"It's fuckin' spooky, boss," Burke said.

"Yeah," Savoy whispered as he stepped up to the huge rend in the hull of the lander, "tell me about it."

No one had anything to say to that, so Savoy just swung his rifle around the corner of the rip, watching the results from the built-in camera that beamed back to his HUD as he swept the interior.

"Looks clear," he said, pulling back. "Mehn, cover me."

"You got it, boss."

Savoy crouched down and jumped up in a calculated motion that brought him up to the lip of the tear, landing just inside. His suit systems automatically adjusted to the low-light levels, bringing up a computer enhancement over his HUD that included thermal and light amplification. Savoy automatically rejected the suit's query concerning active night-vision systems while stepping inside cautiously.

"It's a wreck in here," he muttered after a moment.

"Say that again, boss," Burke replied, landing just where Savoy had been and looking around for himself. "Must have been one rough landing."

"Don't let your guard down," Mehn reminded them both. "We saw that these things are tougher than you'd expect."

"Right," Savoy nodded, pushing forward slowly as he looked around. "More to the point, I don't see any bodies, boys."

"Shit," Burke muttered, crouching just beside the tear as Mehn jumped up. "I don't like the sounds of that."

"Can't say I much like it, either," Savoy said. "But them's the cards we've been dealt. I'm going to move farther in. Give me some cover, okay, you two?"

"We got your back, boss," Mehn said.

Savoy swung his rifle around a corner, scanning quickly before he ducked around in a crouch to let his suit's more effective sensors give him a second opinion. Nothing was in sight, so he rose to his feet and moved forward.

▶▶▶

Admiral Tanner looked at the face on the screen and frowned. "What is it, Saren?"

"The ithan wishes to speak to you," the man said stiffly.

"I told you to bring her here as fast as possible…"

"I am…we are…that is," the man replied. "However, she insists on speaking to you as we travel."

"Very well," Tanner sighed. "Hand her the com."

The image jiggled a little and came to rest on the smooth, faceless armor that was even disconcerting over a com.

"Admiral."

"What is it, Ithan? I'm quite occupied at the moment—" Tanner began.

"The soldiers from the *Odyssey* have incurred injuries," Milla interrupted him. "Their emergency craft has been redirected to rescue pilots lost in the outer system, so they have no local medical support at this instant. I'm told that they can, of course, redirect a shuttle to supply them with what they need, but it will take time…"

Tanner nodded. "One moment, Ithan."

He stepped back while moving over to the control pit that handled ground operations. "Nero!"

"Yes, Rael?" the big man asked, stepping up.

"The soldiers from the ship have had casualties. They would appreciate medical aid," Tanner told his counterpart. "Would security concerns permit redirecting them to one of your hospitals?"

"Of course," Nero replied. "I'll provide you with a list immediately and—"

"No need," Tanner said. "It's in Central. I'll inform Ithan Chans of the locations."

"Please do not neglect to inform me of which ones they are directed to," Nero said. "I will ensure that they are received without undue trouble."

Tanner nodded and headed back.

▶ ▶ ▶

"Roger that, Miss Chans. Can you locate these sites on an aerial map?" Brinks asked, looking at Milla's tense face over his HUD.

"I…I think so," she said hesitantly. "Can you show me this map?"

"One second…" Brinks activated one of the command override circuits while snaking into her system using the boot camp back door. He called up the carnivore data and fed it to her via the HUD.

Milla watched, surprised at the image of the city floating in front of her, translucent but clear enough to see. Wherever she looked, a blue circle seemed to follow, and she quickly realized that it was somehow tracking her eyesight.

"Here…" she said, looking at one of the hospital sites. "This is one of the places."

Brinks downloaded the information. "All right. Thank you, Miss Chans. I'm redirecting our wounded there now."

"It is…nothing, Major," she told him. "It's the least we owe you."

"Just get to your superiors, Miss Chans. We need to coordinate with your leadership if we want to finish this off," Brinks told her, shutting down the HUD back door and returning her to normal operations.

Redirecting the wounded to the new site took only a couple commands. He summoned another chute for himself.

There was no way he was going to entrust his people to a place he hadn't checked out first, if he had any choice in the matter.

▶ ▶ ▶

"This cannot be good," Lieutenant Savoy said after a long moment of silence while his team examined the interior of the wrecked pod.

"What is it, boss?" Burke asked, coming up behind him and stumbling to a halt as he saw what Savoy was looking at. "Oh shit."

"Eloquent, Burke. Worthy of the bards," Savoy said as he blew out a long breath, letting his armor's air-conditioning catch the moist air and whisk it away from the faceplate HUD.

"What the hell are you two blathering about?" Mehn asked as he stepped up, coming to a dead stop between the two of them and looking down—a long way down.

The hole in the deck was about five meters in diameter and seemed to bore right through the hull of the landing craft and into the hard ground beneath them.

"I'm getting a depth reading...Jesus...thirty meters... How'd they manage to dig that this fast?"

"Don't know, boss...But it can't be a good thing."

"Yeah..." Savoy shook his head. "All right, Burke, head back out and get one of the chutes in here."

"How come?" Burke objected. "The sensors on those things aren't gonna be worth much in that tight an area."

"I know that..." Savoy responded. "But my suit sensors will be. I'm going down there."

▶▶▶

Weston was sipping a steaming mug of coffee when the alert came in.

He dropped the mug unceremoniously into a recycling hatch and turned to the even younger ensign who was taking Waters's position. "What is it, Ensign?"

"Tachyon wakes, sir," she replied tensely, her eyes darting across her board. "I...I think its several ships decelerating from FTL."

"Put your readings up on the screen," he ordered.

The screen flickered, showing a computer enhancement of nicely animated blue particles being pushed ahead of something and breaking out and around, like the bow wave of a boat pushing itself through a calm lake.

Only there were five of them.

"Oh my God," someone whispered.

Weston ignored them.

At least now he knew what the last ship was waiting for.

And he'd been right, too.

He didn't like it.

CHAPTER 25

▶ LIEUTENANT SAVOY FLOATED in a nonexistent breeze as he dropped down the five-meter-wide hole, the CM chute lowering him slowly into the pit.

"Heat dissipation is roughly even," he reported, looking down through the thermal overlay that decorated his suit's HUD. "The walls are almost smooth, very regularly cut...but not glassy like a laser drill..."

His running commentary was relayed up to his tech squad and from them to the major and the *Odyssey*, so he kept speaking for the record as the walls continued to loom farther and farther above him.

"I'm approaching the bottom now...slowing chute deployment," he said, bringing himself to a stop just above the turn in the tunnel.

Savoy inverted himself, hooking one leg up and around the cable that held him suspended in the air, and commanded the chute to descend again. His head dipped below the curve of the tunnel a few seconds later and he stopped it again, watching through the thermal overlay down the tunnel, looking for any heat sources that might be the enemy drones.

"It's quiet down here," he said after a moment. "Nothing to indicate enemy activity."

Other than the tunnel itself, of course, he thought, without stating the obvious. After a long look, he made a choice. "All right, guys, I'm cutting the tether."

He unhooked his leg from the cable and snapped back upright as he triggered the release and dropped the remaining four meters to the ground. The sound of his landing echoed around him as he came down in a crouch, retrieving his rifle from where it was latched to the back of his armor.

In the passive night vision of his HUD, the tunnel appeared endless, vanishing off into eternity with only minor thermal variations apparent. The space around him cooled, only a few degrees above the air temperature, which was running at a relatively high thirty degrees Celsius.

Savoy took a few steps down the tunnel. "I'm switching to active night vision now."

A few motions brought up the options, and then he turned on the infrared spotlights built into the helmet and shoulders of his armor. The HUD lit up bright green. For a second, it instantly darkened as its filters kicked in. Now he could see a tunnel he estimated at about fifty meters long, with branches moving off to either side at roughly ten-meter intervals.

"Industrious little bastards," he muttered as he moved forward one foot in front of the other. Dry dirt and gravel crackled and crunched with each step as he began to plumb the depths of the alien tunnel system.

▶ ▶ ▶

The three small flying devices approached the medical center together, something that might have prompted an attempt at defending the building if the military command hadn't placed a call through several minutes earlier to warn the guards of the approach.

They spread out slightly as the lead device swooped in and dropped off a hulking figure that carried a weapon at least three times the size of their laser rifles. He, or it, walked directly to the closest guard, not showing any sign of caution or fear and spoke sharply.

"Is this the medical center?"

The guard nodded, blinking in surprise at the odd accent. He'd never heard anything quite like it; it was almost like a total lack of accent, a flatness that he couldn't place.

"Good," the hulking figure said, not moving but somehow giving the impression that he was doing something.

The other two devices approached, and the guards saw the limp figures dangling from them.

"Doctor!" the guard yelled over his shoulder, nodding at two of the others.

The other two guards stepped aside, and three of the medical staff rushed out with a hovering platform sliding obediently along behind them.

Immediately behind them were another three and another platform.

The guard turned back to the hulking figure and was surprised to see that the anonymous faceplate was no longer blacked out. He could see the face behind it, lit up by a series of soft-red lights. The grim-looking man actually looked a great deal more frightful than the impersonal black of the faceplate.

"Your people will need my help to open the armor," he said, walking toward the medical teams.

The guard signaled to the others and rushed along behind the hulking figure as he reached the first medical team.

They were puzzling over how to treat a man they couldn't seem to get onto their platform, let along physically reach. The hulking figure just grabbed the limp figure, disconnecting the cable that supported him effortlessly, and slung him onto the platform.

"The suit has a subsurface breach in case of medical emergencies," he told him in that curiously flat tone as he placed a finger alongside the prone man's helmet.

They couldn't see it, but Major Brinks initiated a physical link to the suit so that he could access a command set that wasn't available over any wireless link, for obvious reasons. Once the link was established, he ordered the suit to breach.

A hiss of escaping gas startled the team, causing many of them to jump back, and the suit split along the center of the chest, down along the abdomen. It then slid open on hidden pneumatics as Brinks popped the helmet seal and pried the clamshell armor from Lieutenant Mackay's head.

"You can treat him in the armor, or pull him out if you have to," Brinks told them brusquely, then turned and moved over to where Jaime Curtis was still hanging suspended above the ground by her cable connection to the chute.

The medical team stared after him for a second before the lead doctor shook her head and snapped at them. A few seconds later, the platform retreated into the facility with the three of them jogging alongside as they scanned and attached devices to their new patient.

▶▶▶

"If they continue their current deceleration," Waters told his captain, "they'll rendezvous with the other ship in eight hours. If he accelerates to match course with them on a least-time approach, we'll be facing all six of them in about twelve, sir."

Weston looked at the status board. The *Odyssey* would have its forward armor repaired long before that, but its flight deck would still be breached, though the circuits for the traps should be repaired by then. That would put the *Odyssey* in near-fighting trim, along with a full charge on her pulse torpedoes. This, even under ideal circumstances, placed the *Odyssey* at the wrong side of long odds. Weston shook his head, letting his PDA clatter to the console in front of him and looking over at Susan Lamont.

"All right, what's the status on the Archangels?"

"Not as bad as we'd feared, but they're still down by four pilots. No fatalities, but three of the injured pilots have major radiation burns from cockpit hits, and we have one man with a head injury. We think his CM field collapsed when he ejected his cockpit," Ensign Lamont said. "Counting Clarke, that brings our total fighter complement down by just over a third."

Weston nodded.

"Further," Waters spoke up again, "I'm afraid that the Archangels just don't seem to be carrying enough firepower to really damage the enemy cruisers. We'll need them for fighter coverage, but they're not going to shift the odds substantially."

Weston didn't like to admit it, but the young man was most likely right. The weapons load for the Archangels wasn't intended for the level of power being thrown around in these engagements. Even the heaviest missiles they had available for the fighters were originally intended to sink seaborne battleships and dreadnaughts. Weapons that appeared to be roughly the equivalent of popguns against these alien cruisers.

"All right, I need alternatives here. Waters, talk to your department, talk to the civilian researchers, talk to God himself if you have to, but get them to me. If I can't use the Archangels, find me something I *can* use," he told the young man, then turned to Lamont. "Get as many people on the repairs as you can, and have Engineering start siphoning off more power from the reactor to the auxiliary capacitors. I want as many charges in the pulse tubes as I can get this time."

"Aye, aye, Captain," they both replied, stiffening as they gave him a quick salute and turned to their tasks.

Weston picked up his induction mic and slapped it onto his jaw. "Commander Roberts."

"Yes, Captain?" the commander's voice returned a moment later.

"I'm coming up to the auxiliary bridge to discuss the current situation."

"Yes, sir, I'll be waiting."

Weston closed the link and turned to Waters. "Lieutenant, you have the watch."

"I have the watch, sir."

Bermont snarled under his armored helm, the vibrations of the whining, roaring weapon only reaching him in his imagination as he fired another burst into the scampering, skittering drones. They'd appeared from some crevice or another like wraiths, firing a burst at his team, vanishing around a corner or into some hole they'd found.

The soldiers had managed to avoid any serious injuries, though Bermont himself was sporting a burn on his thigh that was going to sting like a bitch once the local anesthetic started wearing off. It had been a glancing blow from the enemy's beam weapons, but it had been enough to cook his armor—and by extension, his thigh—before he'd managed to roll free.

Most of the others now sported similar wounds, or at least scarred patches on their armor to show how close they'd come to joining the club, but they were getting wise to the enemy's tactics now and it was showing. The last attack hadn't scorched anybody, and the Drasin had lost another drone in the attempt.

It was a pity, Bermont thought, that the thermal guidance on their bullets wasn't able to manage ninety-degree turns. They'd have fried a great deal more of the spiderlike things if they could, but the system only allowed relatively minor course corrections, especially over short distances.

The mission was turning into a grueling manhunt—or rather, alien hunt—through the bewildering streets and alleys of the alien city, sometimes climbing up through immense arcing roads and sometimes digging down into the depths of the city as they went practically underground in their pursuit. And, unfortunately, Bermont's own prediction that they were simply going to have to get down and dirty was proving to be altogether too accurate, and the constant pursuit of the devil-ish bastards was starting to wear on both him and his people.

A light nerve-tingle alarm went off. Bermont let his empty magazine drop to the ground automatically and fell back as others moved ahead of him to take up the slack. Slapping the new one in took a few seconds before he was moving forward again, his foot crunching the spent clip into the ground as he brought his weapon back up to his shoulder and looked for another target.

▶▶▶

"Another empty tunnel," Savoy said, his voice calm despite the beads of sweat that had formed on his forehead.

The silence was deafening, as the saying went, and the lieutenant found himself almost wishing for something to happen. *Anything would be good,* a dark part of his mind whispered.

A dark and stupid part, of course.

Savoy knew that it was just the tension speaking, demanding some form of release, but the voice was seductive, just the same, and it took all of his intellect and trained reflexes to shove it down and maintain his current operational stance. He knew that wishing for action was as useless as it was stupid. For one thing, no one ever answered wishes. And for another, the demon Murphy just might answer this one. So he forced his mind into the job and moved as silently as he could onto the next tunnel.

He paused at the tunnel wall beside the branching point, taking a breath as he gathered his thoughts for a moment and looked around. He wasn't certain what they were doing, this bunch, whether there was a plan for the tunnels or even if maybe the crash had scrambled what passed for brains and they were just acting at random.

This time, there was a soft scratching that reached his armor's sensors and Savoy froze, his mind blanking as he looked into the pits of hell. At the end of this tunnel, there were dozens, fifty or more, of the alien things—he couldn't tell. They were crawling over each other, scraping at the walls and gathering up the material that fell. Savoy watched as the horde seemed to actually eat the rocks, ingesting the minerals and even going so far as to apparently carry certain bits to one or another of their group and feed it to each other.

"Oh man," he muttered, knowing that his helmet would insulate all sound. "This is something else. I think...It might be nest building? Computer, flag this data to be relayed to the research labs on the *Odyssey* immediately...Xeno-Biology Department."

They were eating rocks, or at least ingesting them. Whether they got any nutrients out of it wasn't something he could guess at, but there had to be some reason.

Savoy inched forward, trying to get a better view of the activities, only to freeze when one of them suddenly snapped around and stared right at him.

He hadn't made any noise, but the beast had apparently spotted him anyway, because in a moment, all the others turned as well. Worse, perhaps, from his point of view, was that they did it without any sound or obvious signal. They just seemed to all notice him at the same time.

"Oh shit," Savoy muttered, backing away.

It was like a dam breaking; the sudden charge of the drones was like the rush of water over the broken floodgates, and that was all the signal Savoy needed.

He turned and ran just as another flood burst from a tunnel farther down and came racing straight up at him.

"Shit!" he screamed as he ran. "Mehn! Burke! I'm coming back, and I've got company on my ass!"

He didn't wait for an answer, just bolted up the incline of the tunnel at the best speed his suit could give him, which was fairly impressive. Each step was more of a leap, angled to propel him parallel to the incline, sending him flying for a dozen meters before he would power his other leg down to meet the ground and accelerate him ahead even faster.

The end of the tunnel was approaching at blinding speeds, but his wraparound sensors showed him that the room behind him wasn't all that much better, so he didn't slow down.

He grabbed the cable of the chute mid-leap, keying its automatic lift even as he wrapped it around his hand in desperation.

The cable went taut almost instantly, the CM field dropping his weight to near nothing as the chute's thrusters whined and pulled him straight up. Savoy struck the wall as he swung on the end of the chute's line, caroming off it like a billiard ball, but kept his grip on the cable as he shoved the chute's climb rate to maximum.

"Coming through!" he yelled as the chute cleared the tunnel entrance and slammed into the ceiling of the lander, throwing sparks and fragments around as its lateral thrusters kicked in and yanked Savoy suddenly to the right.

His upward motion remained largely unchecked, so he bounced off the ceiling. Before snapping to one side and careening off a wall, he slammed into another bulkhead and finally came to a rest against a charred piece of machinery.

Mehn and Burke didn't have time to watch his rather rough flight, as they were watching the tunnel as he flashed past. They both saw the horrific mass that was scrambling up along the walls like they weren't a smooth, vertical surface.

"TB!" Mehn yelled, twisting a cylinder in his hand and dropping it down into the mass.

"TB!" Burke returned, doing the same thing.

They both turned and sprinted away from the tunnel, grabbing Savoy from where he had fallen, and lunged for the rent in the ship that had given them entrance.

The rumble behind them was enough to inform them when the thermobaric grenades detonated, shaking the entire lander as the overpressure waves erupted in the contained space, each reflected shock wave reinforcing the next as they had been designed to.

A blast of flame and gas erupted out of the tunnel, curving around the bulkheads like a living thing, seeking a way out, just as the soldiers did. It caught up with them as they passed the tear in the hull, slapping them with over ten pounds per square inch of pressure and tossing them from the lander like toys in a hurricane.

▶ ▶ ▶

"Savoy! Burke! Mehn!" Major Brinks growled, eyeing the scrambled signals that were once three of his best men. "Damn!"

He was still standing outside the hospital facility, and his angry body language was apparent to the guards. It took the major a few moments to recognize how nervous they were getting and to move off. He didn't really care about their nerves, but he'd rather not test the discipline of troops he didn't know.

"Goddammit, Lieutenant Savoy, report!" he roared again, keying and rekeying the network-reconnect command.

▶ ▶ ▶

Dust and debris rained down around them, covering the three soldiers in a fine coat of powder and several hundred pounds of what used to be an alien landing craft as the rumbling thunder slowly died out.

"Ohhh...fuck," Burke groaned, pushing himself up to his hands and knees, shunting a half ton of debris off his back. "You guys...dead?"

"Just wishing," Mehn replied as he shifted some more material and they both pulled a chunk of something off Savoy. "Hey, L.T., you okay?"

Savoy didn't move, but his suit sent them a steady stream of medical data when they queried it that showed him to be alive.

"Come on, Sav." Burke hooked him under his arms and dragged him back. "Snap out of it. We might have company any time now..."

Savoy groaned but moved his arm in a flapping motion that really didn't help much.

"Well, he's alive and probably awake," Mehn muttered. "I'll contact the major and get a pickup..."

Burke nodded, dragging Savoy along the ground as they both shot glances at the somewhat more dilapidated-looking landing craft.

"Oh fuck," Mehn muttered.

"What's wrong?"

"Our network link is scrambled," he told Burke. "Long-range frequencies are junked..."

"It'll settle down," Savoy groaned more than spoke.

Burke looked down at him in surprise but chuckled. "Welcome back, boss."

"Yeah, yeah..." Savoy croaked, pulling himself free of Burke and climbing unsteadily to his feet. "Reboot the com-suite, both of you."

"You got it," they told him, following his instructions.

The software reboot took a few seconds. The network connection wizard activated and sent out a query signal. A few nanoseconds later, after two handshakes, three passwords, and a gigabit encryption code, the network connected again.

"Major..." Savoy staggered in pain as he tried to walk. "We've got trouble."

CHAPTER 26

▶"TUNNELS?" COMMANDER ROBERTS demanded, fists tightening into a clench as he looked at the face on the large screen. "To what end?"

"According to Lieutenant Savoy, they seem to be...eating the minerals in the ground, Commander," Major Brinks said. "Using it as resources for breeding or something similar."

Roberts's eyes flickered around the room for an instant, taking in the reactions of the others sitting on the auxiliary bridge, strapped down against the zero-gravity environment. Their eyes widened. Some of them seemed to understand the implications more than others, paling at the thought. Roberts himself had enough of a base in concept technology to understand what was being implied, though he wasn't certain he was ready to believe that it could possibly exist in a naturally evolved species.

"Major, are you aware of what you're saying?" he asked grimly.

"I'm afraid so, Commander," Brinks said. "But it does make the pieces fit, Commander. If they're able to process minerals in order to fuel themselves, it explains their rate of reproduction."

"What evidence did the lieutenant give?"

"His suit's computer counted no less than two hundred of the drones in those tunnels," Brinks replied. "Our worst-case estimate is that a lander can't hold more than a hundred, maybe a hundred and fifty. Unless they've got some other twist that they're working, I think his theory is sound."

"Damn." Roberts closed his eyes. "Major, the situation up here is deteriorating quickly. In less than twelve hours, unless we withdraw, we'll be facing six of the enemy cruisers. If you're still on the ground then…" He let the words draw out.

"Understood, Commander. Do we know what the captain intends to do?"

"Not yet," Roberts replied. "I'll be meeting with him shortly in order to confer…However, I doubt that we'll abandon the planet easily."

"All right. I have to get back to work, Commander. I'll contact you later with an updated sitrep."

"Very well, Major. Godspeed."

The connection closed and Roberts forced his fists to relax. The situation was turning from bad to worse, and even at best, there was no way that they could take on six of those alien cruisers. The computer had run the scenarios, and even adjusting for the severe lack of imagination in any simulation, the best they could hope for would be to eliminate or disable four of the enemy ships.

The damages they were likely to incur while dealing with those four would make the *Odyssey* a sitting duck for the remaining ships. Those were best-case scenarios as well, assuming that the enemy followed patterns of behavior consistent with their last engagement and that the *Odyssey* made no mistakes and suffered no interference from Mr. Murphy.

Roberts thought that they'd be lucky if they successfully took on two enemy cruisers at once, forget the added disadvantage of the additional four. Two of the enemy ships attacking from a similar tangent would turn their armor advantage into a joke. The phase shift in the armor would work against one of the lasers, but the second would cut them up like a hot knife through butter.

The problem was that he couldn't see any way out of the encounter.

Certainly, they could turn tail and run, but the thought left a bitter taste in his mouth to even contemplate. Military units were only as good as their traditions, in Roberts's opinion. The NAC had a short history, but its military traditions went back hundreds of years, just the same.

To begin the NAC Interstellar Armed Forces with the act of abandoning a world to genocide would be setting a precedent of the worst kind. A tacit approval of the act in implication, even if not in fact. It would be a tradition not only of dishonor but of perceived cowardice.

The problem, however, wasn't in the dying.

Commander Roberts was willing to die for his own people or for the strangers, because that was what his duty demanded. However, his intellect would not permit his emotion to forget the fact that Earth knew nothing of their situation, and if they died out here on this day, Earth could well follow them into the abyss because they had failed to provide data vital to the survival of the human—the Terran—species.

In the middle of his contemplation, the door behind him whisked open and he saw the people around him stiffen. Roberts shook his mind clear.

"Captain."

▶▶▶

"Bring that carnivore down to three thousand meters," Lieutenant Savoy ordered as he and his team stood observing the great wreck they had made of the already wrecked lander.

They were standing about a hundred meters from it now, watching the settling debris through their enhanced HUDs as they waited for the information from the carnivore's ground-penetrating radar to come back.

The signal was fuzzy at first, the initial pass only returning a low-resolution scan, but their fears were confirmed as subsequent passes cleared up the signal.

The tunnels showed up plainly, long lines extending dozens of meters down and out from the lander, with several branches that extended in all directions like the limbs of an inverted tree.

Or perhaps like the roots of a virulent weed.

Inside the tunnel spaces, some pictures showed places that were blocked in, while others would later show those spaces to be quite clear. The pattern was overlaid rapidly, scans being taken every few milliseconds apart, while played back in a real-time sequence.

They could almost make out the flailing limbs of the drones as they crawled through the tunnels and continued their digging.

"The estimates are coming back now, boss," Mehn said. "The computer says that there's a ninety percent probability that there are over two hundred and eighty of them down there."

Savoy nodded. "Tell it to keep counting."

"You've got it, boss."

Savoy flicked over to another com-channel, accessing into the command. "Well it's confirmed, Major. We've got a nest or something being built under our feet."

"We've also got the sky about to fall on us, Lieutenant."

"Sir?"

"Six more cruisers are up there. In less than twelve hours we're going to have to fight or flee," Brinks said, his voice grim.

Savoy grimaced. "I can't say I like the thought of turning tail, sir."

"Not our call," Brinks replied. "In the meantime, we've got twelve hours to try and get a handle on the situation. I'm open to suggestions, Lieutenant."

Savoy frowned. "We should redirect one or more of the carnivores back to the *Odyssey* for rearming. Right now they're equipped with air-to-ground missiles, but if we load them up with some bunker busters, we might have a chance—maybe at taking the nest out with minimal risk."

"Time to rearm?"

"An hour, including flight time," Savoy responded.

Brinks considered it. "All right. But we'll keep our drones where they are and have the commander detail two more with the appropriate hardware. That'll save us some time and let us keep on with our own work."

"Yes, sir," Savoy said.

"In the meantime, do what you can. Miss Chans is being transported to the local alien command center now. With luck, we might be able to get some coordination with the locals," Brinks said, glancing over his shoulder. "Their medical facility seems competently run. Makes me wonder why their military is just a fuckup."

"Sir, I'm not sure if I'd put it that way, exactly," Savoy replied, a little cautiously.

"Are you kidding, Lieutenant?" Brinks snorted. "They're getting their butts handed to them."

"That's true, sir. However, it's not due to a lack of power. Bermont's little test with that laser rifle proves that." Savoy shook his head. "And while they're a little rudimentary by our standards, sir, they're probably on par with most conventional forces I've seen."

"I suppose you've got a theory for why these Drasin things are kicking ass and taking names, then?"

"Sir, they seem to be two steps ahead of their opposition," Savoy replied. "Nothing more than that. Power-wise, they appear to be at parity with each other…The Drasin simply seem…I don't know, more prepared. Like they knew what they were getting into and packed for the job."

Brinks pushed the thought aside. Whatever it was, it didn't matter at the moment. What did matter was the situation as it stood, so the major just had to play the cards he was dealt.

No matter how badly the hand sucked.

▶▶▶

"Admiral!" someone shouted, a twinge of shock and fear in their voice, causing Tanner to spin around just as the doors to the rear of the command pit burst open.

Burst being the operative word, since the heavy metal doors literally were pulled off their equally heavy hinges as a hulking figure stepped through, paused, and looked around. For a crazy moment, Tanner could have sworn that the figure seemed chagrined.

Then she spoke.

"Oops," a decidedly tiny and feminine voice came from the hulk, sounding embarrassed, as if she had just accidentally jarred someone's elbow, or something equally inane, rather than having just ripped two security doors off their hinges.

"Ithan Chans, I presume?" Admiral Tanner asked calmly, his voice causing the guards to pause and lower their weapons, just slightly.

The hulk snapped to a rigid stance and nodded in salute. "Ithan Milla Chans reporting, Admiral."

"Relax," he ordered, stepping out of the pit to come face-to-face with the ithan.

Or as close to it as he could manage since the armored suit placed her faceplate about two feet over his head. Tanner didn't flinch, though, or alter his expression as he looked up at the faceless features of the armor.

"What can you tell me about the...*Odyssey*, Ithan?" he asked.

"They belong to the...to a human world that is not part of the colonies, sir," she told him, obviously correcting herself as she almost mentioned the mythical Others again. "Their technology is largely of inferior quality to ours; however, they have markedly superior weapons systems and an ingenious, though disconcerting, trans-light drive."

The admiral's eyebrows went up. "And their intentions?"

"Sir"—the hulking figure seemed to relax a bit, her stance shifting and becoming more pensive—"they rescued me and the survivors at Port Fuielles without second considerations. In this system, they were reluctant to engage the Drasin until it became obvious that the Drasin would continue on to kill the civilians of this world." She paused. "They don't wish to be involved in this war, Admiral. But they...I don't think that they can turn their backs on the annihilation of an entire world."

Tanner nodded. "Are you in contact with them now?"

"Yes, sir."

"Very well," Tanner nodded. "Give them my thanks for their aid and ask them what my people can do to help."

▶▶▶

"That's it?" Brinks blinked.

It couldn't be that simple.

"What is it?" Milla asked him over the link, her voice as puzzled as the computer translation could manage.

"What can he do to help?" Brinks repeated. "No demands, no posturing, no questions?"

"We have very little time, Major," Milla reminded him.

This was true, the major had to admit, but it still seemed insane to him. If nothing else, the admiral should be talking about how to integrate Brinks's people into his own strategies. Military people didn't just let some rogue group pop onto their turf and start shooting things up.

Brinks shook it off, chalking it up to a complete alien mentality.

"Fine. Inform him that we'll need to start coordinating the sweeps of the city if we want to be sure that we get them all. We also have a problem where one of the landers apparently crashed."

▶▶▶

"Tunnels?" Admiral Tanner asked, his eyes narrowing. "Where?"

Milla's eyes flickered over the map on her suit's HUD. She looked up to the large display that showed a similar map at the front of the large room. "There."

Tanner turned to look where she was pointing. "Nero!"

The big man came up from the ground forces control pit, standing almost as tall as Milla in her armor, and looked curiously at her. "This must be your missing ithan?"

"It is...or so I believe." Tanner's lips twisted. "It is difficult to say, of course, as I have yet to see her face."

Milla's eyes widened under her helm, and she uttered a shocked "ohh."

She immediately started fumbling with the controls until she located the shield that Brinks had shown her before and activated the control.

"Sorry," she told them, her faceplate shimmering from a flat, opaque black to a transparent form backlit by internal lights. "I require the helmet to communicate with the others, however."

Tanner nodded, and Nero just gazed evenly at her.

"Nero, the ithan tells me that the Drasin are digging tunnels under the Corinth landing site," Tanner said.

"Corinth?" Nero frowned. "That was a crash. Nothing could have survived."

"I'm aware of that. However, I believe that we may want to check, just the same."

The big man nodded gruffly. "Agreed. I'll correct the oversight."

"I'm certain you will," Tanner said confidently. "However, if what our...friends are saying is true, we may have a serious situation developing."

"Agreed," Nero said.

"Their scans indicate that there are over two hundred Drasin in those tunnels at the moment, Admiral," Milla said. "They have ordered two assault drones from the *Odyssey* with weapons they believe might be able to eliminate the Drasin."

"Then act quickly," Nero intoned, his voice not giving any indication of his opinions of that speed.

"Indeed," Tanner nodded. "Let us act as quickly."

"Agreed," Nero replied, then turned away without another word.

"Now, Ithan," Tanner said, looking up at Milla without any hint of discomfort in having to look so far up to meet her eyes. "I believe that you and I should have a conversation that includes the captain of the *Odyssey*?"

Milla nodded at once. "Yes, Admiral."

▼

CHAPTER 27

▲

▶ "CAPTAIN…WESTON, I presume?"

The translation came through clear enough, though the computer seemed to hitch up on the last word, and for a moment, Weston could have sworn that it was going to go with the clichéd "Doctor Livingston, I presume?" rather than what he hoped was the more accurate translation.

Weston pushed the trivial thought from his mind, though he knew that, unlike himself, the other man couldn't see whom he was talking to. "That's correct. You're Admiral Tanner?"

"That is correct." The slimly built man looked out of the screen with every appearance of examining the auxiliary bridge where Weston had taken the transmission.

He wasn't, of course, seeing the bridge. Rather, what Admiral Tanner was looking at was Miss Chans's face while her suit systems transmitted his image to Weston. The reverse wasn't possible, of course, but Weston was able to speak out of the suit speaker system so that they could hold something that at least resembled a coherent conversation.

Admiral Tanner was an unassuming man, Weston noted, the type that you would probably overlook if you saw him on the street. His uniform seemed oddly rudimentary, more like work clothes than something any Terran admiral would wear, but it was spotless and well kept.

There was something about his eyes, though. Weston couldn't pin it down, but it was a look he'd seen before.

"Captain." The Admiral was speaking again, forcing Weston to pay attention. "We all owe you our thanks for your intervention. I do not believe that my world could ever repay you for what you have done."

Weston waved a hand, almost irritated by the suggestion. "Nonsense. Gratitude is fine, Admiral, but beyond that, it isn't of any concern to me. We wouldn't let anyone do what these things were planning to do. They killed two worlds, Admiral. My people wouldn't let them take a third—not unchallenged."

"Yes…" Tanner glanced down, his eyes flickering shut. "I was pained to hear of Port Fuielles. Is the system titualar there with you?"

"She is with her people at the moment, Admiral, though they are still sedated," Weston said.

"Sedated?"

"When we're finished, Milla can fill you in. Suffice to say that the sedation was as much for their sake as for ours. We would have woken them already, but given the situation, I didn't want panicked civilians adding to our problems."

"Yes," the admiral nodded, "I can see that. We shall, of course, prepare a place for them immediately."

"That would be welcome, sir." Weston replied. "However, we have something else to discuss at this point. You are aware, of course, of the five ships currently approaching to join the one already in-system?"

"Yes, Captain," Tanner replied grimly. "We have them on our long-range sensors now. It's worse than I had hoped but much as I'd feared."

"Admiral, I have to be frank, sir." Weston leaned forward as he talked, clasping his hands in front of him. "The odds of the *Odyssey* mounting a successful defense against six of those cruisers is very nearly zero."

Milla held herself still as the captain's words came over the speakers, but her heart was in her throat at the admission. She'd known it, at least that it was likely, but to hear it put into words by Captain Weston was something else.

Was he going to leave them? Could he justify fighting a lost cause for a world that wasn't his own? She didn't know.

Words spoken with a calm assurance brought her back as she realized that Admiral Tanner was speaking again, so she tried to focus on what he was saying.

"I expected that might be the case, Captain," the admiral said, sounding almost resigned. "Part of me wishes very much to ask you to stay; however, I understand that we are not your people."

"I didn't say I was ready to run out on you just yet, Admiral," Weston's voice came back over the suit's systems. "I'm just giving you the odds."

"I'm afraid that I don't understand," Tanner said, trying very hard not to sound confused.

"Admiral, the way I see it…Judging from reports from our ground forces, it's not totally impossible to fight off these things on the ground," Weston said. "I understand that your weapons aren't as effective as you might like; however, if you were to adjust your tactics, you should have the people to take out any invasion force that might land—assuming you do it fast enough."

"I'm afraid that isn't my specialty, Captain," Tanner smiled, glancing over his shoulder. "However, I can speak with our ground forces commander."

"I expect you can," Weston said. "In that case, what we might be able to do for you is to help cut down the opposition somewhat. Every ship we can take out for you is one less that you'll have to deal with on the ground."

Admiral Tanner took a deep breath, understanding entering his eyes. "I understand, and I thank you for your help, Captain."

There was a moment of silence from the speakers, and Captain Weston's voice returned, its tone serious.

"It's what we do, Admiral."

▶▶▶

Traditions.

They mattered more than most people realized, especially in military units.

Commander Roberts knew this, and he had always felt that the best units were those that had traditions of excellence that every member could aspire to. Few were those who both saw the birth of those traditions and who realized just what it was they were seeing. Something told him, deep inside, that he was now among those few.

When the captain said those words, Roberts lifted his chin a little higher on reflex, though he knew that no one was looking at him. And around him, he could see the same effect on the others sitting there.

The young men and women assigned to the auxiliary bridge weren't the *Odyssey*'s primary command crew; they were a little younger, and in what was already a young man's navy, that meant they were practically in nappies. They had joined after the war, most of them, probably out of the same ideals, misguided though they may be, that the captain was now espousing.

They stood just a little taller, sat just a little straighter, and Roberts caught a gleam in the eyes of one of them as he glanced over his shoulder at the captain.

The commander risked a look at Weston, wondering if the captain had done it on purpose, but couldn't tell from the other man's stance. Weston was intent on his conversation with the alien admiral and wasn't paying attention to the effect his words had.

Before the next shift was out, Roberts knew, the word would be spread across the ship. Everyone would know the gist, if not the details, of the captain's proclamation.

It's what we do.

Roberts doubted that the captain meant it the way it would be interpreted. It was just what soldiers said when they were complimented or thanked. In another time, another place, the words would be just that—words.

Here, though, and now, they had already taken on a new meaning. Traditions, Commander Roberts mused silently, were funny things. They started when you least expected them and endured through everything the universe could throw at them. And the captain had just started one hell of a tradition—assuming, of course, that anyone survived to pass it on.

It's what we do.

Spoken to an alien admiral by a Terran captain in the defense of a world that wasn't his own. The rest of the fleet, and all those that followed, would have one hell of a tradition to live up to.

Comdr. Jason Roberts just had to wonder if it was a good thing or not.

▶ ▶ ▶

"Yes...well..." The admiral seemed flustered, something that didn't look quite right on him, Weston noted. "We still owe you greatly, Captain."

"All you have to do for the moment, Admiral, is fight," Weston told him. "We're willing to lend a hand, but we can't do this for you, sir. So fight."

Tanner inclined his head, nodding in acceptance. "I believe that you may count on that, Captain."

"Good," Weston said.

Admiral Tanner looked up again. "If I may know, though, how do you intend to fight six cruisers at once?"

Weston grinned, almost ferally, the effect sadly lost on the admiral, who couldn't see it. The members of the crew around him, however, noted the smile and shivered in response.

"There is an old expression where we come from for people in our position," Captain Weston replied, his tone edged with a hint of dark humor. "A piece of advice from the past, you might say."

"Really, Captain?" The Admiral had a hint of a smile as well. "Do your people make a habit of getting into situations like this?"

Weston's chuckle washed across the bridge. "Not this precise situation, but close enough, perhaps."

"I see," Tanner replied, that same hint of a smile gracing his fine features. "And what is this advice from the past?"

"Run silent, Admiral," Weston replied. "Run silent, and run deep."

There was a moment of silence, the admiral looking genuinely puzzled. "I'm afraid that I don't understand…"

"I didn't expect you to, Admiral," Weston replied. "So I just hope that the enemy doesn't understand it, either."

"I…see…"

"I'm afraid that I have duties to attend to, Admiral," Weston said. "I'll contact you before making any moves."

"I…very well, Captain. Again, thank you for your help."

"Not at all, Admiral," Weston replied. "Until the next time we speak…"

Admiral Tanner nodded, and Weston cut the connection.

"Sir," Roberts spoke up after a moment. "Are you sure…?"

"I am," Weston said, not looking back.

"Yes, sir."

"Ensign," the captain said, glancing to one side.

"Sir!"

"Contact the bridge. Inform them that I'm on my way back, and have them recall the senior officers."

"Aye, aye, Captain," the ensign replied crisply.

Weston loosened his restraints, floating up into the air and kicking off the command chair toward the rear door. "Commander Roberts."

"Yes, Captain."

"You're with me."

"Aye, sir." Roberts waved a hand to the lieutenant at the auxiliary conn.

As Roberts followed Captain Weston from the auxiliary bridge, the lieutenant shifted himself over to the command seat and snapped in his restraints, his eyes on the screens that displayed the bow wake of the decelerating ships, a hint of steely determination in them that had been missing an hour earlier.

▼

CHAPTER 28

▲

▶ TANNER FOCUSED ON the young ithan who was standing stock still in the center of his command pit, apparently not in the least tired or inclined to sit down, despite the fact that it had been quite some time since she'd arrived.

"Are you certain you won't take a seat, Ithan?" he asked once more, ingrained civility forcing him to do so, despite the irritation that washed over him at the repetition.

"No, Admiral," Milla replied. "I am fine. This armor seems to keep pressure off my feet, so in a strange way, I'm already sitting."

"Ah," Tanner nodded. "Very well. Ithan, tell me something…"

"Certainly, Admiral."

"The *Carlache…*"

Milla winced visibly under her helm, but he pressed on.

"Her captain and I were old friends," he said. "I would appreciate knowing…how it happened."

Milla was silent for a moment. "After he ordered the evacuation, Captain Tal remained on the bridge, controlling the defense weapons. The last I saw of him was when he ordered me to leave, sir."

Tanner nodded, his face thoughtful.

"Yes, I see," he said, a small smile on his face. "Oddly, I believe that it was not the worst way Tal could have imagined dying."

Milla didn't have anything to say to that.

▶▶▶

Work crews on the *Odyssey* were hanging, literally, out of the ship as they welded new armor joints to the flight deck, carefully applying patches around the powerful coils that controlled the fighter traps. The work had been going on for hours and continued for a good many more—that is, until Chief Corrin stormed onto the deck in her hard suit, snapping orders.

"Rowley! Get those men out of there!" she growled. "New orders came down. We're gonna forget the armor."

"What?" Alistair Rowley, machinist's mate first class, looked up in confusion. "We need this deck back, Chief!"

"And we're gonna get it back—fast," Corrin said, grabbing a crewman and pointing across the deck. "We've got some steel plate coming down through the lock. Grab a crew and bring it over here."

"Yes, ma'am," the crewman nodded, clunking off instantly toward the lock.

"What's going on, Chief?" Rowley crawled up out of the gash the enemy lasers had ripped.

"We're gonna fill the gash with laser-reflective foam, then laser-weld some plates down over it. You've got the trap fixed, right?"

"Yes, ma'am," he nodded. "But the armor—"

"We don't have time for the armor, Rowley," Corrin told him. "Just get the deck operational and let me and the captain worry about the armor."

"You want it that way, Chief, you got it," Rowley said, with a shrug. "I'll have the deck ready to use inside of…say, two hours?"

"Good man," Corrin said. "I'll be back in an hour to have a look. In the meantime, I've got some bad news to drop on a couple other departments."

"What's going on, Chief?" Rowley asked a second time, his voice tense.

"We're going to war, Rowley. Got a problem with that?"

"No, ma'am."

"Good," the chief said, nodding once in her helmet. "Get your crew back to work."

"You got it, Chief!"

Rowley switched over to his crew's frequency. "All right, you bums, we've got a deadline. Franks! Get me a couple canisters of that insulating foam from storage. We're gonna patch this bitch the dirty way!"

▶▶▶

"Sir," Commander Roberts hesitated, "I'm not sure this plan of yours is going to work."

"Join the club, Commander," Weston said as he took a seat behind his desk.

"Sir, it relies on too many unknowns."

Weston nodded. "Agreed. But you and I both know that we can't hope to win in a stand-up fight, Jason."

Commander Roberts paused, blinking back a bit of surprise as Weston used his first name for the first time. After a moment, he shook his head. "Even so, you're risking a lot on our stealth systems. We don't know what kind of sensors the enemy has."

"True. But I think that we can pretty much imitate a hole in space for anything short of an active tachyon scan."

"For anything using conventional frequency scans, you mean," Roberts corrected, though he had to concede the point.

The *Odyssey* had been built with the cam-plates for two reasons. The first—or rather, the first that became important to them—was the fact that, with appropriate modifications, the cam-plate system could reflect over 98 percent of laser energy away from the ship. It was, against energy weapons, the ultimate form of armor.

However, the original design wasn't built with armor specifically in mind. The cam-plate technology was based on the development of carbon nano-tubes designed to shift reflective frequencies as an active camouflage for main battle tanks. An appropriate program shunted through the armor coating so as to allow a tank to blend into practically any environment with a nearly perfect camouflage.

At the far end of its ability was the black hole setting, a phase-shifted armor that would absorb everything in the EM range sent its way, including radar, laser, and all other conventional detection systems. The net effect was to reduce the electronic and sensor profile of any unit coated in it to less than 2 percent of its normal signal.

Of course, Roberts knew that particular use had one rather nasty side effect. "You do know what will happen if one of their lasers nails us while we're using the black hole settings?"

"We'll probably be vaporized before we know we're hit," Weston told him flatly.

Since the net effect of the black hole setting was to *absorb* over 98 percent of all energy directed against it, it would actually behave like an inverse of the normal armor and offer absolute minimal resistance to enemy lasers.

And given how powerful those lasers were, one shot would be all it would take.

"It's reckless, sir," Roberts said calmly, finally taking a seat across from Weston.

"I know."

▶▶▶

"Hey, L.T.," Burke called out. "We've got some company coming up here."

Savoy glanced over in the direction that Burke had indicated and noted the armed forces converging on their position. "Great. Don't make any fast moves, guys. I'd hate to get toasted by the guys we came here to save."

"Don't worry," Burke muttered.

The team watched as the militia came up, finally stopping just in front of them, and one of the figures stepped forward.

He was a big man, Savoy noted, his face craggy with exposure to the elements, and he handled the laser rifle in his hands like it was a toy.

"You are Ithan Savoy?" the man grumbled.

Savoy frowned. The translator either scrambled the word or he'd just gotten a new rank. In either case, it didn't matter, so he nodded in an exaggerated fashion so the big man would be able to tell. "That's correct."

"Kimbo Yulth," the man said, gesturing in what might have been a salute. "We are assigned to you."

Savoy blinked, toggling into the command channel reflexively. "Hey, boss?"

Brinks's growl came back, "What is it, Lieutenant? I've got mopping-up operations in three quadrants and a firefight in a civilian building in the fourth."

"You know anything about local reinforcements?"

"They get to you already?" Brinks muttered. "Shit. I meant to warn you that they were coming. Didn't think they'd be so fast."

"I guess Milla got through to the local boss man," Savoy said.

"That's affirmative, Lieutenant," Brinks told him. "They're yours. Use them as you see fit. The local guy has given us the lead."

Savoy almost cursed from the surprise, blinking furiously as his mind whirred.

"Sir?" he said.

"I know, I know," Brinks said. "I don't know what to make of it, either. I can't say I'm opposed to it, mind you, just doesn't make sense. The local military is acting more like a militia group or something…"

"Could be that's all they are, sir."

"Whatever," Brinks muttered. "Doesn't matter. They're yours. Deal with it."

"Yes, sir," Savoy replied just before the channel went dead.

When he turned his attention back to Yulth, the man was waiting patiently for him to say something, to all appearances completely at peace with the world. Savoy tried to shake off the disturbing feeling it gave him and started speaking.

"All right, Yulth," he said through the suit speakers. "Here's the situation: We've got over two hundred of those Drasin things down in tunnels under our feet. We can't ignore them, or they'll rip this city out from under us. Got that?"

Yulth nodded.

"All right, here's what I need to know." Savoy stepped forward, placing a hand on Yulth's shoulder and turning him around. He pointed down toward the wreckage, moving his hand expansively to either side. "Are there any civilians in that area, and if there are, how fast can you boys clear them out?"

Yulth frowned, and for a moment, Savoy was worried that the interpreter had messed up the translation.

Finally, the immense man spoke. "There are civilians. Many. Too many to evacuate. It will take time."

Savoy sighed. "We don't have much of that, so you'd better get to work."

Yulth turned with an almost alarming speed and started shouting orders to his men. Savoy and his team watched them break up and rush off, impressed with their speed, if nothing else.

Whether they will be as effective as they were fast, Savoy thought, *is another matter.*

▶ ▶ ▶

"Get those circuits degaussed!"

"Yes, sir!" the tachyon specialist on the *Odyssey* said, not looking up as the chief engineer cursed under his breath while they all but dismantled his babies.

The transition drive was first, but it was also the most painful.

Captain Weston's orders had come down, and at first, no one really wanted to believe it. It was insane, for one, but the orders were quickly confirmed, and the Engineering team had gotten to work in short order.

All the ship's tachyon generation systems were being discharged, degaussed, and taken offline. Since that list included the FTL sensor systems, as well as the transition drive, the net effect was to make the *Odyssey* blind as well as lame.

Yet, those were the captain's orders, so the teams got to work and sailored on.

▶▶▶

"Admiral Tanner, we have the orbiters prepared."

"Ah, excellent, thank you," Rael said, turning to Milla. "Pardon me, Ithan, could you contact Captain Weston?"

"One moment," she said, her eyes refocusing.

Tanner saw the young woman's eyes flicker around, looking at something he couldn't see. He wasn't sure if she knew how to use the system effectively, but from the outside, it looked very odd and impressive as well.

His reverie was cut short when he heard a distinctly non-female voice address him.

"Yes, Admiral?"

"Ah, Captain Weston, we have prepared four orbiters, if you wish to unload your passengers."

"Thank you, Admiral. That will be fine," Weston's voice said. "What is the size of these…orbiters?"

Tanner waved a hand at one of his subordinates.

The answer came back in a few seconds in the form of a plate dropped into his hands, so he rattled off the numbers from the display.

There was a long pause.

"Uh…"

Tanner blinked. The sound made no sense whatsoever.

"Perhaps you should send one up and we'll just scan it," Weston continued after a moment. "I'm afraid that the translator is missing a few important modules."

"I see," Tanner replied, not entirely certain that he did. "Very well, I'll authorize their departure immediately."

"Thank you, Admiral. I'll be in touch."

The signal went dead, leaving Tanner blinking owlishly at Milla as she looked back, just as confused.

"How will he be 'in touch' from orbit?" Tanner asked after a moment.

"I do not know, Admiral. I said that they were human, not that they were normal."

▶▶▶

Weston looked over to Ensign Waters. "Scan those 'orbiters' when they lift off. I'm hoping that they built them small enough to fit our locks."

"Yes, sir."

Weston turned and walked over to Ensign Lamont's station. "How are the preparations coming?"

"They're about as expected, sir. The primary- and secondary-sensor arrays have been degaussed as you ordered, and the tachyon generator has been taken offline."

"And the transition drives?"

"Should be completely offline in an hour, sir."

"All right, good," Weston nodded. "Thank you, Ensign."

Weston turned back, thinking.

The tachyon systems were among the most delicate on the *Odyssey*, engineered to tolerances determined in nanometers. Taking them offline was a risk, particularly with the tokamak generator that fueled the active systems and the transition drive.

Bringing that back online would take at least an hour, under normal circumstances. The chief had assured him that she could actually cut that back to fifteen minutes, and he hadn't questioned her on it despite the shiver that ran down his spine when she said it. He hadn't really wanted to know what corners she was going to cut to get that done.

She couldn't cause any more damage than those alien warships could, anyway.

Well, not much more.

▶▶▶

"We have two more drones inbound from the *Odyssey*, Lieutenant," Brinks transmitted.

Savoy nodded, flipping his HUD over from the ground-penetrating radar display to the drone control screen. The two new drones flashed red as they approached, indicating that they were loaded with the bunker-buster weapons he'd requested.

He ordered them into an orbit of the area while he waited for news concerning the civilians.

"Burke!"

"Yeah, L.T.?"

"Start calculating the impact point and program the GBU Ninety-eights for the job," he ordered his explosives man. "I want to launch as soon as we get this area cleared."

"You got it, boss," Burke replied, automatically working as he talked. "We've got four of the Ninety-eights to work with. Do you want to use them all?"

Savoy frowned, thinking.

The GBU (guided bomb unit) 98s weren't exactly cheap, nor were they small, either in stature or payload. The five thousand–kilogram penetrators were loaded with the equivalent of five-kiloton payloads and weren't something he'd want someone setting off indiscriminately in his backyard. However, given what they knew about these little alien monsters, Savoy didn't want to take any chances, either.

"Give me a plan for two- and four-bomb placements," he ordered. "I'm sending the ground-penetrating radar readings back up to the *Odyssey*'s exo-geology lab for analysis. If they say that you're not going to sink the city or something, we'll go with the full blast."

"Yes, sir," Burke replied, just a little too eagerly.

Savoy shook his head. Burke loved his explosions just a little too much for the comfort of those who had to bunk anywhere near him.

▶▶▶

"Captain?" Waters asked.

"Yes, Ensign?" Weston said, looking up.

"I think I've got the orbiters on sensors now."

"What's the verdict?"

Ensign Waters shrugged, looking a little confused. "They'll…Well, they'll fit, sir."

"That's good," Weston said, frowning. "What is it, Waters?"

"Sir?"

"What's wrong?" he asked.

"Nothing, sir…it's just…" Waters shook his head. "Here, sir, look for yourself."

Weston watched as the information was relayed to the main screen. "Are those dimensions correct, Ensign?"

"As far as I can tell, Captain."

"How many are coming up?"

"Four, sir."

"How in the hell are they going to fit five hundred people on board four of those things?" Weston asked, looking at the tiny approaching craft.

They were roughly two-thirds the size of one of the *Odyssey*'s shuttles and looked like ugly, squat, flying bricks.

"We're getting minimal energy readings off them, Captain. Their drive systems must be very efficient. Probably a lot smaller than our own."

That made sense. The drive systems on the shuttles, Archangel fighters, and even the *Odyssey* itself made up over a third of the ship's total mass. If they had a considerably smaller drive mass, then it was just remotely possible that they could cram five hundred people onto four of those things.

"I'd hate to try dead-sticking one of those suckers in," Weston muttered, not realizing that he was speaking out loud.

"Excuse me, sir?" Waters asked, half turning.

"Nothing, Ensign," Weston said. "Link me back through to Miss Chans."

"Aye, Captain."

Weston watched the approaching ships for another second, eyeing their ugly, completely non-aerodynamic design, and repeated his comment, mentally this time. Dead-sticking one of those things would be suicide—of that he was certain.

There was a reason why the Archangels and other craft were still designed to fly, more or less, in an atmosphere despite the abilities of the CM generators. No pilot wanted to fly something that would become a crater the first time there was a power glitch.

"I have Miss Chans now, sir."

He turned his focus to the screen, where Admiral Tanner was already looking out at him.

"Admiral," Weston started.

"Captain," the admiral replied, "I trust that you have scanned the orbiters."

"Yes, sir, and we won't have any trouble with them," Weston said.

"That is good."

"Please inform your pilots that I will be launching a drone. They are to follow it into our flight deck. We'll have the refugees waiting."

"Thank you, Captain." The admiral half bowed. "I'll pass your message along."

"Excellent. Weston out."

Waters cut the signal automatically.

"Ensign Waters."

"Yes, sir?"

"Full scans on the incoming craft, if you please."

"Aye, Captain."

It was highly unlikely that they'd be trying anything, given that the *Odyssey* was the only thing standing between them and the approaching alien warships, but Weston had all but grown up in one warzone after another. You didn't take unnecessary chances with your life, or the lives of your people.

If he didn't need to get those people off the *Odyssey* in the worst way, he'd have taken the time to use the ship's own shuttles, just on principle. However, at the moment, they were not only using up his air, but they were also closing off an entire deck and taking up the time of his medical staff.

To say nothing of the fact that he had no suits on hand for these people, and in the battle to come, a hull breach was all too likely. One glancing-laser strike could kill every single one of them, rendering the whole operation to rescue them a particularly bad joke.

CHAPTER 29

▶ "CLEAR THAT DECK!" The landing signals officer (LSO) screamed, though he didn't technically have to raise his voice. The com-net intercepted and normalized the volume before it shot across the vacuum of the flight deck. "Inbound on the ball!"

The computer filtered out the mass of acknowledgments, its programming designed to bring problems to his attention rather than highlight what was going right. This time, everything seemed to be working well, and the software didn't raise any flags.

Not that Chief Mackenzie was going to take that for granted.

His eyes roved the *Odyssey*'s flight deck, looking for anything that might inflict foreign object damage (FOD) on the incoming craft. He wasn't sure if the alien ships were likely to suffer any bad effects from a FOD strike, but it was better to be sure.

When the deck was cleared to his satisfaction, he nodded and waved to one of the cat-control crews standing well out of the way in their green-accented suits. The crew chief flashed him a thumbs-up rather than clutter the network with chatter, and Mac turned back to the front of the immense flight deck.

The unblinking stare of the stars beyond the maw of the deck was a little unnerving, but he'd seen it before and was finally starting to get used to it. Certainly, it wasn't as bad as trying to launch fighters in a hurricane, though it was close, he had to admit. He had two men down by the opening, clearing the deck, and didn't envy them that job in the slightest.

Once they were clear and out of the way, he switched over to a control channel. "Deck is clear for landing."

"Roger that," the answer came back instantly. "Drone will lead. Watch the followers."

"Right," Mac muttered, cutting his channel just after.

Who thought up this idea? He didn't want to know. Chances were that it was Captain Weston, and in that case, he'd really *rather* not know. Because he and his crew were duty bound to curse the idiot's soul for this, and Mac rather liked the captain.

The problem was, of course, that the incoming ships didn't have any active communications with the *Odyssey*, let alone Mac's deck crew. Which was the closest thing to insanity he'd run into since the war.

Four alien ships who don't know fuck all about our systems, procedures, or technology…And we're landing them on a closed flight deck that has a damned field patch running up its center… Mac shook his head.

Total lunacy.

Someone yelled and it was patched through his suit.

"I've got the drone in sight!"

Mac looked up quickly, his eyes sharp as he scanned the maw of the deck.

"There it is!" One of his men pointed.

Mac spotted the drone a second later as it dropped into view, settling in on an approach course that would bring it right down the center of the deck.

The LSO grimaced. Normally, that was the optimal course, but with the steel sheets patching the gash in the center of their deck, it might be a bit rough on the smaller size of the drone and could even damage the systems.

He shrugged that off, as it wasn't his problem, but made a note to have the deck FOD checked again as soon as he could, just in case something got jolted off the drone in the process.

That was about the time that someone screamed.

The yell was logged into the system, its source noted. Mac's HUD lit up like a Christmas tree as he spun around.

The man who had yelled was pointing outside and was still yelling.

"Sweet Jesus! Look!"

Mac looked.

The experienced LSO went pale in his vacuum suit as he saw what had scared the crewman. The four alien shuttles, such as they were, were coming in practically right on each other's tails!

"Wave them off!" Mac yelled, flashing signals with his arms. "Wave them off!"

Men were darting out of the way, gluing themselves to the walls of the flight deck as part of his signal corps held their ground, signaling desperately to the alien crews with lighted batons.

The four ships ignored—or more likely, perhaps, didn't understand—the signals, and kept on barreling in.

Men dove for cover on both sides, and even Mac kicked off his position and flew for the nearby blast shield. He hooked his hand in the grip and swung down into the bunker, where two men from the crash and salvage crews were tensing to jump into motion if the worst came to happen.

Mac pulled himself out of the way of the figures in the red-accented suits, grabbing a handle so he could look through the clear blast shield.

His eyes widened as the four ships came in like a god-damned freight train, barreling into the deck, well past any sane speed, then came to a smooth stop like they were bolted together.

The four shuttles came to a rest just meters from where he was hunkered down, maintaining precise distance from each other, and for a moment, Mac found himself looking for the braces that must be connecting them.

He didn't find any and wasted minutes staring until his heart slowed back down to normal. Finally, he climbed out of the blast bunker and walked over to the shuttles, wondering if anyone inside had seen the scramble.

A flash of embarrassment and anger rose up in him, but the experienced LSO forced it down and pulled the two lighted batons from his hand. He flicked them over to the brilliant green setting and waved both of them to the nearest lock.

Slowly, the first of the ships began to move in that direction, this time at a decent pace, and Mac walked it to the lock.

"Gregor! You get the next one."

"You got it, Chief," a shaky voice came back.

Business gradually returned to normal on the flight deck.

"They're aboard, Captain."

Weston nodded at the unneeded comment, still staring at the screen. "Any injuries?"

"No, sir."

"Thank God for that," he said, standing up. "Commander, you have the bridge. I'm going to have a chat with the pilot of the lead 'orbiter.'"

"Aye, Captain." Roberts moved to take Weston's place as the captain turned and strode back to the lift.

Weston sat down in the lift and told it where to take him. He wasn't certain what he could say to the man, or woman, flying that heap, other than to inform them of proper flight protocols.

Proper protocols for this ship, at any rate, he corrected himself.

It was obvious that the alien drive technology was entirely different than the reaction-based system that the *Odyssey* and its onboard complement used. The Archangels could match that kind of precision flying and often did, but no other craft built on Earth could hope to do it, and even the Angels would never try it on a *landing*.

The pilots were obviously used to maneuvers that made Earth's precision flying look like child's play, so Weston wondered what would happen to flight teams like the Blue Angels and the Snowbirds, if and when this drive technology became part of the Earth tech base.

Probably nothing, he thought after a moment. *Fighters will always look impressive and dangerous to crowds, even if freighters are able to match their maneuvers.*

Still, it wasn't a happy thought to the former fighter pilot.

As the lift stopped, Weston pushed the thoughts away and grabbed a pair of Magboots as he kicked out into the zero-g deck.

▶▶▶

Impressive drives or not, they were still ugly as sin.

Weston floated along the wall as the first of the orbiters rose up from the evacuated deck below, riding the massive airlock up into the parking level.

The squat ship was little more than a flying box, without even the bristling sensor antennae to give it a vaguely utilitarian look. Instead, it looked like someone had attached some kind of drive system to a cargo container and wished its crew the best of luck.

Weston waited for the orbiter to come to a halt in one of the parking places normally reserved for the *Odyssey*'s shuttles, then walked over as a small crowd gathered around it.

"Where's the door?" someone called out.

"Damn if know." Another of the flight-op crew shrugged. "Looks like a brick without the wings."

"Captain on deck!" someone snapped out as Weston approached.

The men snapped to attention as Weston touched down, the echoing clanks of his boots rebounding through the deck.

"As you were," he said, waving them off.

The crowd began dispersing as the airlock rumbled again.

Weston and the deck chief were startled when a section of its sidewall melted away.

"Hol-y shit," the deck chief muttered, actually taking a step back, flushing. "Sorry, Cap..."

"No need. I know the feeling," Weston replied, watching the fluid motion of the metal as it pooled on the floor of the deck and built up a ramp.

It looked impressive, but Weston had to admit that he didn't like the idea of flying in a ship that could melt around him without warning.

Someone appeared at the hatch and walked down the ramp. She, Weston realized noting the figure in the utilitarian coveralls, stopped just before stepping onto the *Odyssey*'s deck and made a motion with her hand, crossing her chest, palm up and open. It struck him that it was probably a salute or something similar, so Weston snapped to attention and brought his fingers up to his temple, while he saw the chief do the same at his side.

"I would like permission to set foot on your vessel, Captain," the woman's voice came through the translator clearly.

Weston nodded and dropped his salute. "Granted."

"Thank you," she nodded, stepping off onto the deck, only to float free as her feet no longer wanted to remain connected to the ground.

"Chief!" Weston yelled.

"Got it, Cap!" the chief said, boots clanging on the deck as he grabbed the woman's arm mid-tumble and pulled her down to the deck.

She was none the worse for wear, but her face was flush with embarrassment and anger as she muttered something the translator didn't catch.

"My apologies," Weston said as he motioned the chief to find her a pair of over-boots. "I forgot to mention that our lower decks are all in zero-g."

"My mistake, Captaine," she said, her flowing accent quite crisp from her annoyance. "I should have checked my instruments."

"Nonsense." Weston waved a hand. "It's my understanding that your ships all have artificial gravity. Why would you check?"

"Perhaps," she grated, obviously distressed by the rather ignominious impression she'd left. She took a deep breath as they reached the wall, turning back to Weston. "I am Ithan Cora Sienthe."

"Captain Eric Weston…pleased to meet you."

"I as well," she said.

"Now," Weston smiled thinly as the deck chief fetched a pair of Magboots. "Let us talk about your landing protocols and how they impact on my ship."

▶▶▶

Dr. Rame moved slowly through the ranks of patients who were gradually returning to consciousness.

"How are they, Nurse?"

"No obvious allergic reactions, and they seem to be reacting to the stimulant as expected."

Rame nodded. "Good. As soon as they can walk, get them divided up into groups. Keep families together, but speed matters. We have to get these people off the *Odyssey* before we break orbit."

The nurse nodded professionally, returning to her task as Rame continued on, masking a grim look on his face.

The doctor didn't like being pushed on such a tight schedule, but the captain had given him his orders in no uncertain terms. Get these people off the *Odyssey*, upright or on their backs, within three hours, or the *Odyssey* would be entering battle with them on board.

Being the chief medical officer gave him quite a lot of power, even over the captain, but none of it concerned tactical decisions. So he found himself pushing the envelope of what he'd recommend under similar circumstances, trying to get as many of the patients moving under their own power as possible. Any others they'd carry off if they had to.

A ship in combat was no place for an innocent bystander.

Not even when the ship was, itself, an innocent bystander of sorts.

▶ ▶ ▶

Weston watched the first flood of shaky passengers being led to the small orbiter parked on his deck. A junior lieutenant moved to his side, catching his attention.

"Lieutenant."

"Begging the captain's pardon, sir, but I just came back from the Archangel's berth."

"Did you deliver my request to speak with Commander Michaels?"

"Yes, sir." The lieutenant was sweating, Weston noted.

"Then why is the commander not here, Lieutenant?"

"Sir, I...sir...that is, Lieutenant Amherst...sir, he..."

"Spit it out," Weston snapped, wondering why the young kid was so worked up. Amherst was Steph's second in the Angels, but if something had happened to Steph, Weston should have been told about it.

"Sir!" The young man snapped straight. "Lieutenant Amherst told me that, unless the ship was about to be blown to hell, I wasn't getting within twenty feet of Commander Michaels, sir."

Weston kept a straight face. "Very well. If you'll inform Mr. Amherst that I would like to speak with him, I would be appreciative."

"Aye, aye, Captain!" The young man snapped a salute and beat a hasty retreat.

Weston watched him go with an amused look. Amherst was just doing his job, even if it sounded like he'd been a little rougher than he had to be. If he felt that Steph needed more sleep, and Weston wasn't going to argue with him on the subject—not until the attack was underway, at any rate.

Still, if Amherst wanted to play that game, he was going to have to learn the consequences one had to suffer as a good XO.

Weston turned his attention back to the refugee exodus.

Things were going as well as could be expected, he supposed, given that most of the refugees were still at least somewhat under the effects of the sedatives and weren't in the most lucid state of mind.

The pilots of the orbiters had pitched in and seemed to be trained medical personnel as well as pilots, which made things a lot easier.

Their efficiency almost made Weston sorry for ripping a strip off each one of their backs in turn for their landing.

Almost.

▶▶▶

"Commander! Enemy status changed!"

Roberts turned and approached Waters's bridge station. "What happened, Ensign?"

"They accelerated once they rendezvoused with the sixth ship, sir. New ETA is still being calculated, but it'll be less than eight hours."

"All right. I'll inform the captain. Are all our people back yet?" Roberts asked as he turned around.

"Yes, sir," Ensign Lamont replied. "The last SAR flight just came back in. All we have left out there are dirt-side, sir."

"Major Brinks and his team are going to be on their own shortly," Roberts said.

"Yes, sir."

"Lamont, contact the captain. Inform him of the new ETA."

"Aye, aye, sir."

▶▶▶

Chief Corrin smiled under her hard suit helmet, knowing that no one could see her. The work on the flight deck had been superb, and she was proud of the damage-control team that had guided and done most of it. Not that she was going to tell them that.

"Not bad," she said over the com-channels. "Not half bad at all."

The figures around her relaxed noticeably.

Well, she wouldn't tell them in so many words. Good crews knew without being told. That was what made them good crews.

"Awright," she said.

The men and women snapped back to attention, each of them focusing on her.

"We're going to war, ladies. That means that damage control just got bumped up to the front lines on this here tub. You're all off shift starting now, but by God, you better be ready when I call."

A chorus of acknowledgments came from the fatigued group. Corrin waved a half salute and dismissed them without a word. They quickly made for the locks, and she knew they'd be riding them up to the crew berths in short order.

The chief looked over the repair job one last time, noting the smooth bead on the laser weld.

"Not half bad at all."

▶▶▶

"Captain." Lieutenant Amherst saluted as his feet clanged together on the deck. "You asked for me, sir?"

"I understand that you refused to allow my message to reach Stephanos," Weston said.

"Sir, I decided that the commander needed the rest, sir."

Weston suppressed both the urge to smirk at the format of the response and the desire to club Amherst in the back of his head. "I see."

Amherst didn't respond.

"Well, in that case, Lieutenant, I believe that you have some decisions to make."

"Me, sir?"

"You are the XO of the flight group, are you not?"

"Yes, sir but…" Amherst paled.

"Well, then you make the decisions, and Steph will rubber-stamp them when you decide he's had enough sleepy time," Weston said, with just a hint of sarcasm to his voice.

"Uh…yes, sir."

"Good. First, what's the status of the flight?"

"We're down by four pilots and planes, sir. Two losses, not counting Flare, and Brute is in the med-lab."

Weston nodded. "We'll need you to be at your best in a few hours…"

"Sir, the Archangels are always ready."

"I remember that, Lieutenant, but you're badly weakened, and despite the downtime, you're going to be tired, too."

"Sir…Captain, we won't let you down."

"I'm sure you won't, Lieutenant," Weston told him. "But I was thinking about giving you at least one more pilot."

"Sir?" Amherst frowned. "I'm afraid I don't see how that's possible. We're missing four planes, and we don't have any replacements—even if we did have another pilot."

"We have at least one more pilot on the *Odyssey*, Lieutenant," Weston replied, his voice brittle.

Amherst paled. "Captain, with all due respect, you can't mean yourself!"

Weston let the moment stretch out while the pilot paled even more. "No, Lieutenant. I wasn't referring to myself."

Amherst let out a breath.

"You don't need to sound *quite* so relieved, Lieutenant."

"Sir, you know it's not that. But you're needed here," Amherst said.

"Well, be that as it may, what's your opinion on Jennifer Samuels?"

"Jenny, sir? She's good people," Amherst replied. "Tried out for the Angels, didn't make the cut."

"She made the cut, Lieutenant," Weston corrected him.

"Pardon?" Amherst blinked.

"Samuels's flight scores were well above minimum standards," Weston said.

"Begging the captain's pardon, sir, but why the hell isn't she in the flight?"

Weston heard the incredulity in the man's voice and didn't blame him. Finding qualified pilots for the limited neural interface system on the Archangel fighter craft wasn't easy. During the war, the main limitation wasn't in how many of them they could build, but rather, how many of them they could man.

"The war was over before she could be accepted, Lieutenant," Weston replied. "We Archangels aren't that much of an asset in peacetime, you see."

Amherst winced.

"However," Weston said, with a thin smile, "I don't believe that I see any peacetime in our immediate area. Do you, Lieutenant?"

"Um...no, sir," Amherst returned, still frowning. "But we're still down by a plane."

"Are we, Lieutenant?" Weston asked, gazing across the deck.

Amherst followed his captain's gaze as his eyes settled on Archangel One, the captain's own.

"Inform the lieutenant of her promotion," Weston replied.

"Aye, aye, sir."

▼

CHAPTER 30

▲

▶ SAVOY WATCHED THE display trail off and then blinked away the information. The tunnels under the city were still small enough to be taken out, but they didn't have a lot of time left if he were to judge by the changes he saw in the ground-penetrating radar map.

"Burke!"

"Sir!"

"We're cleared for a four-point detonation," he told the explosives expert. "You have the blast map for me?"

"Yes, sir, I'm dropping it in your slot now."

Savoy accessed his memory slot on the network. Sure enough, the map file was waiting for him, so he tabbed it and watched as it opened in 50 percent transparency over his HUD.

The map was thorough, as he'd expected, so he gave it a quick glance over before he tagged it with his electronic signature and approved the plan. The suit's computer automatically attached the geological estimate provided by the exogeology lab, just to cover the paperwork required to release the powerful explosives.

"Where are we coming on the evacuation?" He turned, looking for Mehn.

"Those local boys say they've almost got the place empty!" the other soldier replied, his voice a bit stressed.

"Are you all right?" Savoy asked.

His HUD flickered, a video window opening up in half transparency, and the sweating face of Eddy Mehn appeared.

"I'm fine, L.T.," he panted. "Just having a little trouble here."

"Do you need backup?"

"Negative," the soldier replied. "I'm almost done. There was some structural damage when the ship impacted. I'm just holding up a wall while some kids get out."

"All right," Savoy said, "report back when the area is clear."

"Yes, sir."

▶ ▶ ▶

Commander Stephanos groaned and stretched as he stepped out of his berth and looked around.

"What?" he asked, frowning in confusion as the Archangel flight crew was there, staring at him.

"You tell him, Amherst. I didn't have anything to do with it," one of them said.

"Oh, this is gonna be good." Steph smirked, his eyes settling on Lieutenant Amherst.

"Well, you see, sir. It's like this…"

Stephanos knew that it was going to be one of those days when Amherst called him "sir." Informality was the formality of the Archangels, so when his XO retreated to proper military decorum, he'd done something he was half expecting to get spanked for.

"All right, Amherst, why don't you tell me what's going on?"

▶▶▶

Lt. Jennifer Samuels lowered herself into the cockpit of the fighter reverently. She knew its every control forward and backward, her hands sliding over each in turn, lightly fingering the firing studs and arming switches. She had a hard time believing that she was sitting in a fighter, let along this particular one.

Archangel One.

The captain's own.

She settled her feet onto the form-molded pedals, letting them rest there without pressure, and sat back in the bolster seat that was just a touch too big for comfort. That would be fixed when she suited up, she knew from experience, but it still felt unreal to be here. She was lost in those thoughts when the voice startled her from behind.

"Like a dream, isn't it?"

Jennifer Samuels twisted in her seat, her eyes wide with surprise. "Captain! I…sorry, sir. I shouldn't be…"

"Relax," Weston said. "I hear you've accepted the posting."

She swallowed. "I…that is, yes, sir. Thank you, sir."

He nodded, his face serious. "It won't be a cakewalk, you know."

"I know, sir."

"I've checked your records, Lieutenant. You'll do just fine. Just don't get fancy, and remember to stay with your wingman. You'll have the least experience of any of them out there, so you might have some trouble keeping up at first. Don't let it get under your skin. If you let the little mistakes get to you, they'll pile up into a big one."

"Yes, sir."

Weston smiled, kicked off the fighter, and floated toward the wall. "I'll let you two get acquainted, Lieutenant. Treat her well, as she's an old friend of mine. I'd like to have her back in one piece."

"Aye, aye, sir," Jennifer replied, throwing the departing officer a salute as she felt her attention being drawn back to the fighter she was strapping into.

It was good to be home.

▶▶▶

Admiral Tanner watched the displays as the first of the orbiters departed the *Odyssey* and began its downward spiral. It seemed foolish in so many ways, evacuating people from one danger just to plant them smack in the middle of another.

If the *Odyssey* failed to eliminate the ships, if the Forge failed to finish the work they were so desperately trying to accomplish, if the ground forces now on Mons Systema failed to account for each and every Drasin…

If any one of those things occurred, those people would die here on the planet instead of there, in space.

It hardly seems fair, Tanner thought, *that they should survive so much on their own, live through the destruction of their own world, just to die here on someone else's. So this is war,* he thought grimly to himself. *Such an innocuous word for something so horrific.*

Millennia of peace didn't prepare a man for this. Tanner wasn't a warrior; he wasn't like his old friend, Nero. He was in charge of a mining and exploration fleet, scouring the galaxy for new worlds, new resources, and new things to see. And now he was here, defending a world, with no assets of his own, and forced to rely on gifts from the gods to save his people.

That wasn't the way it was supposed to work.

▶▶▶

"Captain!"

Weston paused mid-step, glancing over his shoulder. He nodded as he saw Stephanos jogging to catch up with him.

"I need to speak with you, Captain," the pilot said.

"Walk with me, Commander," Weston said. "I have to get to the bridge. We've almost got the refugees off my ship, and we've got some tricky maneuvers to plan."

"Sir, about Lieutenant Samuels…" Steph started earnestly. "You can't be serious about assigning her to the flight."

"And why would that be, Commander?" Weston asked smoothly as they walked.

"Sir, Jenny's a good pilot, but she's not been drilled with the flight," Stephanos said. "The Archangels aren't just any fighter group…"

"I like to think that I know that, Commander."

Stephanos flushed. "I know you do, Captain, but…dammit, sir!"

"Watch yourself, Commander," Weston snapped, coming to a stop so fast that Stephanos was past him before he knew it. "You're overstepping yourself."

"Maybe I am, sir," he said, turning back, "but you're asking me to take a rookie out on a hot run for her first mission. Sir, I'd rather go underpowered than do that. If she messes up, she could take my flight with her."

"Perhaps," Weston said, conceding the point. "But I think that you're forgetting something."

"Like what?"

Weston ignored the challenging tone in his friend's voice and responded, "You aren't going a little underpowered, Steph. You're down by four planes and pilots; that's a full quarter of your flight."

Stephanos scowled. "I'm aware of that."

"Are you also aware that Lieutenant Samuels passed her NICS exam with a point-three-nine variance?" Weston retorted. "Or that she trained at the Angels flight camp for nine months before the war ended? Or that she was in line for a commission with the flight until the congressional decision to stop 'antagonizing' the Block by dangling our feathered butts in their face?"

Steph paled as the captain spoke with hard edge in his voice. "No, sir, I wasn't aware of that."

"Then I suggest you review her file," Weston said.

"Aye, aye, sir."

Weston watched as Stephen walked away. "Steph," he said as the commander reached the corner.

Stephanos paused, glancing back. "Sir?"

"I understand your worry, but you need every able body you can get. If I had my way, I'd be out there, too."

"I don't think we're quite that bad off, begging the captain's pardon," Steph replied, with a smirk.

"Wiseass." Weston shook his head, turning away.

"Always, sir."

▶ ▶ ▶

"Captain on the bridge!"

"At ease," Weston said, accepting his seat back from Commander Roberts. "Status report?"

"The last of the refugees will be departing in the next twenty minutes, sir."

"All right, Mr. Daniels, have you prepared the course information I requested?"

"Aye, sir," Lieutenant Daniels replied, tapping out a command on the navigation board. "Using nothing but thrusters will be tough on the ship, sir, but we can mount a successful intercept if we use minimal CM generation."

"How minimal?" Weston's voice was clipped.

"Eight percent, sir. For the first hour of the burn only."

Weston thought about the CM technology that allowed both the heavy lift capability of the *Odyssey*'s shuttles and the lethal speed of the Archangels, not to mention the acceleration of the *Odyssey* itself. The downside of the technology was that it created a rather large sinkhole in normal space that was the equivalent of a searchlight to someone with eyes to see it.

It was also a large part of what kept the acceleration from plastering the crew over the rear bulkheads of the ship. Since their mass was reduced, along with the rest of the ship, their personal inertia was affected by the laws of the little pocket of reality that the *Odyssey* dragged around with her at all times.

"I'm sorry, sir, it's the best I can do with the time restraint."

Weston studied the data. Daniels was right. Without 8 percent, they'd never be able to intercept the ships far enough from the planet to ensure that they could prevent more landers from being dispatched.

"All right. Approved," Weston said, signing off on the order. "Lamont?"

Susan Lamont stiffened. "Sir?"

"Status of the preparations?"

"We're ready to run silent, Captain," she replied, with a satisfied tone.

Weston nodded, not noticing the sharp look Commander Roberts threw across the bridge as he noted the use of the term.

"All right. Let's test the system, then, while we still can," Weston said, settling in. "Engage black hole stealth systems. Kill all unnecessary power use. Make us invisible."

"Aye, aye, Captain."

▶▶▶

An unseemly shout jerked Admiral Tanner around in surprise, pulling him away from his status board.

"What?"

"The alien ship, Admiral…She's gone." The technician's face was pale.

"She left orbit already?"

"No, sir. She just…We lost visual, sir."

"What about sensors?" Tanner frowned, reaching over the man's shoulder and tapping in commands.

Nothing. Every system he checked said the same thing: there was nothing there. He accessed the logs with a few quick taps and blinked as he watched the oddly configured ship simply vanish.

"Sir…I…I think they're still there," a young woman said, pointing at the screen.

Tanner looked at the screen for several seconds, wondering what the woman was talking about, until he saw it himself. There was a black spot in the middle of the screen where the ship was supposed to be, one that moved against the background of stars as it orbited the world.

"Fascinating," he whispered, a touch of a smile showing on his lips.

"Admiral?" Milla said.

"They're still there, Ithan," he said absently, pointing out the screen. "Watch the stars."

With that comment, Tanner headed over to another console. "Casa," he said to the young woman seated there. "Active scan, if you please."

"Yes, Admiral," she replied, tapping out a command.

▶▶▶

"We're being scanned, Captain," Waters said, looking up from his console. "All across the spectrum, very high power."

"Source?"

"The planet, sir."

Weston nodded. "Good. That means they noticed something when we shifted. Let's hope our signal is low on their systems."

"Aye, sir."

"Lamont?"

"Sir," Susan Lamont responded.

"Have all decks made ready for acceleration drills," Weston told her. "We'll have a rough ride for the first hour or so."

"Aye, sir."

"And in the meantime, put me through to Milla and the admiral."

"Aye, aye, Captain."

▶▶▶

"Incredible," Admiral Tanner said in a low voice. "They really are there, aren't they?"

"Yes, Admiral, but their signal has dimmed considerably. Even knowing where to focus our sensors, all we get is a marginal return," the technician said. "Admiral…if they wished to sneak up on any of our ships…"

"Our captains would have to know that they were coming to have a chance of spotting them," Tanner finished for her. "Let us hope that the Drasin are the same."

"Yes, Admiral."

"Admiral…"

Tanner turned and saw that Milla was approaching in her impressively sized armor. "May I assume that Captain Weston wishes to make contact?"

"He does, Admiral."

Tanner took a moment to straighten his clothing, stepping into the full view of the armor.

"Captain Weston." He nodded gravely.

Weston hid a smile as he watched the admiral adjust his clothing before stepping around to the front of the armor and wondered if he should inform the man that infantry special warfare armor had 360-degree sensor coverage.

Maybe another time, he thought as Tanner spoke.

"Captain Weston," the small man began.

"Admiral Tanner." Weston permitted himself a slight smile. "May I assume that you noticed a change in our current stance?"

"You may," Tanner replied.

"Might I inquire as to the effect?" Weston probed.

"Your vessel vanished almost entirely from our passive sensors," the small man replied, "and even though we knew your location, our active sensors were unable to uncover more than a shadow of your previous signature."

There was a low breath of relief that passed through the bridge, but Weston ignored it in favor of masking his own breath of relief. "That was what we were hoping for, Admiral. Now, if only the enemy finds us equally difficult to see."

"One can only hope."

"Indeed," Weston replied. "We'll be leaving orbit shortly, Admiral."

"May I inquire as to your plans?"

"Wouldn't do you any good, Admiral," Weston replied, "and I'm afraid that we don't have the time."

"I understand, Captain," Tanner said. "In that case, I wish you the very best and…"

"And?" Weston blinked, hearing something in the other man's tone.

Tanner paused, looking like he wanted to say more, then shook his head. "It is nothing, Captain. May the Maker journey with you…"

"And you," Weston replied automatically, as he always did when someone wished him well in one way or another.

The signal was dropped and Commander Roberts leaned over.

"Just as long as we don't have to meet our 'Maker' before he journeys with us."

Weston stifled a snort. "Why, Commander Roberts, I do believe you just made a joke."

Roberts looked evenly back at him. "I wish I had."

"Right," Weston said. "Sound general quarters."

"Aye, Captain. General quarters."

"And get me Major Brinks, if you please."

"Aye, aye, Captain."

▶▶▶

Brinks rumbled into the intercom, keeping most of his attention on the squad that worked to clear out a large promenade or something similar.

"Major, how are things?"

"They're coming along, Captain."

"Good. I'm calling to inform you that we will be leaving orbit shortly."

"Understood." Brinks paused. "Godspeed, Captain."

"And you, Major."

"Yes, sir. Brinks out."

▶▶▶

The lights across the ship flickered and came back in muted red as the ship-wide intercom began speaking over the commotion.

"General quarters. This is a call to general quarters."

"You heard the lady!" Chief Corrin yelled over the ruckus. "Get movin' 'fore I have your hides pinned to the bulkheads!"

"All stations, secure for acceleration. This is no drill. I say again, this is no drill."

Corrin paused mid-step, slapping a crewman on the shoulder. "Strap that PDA down, Rickman! You want it to bat you upside the head? And do up that restraint good and proper!"

She grabbed the seat restraint and cinched it tight enough to bruise the man, growling the whole time, "I swear to God, all of you, if I catch you in the medical bay with a broken leg because you fell out of your damned chair, I'll wring your necks good and proper!"

There was no verbal response, but before she moved onto the next station, they had all triple-checked their belts.

▶▶▶

"All stations report ready, Captain," Lieutenant Daniels said.

"And our current orbit?"

Daniels looked up. "We'll pass the meridian in two minutes, sir. At that point, we'll be completely behind the planet and should be shielded by its mass."

"Very well, Mr. Daniels, you may execute when ready."

"Aye, aye, Captain." Daniels tapped in a command and watched the course change. On the screen, a diagram of the system ticked by, moment by moment, until the navigator leaned eagerly forward. "Firing thrusters now!"

The ship began to vibrate, a low rumble filling the air around the crew, and the force shoved them back into their seats. For the first few seconds, it was a gentle pressure. Then it climbed until the acceleration on the bridge had equalized with the centrifugal force of the habitat, and they all felt like they were half lying down as the bridge angled upward.

"One gravity acceleration," Daniels announced. "Increasing power in fifteen seconds."

The countdown was silent but poignant as the *Odyssey* poured on the power. The big ship looped low around the planet, almost skimming the atmosphere as it followed the course, using the planet's gravity as part of his calculations.

Then the second-stage thrust kicked in and they felt the bridge flip end for end around them as the force slapped them back even harder.

"Crossing the second meridian in forty-five seconds." Daniels's voice was strained this time, but he managed to speak clearly as his hands worked the controls. "Main thrust cutoff in forty."

Weston didn't say a word as he watched the numbers on his personal display, noting that the entire ship's company was currently pulling over three g's due to the firing of the powerful main engines without full compensation from the CM generators.

"Main thruster cutout!"

The sudden lack of acceleration was like being thrown forward in a braking vehicle, but the seat restraints held everyone in place as the heavy rumble faded, leaving only a bare hint of its former glory in the air, and everyone started breathing a little easier.

"We're clearing the meridian...now," Daniels said, a hint of satisfaction in his voice as the *Odyssey* whipped around the planet and flung itself out into the depths of space once more.

CHAPTER 31

▶ "WELL THAT'S IT, gentlemen," Major Brinks said as the connection to the *Odyssey* blinked off. "We're on our own from here on out. I hope everyone packed their underwear."

A few muffled chuckles greeted his words, but for the most part, the men on the link were too busy fighting, running, or hiding to respond.

Brinks checked his HUD before leaping the forty-meter gap to the next building, where he landed with a solid smack, the nano-servos in his armor absorbing and storing the energy as he flexed his legs. The situation wasn't as bad as all that, actually. For the most part, the drones were being mopped up whenever they stuck their disturbing little mandibles out to be seen.

That was the good news.

The bad news was that fewer and fewer of them were sticking their disturbing little mandibles out to have them shot off. Brinks might have considered that a good sign, that perhaps they were cleaning the last of them out, but judging from the reports he was getting back through the link, it was obvious that the survivors were still numerous. They were just getting smarter.

Nothing worse than an enemy who's a quick learner, the major grumbled as he stepped over to the edge of the scraper and looked down at the public promenade below.

▶ ▶ ▶

The whining crack of the bullets was joined by the pure-white contrails as they accelerated across the huge promenade, twisting and turning as they locked in on the heat sources on the other side and adjusted their courses. The firefight raged around him as Sean Bermont held the trigger of his rifle down and poured the last of his magazine into the maelstrom. He kept moving as the now empty magazine hit the ground at his feet. He didn't flinch, or even notice, except in a visceral way, when a ray of energy blew up a stone column only a few feet away. Bermont slapped the mag into the receiver as he and the others continued to approach through the enemy fire. He lifted the weapon to his shoulder and held the trigger down again.

It wasn't a firefight as much as a rout when it came to dealing with the drones that came out into the open. The enemy weapons were technically impressive, their whining power enough to actually cause solid stone to explode when the beams intersected it, but the MX-112s were their equal in effectiveness, if not technical prowess, and the battles between the two were short, furious, and final.

The guided ability of the MX-112 gave the humans the advantage, however, since they didn't have to be perfectly on target with every shot. A near miss without guidance was a bull's-eye with even the minimal course corrections that each bullet was capable of. If the minimal intelligence of the scramjet-propelled round was capable of seeing the enemy, the enemy was already dead. The problem was when the drones hid within buildings and alcoves and forced the humans to approach too close for the guidance system to be effective.

The heavy, little rounds were lethal killers at any range, of course, but the MX-112 was designed for the modern battlefield, not the sort of close-quarters room clearing that this fight was turning into. At short range, the weapon's effectiveness was less than half what it could do at its optimum engagement range. Of course, the armor-piercing rounds tended to compensate for any shortcomings from a lack of a kinetic kill.

In short, it was a good thing that the squad was wearing full environmental body armor. An explosive blowback and incidental shrapnel from your own bullet was a bitch of a way to die.

▶▶▶

"All right, boss. Looks like we're clear," Eddy Mehn said as he double-checked the status of the evacuations. The locals had moved fast and seemed on the ball, so they were about to have a front-row seat to a big boom.

Savoy nodded. "Thanks, Mehn. Burke…You're up."

"Yes, sir!" Burke said eagerly.

"Could you at least *try* to not sound so happy about it?" Savoy groaned.

"Sorry, sir."

Bullshit, Savoy thought but didn't comment. "Mehn, get those locals over here and under cover!"

"On our way, boss."

Good. One less thing to worry about, Savoy thought as he looked around for a likely spot.

There was a solid-looking building a short distance away that looked tough enough, so he jumped over to it and checked the area behind it.

"This'll do. Hey, Mehn, those locals got one of their ray guns?"

"Sure do, sir. What's up?" the response came back.

"Bring 'em here." Savoy grinned.

Mehn acknowledged the order, so Savoy turned his focus to Burke as the explosives man finished up the last-minute preparations. Mostly, it was just a lot of higher-level math, trying to work out the best positioning for the bunker busters so that the pressure waves of the explosions took out everything below in one hit. Normally, missing one or two people was hardly a mission-critical error, but the last thing they wanted to do was leave any of those creatures alive, kicking and *eating*.

"Can we do this and be sure?" Savoy prodded Burke. His eyes tracked the inbound carnivore drone on his HUD.

Burke raised a fist, signaling the affirmative. "Can do, boss. I've got data from the thermobarics earlier, and the GPR has given us a good idea of the composition of the soil and the extent of their tunnels. I could probably do it with half the firepower, but since we've got it…"

"Use it. Be sure." Savoy made a fist of his own and thudded it against Burke's raised one.

▶▶▶

Nero Jehan grumbled as he listened to the incoming reports from all over the city.

Less than half of them were from his soldiers. The rest were routed to him from various other sectors and were almost entirely composed of complaints from the civilians.

He didn't have time for this!

The big man's fist cracked the obsidian surface of the console in front of him, and half his staff shrank away in fear as he snarled in annoyance.

The rest were more used to him, it seemed, and didn't do more than jump a little, but it was enough for Jehan to calm himself and turn back to his work. He grumbled as he wiped the complaints from his screen. Let someone else handle that idiocy.

"Reassign Fourth Squad to the promenade in Calisma," he said, glancing over at one of his staff. "Make sure that they are careful to announce their arrival. I don't want them killed by our allies."

"Yes, sir."

"Are you all right, Nero?"

He looked around to see Tanner approaching. "Shouldn't you be busy?"

"I have no fleet to command, and the alien ship has left orbit...to fight for us," the small man completed, his tone bitter.

"Welcome to my hell, Tanner."

"Why, I wonder, does it feel like we are paying the price for millennia of peace?" the admiral asked, mostly rhetorically.

Nero just snorted.

"You don't agree?"

"I'm from the outer colonies," Nero responded. "My people left the inner systems because we couldn't handle the 'peace.' I'm probably not the best person to ask."

Tanner nodded. "I understand that...This is why you are in charge of our ground forces..."

"Ground forces!" Nero snapped, his voice laced with disgust. "Is that what you call them? Tanner, my friend, they are no more 'ground forces' than your ships were a 'navy.' They are, at best, police playacting at being soldiers. If the Drasin were parking their ships illegally—or perhaps, stealing trinkets on the street—then they might know what to do. They aren't soldiers, Tanner. No matter how well you dress them up."

"I think you are letting your frustration get the best of you, Nero," Tanner told him mildly. "And it is bothering your staff."

Nero looked around and grimaced.

Tanner had a point. If nothing else, he should keep his mouth shut in front of the others. There was no reason for them to lose hope, as he had.

Nero Jehan nodded. "You are right, my friend. Perhaps I'm just tired."

Tanner stiffened as the big man moved past him and leaned down to whisper.

"How can they be soldiers, old friend," Nero asked in a whisper as he moved past, "when the person they look to for leadership doesn't even know what a soldier is?"

▶▶▶

Sean Bermont threw himself up against a wall as he checked his gun's status in the HUD and grimaced.

"I'm out!" he said over the link, taking a few deep breaths to relax as stray ray gun blasts whined around him.

"Hold for reload," Brinks's voice came over the link, but all Bermont could do was nod uselessly.

The powered armor increased a soldier's endurance practically exponentially, but he always seemed to get winded in combat, just the same. Something about the adrenaline rush, perhaps, or maybe it was the fear, plain and simple.

He didn't know what it was, but when he started to come down from the battle rush, it was like he'd run a marathon, even when it was the suit taking up most of the slack.

A scraping hiss startled the former JTF2 soldier into action as he turned against the wall and fell into a crouch with his empty rifle braced against his knee. He poked the muzzle around the corner, linking his HUD into the rifle's camera, and swept it around in an attempt to locate the source of the sound.

When he found it, all thought of a post-battle crash was gone as another surge of adrenaline struck him.

"Oh fuck."

Those two words were all he had time to get out as one of the drones surged around the corner and practically ran him over in what *had* to be a shock of the ages for both of them. Bermont was out of ammo in his rifle, too close to draw his pistol, and knocked back on his ass by a multiton insect that may or may not have been as surprised as he was. Either way, it had the advantage of weight and position, and it became clear in an instant that it wasn't planning on wasting either.

The heavy smack sent Bermont's MX-112 flying before he could pull it back, leaving the soldier barely enough time to roll clear before the heavy blow cleaved into the structure where his head had been.

The drone gave an odd hiss as it rushed around the corner, striking again at him as the armored soldier rolled desperately, then slapped his right hand down into the ground with a full-powered strike.

The slap cracked against the smooth, glassy material of the promenade floor, its force lifting him off the ground as another cleaving strike landed where he had been. He tucked his arms into his torso as he spun in the air, using his feet and legs to control his spin as he landed back on his feet.

The move left him facing the wrong direction when he landed, but the 360-degree panorama the suit afforded kept him informed of what the enemy at his back was doing, just in time to sidestep another strike and spin as he pulled his carbon-steel kukri from the sheath in the thigh of his armor.

The blade was curved and honed to a fine, though not razor, edge and it actually swooshed as it parted the air and the armor-assisted strike went through. The blade bit into the drone's mandible, causing it to jump back before it hissed again and lifted its leg up over four meters above Bermont's head.

He saw the blow coming, his mind already running at that insane speed combat seemed to induce, but his own reactions felt as sluggish as the fluid motion of his foe. He let go of the kukri, bringing his right hand up to block the blow as the leg came crashing down into his shoulder with force enough to rupture the carbon-fiber armor and dig deep into his shoulder.

His HUD went wild, but he only noted it instinctively as he screamed both in pain and outraged exertion. He kept his right arm moving by some force of will and locked it onto the carapace of the leg that had impaled him.

He screamed at the drone, anything to distract himself from the torturous pain as he began twisting the leg to the side. The leg gave way slowly but surely as his armor-enhanced muscles continued to pressure it down in a twisting motion, like one might use when breaking off a lobster's claw at a fine meal.

There was a sickening crack as the leg broke, and the drone squealed in shock or pain, Bermont didn't know or care which. He ripped it loose, twisting his entire body back and yanking until the leg burst from the main body in a spray of steaming fluids.

Both fell apart at that moment, the human collapsing to the ground and the alien staggering as it tried to balance itself on a limb that was no longer there.

Bermont screamed yet again as he pulled the impaling limb from his shoulder, while feeling the cooling rush of the suit's automatic foam systems sealing the wound. He looked at the tip of the limb where it was coated in his own blood, giving the carapace a sinister, oily appearance. It was shaped like a spear point, with jagged edges that he assumed were to aid it in climbing but had also done a wicked job on his flesh.

His attention came back to the real world when the creature charged at him again. Bermont howled, covering his pain with sound as he drove upward and flipped the alien limb over in his wounded hand, then passed it to his good one. He met the charge like a pikeman from some long-forgotten war, grunting in pain and exertion as he drove the alien's own leg deep into its guts.

It screamed this time, and Bermont grunted in satisfaction as he gave the limb a twist and fell back. The steaming and sizzling fluid that filled the alien poured around him, bubbling against his armor and the ground, but he didn't have the strength to get up and fell back where he was and lay on the ground.

"One...This is Five. Scratch the rearm and send me a medevac," he grunted into the tac-net.

"Confirmed, Five. You all right, Sean?"

Bermont grimaced as a rough chuckle echoed through him. "I'll live—probably."

"Chute is coming in now."

"Good."

▶ ▶ ▶

Savoy looked up as the local military came around the corner at a dead run, Mehn's easy jog placing him at their rear as his rifle swept their six.

"Here," Savoy snapped, slapping his rifle into the arms of the closest of the locals, startling the man into grabbing it as he appropriated the man's laser rifle.

"What...?" the man blurted, but Savoy ignored him.

The Terran lieutenant stepped away from them and examined the rifle, comparing it to the log recordings of Bermont's experimentation. In a few seconds, he had the controls more or less figured out, and if he was right, it was already set to maximum power.

That done, he leveled the weapon at the ground and triggered the firing stud.

The rifle whined in his hands, and its beam cut into the ground. Savoy held it steady for a couple seconds and began to play it along the ground in a straight line. Acrid smoke rose around him, but he ignored it as he watched the glowing of the heated ground through his thermal overlay.

He was finished with the test a few seconds later. Savoy shouldered the rifle and walked back to the group, even as he thumbed in an order for one of the chutes floating above them.

"Here." He tossed the rifle back to the man he'd taken it from and nodded to Mehn, who had come to the front of the group.

Mehn reclaimed Savoy's weapon from the startled man and glanced skyward as one of the CM packs descended. "You doing what I think you're doing, L.T.?"

"Yup."

"Cool." Mehn held both rifles against his shoulders and leaned back against the building.

Savoy settled the pack over the still-glowing trench and walked over to it. The heat coming from the superheated ground was searing, but his suit could handle worse if it had to, so he ignored it and pulled a panel off the chute to access a couple of its controls. In a few seconds, he'd shunted the power circuits to the CM field and stepped back as he tapped in a command.

The resulting burst of energy slapped him like a fist, actually sliding him back along the ground a few inches, but he'd been expecting it. It also drove all the air molecules back for more than half a dozen meters, leaving the entire area engulfed in a miniature vacuum, physically pushing the molecules in place and holding them still. The ground at his feet cracked, though he could only feel it through the suit and not hear it as it cooled under the sudden chill. A short while after, the CM pack failed and the air rushed back with an impressive thunderclap.

Savoy checked the ground temperature and nodded. "All right, everyone, get into the trench and keep your heads *down.*"

Savoy and Mehn had finished herding the locals into the makeshift trench he'd cut when Burke made his appearance again.

"We ready?" Savoy asked, glancing up as the other man approached.

"On your order, boss," Burke told him, checking the trench.

"This good enough?" Savoy asked.

Burke eyed the cut in the ground with a critical glance. It was deep, as such things went, over a meter down, in fact, and was coated with a glassy substance he'd never seen, but it looked like it would suffice to keep everyone clear of the worst of the blast.

He nodded. "It'll do, boss."

"Good," Savoy said, making a notation on his battle log that he had cleared the four GBU-98s for immediate deployment. "You're clear to launch."

"Best get your head down," Burke said.

"Everyone down!" Savoy ordered, reaching out and hauling a couple of the locals down as Mehn did the same.

The rest got the idea, and they all hunkered down as deep as they could in the still-warm trench, while Burke stood up with a silly smirk plastered across his face, where no one could hope to see it. Above them, the two armed carnivore recon drones orbited lazily at over thirteen thousand meters, the target below them nothing more than a mere spec to the human eye. But it wasn't a human eye that they relied on, so the two weapons of war could see with crystal clarity as their systems blinked to life and they prepared to launch.

Power fed into the GBU-98s from the drones, charging the superconducting capacitance coils that encircled each weapon's interior until the telltale LEDs all went green. Then the four weapons, two to a drone, fell free of their shackles.

Four fins snapped out a quarter second after release, pulling the rear ends of the weapons up until their noses pointed at the desired location, the relatively small rocket motors whined, and the bombs leapt to life.

Downward they rushed, entering terminal attack mode only three seconds after they were released, their onboard computers making final adjustments in the last instant before the point of no return, activating the weapon's terminal program.

Designed late in the so-called terror wars, the GBU-98 carried a payload sufficient to destroy any bunker ever built, assuming it could penetrate it. That problem, in particular, had been a plague on the forces of the so-called civilized nations early in the terror wars, because many of their targets were effectively proofed against even nuclear attacks by a simple insulating layer of earth.

Initial designs had depended on an earth-penetrating steel casing to get the weapon deep enough before detonation.

The GBU-98s used that in addition to a more...refined approach.

The powerful, though short-lived, lasers built into the nose cones of each weapon whined to life as the weapons went terminal, cutting into the ground where they were aimed like an industrial drill, opening the door, so to speak.

And then it was done. The lasers burned out under the powerful energy pulse released through them, and the weapons slammed into the ground right through the holes they had cut and kept on boring down on pure kinetic power until they blew through into the caverns below and came to a sudden, jarring stop.

The earth under them heaved, throwing the men in the trench into the air from the sheer force of it. Savoy and Mehn had been expecting something along those lines and landed easily, but the others just slammed back down to the ground as four pillars of fire rose up from the strike zones and huge gouts of flames and dust erupted from the Drasin tunnels.

Burke dropped back into the trench, whistling happily over the network as he threw himself over three of the locals. "Incoming!"

Mehn and Savoy followed his example, covering as many of the locals as they could with their armor as dirt and debris rained down around them and a stiff wind whistled over their heads. There wasn't as much of it as one might expect, since the vast majority of the blast had been directed downward by the shaped detonations of the GBU-98s.

When it stopped, the three soldiers climbed back up to the lip of the trench and looked out over the damage.

Savoy whistled appreciatively when he saw the impact sites. The ground was burning there now, four deep craters spewing flame and smoke as the ground caved in farther, hopefully crushing anything that might be left in there.

"Nice work, Burke," Savoy said, already accessing the carnivore drones and bringing them back around for another look with their ground-penetrating radar. "Let's make sure we got them all."

▶ ▶ ▶

"What in the Maker was *that?*" Tanner asked incredulously as the ground stopped shaking and quaking around him.

"An explosion in the Corinth Sector, Admiral."

Tanner cast a glance at Milla. "Your friends don't believe in doing things lightly, now, do they?"

Milla tried to shrug, but the effect was wasted in a suit.

"Never mind." He shook his head. "Damage?"

"That is my concern, Admiral," Nero stated. "My people are there, and the area was evacuated. We're trying to get confirmation on the elimination of the Drasin now. Leave it to my people."

Tanner nodded grimly. "Very well, Nero."

Tanner turned back to his own people. "Do we know where the *Odyssey* is now?"

"I'm afraid not, Admiral."

He just sat back in his chair.

Then what good am I, I wonder?

▼

CHAPTER 32

▲

▶ "KILL THE THRUSTERS."

"Aye, aye, sir," Daniels responded, hitting the command on cue.

The background rumble went dead and the deck seemed to tilt back to a level keel as the acceleration died off. Weston leaned back in his seat, partly to keep his head from spinning from the sudden change and partly in an attempt to think.

The *Odyssey* had spent the last hour at one-g subjective acceleration, meaning, with the eight percent CM field, they had been able to pull approximately fifty gravities. With the initial full burn they'd used at the start, that left its current ballistic speed at just under seventy-five thousand kilometers per second, or roughly one-quarter light-speed.

"Enemy status?" Weston asked.

"Still on course for the planet, Captain," Waters responded. "No sign that they've seen us."

Weston tried not to think about the risks he was taking or the dangers ahead. He could see from the display that they'd reach the interception point in just under an hour. Their crossing velocity would be such that the *Odyssey* would get one round of shots free of charge—no more.

After that, it all depended on the enemy.

And that, Weston knew, was a bad way to plan your action.

"Relief crews to the bridge," he ordered, with no sign of his thoughts on his face.

"Aye, sir."

"Commander, take first watch," Weston said, standing up. "I'll be back in twenty minutes to relieve you."

"That's not necessary, sir. I don't need any time," the commander told him.

Weston half smiled. "In twenty minutes, Commander, you will go down to your room. You will take a quick shower, then go and get a light meal. When this is done, and only when this is done, will I allow you to return to the bridge. Am I understood?"

"Understood, sir."

"Good." Weston turned, stepping toward the lift as it arrived with the relief crew. "Then I'll see you in twenty minutes."

"Aye, Captain."

▶▶▶

"Doctor...I..."

"What is it, Nurse?" Dr. Rame asked as he took a packet of antibiotics from a cooler and carried it across the med-lab to an operating table. He loaded it into a pressurized pump designed to deliver the drugs, even if they lost rotational gravity.

"What's going to happen, doctor?"

Rame paused, glancing back at the young woman, then crossed back to the cooler for a supply of morphine. "We're going to receive injured personnel," he said as he worked. "If we're lucky, we'll receive a great many of them."

"Lucky?"

"Sandra...If we're not lucky, they'll be dead before they get here," Rame said quite seriously. "You're too young to have served in the war, right?"

"I served on the USS *Enterprise* in the last few months," she said defensively.

Rame nodded. "This will be worse."

"I almost wish something would happen...the waiting..."

"I know," Rame said, his voice soft. "Go check the portable power modules and see that they have a full charge. I don't want to lose instruments or the infrareds if we take a bad hit."

"Yes, Doctor."

Rame watched her go. Resigned, he checked the plasma supplies one more time.

▶ ▶ ▶

"Hey, Steph, you up for a few more kills?"

Stephanos acknowledged the crewman as he approached Archangel Lead. The kills from his last fight had been tallied under his cockpit already, but he ignored the new alien silhouettes that had been painted there. They had always been more for the ground crews than for him, anyway, and he didn't like to look at them before a fight.

The crewman backed off as Stephanos caught the edge of his cockpit and slowly lowered himself into the fighter. Once he'd settled in a bit, he flipped on the primary power to the computers and opened up the diagnostic windows. They'd already have been run, of course, but Stephanos was old school. As always, he didn't go out in a plane he hadn't checked for himself.

Around the bay, the Archangels were mostly following the same ritual, though he knew that some of them were less interested in diagnostics and were just taking a few minutes to communicate with the gods that watched out for crazy aviators.

"Got another one coming up, girl," he whispered softly to the plane as he ran a hand along the molded control stick. "You up for it?"

He closed his eyes, letting his mind drift until he could almost hear the voice of the fighter speaking back to him. The voice told him what he wanted to hear.

▶▶▶

"Chief."

Chief Corrin glanced up, startled by the calm greeting. "Captain."

Weston waved his free hand. "Don't get up, Chief. You mind if I join you?"

She glanced at the food in front of her and nodded. "Please."

"Thank you," he said, taking a seat across from her. "I wanted to congratulate you on the repairs you pushed through earlier."

"We've got some good people on this boat, sir," she said. "They're rough 'round the edges, but I'm knocking the corners off."

The captain took a bite of his sandwich. "I'm sure you are, Chief."

"I have to admit, I didn't think it would work so well, what with all the different branches tossed together," she admitted as she drank some of her soup. "But they pulled together tight in the pinch. Good swabs, all of 'em—even the air force pukes."

Weston chuckled. "That's how they got here, Chief. Best of the best across the board."

"Now, I wouldn't go that far." Corrin grinned back. "They're good swabs, yeah, but they're not up to my old crew on the *Tico*. Not yet."

"I have no doubt that you'll find a way to get them there," Weston said.

She glanced around the cafeteria. "They're good kids, sir. But they're nervous."

"Yeah, I figured they would be."

"You might want to have a talk with 'em, just a few words before we get started," she suggested.

He cocked his head and shrugged. "Maybe I will, at that, Chief."

"Might do you some good, too, Cap'n," she said. "If you don't mind my saying."

"I learned a long time ago not to argue with a chief," Weston smiled. "Saves time."

Corrin grinned from ear to ear. "Sounds like you had a good teacher somewhere along the line, sir."

▶▶▶

"Doctor...What are you doing?"

Palin looked up, confused, into the wide eyes of one of the lab techs. "I'm refining the translation matrix. Why?"

"Doctor…We're about to go into battle!" the lab-coated young man blurted out.

"So?"

"So…*so*? Dr. Palin, what good is that going to do us?"

Palin shrugged. "I'm not a soldier, Evan. I'm a scientist, who happens to be quite good with languages. My skills are unlikely to affect the outcome of this battle, but should we survive it, they might have an impact on our future relations with these people. So why shouldn't I continue to work?"

The lab tech just stared wide-eyed.

Palin shoved a chair over to the young man. "Here, sit— unless you have something more pressing to do."

The young man sat down numbly, and Palin passed him a PDA displaying a translation algorithm.

He stared at it. "What's this?"

"That's the sole transmission we've detected from the enemy ships," Palin said. "Our best guess is that it's a request for reinforcements. Why don't you run it through the computer and see if we have any historical analogues for it?"

"Historical analogues for an alien combat cipher?"

Palin shrugged. "One never knows, Evan. One never knows."

▶ ▶ ▶

Lt. Jennifer Samuels tried to make herself relax as she sat in the cockpit of the fighter. She couldn't quite make the preflight jitters go away, something she hadn't experienced in years. Not since her first shuttle flight.

Come on, Sam, she chastened herself, *this is what you wanted, what you trained for. Don't lose it now.*

The words sounded nice, but they didn't make her any calmer as she sat there.

Archangel One was parked alongside the other Angels, and she could feel them staring at her as they checked their own fighters. She knew they were questioning if she was up for it, just as she was wondering the same thing.

She'd already heard how Commander Michaels had cornered the captain and all but risked court martial over her assignment to the flight. The worst thing was, at that moment, she wasn't sure she blamed him. Michaels was a legend; he'd been with the Angels almost from the beginning and had tallied up a long list of victories flying under the command of Captain Weston.

The captain, even more so. Between the two of them, they had been responsible for some of the greatest victories of the Block War, and on Earth. Their names were synonymous with the Archangel Flight Group, even as the flight group had become synonymous with victory in the postwar world.

Powerful images to live up to, yet that was what she'd wanted to do, ever since the first reports of Archangel missions filtered out through the news. In a world wired for sight and sound, it had still been a riveting image of the war when the government public relations people began releasing the unedited mission records of the flight group.

For a nation struggling with the first devastating defeats of the World War and the oppressive weight of the Block's troops pushing in from all sides, the Angels had been one of the symbols that turned things around.

Samuels had to wonder, now that she was confronted with what she had wished for, how well she was going to stack up against those giants.

"Nervous?"

Samuels jumped. Or rather, she jerked and went flying off the seat in the null gravity. Her quick reflexes let her hook the cockpit canopy with her fingers and push herself back as she looked to the source of the voice. She almost wished she'd just kept flying off when she recognized Commander Michaels.

"No, sir," she told him evenly.

"Bullshit," he snorted in response. "Lieutenant, let me clue you into one thing, something Weston told me before my first flight."

She swallowed at his tone.

"You can bullshit yourself all you want, I don't care. You can lie to your mates about how scared you are, 'cause, Lord knows, they're going to lie to you." He flashed a crooked grin, then looked serious again. "But I'm the honcho of this circus, and if I ask you a question—any question—you can damn well bet I have a good reason for asking. So when I ask, you give me the truth. We clear?"

She nodded. "Crystal."

"Good." He glared at her. "Nervous?"

"Yes, sir," she said.

"Also good," he said. "Don't lose those butterflies. They'll keep you alive long enough to become an old-timer like me."

She risked a smile at that, since Michaels wasn't even twenty-eight yet.

"But when we engage the interface, watch out for your nerves," he told her. "You can mess up your stabilizers pretty bad if the plane can't figure out what direction you want to jump. So nerves are okay; just don't let them screw up your flying."

Samuels nodded. "Yes, sir."

"Good." He clapped the canopy with his hand. "Then I'll let you get back to communing."

"Sir?" She looked confused.

"Talking to your plane," he smiled. "We all do it, Lieutenant. Stark-raving lunatics, the lot of us."

"Yes, sir." She grinned in response. "I think I'll fit in fine."

"I'm sure you will, Lieutenant. I'm sure you will."

▶▶▶

Captain Weston stepped back on the bridge twenty minutes to the second after he'd left and shot Commander Roberts a look as he crossed the deck to the central chair.

The commander rose without comment, nodding respectfully as Weston sat down, then excused himself and left the bridge.

"Enemy status?"

"Still on the predicted course, Captain," Waters replied. "We're now within one AU of the task group."

"Understood," Weston replied. "Lamont, inform all decks that we're going to drop all nonessential power consumption until further notice."

"Aye, Captain. Powering down all nonessentials," Lamont replied, tapping the order.

The lights dimmed immediately, as did many of the displays littering the bridge. In a few moments, they were sitting in near darkness, only the low-powered red lamps joining the dim glow of the combat displays as they counted down the time to intercept.

Weston reached down to the arm of his chair, feeling out the controls by touch, toggling the ship-wide communicator.

"This is the captain speaking," he said, looking ahead at the display. "I'd like to say a few words to everyone, so if you can...take a moment to listen."

▶▶▶

The ship hushed, everyone looking up at the speakers in the walls and ceiling.

"In…a little over thirty minutes, we'll be going into battle once more. The enemy has proven itself to be ruthless, having destroyed at least two entire worlds—that we know of—and has obvious designs on a populated planet in this system.

"I…We won't stand by and simply allow this. I don't know if we'll be able to stop it, but I do know that to let it simply… happen…would be a crime in itself."

▶▶▶

Commander Roberts looked up as he finished stripping off his uniform, his hand a few inches from the shower controls, and continued to listen to the captain.

"We've already become more involved in this war than I would have liked, but each time, we have proven that we are not playing out of our league, as many might have believed. Further, and more important, we…You have proven that you are exactly what Earth believed you to be when they assigned you to the *Odyssey*…that you are the very best that Earth has to offer."

▶▶▶

Jennifer Samuels let out a long breath, laying her head back against the seat as the captain's voice filled the deck around her and the other Archangels.

"You've proven that, and proven yourselves beyond all doubt, and I am honored to serve with each and every one of you," he said.

Her nerves dimmed a little as she felt herself nodding in agreement.

"So, in this last battle before we go home, with one of the greatest discoveries ever made by man, I want you all to continue doing just what you have done and know that you have all secured your places in history."

▶▶▶

Dr. Palin glanced up disinterestedly at the speakers and reached over to shut them off. He stayed his hand when he saw the awed look on the technician's face and sighed, rolling his eyes and letting the captain drone on.

"Just one more fight," Weston said over the speaker. "One more fight against an enemy as ruthless as any we've seen. Then we'll be heading home."

▶▶▶

Capt. Eric Weston took a breath, glancing around the bridge to where everyone had turned to look at him.

Then he continued to speak.

"So, if this is our last battle for a while," he let his voice grow a little harder, "let us make it *their* last battle—ever. I want to go home with a victory painted on our bow, ladies and gentlemen. It's not every day that we get to save a world. Let's make sure that the name *Odyssey* is one hell of a challenge to live up to."

He reached for the controls to the ship-wide communications again.

"That is all. Weston out."

▼

CHAPTER 33

▲

▶ COMMANDER ROBERTS STEPPED onto the bridge twenty-five minutes later and noted that the rest of the senior staff had already manned their stations.

"Ensign, what's the current status of our friends out there?" Captain Weston asked as he nodded in greeting.

Roberts returned the greeting and stood at his station as Waters looked up from his board.

"Our soft lock has been upgraded to a seventy percent solution, Captain. Our current estimates have them right...here."

Roberts looked at the section highlighted in red on the board while the *Odyssey*'s current position glowed a steady blue. The two points in space were closing rapidly as the icons and spatial reference points were constantly updated to include the latest ranging estimates.

"How long to our outer engagement range?"

"We're looking at five minutes to extreme pulse torpedo range, Captain," Waters replied, "but without a real time lock, we'd probably just give away our position for nothing."

"Understood. Give me a range chart with incremental adjustments to our probable targeting solutions."

"Aye, Captain," Waters replied, tapping in a comment.

The screen lit up again, this time with a timeline counting up from 0 to 100 percent in increments of five light-seconds across the board.

"When we launch, we'll be giving away our position, anyway," Weston said, frowning at the board. "So I don't want us too close. Lay in firing commands for one hundred light-seconds."

"Aye, aye, Captain," Waters replied, going back to work.

"Commander," Weston beckoned Roberts over.

The executive officer walked to the central command chair and came to a stop at Weston's right hand. "Yes, sir?"

"I'll want you manning the auxiliary bridge again, Commander," Weston said. "It's vital that we don't lose the chain of command in the event of a shipboard strike."

Roberts nodded. "Aye, sir."

The captain looked intently at Roberts. "You and I both know that the auxiliary bridge is a lot more vulnerable than here, so I appreciate your willingness, Commander."

"It's for the best, sir," Roberts responded. "As you say, we can't afford to lose the chain of command if worse comes to worst."

"I know that, Jason, which is why I'm also going to attach an addendum to your orders."

"Sir?"

"In the event that the main bridge is incapacitated, under no circumstances are you to close with the enemy," Weston affirmed. "I don't believe that this is a necessary order, given your thoughts on our situation, but I want it on record. If you lose the ability to engage the enemy from a distance, you are to abandon the defense of this world and return to Earth via a circuitous route. Is that understood?"

"Aye, sir," Roberts frowned. "Sir...the troops dirt-side?"

"If you can get them out without risking my ship, do so. Otherwise, they're on their own."

"Aye, aye, Captain."

Weston and Roberts looked at each other for a moment. "Now get off my bridge and do your duty, Commander."

"Aye, aye, Captain." The commander turned on his heel and marched off the bridge.

Weston leaned forward, looking into the eyes of young Waters, who handled the big guns of the NACS *Odyssey*. "All right, Mr. Waters. Let's have a look at your combat programs. I want to see what you've put together from the data we gathered on these bastards."

"Yes, sir. I'm sending it to—"

"No, put in on the main screen."

"Aye, sir."

►►►

Stephanos watched as Paladin flipped a card across the twenty-foot gap between him and Lt. Gabrielle "Racer" Tracey. The lieutenant caught the card easily and palmed it as Paladin flipped the next one from the deck to the next player in the circle.

"Hey, Sammy baby!" Paladin yelled across to Samuels, smacking his gum. "You in?"

"What?" Samuels looked up, confused.

"You in?" Paladin repeated.

She saw the cards in his hands and stared for a minute before looking back at her instruments.

"Don't look at those." Paladin shook his head, a crooked grin on his face. "If you ain't got it together by now, you're checking out, anyway."

"For Christ's sakes, Alex!" Racer snapped, her face flaring.

"Hey, I'm just saying…" the cocky pilot shrugged defensively. "You know it's true."

"Yeah, and I also know that's the captain's plane, Paladin." Racer glared at him. "It's fuckin' ready to fly, so don't spook her."

Paladin just shrugged again, still chewing the gum that had replaced the cigar that would normally be clenched in his teeth, while looking back at Samuels. "So? You in?"

Samuels looked at him for another minute and shrugged as she pulled herself up and out of the cockpit. She settled down on the nose of the fighter, straddling it in the zero gravity to hold her place. "Sure. What's the game?"

"Five-Card Stud." Paladin smirked, flipping a card. "We'll keep it simple for ya. Deuces wild. Five buck ante and the table limit is a fifty-dollar bet, fair 'nuff?"

The card spun through the air in the zero-gravity compartment, and Samuels snatched it as it twisted past.

"Sure," she smirked. "We gonna float the pot in the middle of us all?"

"Nah." Paladin flashed a toothy smile. "That's the fun part. You gotta keep tally in yer head. Up to it?"

"Keep dealing the cards."

▶ ▶ ▶

"We're entering the engagement envelope now, Commander."

"Thank you, Ensign," Roberts said, not looking up.

He knew that the captain wasn't going to engage at extreme range, so there was no rush. "What's the disposition of enemy forces?"

"Still continuing on course to the planet, Commander. They don't appear to have changed their formation."

Running fat and slow, Roberts hoped. He'd been looking over the reports from the ground fighting as well as comparing the after-action reports filed from each station concerning the alien ships. They weren't too bright when it came to combat maneuvers, but they seemed to learn fast.

That bothered him, perhaps more than anything else, because there was something about that itching at the back of his skull.

Something he was missing.

Something important.

A warning buzzer sounded, interrupting his train of thought, and he looked up sharply. "Ensign?"

"The captain's set all stations to action alert," the ensign said.

Roberts looked over the board, noting that the scale of the battle zone was rapidly dwindling as the range closed. "The captain will open the engagement shortly. Stand to for battle stations."

"Aye, aye, sir."

▶ ▶ ▶

"What's our lock status?"

"Soft lock, sir, but we're approaching sixty-five percent," Waters responded.

"Charge even tubes two through twelve."

"Aye, Captain. Charging tubes."

In one of the old submarines, or any navy ship, that order would have sent people on the weapons decks scrambling to load torpedoes into the tubes, or even double-checking all the systems involved, but on the *Odyssey*, the military had been forced to bow even more to the gods of automation.

The pulse tubes charged from the capacitor banks that circled the habitats of the *Odyssey,* draining the charge in mere seconds to bring themselves up to full battle-ready status. They could only hold that charge for a mere eight minutes before they would lose the power needed to generate and fire one of the lethal bursts, but Captain Weston didn't plan to hold them that long.

Not that long at all.

"Lamont, have Engineering begin recharging the coils."

"Sir…but…aye, sir," Lamont caught herself and tapped in the order.

Down in the bowels of the ship, cold reactors hummed back to life in response, while on the bridge, the senior staff watched the range tick down as the lock slowly firmed up.

"One hundred fifty light-seconds, Captain. Lock is now seventy-five percent."

Weston nodded but said nothing.

The tension began to climb as the numbers fell, until Waters spoke up a minute later.

"One hundred twenty light-seconds."

"Prepare for firing sequence," Weston ordered.

"Aye, Captain. Firing sequence entered."

"Lock it into the computer."

"Locked."

"Engage the sequence."

Waters nodded. "Sequence engaged."

With that command, the ensign sat back, watching as the computer took over.

His program was in control now, and all he could do was watch the data it threw back and step in if something changed drastically. The actual firing would be up to the computer, because at the ranges they were dealing with, any minute variance in timing or arc would result in a miss of spectacular proportions.

The *Odyssey* had to close another eighteen light-seconds before the program would open fire, which translated into another seventy seconds of waiting. Give or take.

▶▶▶

An audible hum distracted Samuels as she tossed two cards back across ten meters of open space to the dealer, forcing Paladin to dislodge himself to catch the cards. He scowled at her as he pulled himself back into place.

"Be careful, would ya? I don't feel like swimming all over this hold looking for the cards," he growled, thumbing another pair from the deck and sending them back to her.

She caught them, still looking around.

"Relax," Stephanos said, looking up from a PDA he was working on. "That's just the secondary generators coming online. We're getting ready to fire."

She nodded, taking a breath. "I knew that, sir. Just—"

"First time you heard them from the nose of an Archangel." Paladin smirked. "Everything sounds just a bit more dangerous, don't it?"

"Well, I know that your voice keeps sending chills down my spine," she said sarcastically as she settled back down. "That count?"

Racer laughed. "Naw. Trust me, girl, his voice scares all of us, anyway."

A few of the pilots chuckled along with them, even Paladin himself, and the card game went on, the feeling of life returning to the ship.

▶▶▶

"Firing in ten seconds, Captain," Waters said, unnecessarily.

"Understood, Ensign," Weston replied. "Lieutenant Daniels?"

"Yes, sir?" The navigator glanced over at him.

"Prepare for evasive maneuvering, Lieutenant. Thrusters only."

"Thrusters only, aye, sir."

"Lamont?"

"Yes, sir?" Susan Lamont stiffened.

Weston looked at the clock. "Sound battle stations, Ensign."

"Aye, aye, Cap…Captain," Susan stumbled over her words as the deck transmitted the high-frequency pulse of the tubes firing through her feet. "Sounding battle stations."

▶▶▶

From the outside of the NACS *Odyssey*, no sound was heard when the brilliant flashes of light marked the launch of the six bursts of charged energy.

The pulse torpedoes flashed into existence in front of the proud ship and then off through the black just as quickly, until they were nothing but another star in the wasteland to the unaided human eye. Though they were not light-speed weapons, they were very close, as the total mass of each of the weapons actually approached zero, give or take a few nanograms. They left the *Odyssey* at just over 0.9c and would take about ten seconds more to cross the gulf than the light they cast.

Which would give their targets ten seconds to see what was coming, and marginally less time to react.

▶▶▶

"Thrusters!" Weston called. "Take us below the system ecliptic, relative to the enemy!"

"Aye, sir," Daniels said, entering the precoded maneuver with a single tap of his fingers. "Engaging thrusters now."

The *Odyssey* shivered as its maneuvering thrusters, usually intended for low-velocity maneuvers while under port speed restrictions, kicked into action and flared hotly, straining to shove the big ship out of the line of any likely fire.

"Keep an eye on passive sensors," Weston ordered. "I want to know if we get pinged."

"Aye, Captain," Waters responded.

▶▶▶

Samuels tightened her grip on the fighter's nose with her legs as the deck seemed to pitch and a wail of steel and groan of metal echoed through the deck.

This time she was ready for it and didn't miss her throw as she sent her card back to the dealer. The CM field was less effective at muffling sharp maneuvers below decks due to the absence of gravity, so the stress on the ship and the littler inertia of her body, and everything else relative to the real universe, was pushed a bit more in null gravity.

"Captain's got Daniels standing on the stick," Racer said, with a half smile.

"That's what you get when you put a fighter pilot in command of a ship," Paladin said, continuing flipping three cards to another pilot. "One seriously neurotic ship."

Low chuckles passed around the deck, the pilots willing to take any chance to burn away unneeded stress.

"Say," Samuels spoke up, "where did you guys pick up the poker thing? I mean, I get the game and all but…"

"How'd we get the idea to try it in null?" Paladin asked.

"Well…yeah," she admitted. "I mean, this is your first tour in space, right? I mean—"

"We know what you mean," Racer replied. "The poker game is traditional. Goes back a lot of years. The null deal… Well, we figured out how to manage that during our null-grav training."

Another pilot laughed. "Yeah. We almost went bonkers that first week. Took us forever to decide that there just was no good way to float the pot between us."

"Yeah," Paladin said. "Remember the ziplock incident?"

Several laughed, but Racer looked more than a little chagrined.

"Hey, my wristwatch got caught in the bag, all right?"

"Says you," Paladin returned, not missing a beat in his dealing. "I still think you were trying to palm the pot."

Racer rolled her eyes. "Oh yes, like I really needed twenty-two bucks in loose change."

Steaphanos watched the banter with a half smile, remembering the game himself. As he recalled, Gabrielle had won that hand, anyway, on a straight flush, so any accusations of stealing the pot were more than slightly due to sour grapes.

▶ ▶ ▶

"Time?" Weston asked.

"Weapons will be TOT in thirty-two seconds, Captain."

"Keep us moving, Lieutenant," Weston ordered, rapidly making calculations in his head.

If the torpedoes were going to strike in just over thirty seconds, the enemy forces would be picking up the first light-speed evidence of their strike in just over twenty. Given that the *Odyssey* was now altering its course to a slightly more divergent tack, they were still over ninety light-seconds from the target ships and about two minutes from being able to read any solid reactions in the enemy fleet.

Unless he ordered the active sensors back online.

The back of Weston's knuckles itched as he contemplated the satisfying influx of data that would follow that order.

Targeting solutions, enemy positions, full course vectors, and even weapon energy signatures would be at his fingertips, if he could only give that order.

However, it would also give the enemy a positive lock on his position, and even though they might have it already, they may well not have it yet.

So he kept his peace and watched as the *Odyssey*'s course continued to drop under the system ecliptic as its thrusters sought valiantly to shove the warship along a new path.

▶▶▶

Across the reaches of space that lay between them and the alien taskforce, an alien commander was thinking many of the same thoughts as Capt. Eric Weston.

They didn't know their enemy or his weapons, and the tactics he used didn't match the target they had been sent to eliminate.

The ship profile was unknown.

Its power signature absurdly weak.

And yet it was ripping through warships with an ease that was…disturbing.

The Masters would not be concerned with the loss of a few ships, or even all of them, if the task was accomplished. However, because of this one ship, five warrior ships had to be diverted from other priority targets in order to take this system according to plan.

That wasn't an acceptable situation, even if it was a necessary one.

The command of the ship was considering the impact the diversion would have on the extermination when the first warning sensor went off. It was just a minor alert, but the response was quick, just the same. In three seconds, it had been determined that the alert wasn't tripped by any natural satellite of this system, as this alert was wont to do.

Two seconds more were required to confirm that it didn't match any known configuration in the target species inventory.

Another four identified the source of the alert positively as weapons fire from the unknown ship.

Three more seconds would have been required to mount an attempt at defense.

However, two seconds shy of that limit, all hell broke loose across the small armada.

▶▶▶

The *Odyssey*'s pulse torpedoes carried a very small electrical charge designed to prevent the weapons from accidently intersecting the position of another torpedo or, obviously, the walls of the launching tubes.

This tended to cause the weapons to spread slightly as they flew, which made the targeting calculations that much more important, especially at long ranges. So by the time the torpedoes reached their target location, they had spread enough that three of the weapons were outside positive lock range of any of the enemy ships and kept on flying past as their three identical siblings went into terminal guidance, their very nature causing them to be attracted to any matter in their path. They corkscrewed suddenly as they came into range and slammed into a ship apiece, sending plumes of plasma into space as they annihilated huge chunks of matter with their explosions.

The three damaged ships faltered in their course, shifting under the impact, then slowly returned to their place in formation as their power came back.

By that time, they had calculated the direction of the attack and had turned their sensors outward, pouring more and more power in the search for their unseen foe as they altered their course to intercept.

▶▶▶

"They're coming around, Captain!" Waters snapped as the changes in the enemy task force finally showed on the plot.

"All of them?"

"Aye, sir, all of them." The young man's tone was grim.

Weston frowned. The thermal bloom on the sensors a few seconds earlier had confirmed at least three separate strikes, which seemed to tally with their track of the pulse torpedoes. A fifty-fifty hit-miss ratio wasn't great, but if his luck held through, Weston would take it and be glad.

"Course?" he asked tensely.

"Looks like…" Daniels frowned, tapping out a confirmation. Finally, he let out a long breath and half smiled, not in amusement, but in relief. "Heading for our previous position."

"They haven't seen us yet…" someone whispered.

If that were true, Weston thought, *we still hold the advantage.* They knew, more or less, where the enemy was, and the enemy didn't have a clue where the *Odyssey* was lurking.

"Kill thrusters!"

"Killing thrusters, aye, sir," Daniels responded, instantly killing the thrusters with a tap of his fingers.

"Mr. Daniels, adjust our stance—one percent thrust only," Weston ordered. "Put our nose in line with the enemy's projected position in…one minute."

"Adjusting stance, aye, Captain."

Outside, in the cold silence of space, a tiny series of puffs silently pushed the nose of the *Odyssey* around until they were pointing almost back in the direction they had come.

"Waters, calculate targeting coordinates for odd-numbered tubes one through eleven."

"Aye, Captain. Calculating for tubes one through eleven."

"Lamont." Weston half turned. "Charge status on tubes two through twelve?"

"Two and four are now charging, Captain. We'll be ready to fire in five minutes. Six through twelve will take another ten."

Weston turned back to his displays. Having all the capacitors charged and ready, and not drained by a recent transition, meant that he'd get a second round of shots from all tubes in this battle.

It might be enough.

Probably not, but it might.

▶▶▶

On the alien ship, the commander pondered how, once again, the unknown enemy was proving to be an unforeseen obstacle to the plan. The ship was not along the projected path that its weapons had followed, and the fleet had wasted time in the search. The vessel had to be of unprecedented technology in order to deploy as much power as it held and yet register so low on the threat-rating system.

This was disturbing on many levels, of course, but mostly because the weapons and warriors the fleet had deployed were intended for use against the target. This new enemy was not in its database, and there were no appropriate counteractions it could take.

Reluctantly, he ordered the fleet sensors to full spread.

▶▶▶

"We're getting heavy spikes all through the EM range, Captain!"

"Have they spotted us?" Weston asked, intently watching the countdown to firing. It was too soon; they needed another few seconds to fire, then almost a full minute and a half for the shots to land.

"I don't think so, Captain," Waters answered first. "I think… It looks like an omnidirectional burst, and we're far enough out that the pulse density is under our detection threshold."

"But is it under theirs?" Weston muttered under his breath.

"What was that, sir?"

"Nothing, Lieutenant. Hold our course."

"Aye, aye, Captain."

The tension continued to mount as the timer counted down; then the odd-numbered pulse tubes opened fire.

"Thrusters! Half power, Lieutenant," Weston ordered. "Take us up above the enemy this time, but maintain our current horizontal heading."

"Aye, aye, Captain. Firing thrusters."

The *Odyssey* groaned again, though quieter this time, as she tipped her nose up and began to climb back toward the ecliptic. This time the big ship only fired thrusters that were pointed more or less away from the enemy as she sought once more to evade detection.

▶▶▶

In a conventional battlefield, one minute was a lifetime, ninety seconds a lifetime and a half. Hell, in Weston's fighter, lifetimes were counted in tenths of seconds at times, but in space, such time felt like eternity, especially when waiting on information that had to travel that distance just to get to you before you could make any choices based on it.

The torpedoes were the first legs of that data transfer, though the only message they carried was death. They crossed the expanse, blazing a trail across the black with the impunity that belonged to single-minded things, and came flashing right in on their targets, just as calculated.

He knew the alien command probably noted their arrival nine seconds before impact and would begin standard countermeasures against projectile attacks less than one second after that.

The ships would maneuver away from each other, spreading out as they targeted the incoming weapons with lasers and opened fire. Given the enemy's performance to date, they'd hit the incoming weapons with laser fire within four seconds, not that they would have the slightest effect on the incoming energy pulses, as five of the six slammed into the fleet and more plumes of destruction rose up.

▶▶▶

"Hit!" Waters's fist clenched, a tight grin on his face. "They spread their formation at the last second, Captain."

Weston grimaced, his professionalism offended, though it was good news. Against a pulse-torpedo attack, your best defense was to tighten your formation, presenting a smaller target for the charged weapons to lock on to. You would probably still suffer a strike or two, but the spread of the weapons was likely to push at least some of the shots out of range.

"Captain...I think we got one of them," Waters said a moment later, looking at his boards. "In fact, I'm almost certain that I'm looking at a catastrophic failure of a reactor here."

Weston called up the information and found he had to agree. It looked that the odds were down to five to one.

"All right, lock in firing coordinates for—"

"Captain!" Waters interrupted him. "They're up to something! Fleet formation is breaking up..."

"He's right, Captain," Daniels added. "It looks like they're spreading out...It might be a search patter—"

"Shit!"

"Waters!" Weston snapped.

"Sorry, sir." The young man blinked. "But, Captain...I think they just engaged whatever stealth systems they've got... We're losing them, sir."

Weston glared at the young man, then flipped his display up, looking at the information as the hostile red icons faded, then finally vanished one by one from the plotter screen. *Shit.* "Hide-and-seek."

"Excuse me, sir?"

"Hide-and-seek," he repeated. "And they're *it.*"

CHAPTER 34

▶ "WHERE ARE THEY, Ithan?"

The young woman started as Tanner stepped up behind her, glancing back in surprise, then quickly caught herself and turned to the board she was watching.

"We're not certain, Admiral," she said. "We think that there are Drasin ships at these points..."

Tanner saw three fuzzy and indistinct symbols appear on the projection, separating quickly at the scale the system map was set at. "The others?"

"We don't know," she said reluctantly. "They must have some sort of cloaking systems, Admiral. They've vanished from our sight. We only catch intermittent signals from them now, and it's not reliable."

Tanner patted the woman's shoulder. "And the *Odyssey*?"

"Gone from our scanners," she said. "We lost them after they fired the second time."

Rael Tanner, admiral of a nonexistent fleet, took a step back. The *Odyssey* had eliminated one ship—that they could tell—its reactor explosion illuminating its death for all the system to see. That on its own was a feat unmatched by any ship in the colonies' fleet to this point.

Two others were possible kills, though they had not been able to confirm those. And that left three of the Drasin still out there, looking to kill the men and women of the *Odyssey*.

And the entire people of the planet on which he stood.

Tanner hissed in frustration, fists clenched, nails biting into his palm. "Very well, Ithan. Thank you."

▶▶▶

"Find them for me, Mr. Waters."

"Aye, aye, sir," the young man said, his eyes staring at his displays as he tried to ignore his mounting dread.

It had been over a half hour since the enemy had gone to stealth, their last vectors indicating they had broken up their formation in a possible search pattern. In that time, Captain Weston had brought the *Odyssey* above the system ecliptic and slowed it to a relative stop with an asteroid belt only a few thousand kilometers under her keel.

With luck, even if they were spotted, they'd appear to be a rogue rock that had been knocked from the Trojan point by a comet or other stellar event.

"Pulse transmission!" Lamont yelled as the event was communicated to her from the electronic warfare people.

"Locate it!"

"They're working on it, sir," she told him tightly, waiting.

Always the waiting.

Finally, Lamont shook her head. "Couldn't do it, sir. We've got a tangent, but it's fuzzy."

"Damn," Weston muttered. "All right...Helm, I want our nose pointed down that tangent—softly."

"Aye, aye, sir. Softly, sir," Daniels responded, taking the controls and tapping out a few puffs of the propellant.

The big ship came around on its axis, slowly pointing its nose along the direction they'd been given.

"Anything on the main passives?"

"Negative, Captain." Waters shook his head. "It's all quiet."

"Ahead, dead slow, Lieutenant."

"Dead slow. Aye, Captain," Daniels repeated, easing the thrusters on.

A low rumble shook the ship as it fought against its own inertia to start moving, then died out as they came underway.

"Keep your eyes on those sensors."

"Aye, sir."

"Yes, sir."

Weston leaned back in his chair and wished that he were back in a fighter, where things were simpler.

▶▶▶

"Dammit, I wish we were out there doing something."

"Shut up, Paladin," Racer said, checking her cards before tucking them into the oxygen hose of her flight suit. "We go out when we go out, you know that."

"I know, I know," the sharp-faced man said. "It's just the waiting…It gets to me."

"Gets to everyone, Alex," Stephenos said, looking up. "Don't worry, we'll get our shot soon enough."

Alexander "Paladin" Kerry nodded in agreement, glancing over at Samuels. "You betting or folding?"

She glanced down at her cards, frowning as she tried to remember the pot total. *Let's see, Paladin opened with a two-dollar raise, everyone went in, and Racer saw him and bumped him up another three. Crys and Ice folded. Paladin stayed in…So that brings the total up to…hmmm…carry the three…forty-one bucks.*

"I'm in," she said. "I'll see the three and raise you five."

"Ooo, big spender." Paladin grinned.

"I'm out," Racer shrugged, slipping her cards from the hose and sending them spinning in front of her.

"It's you and me, coal baby," Paladin smirked. "You got the assets to back up your play?"

"You wanna see 'em, you gotta pay the toll." Samuels smirked.

The deck rumbled around them again, and they all looked up for a moment.

"Those were the secondary thrusters," Racer said, looking back. "We're moving again."

Paladin looked back toward Samuels and tried to gauge her face.

"Screw it," he muttered. "I fold."

"I'd say come to Mamma while chortling and grabbing the chips, but…" Jennifer smirked as she flipped her cards back.

Paladin caught them, glancing at them as he tucked the cards back in the deck. His eyes widened. "You were fucking bluffing!"

"Hey! You don't pay, you don't peek, boyo!" she growled, stabbing a finger at him.

"Yeah…but!"

"No buts, Paladin. Try that again, you'll eat the deck," she told him in no uncertain words.

"Yikes…" Racer grinned. "Don't wanna mess with this one, Pal. She's a cardsharp."

"Yeah. I think she is. Howzabout it, Cardsharp? Another hand?"

Samuels stared for a moment and then smiled as she realized that she'd just been pegged with a call sign. "Deal 'em, Pally."

▶▶▶

"There's something on the passives, Captain," Waters said, his voice uncertain.

"What have you got?"

"An intermittent signal—twenty degrees left declination from our course. It's almost directly on the ecliptic, but I can't...quite...see it."

"Visual spectrum?"

"A shadow, sir," Waters replied. "I keep losing it in the background."

That could be anything, Weston thought bleakly. *Only there was a signal in this direction.*

"Adjust our heading to intercept," he said, making his choice.

"Aye, aye, Captain," Daniels responded, making the changes in his board.

▶▶▶

On the auxiliary bridge, Commander Roberts watched the same displays. His dark eyes narrowed as he tried to fathom the immense game of hide-and-seek they were currently engaged in.

Out there, somewhere in the immensity of space, were five ships trying to annihilate them. Here on the *Odyssey*, five hundred people turned everything they had to destroying those ships in turn. It was an old game, just being played on a brand-new playground.

"Anything on that bogey yet?" Roberts asked.

"Nothing, sir." The woman at the tactical slot shook her head. "It's just a shadow."

The commander nodded, his eyes boring into the screen as the tension around him became palpable.

It must be what the submariners felt when hunting a surface fleet, or even more so when they hunted one of their own. This feeling of vulnerability that wouldn't go away, like the only defense they had was a fragile silence that could be pierced at any moment. That, somewhere, there was someone who was watching them, even now.

The skin between Roberts's shoulder blades itched as he tried to shake the feeling.

▶▶▶

"This is impossible!" The young tech looked over the indecipherable rows of numbers for the fiftieth time.

"Nothing is impossible, lad," Palin retorted to the young technician's outburst, not bothered in the slightest by it. "Just improbable."

"Easy for you to say," the young man said. "I can't make heads or tails out of this."

"Nor can I." Palin shrugged. "But that's not the point. Sometimes all it takes is one block falling into place. Everything else will just...come together."

The tech just shook his head and tapped a command into his computer.

Palin stiffened when a new sound played over the speakers.

"That's not the same signal," he said.

"What? Of course it is…" Evan, the tech, replied. "I've been playing it for an hour now…"

"The pitch is different, and the pattern…" Palin pierced the young man with a glare. "Where did you get that?"

"I'm telling you, Doctor, it's the same signal…" Evan replied, exasperated, calling up the folder. He pointed to the screen. "There? See it's…"

Palin waited for a moment and then prompted him. "What? What is it?"

"It's a new file," Evan muttered, staring at it. "Where did this come from, now, I wonder…Oh!"

"Oh?"

"It was just received. A pulse signal came in over the forward spires—"

"Play it."

"Doctor, it's probably just—"

"Play it," Palin repeated, his voice hard.

"Uh…as you wish, Doctor," the technician replied, hitting the play key again.

▶ ▶ ▶

"It's one of them, Captain," Ensign Waters said, "lying quiet down there, but it is one of them."

Weston leaned forward. "How many tubes do we have?"

"All but two are charged, Captain."

Weston gave the order: "Prime tubes one through four for sequential fire."

"Aye, aye, Captain."

"Range to target?" Weston asked.

"Eighty-three light-seconds" came the reply.

"Hold our course. Fire on my command."

The tension mounted as the light-seconds gradually counted down. Each tick of light as the display changed sent an imperceptible shiver down the spines of each man and woman present.

As the range dropped to under seventy-five light-seconds, Weston nodded to Waters and gave the command: "Fire."

This time, the computer had less time to plot a course prediction for the enemy, but the ship was also flying slower than before and the range was closer than either of the previous shots. The tubes fired sequentially, according to the captain's orders, each pulse of energy blasting clear of the ship and given a full half second gap before the next shot followed.

When all four shots had been fired, Weston snapped his next command to the helm: "Alter course, four-one-one-mark-positive-twelve. Thrusters only, Lieutenant. Keep us above the ecliptic, this time."

"Aye, aye, Captain. Course to four-one-one-mark-plus-twelve. Thrusters only," came the automatic repetition.

Around them, the rumble of thrusters groaned from the ship itself as they once again shifted course.

"Stick and move, Lieutenant," Weston told Daniels. "Stick and move."

"Yes, sir."

▶▶▶

The ithan lifted her head from the screen. "I think we just registered the *Odyssey*, Admiral!"

"Where is she?" Tanner asked.

"The green icon, Admiral."

Tanner looked up at the display, noting the information appended to the icon. "What are they shooting at, Ithan?"

"We have a soft reflection in that area, Admiral, but I'm not certain. We'll have to wait for the light-speed return."

Tanner nodded in reluctant acceptance.

▶ ▶ ▶

Seventy-five light-seconds was a long distance for anything to travel, even light itself, when you consider that most cultures take centuries or longer to realize that it even did travel. For anything substantially slower, that distance was a prohibitively long way.

For the four pulse torpedoes from the *Odyssey*, however, it took just over eighty seconds to cross the void and arrive at their target. The range meant a relatively shorter gap between their arrival and the light and energy they projected, which, to the alien warship, meant that much less time to react.

The alien command saw them coming and opened fire with lasers, only to have much the same effect. Firing light at an energy weapon was very nearly pointless, and this reaction had been expected, so the order went out at the same time and fighters began to pour from the big ship.

The problem, such as it was, was that the reaction time had been calculated on a ten-second period in which they could react. In each previous time, that was what the enemy weapons had given them.

This time, they had a little less than eight.

The first of the fighters were just sliding into place as a screen when the initial strike smashed into their formation, obliterating the formation and the vast majority of the fighters and opening a hole in them for the remaining three.

Fired sequentially, the pulse torpedoes exhibited much smaller degrees of variance in their course while in flight, their like charges not being able to push them apart in a shotgun-like spread effect. Instead, they flew straight and true, which was why a sequential attack was preferred against single targets at any range.

The remaining three shots slammed into the ship, even as its fighters scrambled to leave its decks, ripping the alien war craft to pieces in an explosion of light and energy as its reactor containment was annihilated.

▶▶▶

Seventy-four seconds after the torpedoes struck, the *Odyssey's* bridge surged with the exhilarated rush of the kill as the catastrophic display of light and energy etched itself on their sensors.

"It's a kill, sir!" Daniels enthused.

Weston's eyes were glued to the screens for the next one. "We've got four more out there, people. Find them before they find us."

"Aye, aye, Captain," they said together, the energy of the moment carrying their enthusiasm.

That enthusiasm, however, wore thin as the minutes turned to an hour, and still, there was nothing on the screens while they cut through the system on a ballistic course.

Weston considered the empty space of a star system made the battlefields of Earth look like a child's playpen by comparison. Even discounting all the rather large solid objects that one could hide behind, it was impossible to scan more than a small percentage of the skies. And even if you could, there was every chance that you wouldn't know what you were looking at when you saw it.

It made for a very ironic way of literally being bored to death.

▶ ▶ ▶

"That's two," the ithan breathed in near disbelief.

Tanner didn't blame her; it was beyond belief that any one ship could stand up to the force that had ground the best fleet his people had been able to mount to dust. The *Odyssey* and Captain Weston were marvels beyond marvels, as far as he was concerned.

Now if only the Forge would finish their work so *he* could do something productive.

Anything productive.

The admiral gritted his teeth, a decidedly uncivilized snarl, showing them to anyone with the courage to face him.

Had it not been for the *Odyssey* fighting a war that was not theirs, this planet would be dead before the Forge could have become a factor at all.

On such whimsical flickers of the universe rested the fate of an entire world.

▶ ▶ ▶

"Radio pulse!" Waters's voice was excited as he looked at the signal.

"Tracking its source now, Captain," Lamont answered the question he had yet to formulate. "We got a clearer bead on this one. The Electronic Warfare Department is narrowing it down to a tighter tangent."

"Thank you, Susan," Weston said. "My compliments to them. Mr. Daniels, bring our bow around, if you please?"

"Aye, aye, Captain, coming around. Thrusters only."

The *Odyssey* rumbled and moaned as it came around again, its nose dipping down into the gravity well of the red giant star, toward the source of the last transmission.

"We're lined up, sir."

"Very well, Lieutenant. Take us ahead—dead slow."

"Dead slow, aye, Captain."

▶▶▶

A chirp sounded through the lab, startling the young tech as he looked around for the cause.

"Relax," Palin told him. "I inserted a command into the system to alert me if we detected another radio transmission. Call it up, would you please?"

"Ah...yes, Doctor," Evan replied, tapping out a command.

A new signal, audibly identical to the others, as far as Evan was concerned, filled the room, and Palin frowned and leaned back as he closed his eyes.

"Doctor?"

"Shh..." Palin said softly. "Place it on a continuous loop, if you please?"

"Uh...yes, sir."

The file played over and over as Evan watched Palin rock in his chair with his eyes closed.

"It's very close to the last one, but quite different from the first," the linguist said, frowning. "There are three sequences that repeat in both. But they have slight differences from each other...something familiar there...But it escapes me at the moment."

The technician shrugged helplessly.

"Play all three—no, just the last two. Continuous loop."

"Yes, Doctor."

▶▶▶

The tension mounted as the bridge staff found themselves staring at everything their passive arrays could feed them. In this game of cat and mouse, or hide-and-seek, the first side to see the other would be the victor, and they were determined that they would not miss the enemy for the lack of a pair of eyes.

"Nothing yet, Captain," Waters said unnecessarily, his eyes glued to the board.

Weston just grunted in response, his own eyes watching the captain's displays. The enemy had to be there somewhere, though perhaps they learned from their last mistakes.

He expanded his display's range to look outside the cone the RDF tangent had indicated, looking for anything suspicious.

"Dammit…" Waters cursed under his breath. "It's all the interference from the star, Captain. It's making it damn near impossible to see anything."

"I know that, Mr. Waters. Just keep looking," Weston said.

Whether on purpose or by accident, this one had managed to set itself between the system's primary and the *Odyssey*. Normally, this might aid them by providing a bright background in which to look for a dark ship. However, the interference generated by the star was wreaking havoc on the delicate reception systems.

Something about that just didn't sit right with Weston, either. What were the odds of the enemy just happening to appear there, at that angle?

Slim to none was Weston's guess, and he opened his mouth to order them to break off but then frowned and held his peace. Sometimes you went with your gut, but usually, the numbers were the best path. Knowing when to draw the line was the hardest skill you could master, and Weston didn't think it was the time, not just yet.

Their best bet was purely visual-based sensors; however, those were relatively easy to spoof in this situation, as the *Odyssey* itself had proven with the black hole settings on their adaptive armor.

"She could be right there…" Waters whispered. "Right out there, just waiting…"

Weston was about to respond when the intercom went off, blaring as someone dialed into the bridge. He slapped the controls, cutting the noise off, and snarled into the device.

"Goddammit, whoever this is I'm a little busy right now…"

"Captain! Captain!" a very excited voice came over the speakers.

"Dr. Palin?" he asked. "How did you get access to this line?"

"Yes, Captain, I just made a discovery!"

"Doctor, if you don't mind, I'm in the middle of a battle up here…"

"What? Oh, yes, yes…But, you see, it's a coordinate system!"

Weston closed his eyes, rubbing them with his right hand. "What?"

"The transmissions, Captain! They were reporting a series of coordinates!" Palin babbled on. "It's fascinating. You see, they use a trinary numbering system and—"

"Doctor! I'm busy up here…" Weston trailed off, thinking furiously. "Wait! Coordinates? Are you sure?"

"Yes, Captain. Quite sure."

Weston supposed they could be reporting their own positions through a battle network, but if that were the case, he would have expected to have picked up signals like this in their earlier encounters. *So what's different this time?*

Only one thing he could think of.

"I'll have to talk to you later. Weston out." He cut the line as he looked around, trying to make a choice as his gut and his mind argued two different courses.

He paused, then straightened in his seat, slapped open a ship-wide channel, and started snapping orders.

"All stations, this is Captain Weston. We are about to go to full military power. All stations, I say again, full military power." Turning to Waters, he said, "Do we have enough for a full-power tachyon pulse?"

Waters blinked, checking his controls. "Yes, sir, but only if we kill recharge on two of our tubes."

"Do it," Weston ordered. "And for God's sake, kill the black hole settings! Bring the armor back to maximum general deflection!"

"Aye, aye, Captain!"

▶▶▶

The big ship began to hum as its core leapt back to life, power feeding into previously dormant systems as it gave up any pretext at hiding its dull-black exterior, suddenly shifting and changing, until it was visually an almost pure white.

At the same time, its running lights came online, casting out the shadows that had covered up its name and numbers, causing the NACS *Odyssey* to roar to life, even as it announced its resurrection with a sudden blast of tachyons.

The massless little particles jumped out from the ship, spreading far and wide as they went out in every direction, looking for things to bounce off. Omnidirectionally, her detection range was limited, as the *Odyssey* simply didn't have enough power to generate that many tachyons, but this time it didn't matter.

▶▶▶

"Mother of God."

Roberts didn't look up to see who had said that. In fact, he nearly seconded the statement himself.

"How'd they get so close?" someone else demanded.

That was a good question, Roberts knew. One that he couldn't answer. Though, to be honest, he was more interested in how Captain Weston had guessed they were there.

On the screen, previously blank, there were now three icons in hostile bloodred, all closing on the *Odyssey* from less than sixty light-seconds.

▼

CHAPTER 35

▲

▶ "HOSTILE CONTACTS—PORT and starboard!" Waters yelled out as the lights came back to full power from their minimal status. "They're moving dead slow, Captain!"

"That won't last!" Weston snapped. "Ahead, all flank!"

"Aye, sir!" Daniels said, slamming the controls hard forward.

"Sir! We have another one along our course!" Waters warned.

"I'm aware of that, Mr. Waters," Weston said. "Bring all forward weapons online and give me a narrow-arc tachyon ping as soon as we have power."

"Aye, aye, sir."

Weston gripped the arms of his chair tightly as the numbers started to drop, the *Odyssey* racing against the enemy to see who would get their ship to full power first. If he was lucky, he'd taken them by surprise with the sudden surge to full military power, but there was no way to tell how quickly they could respond. If they were on the ball, or if their technology was faster than his, the *Odyssey* was in a seriously bad situation.

"The enemy is accelerating." Waters sounded calmer now.

"Trying to catch us in a pincer, Ensign," Weston said.

"Aye, sir."

"Don't worry about it. Our acceleration curve is almost as good as theirs, and we've got the jump on them. Just pay attention to the one in front of us."

"Aye, sir," Waters said, looking up. "Captain, if they hit us with their lasers, even our best general armor setting isn't likely to—"

"I'm aware of that, too, Ensign," Weston cut him off. "Don't forget, they're still sixty light-seconds out, and they don't know our acceleration curve. No way can they predict where we're going to be when their lasers strike."

"Aye, sir." Waters sounded relieved.

Weston decided not to remind him that the craft down angle from them was staring at an essentially stable target and wouldn't need to do much prediction. The tense look in the man's shoulders told him that he didn't need to; Waters had figured that out on his own.

Weston's eyes glanced to the clock.

Thirty seconds.

▶▶▶

"Move your butts, ladies!" the Engineering chief snapped. He swung himself through the compartment, catching a grip on the wall to arrest his flight, and landed near the control for the tokamak. "The captain's gonna need this puppy online in a hurry, Jenks."

"Working on it, Chief," the young man said, not looking up. "We'll jump-start it cold, just as soon as I clear the tubes."

"Just get it done."

"Go bother someone else. You do *not* want me missing something here," the man replied, his head stuck down inside part of the system.

Normally, the chief would have torn his head off for a comment like that, but it was true. The last thing they needed was stray matter particles in the tokamak stream.

▶▶▶

Commander Roberts's face was ashen as he watched the telemetry plot, but his voice was steady and calm while snapping out orders.

"Contact Point Defense and make sure that they're on the ball, Lieutenant," he said, taking up his primary duties of handling the secondary systems so the captain could focus on the situation at hand.

"Aye, Commander," the lieutenant nodded, turning to her controls and opening the appropriate channels. "PD, this is X-Com. What is your status?" She listened for the answer. A few seconds later, she replied, "Point Defense reports ready to fight, sir."

Roberts nodded, his eyes still on the plot. The *Odyssey* had leapt forward, hurtling itself out of the snare that the enemy had prepared for it, but in doing so, they were flying into the teeth of the tiger.

▶▶▶

"Enemy ships are adjusting their courses. They're going to try to intercept."

"Of course they are," Weston said, still watching the clock. Ten seconds.

"Sideslip, Lieutenant. All thrusters to port," he ordered. "Ten-second burn."

"All thrusters to port, aye, Captain," Daniels said, activating the commands. "Ten seconds."

The ship rumbled and complained but followed the command as its starboard thrusters burned hot and shoved the ship off to port.

Ten seconds later, the rumble died out a little, though the big engines pushing them along still filled up the background with their incessant roar.

"Energy flare!" Waters snapped. "They shot at us, sir!"

"Of course they did," Weston smiled. "Analyze and adapt our forward plates to deflect. Helm, random course alterations along our current path, if you please."

"Aye, aye, sir," both men answered as one.

▶▶▶

Admiral Tanner's mood grew grimmer as the waiting game wore thin and then vanished into nothing but one nerve grating against the other. If only he had a ship, even one of the old converted freighters, anything at all to...

"Admiral!"

Tanner spun around. "What is it, Ithan?"

"Look, sir." The young woman pointed.

Tanner looked up, blanching white as he saw the board lit up with four blazing icons, bright as a noonday sun.

The *Odyssey*'s green flash blazed brightly now. They had obviously dropped any pretense at hiding, and he could easily see why. Three hostile red icons surrounded it on the plot. His stomach twisted as he easily read the trap in the image.

"The *Odyssey* is accelerating, Admiral," the ithan said calmly, eyeing the threat board as well as her own instruments. "We are reading all four on the actual time sensors now—weapons fired from the Drasin ship!"

The screen lit up as a blast from the Drasin ship traced across the stars, obviously in response to the *Odyssey*'s sudden appearance. Tanner grimaced as it closed on the *Odyssey*, perfectly aligned with its target.

Someone groaned. Tanner didn't know who and he didn't care. It was all he could do to not groan himself.

And then, less than ten seconds before it struck, the *Odyssey* coolly slid aside.

Tanner stared, his eyes widening, as people gasped at the clean miss. *How did Captain Weston know?* Then he understood. Weston didn't know that the enemy had fired. What he knew was the time it would take, to the second, for a shot to reach his position from the Drasin's lasers.

Would I have thought of that?

Somehow, Tanner doubted it.

▶▶▶

While the *Odyssey* bucked and wove its way along its course, Captain Weston waited impatiently for news from Engineering on the tokamak status. They'd need its power contribution in order to bring the full power of the ship to bear. Now that the hide-and-seek game was over and done with, he wanted as much punch as he could get when he "tagged" the bad guys.

"The chase ships are gaining on our acceleration advantage," Waters told him, calmer now.

"And the bandit ahead?"

"We're waiting for the return from the targeting laser, Captain," he replied. "If we managed to paint her, we'll have a firm lock."

"Very well, Waters."

The seconds ticked by, seeming to pass like hours as they waited for the return bounce from the laser. Finally, the moment passed, and Waters muffled a curse.

"Sorry, Captain." He shook his head. "They've begun evasive maneuvering."

Weston eyed the closing rates.

At less than fifty light-seconds now, the evasive actions on either side would begin to have limited usefulness in about two minutes. However, until the range closed enough to achieve a good laser lock, the only weapons that Weston had for useful engagement were the pulse torpedoes, and he'd rather save them for the chasers.

"Understood," he said out loud. "Keep an eye out for fighters, Mr. Waters."

"Aye, aye, Captain."

Weston reached down and thumbed a switch. "Archangels, proceed to Ready One launch stations. I say again, Archangel Flight Group is to proceed to Ready One positions."

▶▶▶

"Whoop!" Paladin yelled as the voice boomed around them, and tossed his cards into a bag at his side. "Duty calls."

"Saved by the bell." Jennifer "Cardsharp" Samuels smirked as she kicked back and grabbed the edge of her cockpit.

Paladin just smirked as he executed a perfect backflip in the zero gravity, hooked his hands around the lip of the cockpit, and slid right into his seat. "That's how the chips fall!"

"Right," Samuels grinned, pulling her restraints down as one of the flight crew floated into place and handed over her helmet.

She accepted it as the man took a hold of the restraints and yanked them tight. The pressure seals locked with a twist, and she felt the rush of cool air hit her face, then flashed a thumbs-up to the crewman.

"Good hunting, ma'am." He grinned at her. He finished checking her restraints and pushed back off the plane while he waved the loader in.

She nodded curtly, and as the plane shuddered from the loader's kiss, she thumbed the cockpit, sealing command as soon as the crewman was clear.

The clamshell front and back of the armored shield slid down over her, locking solidly into place and engulfing her in a darkness that was lit only by the soft glow of her backlit controls. She ignored the dark, thumbing her systems online, one by one, until the full-surround HUD lit the cockpit back up, making it appear that she was sitting in a glass bubble with a near-perfect view of all angles.

"Archangel Thirteen…" Her lips twisted at the number, wondering if it was going to haunt her, or make her haunt someone else. "Online, all systems check."

▶▶▶

The *Odyssey* and its prey were locked in a deadly dance across Tanner's screens, and suddenly, he found that the waiting hadn't been so bad, after all.

His sensation of helplessness was a hundredfold now that he was watching men and women with no allegiance to him preparing to fight and die for them all. If he could only send them the details that he could see from here. Let them know what their enemies were doing…

Tanner suddenly wanted to slit his own throat.

Stupid, stupid, stupid! You could have sent a transceiver to them. It would have been a matter of a few seconds' work to set it up for them, he berated himself, cursing his stupidity.

"Admiral…"

Tanner ignored the voice. There was nothing they could do from here, anyway. It was all pointless.

"Admiral."

All he had to do was think! Dammit. Wasn't that what he was entrusted to do?

"Admiral!"

"What?" Tanner snapped furiously, turning on the voice.

The young woman flinched back, paling, but managed to keep her voice. "Sir. It's the Forge. They say it's ready."

▶▶▶

Oddly enough, in the very midst of the terror time, Weston found his mind wandering dangerously. He remembered that someone had once said that war was an interminably long stretch of boredom punctuated by seconds of pure terror. In this battle, at least, that statement had been stretched and distorted beyond all recognition as the hours of boredom gave way to an almost equal stretch of terror.

He watched the *Odyssey* buck and weave, spinning along the axis of its course while it registered energy leakage from the immensely powerful lasers flashing around it. Each punctuating moment brought its own thrill of terror, adding to the general chaos of the battlefield.

The sheer distance involved only served to heighten both the boredom of the hunt and lengthen the time of terror as the battle raged across distances unprecedented in the history of the *Odyssey*'s crew.

Weston forced himself back into the moment with sheer force of will.

"We painted her, Captain!" Waters yelled out eagerly.

"Refraction data?" he demanded.

"Aye, sir. We've got it!" Waters practically snarled, his tone feral. "We have her hull's composition, sir."

"Send the word to the laser crews! Make her ready for war, Mr. Waters."

"Aye, aye, Captain."

With the data from the laser bounce added to what they already knew of the Drasin hulls, they could adapt their laser frequency to perfectly target the enemy. So as Waters sent out the command with the information from the laser return appended, Weston tapped out a few calculations of his own.

"Mr. Daniels. Prepare to steady our course for a controlled fire."

"Aye, Captain," Daniels responded, shifting the evasive program over to automatic while he prepared the new course corrections.

The chase ships were still over fifty-five light-seconds behind the *Odyssey*, Weston noted, which meant that even if they had a real-time lock of the *Odyssey*'s position, it would take more than fifty-five seconds for any weapons fire to reach its position from the rear, not counting the *Odyssey*'s own current acceleration away from them.

That, coupled with the fact that they had a clear reading on the waste energy from the forward ship's lasers, led Weston to his next move.

"Forward laser array has been adjusted, Captain," Waters reported.

"Thank you. Helm," Weston said.

"Yes, sir."

"Prepare to abandon evasive maneuvers and initiate an attack run."

"Aye, aye, Captain."

▶▶▶

"Captain Tianne," Admiral Tanner glared at the screen. "You are late."

"My apologies, Admiral." The tall woman looked embarrassed and more than a little frustrated. "The Forge only just completed the basic systems on the *Cerekus*."

"We have allies in-system currently doing battle with three Drasin warships," Tanner said. "They have eliminated five others already and are being hard-pressed. I would appreciate it if you could arrange that they survive this battle."

The woman gaped at him for a moment, not that Tanner blamed her in the slightest. There was no ally in known space that could stand up to the Drasin one-on-one, let alone eliminate five of the warships and fight a three-to-one duel with even the remotest chance of survival.

"Allies, Admiral?"

"I will explain as you move, Captain," Tanner cut her off. "My staff is sending you the pertinent data as we speak."

The woman glanced to her side. "Received. We are laying in our course now."

"Excellent."

"Admiral…" Captain Tianne frowned. "Our sensors have the battle in actual time as we speak. Who are these people?"

"That, Captain, is a question that I, too, wish to have answered," Tanner said. "But for the moment, they are the saviors of our planet. I would prefer that they do not become its martyrs."

"As you say, Admiral." Tianne came to attention and saluted.

Tanner nodded with some satisfaction as the captain of the newly commissioned *Cerekus* battleship turned to her duties. One ship did not a fleet make, but this wasn't just any ship. The *Cerekus* was the first in a new class, or it might be said, a very old one. A class of warships that the central computer had ordered, spitting out designs for when the Drasin first appeared.

Only the Forge could have built one so fast. The shipyard facility was one of the most advanced in all of the colonies. And the one most perfectly hidden. Tanner permitted himself a slight smile. Even should all the colonies fall, Maker forbid, the Forge would never be discovered.

And from that one port, a fleet would arise, like none Rael Tanner had ever imagined in his worst nightmares.

▶▶▶

Weston held his order as the clock counted down the range, watching until the numbers dropped to under twenty light-seconds between the two onrushing ships.

"Now, Mr. Daniels," he ordered. "Initiate our attack run."

"Aye, aye, sir," Daniels ordered, snapping the *Odyssey* out of the evasive roll and steadying her into a headlong rush at their enemy.

"Paint that ship, Mr. Waters," Weston said.

Waters didn't respond right away, his shoulders already bent to the task as his fingers sent out a dozen low-powered targeting lasers, all seeking the enemy ship as they closed in on it at a madman's pace.

Twenty seconds out, eighteen back, and the tactical officer's face flushed with pleasure. "I've got him, Captain."

"Hold him," Weston ordered. "HVM banks, prepare to fire."

"HVMs are ready."

"Flush the banks. Pattern Trafalgar Twelve!"

"Aye, Captain. Trafalgar Twelve away!"

The *Odyssey* shuddered as the forward HVM banks were flushed, the CM-powered death dealers leaping from the ship and into space, accelerating to their maximum speed of 0.789c in the nearly thirty seconds it took them to cross the gap between the *Odyssey* and her foe.

The spread pattern, Trafalgar Twelve, was a statistically based pattern designed to engage opponents at extreme range and had never been used in combat before. The think tank that had come up with it was mostly just shooting blind as they tried to figure out how to engage threats against the Jovian research platform, or more likely, Earth-based satellites and the Demos repair station that overlooked the site of the Martian Colony Project.

They certainly hadn't envisioned it being used against an alien attacker in a different star system over a hundred light-years from Earth.

So when the impact plumes went up across the enemy ship on their screens, almost seventeen seconds after the impact had occurred, the bridge crew of the NACS *Odyssey* was elated.

"Got him!" someone shouted.

"Status, Mr. Waters," Weston said over the general buzz of relief.

Waters, too, was quiet, watching the numbers carefully. Each of the HVM strikes would have carried the equivalent kinetic energy of a nuke strike when their full mass returned after the destruction of the CM generator on impact. In theory, the solid-core missiles could deliver considerably more energy than any nuke ever devised.

In reality, Waters was no longer certain of that.

"Enemy vessel stabilizing, Captain. She's still coming," he reported a moment later.

A dark silence fell over the bridge, but Weston stayed calm. "Prepare a firing solution for the main laser array."

"Aye, aye," Waters responded.

Weston watched the numbers as they fell. Thirteen seconds was now all that lay between them and the ship ahead. Behind, the chasers had managed to gain another fifteen light-seconds on the *Odyssey*, and it was clear that it had lost its brief acceleration advantage. It would shortly be facing those two behind, assuming it survived the deadly duel it was already engaged in.

"Laser strike!" Waters snapped. "Solid hit on the forward armor!"

"Status?"

"Holding, Captain."

"Hold course."

"Captain?" Daniels blurted in shock, half turning.

"If they're firing at us, Mr. Daniels, they aren't trying to dodge. Mr. Waters, open fire with the main laser array."

"Aye, aye, sir."

▶▶▶

Captain Tianne of the warship *Cerekus* watched the duel as it played out on her screens, not quite able to believe the one-sided reports that had been sent to her from the ground. If they were to be believed, this "ally" of Admiral Tanner's was a giant—on the battlefield, at least.

However, on her sensors, it looked more like a gnat.

Its power curve was practically flat; the generation levels were so low that she had seen freighters that could outpower it. Its weapons were barely detectable on the *Cerekus*'s energy traps—at least the ones it had used since her arrival.

It has to be some kind of trick, she thought in confusion. *Stealth systems, perhaps, masking their energy signatures... something...*

Her own ship was now hurtling toward the battle at best speed, which was impressive enough, but the war was being fought over eight rotations away, which was going to take some time to cross, even with the *Cerekus*'s drive.

This meant that the admiral's allies were simply going to have to survive on their own for a while longer.

▶▶▶

The heterodyne-generated laser from the *Odyssey*'s main array—adjusted and fine-tuned by its operating crews to the best absorption frequency of the enemy's armor characteristics—took a little less than ten seconds to cross the gap when the order to fire was given.

It found, upon arrival, a target that was still busy pouring radiation several hundred times its own meager amount back along its own course toward the *Odyssey* and bathed it in fire as it returned the favor.

A few seconds of exchange later, the alien warship began to bubble as nearly 100 percent of the *Odyssey*'s energy was absorbed into its hull material and turned into magma.

Within ten seconds, the ship suddenly folded in on itself as the energy carved out a hole along its beam, striking the power core and turning its own reactor into a nuke.

▶▶▶

"Got him!" Waters grinned darkly as the enemy went critical on his screens, and at almost the same moment, the warning lights went dead.

"Status of our forward armor?"

"Badly ablated, sir," Waters said, after checking it. "We're intact, but I wouldn't want to take too much more, not on those plates."

"Understood," Weston replied. "Prepare to bring us about, Mr. Daniels. We have to bring our pulse tubes to bear on the chasers."

"Aye, sir, on your order."

"Captain!" Susan Lamont's head snapped up. "Report from the Electronic Warfare Department—we have fighters inbound!"

"They must have launched as a precaution," Weston growled. "I would have."

He considered it, then thumbed open a channel. "Archangels...scramble."

▶▶▶

Tianne stared at her screens in disbelief, unwilling or unable to quite grasp what she had seen. The Drasin ship had the advantage—all of the advantages. It had the more powerful weapons, armor that could defeat lasers that were intensely more powerful than those of the unknown vessel. It was faster, with a greater acceleration curve. It had been the superior vessel, the more powerful warship.

So why was it dead, while the oddly configured ship still lived?

▼

CHAPTER 36

▲

▶ WHAT SHOULD HAVE been a deafening roar was nothing but a brilliant flash of light and a sudden rush of motion as two more fighter craft hurtled themselves off the flight deck and out into the black beyond. Samuels waited her turn, the purr of the fighter charging her as the deck crews moved about, clearing the ground in front of her.

She checked her system status one more time as the last checks cycled, and looked up when a light caught her eye.

The deck crew didn't talk to her directly; they didn't have to. The figure ahead of her—his bright white-and-yellow vac suit identifying him as one of the handling officers—waved the okay to her and signaled the all clear.

She gave him a thumbs-up back, keyed in the final release on the twin reactors she was riding on, and waited for the final okay.

The handler dropped to a crouch, waving his hand in a sharp arc, and pointed for the black.

Samuels slid the throttle forward all the way, feeling the sudden lurch that slammed her back into the seat despite the

CM field already surrounding her, and the flight deck around her became a blur as she was catapulted out into space.

"Archangels," Stephanos's voice came through clearly. "Form up on me…Give me a tight wedge while we gather some intel on the opposition."

The fighters automatically came together, the bulk of the *Odyssey* dropping back away from them as they turned on all of their advanced sensor systems and activated the full suite of electronic warfare devices in preparation for the battle to come.

Behind, just as the last of them cleared the spires and moved completely out of range, the *Odyssey*'s front-control thrusters burned, lifting its nose up and flipping the big ship until it was on a ballistic course, its nose pointed back toward the enemy.

"All planes, engage the interface," Stephanos ordered.

Samuels's hand reached forward, hesitating for just a moment in painful memory while she flipped up the safety catch and pushed the switch forward.

The sharp bite of the needles digging into her neck caused her to hiss, then it was gone and she forced herself to relax. With the needles in, she felt herself shifting the plane almost by thought alone as she fine-tuned her place in formation and smiled.

This was what she had trained for.

▶▶▶

"Do we have tokamak power yet?" Weston asked, watching the star field change radically as the *Odyssey* completed its flip.

Computer magnification brought the enemy ships into focus as they hurtled on, their faces lit by the light of the star that was now at the *Odyssey*'s back. Two of them glinted darkly in the reflected light at forty light-seconds now and closing fast.

"Spinning up now, Captain."

"Good," Weston said, with some satisfaction.

The tokamak should have taken a great deal longer to bring fully online, but once again, what the chief promised was delivered. For now, he'd do what he could with what he had.

"Pulse torpedoes," he ordered. "How many are in our banks?"

"Ten, Captain," Waters answered.

"Prime them all. Standard spread. Fire on my mark."

"Aye, sir. Priming tubes one through ten." Waters reached out and toggled a series of commands.

"Fire."

▶▶▶

Captain Tianne stared at the data the computer provided for the sudden barrage of energy the small ship had flung at the Drasin. Whatever those were, they weren't the product of a flat power curve, which meant that there was something exceedingly deceptive about that ship.

"Track those shots," she ordered. "I want a full profile of that weapon."

"Yes, Captain," a young man at the weapons station said.

"What is our arrival time?" she asked, glancing over at the helm controls.

"Ten rotations."

She watched the screen and the estimations for enemy contact with the ship designated *Odyssey*. They would have to survive at least four rotations of direct contact with the enemy before the *Cerekus* arrived.

▶▶▶

The spread of torpedoes had left the *Odyssey* almost a full minute earlier, and the sensors were tracking their terminal flight when the enemy ships began spewing fighter craft like angry bees from a hive. The screens became a mash of conflicting signals just as the first pulse torpedo struck home.

The spherical, white blooms of energy lit up the sky, unleashing devastating energy all across the enemy formation, dying out slowly as the burning of secondary fires continued to blot out information on the sensors.

Someone whistled on the bridge, but Weston couldn't tell who did it. He didn't look too hard, either, as he was leaning forward and willing the screens to clear up.

Then the screens darkened, the energy dwindling as the last of the secondary explosions faded away, and a curse died on his lips as he saw the two enemy warships still coming.

"Their fighter wing absorbed the damage, Captain," Waters reported.

Weston had already guessed as much. "I can see that," he said. "Get a count of their remaining fighters."

"Aye, sir."

Weston pulled a display to him and grimly shook his head.

It was going to be bad—that was certain. The problem was that he didn't see a way to make it any better.

▶▶▶

"Team Two. Break formation and engage the lead elements."

Samuels watched as the four-fighter group broke away from the main group at Stephanos's order, accelerating out and away, forming up into a tight, staggered diamond formation as they did.

The alien bandits were coming in from the sun, and it was lousing up all their sensors as they tried to get an accurate count of the opposition.

Coming out of the sun was one of the oldest tricks in aviation, largely because it worked. Even in the latter days of flying, when radar and lidar turned even the most venerable of maneuvers into a trickier proposition, there were still times when the slight edge it gave a pilot was all that they needed. And that was in the atmosphere of Earth, where the worst of the solar radiation had been filtered out by the layers of protection that made the planet habitable. Out here in space, there was nothing to protect the fighters' sensors from the charged solar wind and the intense radiation, and it showed. The best Samuels was getting was an intermittent group of bandits that faded in and out, seemingly at will.

"Angel Lead, this is Racer," Gabrielle's voice echoed over the tac-net. "Fox Three."

And the battle was joined.

▶▶▶

"How many HVMs do we have left in stores, Ensign?" Weston glanced over to Susan Lamont.

She'd put the munitions list on one of her quick-call commands before the battle and had the data quickly. "We've expended about eighty percent of our standard load, sir."

Weston nodded, noting with some amusement that, despite the gravity of the situation, her voice was almost apologetic. "Thank you, Ensign."

It wasn't her fault, of course. There was no way for anyone to know that they'd be in a situation that was anything even remotely like this. Had they planned going into an actual war zone, the load would probably have been ten times that taken aboard.

This meant that they had about half of a full salvo left, totally discharged pulse tubes, and their laser array left to fend off two of the enemy warships.

It could always be worse, Weston thought. *The Block could have succeeded in getting that reporter, Miss Lynn, assigned as an observer.*

He briefly considered the order he had given Commander Roberts to recall the Archangels and make a run for it, but he knew that would be pointless now. The acceleration curves on the alien ships were superior to the *Odyssey*'s, though not by as much as first thought, and that would permit them to run her down long before she reached the heliopause.

So, as instinct and nature did so command, when flight was no longer an option, the human animal had one more option remaining.

And fight it was.

▶ ▶ ▶

"I...I think we got a hit!" Racer's voice called over the tac-net. "It's hard to tell...There was a thermal bloom, but it was masked by the sun!"

"All Archangels," Stephanos's voice smoothly slid over the tac-net, "increase velocity, spread formation."

Samuels pushed the thrust controls forward as the fighter roared at her back. All around her, the others did the same.

The fighters spread out, still accelerating as they closed the distance with the enemy and leapt ahead into the brilliant, yet decidedly ghastly, red glare coming from the system's primary.

"Keep your eyes peeled, Angels," Stephanos ordered. "They're coming."

Samuels did as ordered, her eyes wide open as she stared into the sun, looking for the enemy. They were still fading in and out, like before, until suddenly they weren't. Then they were there, screaming in from the brilliance of the star, but too large to hide completely. She yelled in surprise.

"That's it! Stay sharp!" Stephanos said a moment later as the enemy began to fire. "Make sure your combat computers are automatic adaptive settings and continue to accelerate."

The needles in Jennifer's neck were itching, though she supposed it was all in her mind. They weren't supposed to feel anything once they were inserted. The computer began wailing around her as one of the enemy fighters singled her out for some special attention and a glancing-laser strike tripped her combat computer's automatic adaptive armor. The camplates that surrounded her shimmered, changing their base color to the best reflective surface for the enemy beam, then settled in as the wail died down.

Minimal damage, she thought as she looked over the reports. The surface of her right wing was a little scorched and probably wouldn't take another direct hit too well, since the brief flash had ablated away most of its armor; however, it was only a small surface.

She would survive it—probably.

"Almost there, Angels," Stephanos said tensely, the sounds of damage reports from other fighters chattering over the tacnet. "Hold on course...hold...hold..."

Then the Archangels interpenetrated the enemy ranks, the two forces slamming together at unimaginable speeds as both sides started to turn and burn, trying desperately to claw themselves, fist over fist, into the position of best advantage.

And in that moment, all across the wing, the largest amount of solar interference was gone as the Archangels dropped behind the enemy lines, circling around in tight maneuvers, and got the sun at *their* back.

▶ ▶ ▶

Adm. Rael Tanner's knuckles were bone white as he gripped the board in front of him. "What is he doing? By the Maker and all He has made, what is that insane fool doing?"

The *Odyssey* had stopped accelerating away from the remaining two ships, flipping end for end on the scanners, and while it wasn't accelerating toward the ships, the distance between decreased quickly. The *Odyssey* was merely coasting now as energy discharges roared around them.

"Turn and run!" Tanner hissed, wiping sweat from his face with a stiff hand. "The *Cerekus* is here now, you damned fool. Run."

"Maybe they don't see her?" someone said.

Tanner shook his head. "That's not possible. A ship the size of the *Cerekus* would be visible on any sensors that weren't absolutely blinded."

"The sun, Admiral," a quiet voice spoke up.

"What?" Tanner spun, looking back at Milla, who was standing pale in her borrowed armor.

"The sun. The *Cerekus* is straight from the Forge. That means that Okana is directly behind them, and the *Odyssey's* passive sensors are—"

"Blind." Tanner grimaced, his fist slapping down in realization. "Even the best sensor systems would be overwhelmed by staring right into a star the size of Okana."

"They don't see the *Cerekus*, Admiral," Milla said. "And even if they did…They would as likely believe it to be Drasin as anything else."

Tanner's curse echoed across the pit, making the ratings go pale white and bringing a booming laugh from the army control pit.

"Oh, shut *up*, Nero!" Tanner growled in response, staring at the displays again.

There had to be a way.

▶▶▶

The form-fitted seats kept him from bouncing around as Stephanos pushed the limits of his fighter's capabilities, even with the CM cutting into his personal inertia. He snapped his plane around, not changing his velocity as he first penetrated the enemy line and yanked his finger down on the forward auto-canon.

The gimbal mounted eighty millimeters locked onto the first target he haloed, its roar lost in the vacuum of space, but not on Steph himself. The vibrations shaking the hefty fighter wrapped around him as it sent out a burst.

Forty rounds found the enemy fighter, the explosive ordinance they had loaded in preparation for just this mission ripping it to shreds and sending shrapnel flying along its previous course.

Steph twisted the throttle hard, slamming it forward at the same time, and his plane spun on its axis as its twin reactors opened up fully and his minimized. Personal inertia slammed him back in the seat. The fighter darted off in another direction, in seeming defiance of all the laws of physics.

Around him, the old dance had begun again, the dying over a completely unimportant section of space, merely a repeat of an age-old ritual of which Comdr. Stephen "Stephanos" Michaels was intimately familiar.

The Archangels were acquitting themselves well, as he knew they would, but there was already one emergency beacon blaring on the search and rescue frequency, so they'd taken their hits.

His mind wandered briefly, wondering how the new kid was doing, but he didn't have time to focus on her, so he brought himself back to the moment.

"Angel Two, this is Lead…Make your run. I'll cover," he ordered.

"You got it, boss."

Stephanos tapped his controls, coming up behind Angel Two and prepared to jump back into the fight.

Same old dance, he thought wryly. *Only a different partner.*

▶▶▶

"Ranging bursts," Weston ordered. "Paint them if you can, Mr. Waters."

"Aye, Captain," Waters responded.

The firing of the ranging lasers was silent and did nothing to provide the crew with the same level of comfort or satisfaction that the hum of the main array did. There was something to be said, psychologically, for the noise of a real weapon.

After the bursts were fired, Weston had nothing to do but wait for the return, something that would take just under one minute now.

The waiting is going to drive me out of my mind, Weston thought, watching the numbers fall. His mind reeled under the pressure, something he'd never felt before. In the Archangels, there had been waiting, but it had always been waiting for the order to fly. Not this...this unending battle.

That's what it was. Once battle was joined on Earth, it generally ended in minutes. The winners won and the losers died—or some of the winners won, at least. The distances involved here were just dragging it on and on into a never-ending war.

Weston rubbed his eyes and glanced at the clock—over six hours since the first shots had been fired, more than eight since they had left orbit of the planet. He was getting tired; he could feel it. The ebb and flow of the fight wasn't conducive to maintaining a healthy alert.

"Return fire!" Waters snapped.

Weston bolted straight up in his seat, spotting the sweep of the energy signature coming from the starboard. "Turn us to port and fire all keel thrusters!"

"Aye, Captain!" Daniels snapped.

The *Odyssey* twisted away from the sweeping beam, catching only a glancing shot along the rear habitat before Daniels had the big ship climbing over the beam.

"Damage to the rear habitat!" Lamont snapped. "Teams en route. We're venting air, Captain."

"Lock out the sections," Weston ordered. "We can't afford to lose too much atmosphere."

"Aye, aye, Captain." Lamont checked some of the readings. "Sections are now closed off."

"That was just a glancing blow, Captain," Waters said. "We've got a reading on the laser..."

"Adjust our plates to compensate," Weston said. "Which ship fired that?"

"The angle indicates Bandit One, Captain."

"Very well. Maintain general settings on our port side and adjust all armor to starboard, to the new settings."

"Aye, Captain," Waters said. He hesitated before speaking again. "The general deflection settings just aren't going to do the job."

"I think, Mr. Waters, that you may rest assured that you have just made an understatement of epic proportions," Weston said. "Have we managed to paint either of them yet?"

"Uh…no, sir. Sorry, sir."

"Keep trying."

"Aye, Captain."

▶▶▶

"Move it, you monkeys!" Chief Corrin growled as she and her team roughly shouldered their way through a group evacuating their section before the doors slammed down. "Get your butts to your secondary stations and out of our way!"

The crewmen and women scattered and started moving out as Corrin and her team set up by the bulkhead that led to the damaged section.

"We've got a vacuum on the other side," one of the team reported.

"All right, check your seals. Lock this section off. We're going in," Corrin ordered. "Have an E-med team standing by."

"You got it, Chief."

They sealed the room, each person checking their own suit seal and then the seal of the man or woman next to them.

"We're good to go, Chief."

"Clear the room," Corrin ordered, features setting under her helmet.

▶▶▶

"Damage-control teams are on-site, Captain," Lamont said quietly. "We'll be getting reports back shortly."

"Very well."

"And Engineering reports that we have full power coming off the tokamak."

"Excellent. Mr. Waters, narrow-focus ping. Give me a real-time targeting solution."

"Aye, aye, Captain," Waters replied.

The surge went out, a single, low ping of sound announcing the signal across the bridge and the display in front of them. All snapped into sudden clarity as the enemy positions and formations were readily available to them.

"Main laser array, adjust for best general absorption against enemy materials," Weston ordered.

"Aye, Captain," Waters replied, calling up all the previous examples of enemy armor and ordering the computer to average them out and devise a new beam frequency. In a matter of seconds, it was ready and he nodded. "Coded, Captain."

"Give me a sweeping beam, right across their fighter escort," Weston ordered.

"Aye, aye, Captain."

▶▶▶

The tachyon traps sent a signal through the bridge of the *Cerekus*, bringing Tianne's attention back to the present.

"What was that?"

"The *Odyssey* just registered a light-tachyon pulse, and we received a return off the Drasin, Captain. Probably a sensor system."

Tianne nodded, glancing at the time to arrival.

Six rotations.

She wondered if they'd be able to hold out until she got there. Normally, she'd doubt it; however, this ship was obviously more than it appeared. Perhaps they would survive.

Perhaps.

"Send the details to Admiral Tanner," she ordered. He may find it interesting."

"Yes, Captain."

▶▶▶

The low hum of the main laser firing had died out seconds earlier, and now the waiting had started again. Though the time was now dropping, the wait was no less tense. The fact that it was becoming shorter by the second only meant that the battles were taking up a higher percentage of their time.

"Contact," Waters whispered, drawing Weston's eyes back to the screen.

For a moment, nothing, then a few of the fighters went up like matches in the darkness, flaring brightly under the sweeping gaze of the eye of the *Odyssey*'s main laser. Then a few more went up, and soon an entire formation was blazing ahead of the oncoming vessels.

"That's it, Captain," Waters said.

"Very nice shooting, Ensign."

Weston glanced at the board, the distance was down to under twenty-five light-seconds now. "Change evasive action, Mr. Daniels. Move to Pattern Troy."

"Aye, Captain. Initiating Pattern Troy," Daniels replied, initiating the command set.

The *Odyssey* shifted and groaned as they changed course on thrusters, keeping themselves, hopefully, one step ahead of the enemy attacks.

CHAPTER 37

▶ CHIEF CORRIN LED her crew through into the damaged sector. The decompression had left the section in massive disarray, items as large as chairs and desks scattered around the room.

"Jason, you better see if we've got any survivors," she ordered. "Brian, you and your team follow me. We're going to check that breach."

The two men nodded and split off as Corrin kept walking.

The breach was three rooms over, but either the energy from the laser or the explosive decompression had apparently blown out the automatics on the heavy doors. Corrin cursed as she looked over the place.

"What in the fuck were those doors open for, anyway?" she said, kicking a chair out of the way. "We're on a goddamned battle stations alert. That's a mandatory lockdown!"

"Yes, Chief," Brian Kreuse agreed from behind her. "Someone must have overridden them."

Corrin cursed again, shoving through a door that had half swung closed. Inside the next room, she spotted the deep gash the enemy laser had cut in the *Odyssey* and the moving starscape beyond it.

"Careful now," she said, walking closer to the gash in the floor. "Don't want the spin to toss us right out the hole."

"No, ma'am."

There was a desk jammed in the breach, one of the big aluminum jobs that the scientists liked to use, twisted into a useless hunk of metal that was most certainly going to be in their way.

"Ah shit," Corrin muttered. "You'd better get that cut away, Brian. I'll secure the rest of the compartment."

"You got it, Chief." He waved behind him. "Bring up the laser cutters!"

"Hey," Corrin said. "What's this section for, anyway?"

"Don't know, Chief. This is the eggheads' country." Brian glanced back, pulling a computer from his pocket. "Let's see... Deck Eight, Habitat B...Looks like the linguistics lab, Chief."

"Check with the computer. See if anyone was in here," Chief Corrin ordered, glaring at a section of the bulkhead that had been decorated with scribbled writings.

Scientists, she muttered. *If I ever caught one of my boys writing on the fucking walls...*

▶▶▶

"Fifteen light-seconds, Captain."

"Thank you, Mr. Waters," Weston replied, cocking his head toward the helm. "Daniels, prepare for hard maneuvering and call up Attack Pattern Nimitz."

"Nimitz, aye, sir," Daniels responded.

"Do we have paint on either of the bandits, Mr. Waters?"

"Yes, sir. Laser return off of the port-side bandit is confirmed."

"Very good. Have our laser frequencies adjusted to match."

"Aye, aye, Captain."

Weston watched the preparations, noting with some degree of pleasure that the crew wasn't fumbling over any of them or making any of the fatigue-induced errors that he had been worried about.

This was the end of a marathon battle, and while they were no longer fresh, it was obvious that the people he had been assigned were up to the challenges.

Now they had just one more challenge to surmount—or rather, just two more.

"Laser-control report adjustments prepared, Captain."

"Mr. Daniels...Engage Nimitz Maneuvering."

"Aye, sir. Engaging."

"Mr. Waters. Fire at will."

▶▶▶

Adm. Rael Tanner watched the board, his eyes watering as he practically refused to blink. The battle being carried out in clean, sterile, three-dimensional graphics in front of him was as riveting as it was utterly pointless.

He had to get word to the *Odyssey* to tell them just to run. They didn't have to do this, to die fighting for a world not their own. Not now, when the *Cerekus* was here and ready to defend her people.

"Milla!" he snapped, turning abrubtly.

"Admiral." She stiffened, her armored form whining as it responded to her body's demand.

"Contact the Major Brinks you mentioned. I wish to speak with him."

"Yes, sir. One moment."

▶▶▶

"Major Brinks?" The hesitant voice came softly through the tac-net, catching Brinks's attention as the whine-crack of his rifle died down.

He'd just sniped a stray drone that had evaded the main cleanup teams and didn't see any more, so he relaxed a bit and swung his weapon up onto his shoulder. "Yes, Miss Chans? What is it?"

"The admiral wishes to speak with you," she told him.

Brinks wondered briefly why the word *admiral* translated properly, but Milla's rank, or whatever it was, didn't seem to. He shrugged it off a second later as none of his concern for the moment. "Very well."

An instant later, an image of a very grim man appeared on his HUD, a man who looked like he was fraying on the ragged edge. *Man needs some bunk time in the worst way.*

"Admiral," he said. "Major Wilhelm Brinks, at your service."

"As you have been," the admiral replied with a weary smile. "However, just now I wish to be at the service of your Captain Weston."

"Is there something wrong with the *Odyssey?*" Brinks asked, with a frown.

"Your ship is currently in combat with two Drasin warships and is sustaining damage. I'm afraid that I can't say how badly she has been hurt. However, what disturbs me is that it is no longer needed."

"Pardon me?" Brinks blinked. If there were two ships, at least, still out there, he didn't see how it wasn't needed. One ship had landed enough drones that they'd been hard-pressed to cull them back. If two more dropped ground forces, it would be all over, except for the dying.

"Our own warship, the *Cerekus*, is approaching the battle. If the *Odyssey* would drop back, she could handle the enemy," the admiral replied. "Or, at least, they could engage together. However, the *Odyssey* does not see her."

"Can you generate tachyon particles?"

The admiral blinked, frowning, and Brinks knew that the translator had muffed it. He tried again. "Can you broadcast faster-than-light particles?"

The admiral's face cleared up and he nodded. "Yes. However, so can the Drasin. And if your captain thinks that they have reinforcements…"

"He might do something desperate," Brinks's lips twisted. "All right, I think I can help you out there."

"That would be most acceptable," the admiral said.

▶▶▶

"Archangel Eight, bank hard to port, on my signal."

The acknowledgment came through a moment later as the Drasin twisted in between them, looking for the sweet spot.

"Now!"

Angel Eight spun on its axis like a top, its twin reactors flaring as the plane suddenly shot away in apparent violation of Newton's Laws, and Samuels tightened her finger on the trigger.

"Archangel Thirteen, Fox Three."

The Havoc dropped from its internal pylon, hesitating that brief instant while it massed a full normal amount, then flickered away in an unreal sort of pseudo-motion. It crossed the gap between human and alien and, in a flash, slammed into its target.

The first thing destroyed was the CM generator, and then the fully massed weapon bored right though the enemy fighter at 0.6c, turning it into an expanding fireball.

"Nice shooting, Cardsharp," Archangel Eight called. "Thanks."

"No problem, Paladin," Samuels said. "But you owe me another hand."

Paladin chuckled as they brought their fighters back together while looking around the mess of the battleground around them.

"Looks like we're doing cleanup," Paladin said, tallying up the wrecks around them.

"Yeah," Samuels replied, glancing over her shoulder. "But the *Odyssey* seems to have stepped in it."

The two fighter pilots checked their HUDs and noted that the *Odyssey* and the alien cruisers seemed to be getting more than a little too close for comfort.

"Archangels," Stephanos broke in to the chatter, "form up on me. We're going to give the *Odyssey* a little support."

▶▶▶

"Kick it loose!" Kreuse ordered, slamming his foot down on the smoldering desk still jammed in the breach.

The other men found themselves a handgrip and followed suit, finally kicking the mass out of the breach and into the void beyond. For a moment, they all watched as it floated out, away from them. Then the *Odyssey* shifted its course and the desk vanished from sight.

"All right, let's spec this out," Brian growled. "And for God's sake, people, check your lines!"

The team did just that before anything else, making sure that all the safety lines were in place, and they began the delicate and dangerous work of crawling out through the thick mesh of armor and insulating materials that made up the outer hull of the NACS *Odyssey.*

"How bad is it, Brian?" Chief Corrin called from where she was checking the rest of the lab.

"Nasty rupture here," came the answer. "The laser strike was pretty small. Most of this was caused by explosive decompression."

"Great," Corrin muttered.

"The laser must have weakened the structure," Brian Kreuse said. "This isn't supposed to happen in real life. Looks like some goddamned movie set."

"Just fix it, Kreuse."

"I'm on it, Chief."

Corrin let the man get to his work as she came to a sealed door. The electronics on it were busted all to hell, and it didn't register whether there was atmosphere or not on the other side.

"Great," she muttered, pulling a wrench from her belt.

"What's that, Chief?"

"Nothing," she said, then laid her helmet against the door in question and rapped hard with the wrench three times.

Bang, bang, bang.

Then she waited and repeated the action.

Bang, bang, bang.

Each hit vibrated through her helmet contact, rattling her teeth. Corrin grimaced while turning down the pickups as she waited.

Rap, rap, rap.

Three soft hits came in response.

"I've got a live one in here!" she yelled out. "Get me a portable lock and some evac suits!"

▶▶▶

"Pardon me, Admiral," Captain Tianne said, her eyes wide, "but did I hear you correctly? You wish me to what?"

"Send a message to the *Odyssey*," Admiral Tanner replied. "We have a code you can use that they should be able to decipher."

Tianne waved her hand. "Again. Pardon me, Admiral, but that is a lunatic idea."

"Excuse me?" Tanner glared at her.

"The Drasin have not yet detected us. To follow this…idea of yours would be reckless to the point of criminal behavior."

"Captain Tianne, there are only two Drasin remaining. If you are able to recall the *Odyssey* from a potentially suicidal confrontation, your two vessels would be able to deal with them, together. Should the *Odyssey* lose its current battle, you will be forced to deal with the two Drasin, alone. Are you that confident?" Tanner asked.

"Yes," Tianne said. "The *Cerekus* is unprecedented…"

"Not quite, if you'll recall. Its designs did come from the Central Computer, and Central isn't known for designing warships in its spare time."

"Be that as it may," Tianne said, "the *Cerekus* is more than able to deal with two Drasin warships."

"Good. Then you have no reason not to warn the *Odyssey* of your arrival," Tanner told her. "After all, if the *Cerekus* is as able as you say, what difference will warning make?"

Tianne glared at the screen, her mouth opening for another objection.

"This is an order, Captain," Tanner cut her off. "I want that ship intact."

There was, of course, only one answer to that.

"Yes, Admiral. I will transmit the code," she said, each word grating on her as it passed her teeth.

▶▶▶

"Thermal bloom, Captain!" Waters announced as a section of the threat board was briefly whited-out by an overload in the infrared spectrum.

"Analyze," Weston replied in clipped tones.

"Working on it…"

A moment later, the image stabilized and Waters visibly flinched.

"Sorry, sir. We got a hit, but it wasn't enough. She's still coming."

"Very well. Secure from Nimitz."

"Aye, aye, Captain," Daniels responded, adjusting his program. "New pattern?"

"Evasive. Fractal generation."

"Aye, aye, sir."

Weston called up more information on his personal board, eyeing the distance grimly.

Fifteen light-seconds and still closing.

"Mr. Wat—"

"Captain! Tachyon surge!"

"Pin it down!" Weston ordered. "Where did it come from?"

"Oh…directly astern, sir!" Lamont was the first to reply, paling. "It's coming from—"

"Tachyon surge!" Waters announced again. "We've been pinged again, Captain."

"What the..." Weston stiffened, half twisting in his seat. "That does not make any—"

"Again!"

"What the hell is going on?" Weston thundered, his fist striking the edge of his seat.

▶▶▶

"Tachyon surge!"

"I can see that, Lieutenant," Roberts said, eyeing the screen with morbid curiosity.

"Commander, we're getting pinged all over the place."

"Same source?"

"Aye, sir."

"Huh," Roberts said, not quite believing what he was seeing.

"Sir?"

"Nothing, Lieutenant." Roberts keyed an open channel.

▶▶▶

Weston shifted when the communications network pinged for his attention. He glared at it momentarily, contemplating simply cutting it off. However, Palin aside, those who had access to it were *supposed* to have access to it.

He sighed, slapping the channel open. "Weston here," he growled as the return chirp was heard.

"Captain," Commander Roberts's voice came over the line.

"Commander, I'm a little busy here."

"I can see that. It's concerning the new target, Captain."

"The one with enough power to generate tachyon pings like we turn on cabin lights?" Weston asked.

"That would be the one, Captain. The pings are organized into a code, Captain."

"Like Morse?" Weston glanced back at the signals, his frown slipping.

"More simple…and at the same time, complicated, Captain," Roberts replied. "It's Ranger 'Chirp' Code, Captain. I'm guessing it's from Major Brinks."

"What's it mean, Commander?"

"Rangers lead the way, Captain," Roberts replied, with a hint of humor in his voice. "That usually means that the cavalry is coming over the hill."

Weston looked at the plot, now showing one big honking blimp coming right up their stern. "Are you certain, Commander?"

"I don't joke about the rangers."

"Very well," Weston said. "Thank you for the information. Weston out."

Weston stared at the plot again and mechanically turned toward Daniels. "Helm…Roll ship. Take us toward that bogey, all flank."

"Aye, aye, Captain," Daniels replied. "Preparing to roll."

Weston keyed open the ship-wide. "All hands. This is the captain. Prepare for full military acceleration. I say again, prepare for full military acceleration."

Then he keyed the channel closed and leaned back, letting out a breath. "Rangers lead the way, indeed."

▶ ▶ ▶

"Goddammit, you pukes! Pull!" Kreuse yelled at the top of his lungs, grunting as he grabbed a man's arm and hauled him back inside. "Get those men back in here before we start to—"

The *Odyssey* groaned under their feet, pitching hard as its thrusters tipped it up and over. Kreuse grabbed for the wall, catching himself, and just hung on as the ship swung over.

"That's just the tip!" Corrin yelled, sailing across in a practiced leap that nearly slammed her into the far wall as the ship spun crazily around her. She caught herself, snagging a desk that was bolted down, and joined two others that were hauling in a welder.

"Heave!" she yelled, and the three of them pulled hard, yanking the man back in against the spin-induced gravity.

They had two more men out there, she knew, and the rumble in the decks told Corrin that they weren't going to make it.

Aw shit, she groaned to herself, reaching for another security line.

▶▶▶

"We have men still doing EVA, Captain," Lamont said.

"What?" the Captain said. "Hold acceleration!"

Daniels paused, his hand just millimeters from executing the order. "Holding, Captain."

"Get those people inside, Ensign," Weston ordered.

"Already being done, Captain," Lamont said.

▶▶▶

"Corrin to the bridge," she croaked out, lying back against the floor with one of the men beside her.

Across the gash, she could see Kreuse with the other.

"We're secured for acceleration."

▶▶▶

"All clear, Captain," Lamont said, sounding a little shaky.

"Thank you, Ensign," Weston said, taking a breath. "Mr. Daniels...All ahead flank."

"Aye, aye, Captain. All ahead flank."

The rumble in the decks grew, and the deck pitched slightly, despite the full application of the CM generators. The big ship began to accelerate through space again.

Weston eyed the numbers for a moment, then opened another channel.

"Archangels, we are moving to rendezvous with another contact. Do not engage the enemy, break from your current vectors, and form up on the *Odyssey*."

Only then did he turn back to the board and look at the contact clock.

Twelve light-seconds and still closing, although the closure rate was dropping off slightly.

Weston didn't have to do the math in his head to know that it wasn't going to turn out in his favor this time.

"Maybe I should have stood and fought," he thought, an ironic song suddenly filtering in through his head.

"And the race is on and here comes..."

▶▶▶

"The *Odyssey* has altered her course, Captain."

"Thank you, Ithan. What is their arrival time?" Tianne asked.

"Four rotations."

"And the Drasin intercept?"

"Two rotations."

Tianne scowled, shaking her head. "I suppose that we may as well become somewhat...proactive in this situation, before Admiral Tanner comes up with another brilliant plan."

The men and women around her shifted nervously, but there was no reply.

"Calculate a targeting path for our lasers."

"Yes, Captain."

Tianne watched the plot, eyeing the shrinking line between the two ships. "And do give the *Odyssey* some space to breathe. It would be ludicrous to do all this and then kill them ourselves."

"Yes, Captain."

▶ ▶ ▶

"The *Odyssey* has completed its maneuver and is accelerating away from the Drasin and toward the *Cerekus*, Admiral."

"Thank you, Ithan," Admiral Tanner replied, watching the board. "Has Captain Tianne made her combat plans?"

"She has begun calculating for weapons fire."

"Let us hope that this new class is everything Central claims," Tanner said, pacing the room before he caught himself and forced his body down into a chair.

"Yes, Admiral."

▶ ▶ ▶

"Calculations are in, Captain. We are prepared to fire."

Tianne smiled thinly. "Excellent. Engage the Drasin ships."

"Engaging."

A whining roar vibrated through the deck of the *Cerekus* as power was routed directly to the lasers and the powerful weapons unleashed themselves across the vastness of space.

▶▶▶

"Message from the Archangel Lead, Captain," Lamont said. "Commander Michaels is asking if you want them to come back in."

"Negative." Weston shook his head. "Tell them to keep clear. Something tells me that this isn't going to be—"

"Thermal bloom!"

Weston stiffened. "Where?"

"The new ship, Capt—Holy Mother of GOD!" Waters let out a curse, his eyes bugging out as every warning buzzer on the bridge seemed to go off.

"What the hell was that?"

"Laser fire! Five...ten...no, fifteen beams!" Waters swore. "They bracketed us, sir!"

"Relax, Ensign," Weston advised him. "If they were meant for us, we'd have felt them by now."

"No, sir. We wouldn't," Waters corrected him in a shocked voice. "We're reading intense corona flares—ten times the Drasin weapons levels."

"What?" Weston blurted. "That's insane!"

"Sir...I think we'd better secure for a radiation alert," Waters advised. "These guys are tossing around some serious power."

Waters nodded. "Susan...Issue the alert."

"Aye, Captain." Susan Lamont turned back to her board. "Warning, warning, the *Odyssey* is now under radiation-exposure protocols. I say again, the *Odyssey* is now under radiation-exposure protocols."

▶▶▶

"...say again, the *Odyssey* is now under radiation protocols."

"Ah fuckin' hell!" Kreuse cursed, looking up at the ceiling, though the voice had come through his suit headset. "Now what?"

"Doesn't matter!" Corrin ordered. "Forget trying to repair that breach. We've got to throw a few sheets over it and get the hell out of here!"

"You heard the chief!" Kreuse spun around. "Get those rolls in here!"

While the men were hauling in the huge rolls of carbon-fiber composite they had been intending to use as a base for the repairs, Corrin turned on the crew working on the sealed closet. "And get those people out of there!"

▶▶▶

"Thermal bloom!" Waters announced again. "They've got a direct hit on the port-side warship."

"Analyze," Weston ordered in clipped terms.

"The return signal scrambled the hell out of our sensors, Captain. I'm going to have to reboot the software. Secondary sensors turning into position," Waters replied, working hard.

On the screen, the visible image of the Drasin warship was still there and intact. Though, at the moment, it was glowing practically white-hot from the energy it had absorbed, and for some odd reason, Weston had the impression that it was pissed off.

"Return fire!" Waters called out a second later. "Drasin are firing back."

"Captain…" Daniels spoke up softly. "Course?"

Weston ignored the helmsman for a moment, staring at his boards. The ship coming toward them was now within two light-minutes, and it was finally starting to register on their sensors, despite the solar interference. Which actually bothered Weston, considering that a ship the *Odyssey*'s size would probably be hidden from visual sensors at up to twenty light-seconds.

"Captain?"

How big is that thing? he wondered briefly and shook his head. "Hold course, Helm. Right now they're aiming around us. I don't think I want to bumble into one of their beams by accident."

"Aye, aye, Captain."

▶▶▶

"They are tough, aren't they?" Tianne mused as she watched the Drasin vessel continue to close despite the immense amount of energy they had pelted it with.

"Pardon me, Captain?"

"Nothing, Ithan," she said mildly. "How many beams struck?"

"Two, Captain. We're adjusting the others now."

"Good. Fire again when—"

The *Cerekus* reeled under their feet, sending one young woman into her console and another colliding with the wall.

"Report!"

"Incoming laser attacks. There are more of—"

Then another three beams stabbed into the energy shields of the big ship, overloading power relays all over the ship and blowing out half their defense grid.

"Return fire!" Tianne ordered.

"Yes, Captain! Returning fire!"

▶▶▶

"Thermal bloom!" Waters announced again. "They took a strike, Captain."

"How bad?"

"Just guessing, but from the intensity of the bloom, it looks like they reflected most of the energy away," the young man said. "Too much energy reflected to be a deep strike."

"That's something anyw—"

"They're firing back!"

Weston flinched as the radiation and weapons warnings went off again, throwing the bridge into chaos.

"Why do I feel like I'm caught between two giants fighting with clubs made of oak trees?" Weston growled, shaking his head in annoyance.

"Umm...sir?"

"Nothing, Lieutenant. Hold us steady."

"Aye, sir."

▶▶▶

Lasers crisscrossed the emptiness of space, passing one another through the vacuum, not caring for what the other was doing.

On one side of the raging battle, a trio of beams found their target, unleashing their energy against the hull of an alien vessel. The armor flashed incandescent as it struggled to reflect back the power as best it could. Its best, in fact, was quite good, but there was so very much power to be dealt with, so the heat and radiation inevitably began to pour into the interior of the ship as well.

The Drasin faltered in its flight path, its engines failing for a moment as parts of its hull began to melt.

On the other side of the line, another two beams intersected the *Cerekus*, stabbing through its shields this time and cutting through the armor of the big ship like a pick through soft dirt.

▶▶▶

"We're venting atmosphere, Captain!"

"Seal those decks," Tianne replied. "And continue firing!"

"Aye, Captain."

Unlike the previous encounters with the Drasin, Tianne knew that her ship was something that its predecessors had not been. It was a ship built for war rather than a converted freighter. It had armor to withstand lasers and was built so that the ship could be compartmentalized in the case of massive damage.

The *Cerekus* could absorb far more damage than could the *Carlache*, the previous fleet's flagship vessel.

▶▶▶

"Sweet Jesus," Waters whispered in awe. "She's bleeding air, Captain."

"Bad?"

"Bad," Waters nodded. "But she's still firing."

"Status on the alien warships?"

"One of them is going down, sir. The other seems to be moving to evasive action."

"What's the status of our weapons?"

"Laser array is fully charged. We have a twenty percent load of HVMs, and three tubes are now charged, Captain," Waters replied instantly. "Our PD weapons are, of course, fully charged and ready."

"Thank you, Mr. Waters," Weston said.

Their own laser array, while obviously more versatile than that of either their enemies or their possible allies, was woefully underpowered compared to either. This, along with other concerns, such as their targeting systems, meant that the laser was only useful for relatively close engagement ranges.

The alien warships were already at the limit of that range, and by going to evasive maneuvers, the healthy warship had effectively taken the laser out of consideration.

The HVMs were out for similar reasons as well, because the recorded data from previous attacks made it clear that a 20 percent load wasn't going to cut it.

Similarly, three pulse torpedoes weren't likely to take out one of those things, unless they got lucky.

Weston flinched as the radiation warning alarms all went off again, and slammed his fist down on the armrest.

"Time to get lucky!"

"Captain?"

"Helm, roll the ship. Bring our weapons back to bear on the maneuvering warship," he ordered. "Mr. Waters…Give me a firing solution on that son of a bitch."

"Aye, aye, Captain."

▶▶▶

"Holy Mary, Mother of God," Stephenanos whispered as he watched the battle through the enhanced HUD of the Archangels.

The computer was taking data from all across the network, including the *Odyssey* itself, drawing in the paths of the invisible beams based off their corona leakage, and what it was drawing was a lethal fence trapping the *Odyssey* between a battle of two giants.

"Can you see that shit?" Paladin asked in awe. "They're tossing around more power than a city could use in a year!"

"A lot more," another pilot put in. "Each beam is off the scale…I'm trying to recalibrate, but I'm betting that we're way over the tera-watt range here."

"Jesus," Racer muttered. "Anyone else starting to feel like we're playing out of our league?"

"I might," Stephanos said dryly. "If we hadn't been kicking ass and taking names ever since this shit started."

"You have a point," Racer conceded. "But just think of what happens if these bozos get their shit together."

"I'd rather not," Cardsharp Samuels muttered, her voice low as her HUD lit up with another computer-generated rendering of the crisscross beams.

"Lord! The *Odyssey*!"

The pilots of the Archangels, trapped on the outside of a battle, far beyond their tools and weapons, watched as the *Odyssey* tipped its nose up once more, swinging back around to bring her formidable forward weapons back into play.

"Godspeed, Weston," Stephanos whispered. "Godspeed, Raziel."

"Amen," the rest of the team replied, recognizing the call sign of their old flight leader. "And pity the poor bastards on the receiving end."

Raziel. Secret of God.

Well, it had worked out that way once, Stephanos thought, with a grim smile. *Maybe He'll be smiling on them this time, too.*

If you believed in that sort of thing.

▶▶▶

"Captain! The ship…The *Odyssey* is altering her stance."

"Is she changing course?" Tianne asked, turning her attention to the ship's section of the threat board.

"Not yet, Captain."

"Then ignore her, I don't have time to worry about what some pet of Tanner's is up to. Continue firing."

"Aye, Captain."

Tianne eyed the screen, watching as the alien warship completed its maneuver and began charging its weapons. The power curve for the ship was still distressingly low, and she couldn't quite imagine how anyone had managed to build effective weapons with so little power.

For the moment, however, it wasn't her concern.

Ahead of her still lay two Drasin warships, though one was badly damaged now, and her own *Cerekus* was still on the hunt.

▶▶▶

"Fire sequence loaded!" Waters said, looking up at the main screen.

"Bow armaments coming around," Daniels added. "We will be in firing position on the target in thirty seconds. Firing braking thrusters now."

Weston looked back to the plot, eyeing the approach of what he knew had to be the colonies' ship. The massive vessel just kept getting bigger as it closed, but it was still almost a light-minute behind them despite their relative closing velocities.

Given their current vectors, however, the computer had their rendezvous listed as forty-three seconds. At that point, the *Odyssey* would be officially out of this fight for quite some time, unless Weston ordered her main reactors to power.

"We are locked on, Captain."

Time to decide that later.

"Initiate firing sequence," he ordered, eyeing the board.

▶ ▶ ▶

"The *Odyssey* is firing again."

Rael Tanner looked back to the plot. His own space in the pit was the only part of the command that had more than minimal elbow room, as people had suddenly found reason to gather here and watch the drama unfold above them.

The first energy spike from the *Odyssey* was identified as her main laser array, a pitiful trickle of power, according to the computer, but as they'd seen earlier, a respectable force, just the same.

The computer couldn't track the beam, not the way it did those from the Drasin or the *Cerekus*. The leaked energy from the underpowered beam was well below the system's sensor ability. However, it was able to detect minute fluctuations when the beam crossed paths with stray matter.

Space was, after all, not nearly so empty, as most believed. There was always something out there, somewhere.

The following pulses were more potent, their energy scales quite respectable, even by the colonies' standards; however, only three of the blazing-white charges were thrown into space this time, unlike the normal salvoes of six or more they had registered.

The computer also noted that they were fired sequentially this time, and the lasers were aimed at the single healthy Drasin ship.

The final pulses of energy registered between the other two and were also an underpowered salvo, leaving Tanner to wonder just how badly the *Odyssey* was hurt.

▶▶▶

"All weapons away."

"Good," Weston nodded, eyeing the plot. "That's it, we're spent. No sense getting wasted in the cross fire while we're holding an empty gun. Flip the ship, Daniels."

"Aye, aye, Captain."

Without waiting for the results of their attack, the NACS *Odyssey* fired its thrusters once more, flipping its nose up and over in a graceful maneuver, taking it around to, once more, point in the opposite direction. Then its main reactors fired again, and the ship began to accelerate down the gravity well of the red giant star.

Behind them, their parting shots continued on, unperturbed by the ship's change of course.

"Launch SAR shuttles," Weston ordered. "I see we have three beacons from downed Archangels. I want them back."

"Aye, Captain."

▶▶▶

"All right, we're going to rejoin the *Odyssey*," Stephanos said as they watched the ship roll back. "Loop out and around that big mother, though. I don't feel like getting bug-zapped today."

A few chuckles, mostly very weary ones, were heard, but the flight got back underway again as the fighters responded to their pilots' desire to get back home.

Jennifer Samuels, Cardsharp, flexed her shoulder muscles gingerly, afraid in spite of herself that she might somehow twitch the sensor needles imbedded in her neck. Her shoulders felt so tightly corded that they were made of stone, and her neck was on fire from the tension, so all she could think of was heat—as much of it as she could get, in whatever way it was available.

A shower would do, she decided, but a soak was what the doctor was demanding.

Unfortunately, the *Odyssey* being what it was, she didn't think that a soak was going to happen.

A shower, then, a badly needed one.

God help those aliens if they started anything before she got her shower.

▶▶▶

The laser was a clean miss, Tianne noted as the results of the *Odyssey*'s final shot registered on her sensors. Unsurprising, of course, firing with only one beam at distances greater than a few light-seconds.

The follow-up strike from those energy bursts, however, didn't. At first, they seemed off course, but at the last moment, they spiraled across her sensors and slammed into the Drasin hard and fast, ripping its hull apart.

She had to admit, it was to good effect.

The salvo of projectiles was somewhat less effective, but some of them struck as well, and by the time they had thinned out, the second Drasin was limping away.

"Continue firing on our primary target," she ordered, eyeing the state of affairs and noting with some chagrin that her constant barrage of laser energy was taking almost twice as long to inflict equitable damage as to the first ship.

It was dying, that was certain, but it was taking its time doing so, and now it was grating on her sensibilities.

"Adjust all lasers to target the same point," she ordered, noting that the Drasin wasn't maneuvering anymore, so a firing pattern would merely be wasteful. "And prepare a pursuit course for the escaping ship."

"Yes, Captain."

The *Odyssey* slid past them, launching small ships from its bays as it did. Its armor was scored in a dozen places that she could see on screen, and one of the big rotating drums along its side purchase had a visible gash in it.

So they aren't invulnerable, she thought, eyeing the readings on the strange ship with a skeptical eye. There was something truly off about the power readings, but she couldn't figure out what it was. It was just…off.

She let the ship pass without comment and watched as two small craft paced alongside the *Cerekus,* following her back along their mother ship's previous course.

What are they? Tianne thought, then cut off as one peeled away toward a beaming beacon. *Ah…rescue craft.*

Tianne nodded and then put them out of her mind.

She had work to do.

▶▶▶

"Prepare a course to planetary intercept," Weston ordered tiredly, the last hurrah dying down on the bridge as the sensors recorded their hits.

"Aye, Captain," Daniels replied.

"Waters, keep an eye on those two ships. Let me know if their status changes," he said, looking over at Lamont. "Susan...How bad?"

"We vented about fifteen percent of our O-two when the habitat was blown," she replied. "We're okay on stores, but if the planet can spare us some, it would be helpful."

Weston nodded. "I don't think that they'll mind."

"No, sir." A slight smile played on her lips. "I don't suppose they will."

"What else?"

"The language lab was badly damaged..."

"Language?" Weston's voice sharpened. "Any casualties?"

"Dr. Palin and his assistant were sent to the medical bays with carbon dioxide poisoning, but they're going to be okay. We're doing a headcount to see if anyone else was there," Lamont told him.

Weston slumped back. "Very well. Tell the chief...Just tell her good job."

"Aye, aye, Captain."

"Course prepared, Captain," Daniels spoke up softly.

"Engage it, then," Weston ordered. "We have some people to pick up, some others to talk to, and some to mourn."

"Aye, aye, Captain."

▼

CHAPTER 38

▲

▶ HIS BOOTS CLICKED against the metal floor of the *Odyssey*'s hallways. Behind him, the chorus of similar footfalls announced their passage to anyone within hearing. Crew members melted aside, giving the worn-looking group free passage through the halls. There was a certain level of awe in the air, the way Stephanos knew that there always was after a battle.

He wasn't certain that he and his deserved it, but they had it, just the same. The *Odyssey* itself had probably taken more total damage than the Archangels and had certainly inflicted far more than the small flight had been able to, but there was always that wall between them and the crew of any ship they served upon.

"Lieutenant Commander."

Stephanos paused, noting that one figure had not melted away to the sidelines. A tired smile crossed his face. "Captain."

"Good to have you back aboard, Steph," Weston told his younger friend. "You did good out there. You all did."

Behind him, Steph heard the Angels muttering their thanks, but their hearts weren't in it. Apparently, the captain heard the same thing.

538 • EVAN CURRIE

"You all go get some rest," Weston said. "I need to speak with your commander for a minute."

"Yes, sir," they muttered as they shuffled past.

"Hard one?" Weston asked as they followed, albeit at a slower pace.

"About the same as any other." Steph shrugged. "Felt like a rush while we were out there, but we're all coming down now."

"SAR shuttles picked up Angels Two, Three, and Five. They're okay."

"That's good news, sir," Stephanos said, relief in his voice.

"Once we're in orbit, I'm taking a shuttle down to the surface," Weston said.

"Sir?" Steph paused, frowning.

"It should be safe enough," he said. "Brinks informs me that most of the fighting is dying down and they're just mopping up now."

"I'll detail two of the Angels to escort you."

"That's not necessary."

Stephanos shook his head. "You'll take them, or you'll take the entire squad. Your choice."

Weston chuckled, shaking his head. "Sometimes I wonder who's really in charge of this heap."

"You are." Steph grinned. "And none of the rest of us want to take your place if you get your dumb ass killed, so bear with us, all right?"

Weston nodded. "All right. Two. No more."

"What about the bandits?"

"One of them is down; the other is running for the heliopause," Weston replied. "We're running a plot on it, and it might make it."

Stephanos winced. "Damn."

"Out of our hands now." Weston shrugged. "Nothing to do about it."

"All right. I'll go break the bad news to the pilots," Steph said. "Hey, Raz?"

Weston paused when he heard the more common version of his call sign. "Yeah?"

"You were right about Cardsharp."

Weston shot him a puzzled look. "Who?"

"Samuels. She got pinned with her sign during the poker game."

"You still play that, huh?" Weston asked, with a fond smile, though it was more a statement than a question.

"Of course."

"Good. And I'm glad that she worked out," Weston said. "Now, I've got some work to do…I'll see you later."

"Sir." Stephanos stiffened and saluted.

Weston returned the salute before turning and leaving.

Stephen watched him go for a moment, face blank, and then turned and followed his team into their bunk rooms.

They were spread over practically every available surface of the common room, none of them apparently in the mood for actual sleep and all of them interested in what the captain had to say. He looked them over briefly, smiling as he shook his head.

"I've got good news, and I've got bad news."

They groaned and chuckled.

"We're boned," someone said under their breath, and the chuckles increased.

"The captain wants me to tell you that you did a good job and that there's a shuttle coming home with three of our own on it, alive and kicking," Steph said. "That's the good news."

They laughed, though there was a hint of appreciation in it.

"What's the bad news?"

"His illustrious pampered backside has decided to visit the planet, in person, when we arrive in orbit," Steph said.

The pilots groaned. Then straightened up. "When do we go out?"

"We don't," Steph replied. "I'll take two volunteers for the escort run. The rest of you will get some rest."

"I'm in," Samuels said instantly, though only a few seconds ahead of the rest.

"Good. Cardsharp and Centurion. The rest of you, fall out, shower, and hit your bunks."

The pilots groaned but started to move.

"Oh, and one more thing," Steph said as they paused. He surveyed them again and smiled. "In case you hadn't figured it out, you did good out there. Now get your butts out of my sight."

▶▶▶

"Captain."

"Commander," Weston greeted his first as he stepped onto the bridge.

Roberts got up from the central chair, leaving it to Weston as the captain crossed the floor. "We'll be entering planetary orbit in three minutes."

"Excellent. Have the rest of Brinks's reports finished uploading?"

"Aye, sir," Roberts said, bringing the files up on the captain's displays. "Looks like they had some rough times down there."

Weston winced as he noted the casualty report. "I can see that."

"On the plus side, Brinks has a lot of good to say about the medical facilities made available to our people," Roberts replied. "Apparently, they've got a lot on the ball when it comes to patching people up."

"Nice to know," Weston said. "I suppose I should take Rame down with me, if he can break away from our own casualties."

Roberts shifted uncomfortably. "About this visit, sir…"

"I believe that the hostilities are dying down enough for a diplomatic visit, Commander," Weston said, his voice cool.

Roberts hesitated. "Aye, sir."

"Besides, I think I want to speak with this Admiral Tanner—interesting man."

"Yes, sir. You will be taking an escort?"

"Two Archangels."

"I meant a personal guard, Captain," Roberts said firmly. "I'll assign some men to the job."

Weston started to object, then let it go. If the commander wasn't going to give him a hard time about going down, he may as well reciprocate. "As you wish, Commander."

▶▶▶

"Dr. Rame?"

Rame looked up from checking the blood pressure and oxygen levels of a patient. "Yes, Nurse?"

"You have a message from the bridge, sir."

Rame nodded, setting down his tools, and checked the bank of near-infrared LEDs set over the patient. When he was satisfied that they were all operating at the proscribed pulse pattern, he walked over to his office.

"Rame here."

"Doctor, the captain wishes to inquire as to the status of your patients," the commander's voice came over the intercom.

"As well as they can be," Rame replied curtly. "The ones who survived are out of danger, Commander."

There was a brief pause before Roberts's voice came back. "That's good news, Doctor. The captain also wishes to know if you would be free for a visit to the surface. He would like you to tour the local medical facilities while he speaks with the admiral."

Rame almost told the commander off, then and there, but paused and glanced back out over his lab. The patients were out of danger, and he had two other doctors to handle emergencies—as long as the captain wasn't on board to drag them off into another crisis, at any rate.

"I think I can make the time, Commander," he said after a moment, deciding that one didn't get the chance to tour an alien medical facility very often. Even if they were human aliens.

"Excellent, Doctor. The shuttle is being prepped now. You might want to pack."

Rame stared at the intercom as the channel went dead, then started cursing up a storm as he grabbed his black bag and began throwing things into it.

▶▶▶

Captain Weston stepped off the lift into the zero gravity to see Dr. Rame walking awkwardly toward the shuttle from another lift. He kicked off the ground, ignoring the tacky resistance of his boots, and glided along the ground, out to the doctor's position, before dropping his feet and landing with an abrupt stop.

Rame started and almost lost his footing, but recovered enough to glare at Weston.

"Doctor," Weston smiled.

"Captain."

"Glad you could make it," Weston told him as they walked to the ramp of the shuttle together. Four armored soldiers formed up the ranks behind them.

"Seemed like a once-in-a-lifetime opportunity," Rame said. "In fact, I believe that Dr. Palin is currently cursing his luck for missing it."

"How is the good doctor?"

Rame snorted at the idea of Palin being a "good" anything, but he shrugged. "He'll be fine. He and that boy were lucky. They'll both pull through."

"Excellent," Weston said, checking his restraints as the rating came along and triple-checked everyone.

"We'll be taking off shortly, Captain," he told Weston as he yanked Rame's straps tight.

"Thank you, Crewman."

Weston and the doctor continued talking. Around them, the shuttle slowly wound up, the whine penetrating the deck as the pilot called for clearance. It was given shortly after, and the shuttle pushed them back into their seats as it roared off the deck and into the black.

▶▶▶

Adm. Rael Tanner stood out in the open as the rather large and impressive-looking orbiter slowed for a controlled burn and settled into an easy hover over the landing area.

Tanner had to admit he was suddenly wondering if the area they had chosen was large enough.

His worries proved to be groundless a moment later, when the gleaming white ship settled in for a feather-light landing, its lights flashing in a pattern he didn't know as its reactors powered down.

Above the orbiter, two sleek and lethal-looking fighters hovered in what the admiral was certain was meant to be every bit as menacing a display as it appeared. The nose of each fighter was actually pivoting the barrel of a rather large weapon, giving the craft an angry appearance as it swept over the field.

His eyes were torn from the fighters as the orbiter lowered a plank to the ground and two figures in armor that matched Ithan Chans's marched down and took up positions on either side. Only then did he see his first unarmored human from the *Odyssey*, though Tanner supposed he hadn't seen many armored ones, for that matter.

Two men stepped down next, one wearing a white uniform that matched the gleaming surface of the orbiter, while the other wore a more utilitarian dark blue. Admiral Tanner was suddenly conscious of his own uniform, which was the same as every other member of the Colonial Merchant Exploration Fleet.

He threw back his shoulders to match the stance of the man in white.

"Captain Weston?"

Weston looked down at the man he recognized as Admiral Tanner. He hadn't realized just how small the man was over the screen, and it was a surprise that he stood nearly two heads taller than the admiral. He didn't let the emotion or expression cross his face, however, and stopped with a click of his boots on the obsidian surface, throwing a textbook salute. Beside the admiral, still in her powered armor, Milla stood quietly. He nodded once to her, but focused his attention on the smaller man standing before him.

"Admiral." He held the form for several seconds, then dropped the salute and nodded gravely. "I'm pleased to meet you, sir."

"No more than I," Tanner said. "I...My world, we all owe you a debt. Anything you ask, I am certain we can work something out."

"For the moment, Admiral, I'll settle for some O-two to top off our supplies and a little help with repairs, if you can," Weston replied. "In the long term...Well, I would appreciate if your people gave consideration to sending a representative with the *Odyssey* when we return home."

"As to repairs and O...two?" Tanner frowned. "I'm sure something can be worked out...once I know what O-two is."

Weston smiled involuntarily, shaking his head as he tapped the link on his jaw. "These damn things mess up the oddest words. O-two is oxygen. We lost some of our air during the battle."

"Ah, air." Tanner smiled. "That, I believe, we can provide in plenty. Next, as to a representative, I will have to pass that along to the council. However, I believe that you may be assured that it will be given...a most serious consideration."

"I'm glad to hear that," Weston replied.

"Now, with the preliminaries finished," Tanner motioned to a pair of immense doors attached to an even larger building, "shall we move this inside, as it were?"

"With pleasure...And, Admiral"—Weston motioned to Rame—"this is Dr. Rame. He is interested in touring the medical facility where our soldiers were being treated."

"Absolutely, Captain." Tanner motioned with one hand, and a young woman stepped up. "Show the doctor to the military medical facilities, Ithan."

"Of course, Admiral," she said, with a smile. "Doctor, if you would follow me, I will secure transport."

"Thank you, my dear," Rame said.

She gave him a quizzical look before they headed out.

Tanner turned to Weston with a puzzled look.

"'My dear'?" he asked, frowning.

Weston blinked, and one of the soldiers snorted with laughter behind him. He glanced in irritation over his shoulder, causing the soldier to stiffen immediately. He was going to berate the man but remembered that the armor HUD had probably given him a text definition of the question.

"What is it, Soldier?" He growled.

"Sorry, sir, it's just that the translation matrix is confusing deer and dear," the soldier replied, then backpedaled. "I mean—"

"I know what you mean, sir." Weston remembered Palin's similar conversation with Milla, and he shot a glance over to where she was standing. It wasn't quite the time to be swapping old stories, however, so he turned back to the admiral. "Another translation problem, apparently, sir."

"I see," Tanner said, after waiting for the computer to catch up to what Weston's own, rather harsh, language was saying.

It was difficult enough, Tanner noted, dealing with a translation that was far from perfect, but it was made even more difficult by the fact that the translated words were overlain on top of the original language. He was just as happy that all the colonies spoke the same language; it simplified things greatly despite the occasional dialect issues.

"Well, Captain," he said finally. "If you'd follow me?"

Weston nodded and the two of them stepped into the large building, their entourage walking—or in two cases, thumping—along behind them.

▶▶▶

"Incredible," Rame whispered, watching as the immense city passed around him.

"Pardon, sir?" the ithan asked from where she was sitting at the controls of the flying vehicle.

"It's a very impressive city…ah…Miss…?"

"Rache," she told him. "Ithan Rache."

"Rache," Rame repeated. "As I was saying, it's a very impressive city."

"Mons Systema is the capital city of three worlds," she told him, a touch of what Rame recognized as hometown pride filling her voice.

"Three?"

"That's correct, Docteur," she told him. "Political power is centered here for several star systems, in fact."

"I suppose that's why the aliens used so many ships," Rame said.

She grimaced in response and nodded to a building. "Your wounded were brought here for treatment."

Rame took the hint and shut up.

▶▶▶

"A drink, Captain?"

"Thank you, Admiral." Weston watched as the small man poured a lightly tinted liquid into a long, thin glass.

The admiral started to hand it across, paused, and frowned. "It occurs to me that perhaps we should confirm that there are no poisons in our food or drink that might affect you…"

"I don't believe that would be a problem, Admiral," Weston replied easily, accepting the drink by leaning forward. "Our doctor did extensive cellular examinations when we picked up Miss Chans. We are genetically identical, with the expected minor deviations one would find in any isolated section of the species."

"I see," Tanner replied, pouring a second glass for himself. "I must admit that I find this quite interesting. There have long been legends, of course, concerning other human planets, but I believe that the last time such a thing was found was…several thousand cycles ago, at least."

"That's some history you have there," Weston said, impressed despite not knowing exactly what a cycle was. "How long have you had space travel?"

Tanner shrugged, taking a drink. "I would have to look up the exact number, but it is just marginally over fifteen thousand cycles."

"Cycles?" Weston frowned, tapping his induction mic again, deciding that he'd better get that detail cleared up.

"Pardon, a cycle is the length of time this world takes to circle our sun," Tanner replied.

Weston blinked, pausing with his drink just inches from his lips. "Wow."

"Pardon?" Tanner asked politely, smiling with a look of confusion on his face. "Surely your own worlds have been space faring for some time…"

"Actually, no," Weston said slowly, weighing his words as he tried to decide what exactly to say. Finally, he just decided to go with the truth. "Actually, the *Odyssey* is our first interstellar vessel."

Tanner set his own glass down, laying his hand against the table in surprise. "What was it you said, Captain? Wow?"

Eric chuckled, nodding. "Yes. That was what I said."

"Wow."

"That's a lot of history you have, Admiral," Weston said again. "My own nation, in its current state, actually only goes back about ten years. Until I can get a better comparison, call it ten cycles."

"So young," Tanner said, tilting his head as he considered it. "It's...incredible to me, I must admit."

"Makes two of us," Weston said, picking up his glass again and raising it to his host.

▶▶▶

Sean Bermont looked up in surprise when he recognized the familiar form of the *Odyssey*'s CMO approaching.

"Doctor?" He blinked, his arm itching slightly from where the local med-techs had gone to work on him. "What are you doing down here?"

Rame looked over at the young man, taking a moment to place him. "Ah, Lieutenant. I came down with the captain. I wanted to tour the local medical facilities."

Bermont smirked, then flexed his arm. "They do good work, Doc. Patched me up good as new, 'cept for the itch."

"Oh?" Rame came over, looking for the injury. "Where were you injured?"

"Shoulder," Bermont informed him, then grinned. "But don't bother looking. Nothing to see; they cleaned me up real good."

Rame examined the bare shoulder on the soldier but couldn't find any evidence of an injury other than, perhaps, a patch of pink skin. "Here?"

Bermont rubbed the skin where the doctor had pointed. "Yeah. One of those damned buggy bastards cut right through my armor. They've got feet like spades or something."

"Remarkable," Rame said, looking closer. "And it was as bad you say?"

"Right to the bone. Cut two tendons clean," Bermont said. "In fact, if the armor's artificial muscles hadn't taken up the slack for me, the bastard would have been able to finish me off, easy."

"Most impressive," Rame said, shaking his head. "A wound like that would have lain you up for months at home. Perhaps ended your military career."

"Would that have been such a bad thing?"

Rame and Bermont stiffened at the new voice, turning to see a woman in green coverall-type clothing approaching.

"Yes, Doc," Bermont replied. "It would be. I like my job."

The woman shook her head with a hint of disgust in her features.

"Dr. Rame, this is Dr. Brianne," Bermont spoke up, a hint of tolerant amusement in his voice. "She's the sawbones that patched me up."

Rame wasn't certain what "sawbones" translated into, but the look the woman shot Bermont made it quite clear that it wasn't complimentary. He placed a careful bedside manner smile on his face and greeted the doctor, as much to distract her from Bermont than anything else.

"Pleased to meet you, Doctor," he said. "I'm the chief medical officer of the *Odyssey*."

Dr. Brianne cast him a begrudging look, nodding more or less politely. "So you are the one who normally…What was the phrase? 'Patches them up'?"

Rame smiled. "Unfortunately, yes."

Brianne was about to say something else, but an odd rhythmic thumping caused all three of them to pause and look around. Bermont was the first to recognize it, and he grinned when he saw the first smoke-black figure approach from over a rolling hill.

"Relax," he grinned. "It's just the major and the others. Looks like we're just about done here."

Rame watched the approach of the two ranks of soldiers with interest, not normally in a position to see the powered armor they wore in action.

The powered field armor had been introduced toward the end of the Block Wars, and in his post on board a hospital ship, Rame generally only saw units that had been shot to hell and back. The operational armor was a good deal more impressive, he supposed. Though, as a doctor, he'd often been grateful for the basic lifesaving systems built into each suit.

In this case, the two ranks of soldiers looked like they'd been through the fire—literally. The orbital insertion had burned the surface off their armor, resulting in a patchwork of smoke-gray colors and the coal black of the base armor. The end result was something similar to what was once considered a dark urban camouflage, though with a more random set of patterns.

His eyes shifted to the CM packs that floated along between the ranks, and Rame stared in shock as he realized that each of the packs was hauling what had to be one of the enemy foot soldiers along with it.

His assumption was confirmed when the two ranks were called to a halt by Major Brinks, and the packs unceremoniously dropped their cargo to the ground with a thud.

"Good Lord."

"Doctor?" Major Brinks stepped up, his helm visor shifting to a clear mode as he looked at the doctor. "What are you doing here?"

"He's checking out the local med-techs, sir," Bermont offered. "How'd things go?"

"We got it cleaned up, Lieutenant," Brinks said. "But the locals are going to have to get some seismic sensors scattered around here so they can make sure there's nothing left digging under their feet."

"I'll have a report filed with the captain in twenty minutes," one of the other soldiers spoke up, his black helm preventing Rame from identifying him.

"You do that, Savoy," Brinks said. "And while you're at it, recommend that the locals get some birds in the air with some real down-looking capabilities. The heat difference will let them spot any on the surface."

"Got it, boss," Savoy replied.

"This is the...enemy, is it?" Rame asked, staring at the corpse of an unnaturally large insect-looking thing.

"Damn right," another of the soldiers said, with an obvious grin in his voice. "This is one of the trophies of our bug hunt."

"Goddammit, Deac!" another growled. "I told you to can that sci-fi shit! I'm sick of you talking like we're in some damned movie!"

"Come on, Sarge!" Deacon whined. "Think about it... We're on another planet, fighting giant spider things, in powered armor...Christ, Sarge, that's like every sci-fi cliché ever written!"

Low chuckles passed through the group, as well as a couple groans from soldiers who'd been listening to similar bickering for too long.

"He's got you there, Sarge."

"I don't give a shit!"

"You know...Mr. Deacon, is it?" Rame spoke up idly as he walked around one of the bodies.

"Yeah?"

"One must wonder..."

Everyone shifted, looking at each other as the doctor kneeled down and examined the body closer.

"What's that, Doc?" Deacon asked, curious.

"Well, if we are living a science-fiction scenario," Rame said, standing up, "what will the science fiction writers write about now?"

"Uh..." Deacon just stared for a moment.

"Westerns?" someone else asked, his voice a little hopeful.

"Sacrilege!" Deacon yelled, his voice booming over the speakers of his armor.

Some of the men groaned, but Rame just ignored the comment as he continued examining the body.

"I can't believe that I'm associated with these people," Major Brinks muttered under his breath, but only after he made sure that his comments weren't going out on any frequencies.

▶▶▶

Eric Weston and Rael Tanner were still talking through some details when some of the soldiers Weston had brought with him stepped forward.

"What is it, Evans?" Weston asked, glancing over.

"The major reports that the alien ground forces appear to be mopped up, though he advises that the locals place a seismic network around and a decent CAP to keep an eye out for strays. Lieutenant Savoy will be filing a report shortly."

"Thank you, Corporal."

The young man stepped back.

"What is...CAP?" Tanner asked.

"A combat air patrol, or I suspect, in this case, anything that can fly with heat sensors," Weston said, thinking about the reports already filed. "Those two things should give you a decent warning if they missed any of the drones."

"I will forward the recommendations to Nero," Tanner promised. "It will be his responsibility to organize such defenses."

"He'll probably have to devise new weapons as well. The reports concerning the effectiveness of your laser rifles against the drones weren't promising."

"Indeed not," Tanner grimaced. "Nero has been gnashing his teeth over that very thing for some time. I believe that he even admires your own weapons, though I should not be surprised."

"Pardon?"

"Nero is from a colony that purposely maintains its rough wilderness status. As such, survival for him is a slightly more... hands-on approach than most of my people." Tanner permitted himself a slight smile. "It is why he was asked to join the army."

Weston nodded, still trying to get a full picture painted of the culture he was dealing with. "I see."

"I doubt that you do—not completely, at least."

"Touché," Weston smiled, raising his glass in salute. "But I do believe that I'm at least getting a general idea."

"Perhaps, Captain. Perhaps."

▼

CHAPTER 39

▲

▶ THE SHIPBOARD REPAIRS took two days just to reach the minimum levels before Engineering was willing to certify the ship as transition ready, which Weston had used to the best of his ability while dealing with the citizens of this world they were orbiting.

While Rael Tanner seemed a rather sensible type, and the behemoth of a man in charge of the ground forces was also, the politicos were pretty much what one might expect from experience on Earth. They were a little different in motivation, perhaps, or at least in experience, but they still impeded the progress of pretty much anything they touched, like old hands.

The former UN Council would have been proud.

Of course, it was perhaps a lot to expect for them to make decisions on a forty-eight-hour window, but that was all that Weston was willing to give them. Either they give him a diplomat to take home or he and the *Odyssey* were weighing anchor without them.

They'd mucked around in someone else's war long enough.

So it was perhaps no surprise that Weston's mood was dark as the deadline approached and the planetary council still hadn't contacted the *Odyssey*.

"Ensign Lamont, how are the repairs coming?"

"The crew is welding new armor segments into place over the habitat breach now, Captain," she informed him. "They've also taken the time to rip up the flight deck, and Corrin says that they'll have it ready by the deadline."

He nodded. "I'm sure they will. O-two?"

"The shipments from the surface have replenished our supply," she told him. "As you ordered, we analyzed each tank, and it's sterile and pure."

"Thank you, Ensign."

Weston fell silent, knowing that he had just been marking time, anyway. He didn't need to micromanage his people and he knew it, but he was letting the situation on the planet get to him. He needed some sort of connection with these people when he went home, something the brass could effectively see and touch. Something more than just data banks. Or at least, he really wanted it.

An actual person—preferably people, in all truth—would make his reports at lot more believable to the brass. Weston wasn't worried about being disbelieved, of course—at least not precisely. More, he was worried about his account being given a low priority, comparatively speaking.

So far, by his account, the alien species had committed no less than nine ships to this war of theirs. Along with Milla's account, the number started climbing, even if you assumed that many of the ships the *Odyssey* had destroyed were the ones that originally wrecked the Colonial fleet.

In return, they'd eliminated the planetary populations of a minimum of two star systems, which was a massive breach of all accepted rules of warfare by Earth standards. While civilian casualties were sometimes unavoidable, they were not to be actively pursued. Of course, the term "rules of warfare" was one of the oldest oxymorons in recorded history, but even so, this was a major change from any conflict that Weston had experience in, even through study.

In some ways, the closest example he could think of was World War II. On both sides, the militaries involved sought out civilian targets and destroyed them with no quarter given. The German forces' actions under the command of the SS and the Nazi party were well documented, and the American attacks on Hiroshima and Nagasaki were equally horrific, if somewhat faster.

The Block Wars had never quite reached that level, probably because any attack on a civilian location with modern weapons was largely a waste of weaponry. An HVM rocket fired from an Archangel could tear a city to shreds in its terminal approach; the shock wave alone could kill hundreds.

Combine that fact with the pervasive and persistent use of cameras and the impact they had on world opinion, and even the most hardcore militants on either side weren't stupid enough to do something that might galvanize neutral countries into taking sides.

However, the attacks on the Colonial worlds were something different—or at least that's what he felt in his gut. It was true that they were at least possibly similar to the American strikes on Hiroshima and Nagasaki, intended as proof of ability and will, more than intent to destroy. However, that thought didn't sit right with him, and Weston didn't believe it to be the case.

If that was their intent, then they should have skirted this system with overwhelming force and demanded the

Colonials' surrender. They certainly should never have committed a total of eight ships in an attempt to reach the planet with their drones.

That left option two, but the sort of racial genocide that the other side of the World War II coin showed wasn't quite what he was reading from the alien attacks, either. Why destroy all life in that case? Why turn a world into a wasteland?

No, Weston was certain that there was more to the scenario than he knew. More, certainly, than he was being told by the Colonials, but probably more than even they knew.

There was something new here.

He could feel it.

"Captain?"

Weston shook off the line of thought, glancing over to where Commander Roberts was looking at him. "Yes, Commander?"

"A call for you, sir. Admiral Tanner."

"Thank you."

He turned back to his controls, accessing the com-channel he knew that Tanner would be calling on. They'd reclaimed the armor from Milla, but he had left a portable terminal with a two-way holo-projector in the admiral's keeping. It wasn't rated for combat, but it was top of the line in civilian communications and provided a nice two-way image.

"Good day, Admiral," Weston said.

"Good day to you, Captain," Tanner replied. "I understand that you still intend to leave orbit this day?"

"I'm afraid so, Admiral," Weston said. "I understand that your people need to consider what to do, given the situation, but I can't risk sitting the *Odyssey* in a warzone for any longer."

"I understand," the admiral replied. "And happily, I have managed to cut through some of the process in order to supply you with the...diplomat you requested."

"Thank you, Admiral. I had hoped you would."

"My people are sometimes slow to move, but even we can tell when perhaps speed is a virtue. In this case, I convinced them that it may be so."

Weston nodded.

"I must admit, however, that your particular restrictions in this matter have made things more difficult," Tanner went on.

"I expected as much," Weston said. "However, there was no real choice there, Admiral. Until we have some sort of official relationship, I can't tell you or any of your people the location of our home system...They'll have to come with us."

Tanner shrugged. "I would most likely do the same. However, it was more the problem with scheduling a return that caused serious hesitation."

Weston nodded. That was a given, he'd known from the moment he mentioned it. However, there was no way to predict how the politicians, or anyone, on Earth were going to react to this situation. Contact with an extraterrestrial civilization was one thing—a huge thing, to be certain—but only one thing, just the same. Having been involved, however shortly, in an interstellar war was not going to sit well with a lot of people.

And God alone forbid that the Block got a hold of the information, though Weston knew better than to believe that it wouldn't happen. They would turn the entire event into a three-ring circus, just in an attempt to steal a few more points of world favor for their latest position.

There were no guarantees in life, and less in politics.

"I wish I could be more certain when a second voyage would be authorized, Admiral. But I can't," Weston said.

"I understand. Thankfully, however, it has been decided that the benefits of potential contact with your people is worth the risk of having some of our people caught on another world...They will want your guarantee for their safety, of course."

"They'll have it," Weston replied firmly. "While I can't guarantee that they'll have free access to...my world...I will ensure that they are received as a diplomatic envoy."

"That will be acceptable," Tanner said. "If you can prepare to receive them, I will have an orbiter bring the party to the *Odyssey* before...ah...before you are scheduled to depart."

Weston noted the hesitation. Establishing a common time reference was turning into a real pain. The locals used a system based on a numbering system that the *Odyssey* was still working on deciphering. It had apparently been created to establish some sort of common reference point among their colony worlds.

It didn't distill down into something easily comparable to Earth time units, unfortunately.

"We'll be waiting for them, Admiral," Weston said.

"Excellent. Then I will let you go and see to their preparations. Good day, Captain."

"Good day, Admiral."

Weston turned to Ensign Lamont. "Susan...Have an appropriate reception prepared for our guests."

"Aye, Captain," she replied, her thoughts running back to her earlier research on diplomatic protocol.

She'd had to look that up several times over the last couple days, when it first looked like they might get such an animal aboard, and found the subject to be intensely complicated.

So much depending on cultural differences made things tricky, and she'd been tempted to go with one of the Block ceremonies for their extreme levels of, well, ceremony. In the end, though, she'd decided that simpler was better and had got together with one of the ship's stewards and a few others to prepare.

To that end, she opened a channel after acknowledging the captain's order and turned back to her console.

"Jackie? Yeah, it's Susan. It's on. You want to warn the chef? Thanks. I'll be down in a few to double-check. Thanks."

▶▶▶

"Look sharp, we got another batch of locals landing," Mackenzie said, his teeth exposed in something that wasn't quite a smile.

The men groaned as the chief spoke, thinking about the last time.

"Relax," he grinned. "After the last time, I think that the cap chewed their pilots a new one. We might not have to hit the collision alarms this time."

A few men chuckled, but most of their faces were grim, just the same. Flight deck people had a dangerous-enough task when dealing with pilots who took their job seriously, and whether the locals realized it or not, most of the men on the deck considered their flying to be well up in the "hotdog" category.

On any carrier, let alone one in the vacuous environment of space, trust was integral to the smooth operation of the flight deck. The pilots had to trust the deck crew, and the deck crew had to trust the pilots. A break anywhere in the line could cost lives, either through bad communication or, in the worst situations, intentional misdirection.

Chief Mackenzie knew that, and he knew that his men weren't anywhere near that point just yet, but he figured it wouldn't hurt to remind them of one bit of good news.

"This is the last one of these landings we'll have to deal with—for a while, anyway," he told them with a wry grin. "So stay on your toes, so to speak, and if they rocket the deck... Get the hell out of the way and leave them to me. Got that?"

The men nodded and acknowledged his words.

Mackenzie clapped his hands. "All right, get suited up. We're taking over the deck at oh–fifteen hundred, and I'll want it FOD checked by fifteen past. Move it!"

▶▶▶

In his cabin, Weston sat behind his desk, looking over the proposed course for the trip home that Daniels had prepared according to his wishes. The doglegged flight path made fifteen different transition hops across almost four hundred light-years of space.

The lieutenant had plotted the course to make the best use of the *Odyssey*'s legs, which were pretty impressive despite the limitations her transition drive built into her.

While the transition effect had, in theory, no limit on distance, it did have a practical limit in the case of the *Odyssey*'s power supplies. They could affect a transition over a range of less than thirty light-years at any given jump, after which they had to recharge the massive superconducting capacitors that fed the drive.

The reason, according to the tech boys, was that while a tachyon could transit the entirety of the universe in an instant, it still required the energy to do so. That was the theory that the transition drive was devised to exploit, in actuality.

That, and the fact that nature abhorred tachyons about as much as it abhorred a vacuum.

The universe simply did not seem to like the little buggers and went out of its way to make sure that they didn't stick around any longer than they had to.

The entire tachyon drive was actually little more than a tachyon-based laser system that actually fired itself, along with the entire ship, by forcing every molecule in the *Odyssey* to jump several energy states in one go while keeping the beam coherent over the length of its range.

When the power ran out, the universe exerted its influence on the tachyons to return to their former energy state, allowing the ship and its people to reform.

Not a particularly fun way to travel, Weston would be the first to admit, but it was fast and, hopefully, untraceable.

Each transition did have some energy leakage, just like any laser had a minute corona of energy particles that could be read with the right sensors. The *Odyssey* would pulse a tachyon surge, both when it left a system and when it reappeared. The upside to this was that, like lasers, the energy leakage wasn't much. Calculating it before had only academic value, but recent events had brought that information to the forefront of tactical data.

The corona of a transition jump was calculated as an irrational root of its total length.

Which, to be honest, gave Weston a headache to even consider.

The upshot of it was that they could predict the range at which an observer could see their transition. For a thirty-light-year jump, it would be almost five light-years. This meant that any ship within five light-years of their departure point—or more importantly, their arrival point—would be able to detect their transition.

For a ten-light-year jump, the number was just under two-thirds of a light-year.

The flip side of that was, of course, if they jumped in too small of a transition, then they would increase the risk by broadcasting more tachyons over several smaller zones, rather than over a few larger ones.

Weston had ordered that the last five jumps on their return home be kept to no more than fifteen light-years, but no less than eight.

However, it was the first two that interested him more than anything else.

He was looking at the Port Fuielles system map when the call from the bridge came through. He opened the channel. "Yes?"

"Captain, the orbiter from the planet has lifted off. They'll be landing in about ten minutes."

"Thank you, Susan. Have everything prepared for their arrival. I'll meet you on the parking deck," Weston said, shutting down the holo-display of his desk with a wave.

Enough star maps for the moment; he had guests to greet.

▶▶▶

"Orbiter One has the ball."

"Roger. LSO confirms," Chief Mackenzie said over the network. "All hands, eyes on the inbound plane."

The traditions of carrier crews went back a long way, and though many of the procedures had been changed a hundred times since they had originally been drawn up, some terms just didn't want to die.

Of course, the chief supposed, calling the hunk of material coming his direction a "plane" would undoubtedly piss off a lot of pilots. It was, however, coming in at a more reasonable rate than the last time, and he was relieved to see that no one was going to have to dive for the blast shields as the craft came to a smooth stop about two feet off the deck.

He stepped out and waved it to a lift with his signalers and wished for a moment that he could wipe his brow.

He'd feel a lot better if only he knew for a fact that these locals were carrier qualified.

▶▶▶

On the parking deck, Weston watched, along with Commander Roberts and Ensign Lamont, as the alien orbiter rose through the deck and was directed to a parking position. There, it rested for a time, floating about two feet off the deck like it was nailed there, the image disturbing as its bulkhead melted away.

Weston really didn't like that particular technology—at least not this application for it, he had to amend to himself a moment later.

He forced that thought from his mind and stepped forward as three figures stepped off the orbiter. He was surprised to note that he recognized two of them.

"Ithan Chans," he said formally with a deep nod. "And Ithan Sienthe. A pleasure to see you both again."

"Greetings, Captain," the pilot, Cora Sienthe, said. "Permission to set foot on your vessel?"

"Granted," Weston replied.

The young woman stepped off the plank and onto the deck. Weston hid a smile when he heard her boots make a tacky, sticking sound as she remained well attached to the deck.

Milla did the same. Then both stepped aside for the third person.

Weston turned his attention to this one, an old man who looked quite fit for his obviously advanced age. He stepped onto the deck, his own boots attaching themselves solidly, then nodded to Weston and the other two.

"Captain," he said, his voice gravelly in comparison to the fluid, soft voices he had heard from most of the locals. "I am your…diplomat? I am Benjin Corasc, elder of the Planet Ranquil."

You certainly are, Weston thought, carefully keeping it from his face as he returned the nod. "Welcome aboard the *Odyssey,* Elder Corasc. It is an honor to have you here."

The old man waved the words away. "The honor is mine, Captain. I, and my world, am in your debt."

"One doesn't automatically rule out the other, Elder Corasc."

The old man smiled, laughing in his gravelly voice. "As you say, Captain."

Weston returned the smile, then gestured toward the far wall. "If you'll come with me, sir, I'll show you to your quarters. After that, I'm afraid that I must prepare for our departure from this system. However, I would be honored if you would join my officers and me for supper this evening."

"Of course," Corasc said evenly. "I will need quarters for my attachés as well, however."

Weston glanced back at the two women. "Both of them?"

"Yes, Captain. This will not pose a problem?"

"No, Elder Corasc. It will not," Weston told him. "However, I believe that Commander Roberts and Ithan Sienthe will need to speak concerning the proper securing of the orbiter."

"Excellent," Corasc said. "Then Ithan Chans and I will come with you while they deal with such things."

"Of course." Weston guided the elder toward the lift.

Commander Jason Roberts turned to speak with the young woman concerning her floating spaceship.

▶▶▶

It was some time later when Weston stepped onto the bridge, a little worn out on the polite-o-meter and looking forward to being underway again.

"Captain on the bridge."

"Ah, Commander," he said as he took his position. "Did you get the orbiter secured?"

"Aye, sir. Fascinating piece of technology," Roberts replied.

"Yes, well, I'm certain that they decided that having some evidence of their tech base might be useful."

"Undoubtedly, sir," Roberts said.

"Are we ready to weigh anchor?" Weston asked, a wry tilt of his mouth communicating his humor.

"Aye, sir."

"Good. Helm, take us out of orbit," Weston ordered, settling into the seat. "Thrusters only until we clear the debris, then take us up to full acceleration."

"Aye, sir," Daniels responded. "Thrusters only."

The deck rumbled under them as the ship started to break clear of the planet. Weston was ready. Whatever else happened, they were on their way home now.

EPILOGUE

▶ "Commodore...I think we've got a glitch in that new array they installed."

Commodore Wolfe frowned, leaning forward. "Pipe it up to my station, son."

The young ensign standing watch nodded in response and directed the information up to the commander's pedestal, where Wolfe oversaw the Demos base. The facility was a hybrid between a ship repair base and a terraforming command center for the Martian Colony Project, which meant that the commodore had a lot to deal with on a daily basis.

The sensor glitch, however, brought a smile to his face.

"That's not a glitch, son," he said a moment later. "That's a tachyon surge."

"Sir? But...it didn't match any of the profiles we have in the computer and—"

"It didn't match the profiles because we don't have one for a full-size vessel transitioning in-system," Wolfe said.

"Sir?" The ensign's eyes widened, his voice rising just a little as a smile started to form. "You mean..."

"Let's roll out the welcome mat, boys," Wolfe said, a little louder so everyone in the large command center could hear. "The *Odyssey* just came home."

The command staff—the younger ones, anyway—let out a bit of a cheer. The station's XO let it go for a few seconds, then quickly quieted them down while Wolfe examined the information the sensors had recorded.

His single array of sensors weren't enough to give him an exact lock on the source of the surge, but even as his base obeyed protocol and transmitted the data back to Earth, Earth and the other outposts and ships in the area transmitted their findings to him. It took the better part of a half hour, but by the end of the little storm of signals, he had the transition pinpointed.

Weston's gotten cautious in his old age, Wolfe thought as he locked the entry point right down on the heliopause, the farthest reach of the sun's influence in interstellar space. That put the *Odyssey* about three days out by its fastest cruise, unless Weston planned to use some fancy flying to brake that monster of a ship.

He could have brought it in as close as the heliosphere and cut a day off that number—at least according to all the numbers Wolfe had seen—but Weston was the one on the gun, so it was his call.

That extra day of waiting was going to be one hell of a long time, though.

▶▶▶

"Wolfe here. This better be good," Cdre. Gregory Wolfe muttered as he thumbed open the communication terminal in response to the insistent tone.

"Sorry to wake you, Commodore, but we have a message pulse from the *Odyssey* here."

Wolfe threw his covers off, grabbing for his clothing as he hit the deck. "I'll be right there. Wolfe out."

As he dressed, he checked the clock. Almost twenty-six hours to the minute, just the amount of time for a signal to reach them by radio pulse. He finished getting dressed, checking his uniform only briefly in the mirror, then headed up to the command and control deck.

Once there, he accepted command and settled in to his secure terminal station in order to access the message.

What he had expected to be little more than a greeting from an old friend, with maybe a few bits of fascinating trivia to be shared just between them, turned out to be something entirely different. Wolfe paled at the security encryption, noting that the message was coded and tight beamed directly to him, not broadcast to Fleet Command.

He decoded it as fast as the computer could and started to read through the initial summary.

"Holy shit," he whispered a moment later, his hand slamming down on an alert key, calling his best cryptographer.

A few seconds later, a groggy voice was on the line. "Commodore?"

"Sorry to wake you, Johnson, but I need a secure link to Fleet Command. What's the latest on the security of the FTL pulse system?"

"Intel says that it's still secure, Commodore."

"What do you think?" Wolfe demanded.

The voice hesitated a moment, then came back. "Commodore...What kind of importance are you attaching to this stuff? Your mom's secret recipe for chili or the plans for the fourth-generation adaptive armor?"

"Try something more along the lines of God's phone number," Wolfe replied.

Johnson actually gulped, falling silent for a long time. "Commodore, I think I'd use one of the laser systems."

"I was afraid you'd say that. All right, go back to sleep."

"Are you kidding me, sir?"

Wolfe just shut the line and punched up another channel, linking him to the communications officer. "Jeff, you'd better get me a coded tight beam to Fleet Command."

"Ah, yes, sir. The admiralty base is behind Earth at this time, Commodore...Do you want to use a satellite bounce?"

"How long until we can bounce a signal right off of them directly?"

"Four hours, sir."

Four hours. As much as he hated to waste the time, four hours just didn't mean squat in the scheme of things. Wolfe considered. "I'll wait. Thanks, Jeff."

"No problem, Commodore. I'll have it queued for you, sir."

The channel was cut and Wolfe went back to the report.

"Eric, my old friend, when you step in it, you really step in it," he muttered, opening the file to the first page of the complete report and starting to read.

▶▶▶

"Will we arrive soon?"

Captain Weston looked up as soft words penetrated his thinking. "Yes, Ithan Chans. We'll be entering Earth's orbit shortly."

"Earth," Milla said in return. "And you say that this is really what you named your world? It is not...a distraction so that we may not recognize the real name?"

"I'm afraid not," Milla. "It's been Earth for a long time, now."

Milla shrugged. "Better than simply 'the World,' I suppose, though not by much."

Weston laughed. "We like it."

Milla noted that the captain had grown a lot more relaxed since they had reentered his home system. He was smiling a little freer now, and laughing some as well. It was interesting to see the changes wrought, but she thought that there was still something tense underneath it all.

She couldn't be certain, though, and perhaps it was just her imagination.

"Captain." An ensign approached them.

Weston looked up. "Yes, Ensign?"

"We're about to start braking maneuvers, sir, and we've just established a real-time link to Admiral Gracen."

"Thank you, Ensign. I'll take it on the bridge in a minute."

"Aye, sir."

▶▶▶

"Captain Weston."

"Admiral."

The admiral's stern face had grown no softer in his absence, and Weston couldn't help but note that there was a hard edge of steel in the aristocratic tilt of her eyes.

"Am I to believe that this report you filed is true, Captain?" she asked.

"Yes, ma'am," he told her. "All accounts in the report are verifiable and will be attested to by my crew."

"And these...aliens you have on board?"

"Diplomatic envoy and his staff, ma'am," Weston said clearly. "I've accepted their credentials and promised them a diplomatic reception."

"I see." Her voice was chilly, to say the least. "And you don't believe that somewhere in all of this you might have perhaps overstepped your authority?"

"That's for you to decide, ma'am."

"It is, indeed," Gracen replied, a hint of distaste on her lips. "Very well. I will prepare the reception for your guests. Please, transmit anything we should know about them that might be useful in arranging their stay."

"Will do, Admiral," Weston said. "Though, I'd say that the most important thing would be to avoid taking them to any boxing matches."

"Pardon me?"

He permitted himself a slight smile. "They have a cultural thing about violence, Admiral. They don't much appreciate it."

Gracen's eyebrow went up. "An odd thing for a people under the gun."

Weston shrugged. "I didn't say it was a reasonable thing, ma'am."

Gracen nodded. "Very well. I'll be certain that our people know that."

"Very good, ma'am."

"In the meantime, Captain..." Her voice grew a little darker. "You had best prepare for your debriefing...I don't believe that it will be a simple matter."

"No, ma'am, I didn't believe that it would be."

"I suppose we should make the most of the opportunity you bring us...certainly, since it may have an incredible cost in the long run."

"Yes, ma'am." Weston nodded.

"What would you suggest we discuss with your...envoy?"

"Power, ma'am."

"Power, Captain?"

"Yes, Admiral," Weston said firmly. "If you can do it, get information on their power-generation systems. They'll need information on our class-three or higher lasers and maybe our adaptive armor—second gen would do, I'd say."

"Those are classified technologies, Captain."

"Those are what they'll need to mount a credible defense against their enemies, Admiral," Weston said. "And if we can get their power-generation systems, we'd be able to transition anywhere, ma'am...Our Lasers would be ten times as powerful...You get the idea?"

"Yes, Captain. I suppose I do. Anything else?"

"I'll draw up a list, but I believe that my CMO would like to ensure that you discuss medical exchange, and they also have the ability to generate asymmetrical energy fields."

"Indeed," Gracen said. "Very well, draw up your list...I'll be sure that our negotiators look at it very carefully."

"Yes, ma'am. Oh, one more thing..."

"Yes, Captain?"

"If we decide to get more involved, Admiral..."

"That is a big *if,* Captain."

"I understand that, ma'am," Weston said. "But if we do... I'd suggest we offer them some Green Berets as advisors. They need help setting up their ground forces..."

Admiral Gracen nodded. "And that is what the Green Berets are trained to do. Very well, I'll be sure that it's brought up. For now, Captain...prepare."

"Aye, aye, ma'am."

▶▶▶

Diplomatic receptions, debriefings by a board of admirals, and a great deal of work later, Capt. Eric Weston found himself sitting in the office of Adm. Amanda Gracen, waiting for one more debriefing.

"Captain Weston."

Weston came to his feet, stiffening to attention. "Ma'am."

"Take a seat, Captain," the admiral told him as she circled the room and settled in behind her desk. "This is an informal meeting."

"Yes, ma'am," he said, sitting down again.

"I've gone over your statements, and those of your crew, as they were given to the board," she said, leafing through some loose papers. The admiral was a woman who appreciated the tangibles of paper, it seemed. "However, I'd like to speak with you about it informally, if you don't mind."

"No, ma'am," he said immediately.

"A lot of the admiralty is perturbed that the captain of our flagship would involve us in a war," she said, looking him in the eye. "In fact, there has been more than a little talk of a court martial."

Weston felt a chill but forced himself to nod. "Aye, ma'am. I can't say that I'm surprised."

"And yet you did it anyway?"

"Admiral…" he hesitated. "Yes, ma'am. I did it anyway."

"Why?" Her voice was cool, yet challenging.

Weston took a breath. "Because it wasn't a war, ma'am. It was genocide. I couldn't stand back and watch, Admiral."

"Noble," she told him. "Perhaps not the brightest star in the sky, but noble. I probably shouldn't tell you this just yet, but you may come out of this better than you deserve."

"Ma'am?" Weston asked, confused.

"The initial conferences have left a lot of the brass... impressed. They want the technology these 'Colonials' have to offer. Did you know that Mr. Corasc was approaching his second centennial by our standards?"

Weston nodded.

"Well, we have a few politicians who see themselves 'serving their constituents' well into the next century," Gracen said, a little distastefully. "Beyond that, there have already been a few leaks to the press...So, Captain, you're something of a hero in the Confederation. First contact, and all that junk...The Block has already started a press campaign to discredit you, of course, but it won't have much effect on the home front for the near future."

"So," she went on, "we aren't likely to be able to court martial you...It wouldn't be good PR, or so I'm told."

Weston winced, not certain he liked that being the only reason he may keep his career.

"That's neither here nor there at the moment, however," she said. "I want you to tell me about these...Drah-sin?"

"That's how the Colonials pronounce it, yes, ma'am," he replied. "To be honest, there's not a lot to tell. We have some bodies of the soldier drones on the *Odyssey*, but once they cooled down, it seems like they just petrified, ma'am."

"Petrified?"

"Their internal organs—as near as my people can tell— are suspended in a molten solution that's extremely high in silicon. When they die, they just turn to rock...We can't tell the organs from the rest of the body after that."

"I see."

"To be honest, though, ma'am..." Weston hesitated. "The Drasin don't scare me much."

The admiral looked at him, features perplexed. "Aren't you the one who brought back the images of the planet? What did you call it? Port Fey?"

"Yes, ma'am." Weston swallowed.

The images from Port Fuielles were disturbing, as were those from the first planet they had encountered the Drasin on. Days after the attack on Port Fuielles, the *Odyssey* had made another sweeping pass through the system, intent on seeing the true aftermath of the Drasin attack.

The world had been stripped clean by then, the Drasin literally erasing all evidence of humanity from its surface, along with most traces of life itself. It was well on its way to being a martian-like landscape by the time they had left the system a second time.

The other, however, wasn't merely a nightmare. It was a terror of epic proportions.

The Drasin in the first system had used the intervening weeks from their first attack to multiply completely out of control. When ordered a pass with carnivore drones, all that had been left of the planet was a rapidly degenerating sphere of dead and dying Drasin drones. The things had literally eaten up the entire world in their endless quest to propagate, until the remnants of the planet broke up under a series of volcanic eruptions.

In some mindless instinct, the Drasin had destroyed everything they needed to live—at least as far as the drone had been able to tell. When the atmosphere bled off and the heat from the dying world began to cool, so did the drones. While many of the floating, kicking things were still alive in the orbit that used to hold a planet, the readings indicated that they were rapidly losing their internal heat and dying as well.

The admiral cleared her throat, bringing Weston back to the moment.

"Go on, Captain."

"The Drasin," he said after a moment, "are, in my opinion, bioweapons."

Gracen's eyebrow went up, prompting him to continue.

"The evidence is there, Admiral," he said, leaning forward. "They were just too perfectly suited to attacking the Colonials. Laser resistant on the frequencies their enemy used, both in space and on the ground. They were tailor-made for a job, Admiral…And I don't believe that any species would naturally select for suicide the way these things did. No, ma'am…The Drasin are just a weapon."

"I fail to see, Captain," the admiral said grimly, "why you would not be afraid of them for that reason."

"Because…Admiral, I've never in my life been afraid of a gun," Weston said firmly. "It's the person with their finger on the trigger that worries me."

He let that statement float for a moment and went on. "The Drasin don't bother me much, Admiral. We can take them, with a minimal leadtime to start producing combat ships and defenses. But somewhere out there, there is someone who pointed them at the Colonials and pulled the trigger."

Eric Weston looked the admiral in the eye. "And that person, Admiral, I'm terrified of."

ABOUT THE AUTHOR

 Evan has been writing most of his life in one format or another. Though he studied computer science in his postsecondary education and has worked in the local lobster industry steadily over the last decade, writing has always been his true passion. In his own words, "It's what I do for fun and to relax. There's not much I can imagine better than being a storyteller."